"*Knife Fight and Other Struggles* is ▢▢▢▢ that drops some hi-fidelity weirdness ▢▢▢ ▢▢▢ ▢▢▢ ▢▢▢ prose has gorgeous lines of symmetry and a steel spine."
—Laird Barron, Bram Stoker Award-winning author of *The Beautiful Thing That Awaits Us All*

"David Nickle is my favourite kind of writer. His stories are dark, wildly imaginative, and deeply compassionate—even when they're laced with righteous anger. He's at the top of his game in this new book of short stories, and that's about as good as it gets."
—Nathan Ballingrud, Shirley Jackson Award-winning author of *North American Lake Monsters*

"David Nickle is Canada's answer to Stephen King. His writing charms even as it slices like a blade between the ribs: sharp, subtle, and never less than devastating."
—Helen Marshall, British Fantasy Award-winning author of *Hair Side, Flesh Side*

"David Nickle's *Knife Fight and Other Struggles* is a collection of twelve unique glimpses into the weird. Dynamic imagination, masterful writing of both the every day and the nightmare, characters that breathe, and a dark sense of humour make this a keeper. If you've not yet read Nickle's fiction, *Knife Fight* is a great place to start. If you have, you've no doubt already bought this book."
—Jeffrey Ford, World Fantasy Award-winning author of *Crackpot Palace: Stories*

Praise for *THE 'GEISTERS*

"Anyone who enjoys ghostly yarns or supernatural dark fiction should add this perverse, spine-tingling tome to their collection—stat!"
—*Rue Morgue*

"The language of *The 'Geisters* does an exquisite job of capturing the struggle for language in the face of horror and violence,

the way that the brain can fail to interpret what the eyes are seeing. . . . It is this groping towards making sense of what the characters are seeing and experiencing that makes The 'Geisters succeed in its most wrenching and visceral moments, as horror or fractures in logical reality gradually take shape in the mind of the reader and the characters together. These dawning moments of horror, or spookiness, or dread, or simultaneous arousal and disgust, are what make The 'Geisters at once so desirable and so deeply uncomfortable. This is a book that buzzes in your ears, climbs your crawling skin with multiple barbed feet, feeling with exquisitely sensitive antennae for the next new and terrible revelation."
—The National Post

"Few writers do psychosexual horror as well as Toronto's David Nickle, and with The 'Geisters he's back with another tale of voluptuous terror and the supernatural."
—The Toronto Star

"The book doesn't just explore the attractiveness of terror—it embodies it in a narrative that demands (excites even as it repels) your attention. It's a(nother) strong novel by one of the best, most interesting horror writers working today."
—Bookgasm.com

Praise for *RASPUTIN'S BASTARDS*

"This novel is supernatural eeriness at its best, with intriguing characters, no clear heroes, and a dark passion at its heart. Horror aficionados and fans of Stephen King's larger novels should appreciate this macabre look at the aftermath of the Cold War."
—Library Journal

"Rasputin's Bastards is a testament to the fact Nickle can write anything."
—The Winnipeg Review

"A plot so dissected is not easy to get right, but Nickle juggles it incredibly well. And it's just the right kind of style for this book."
—Newstalk 1010

"*Rasputin's Bastards* is a book with such a vast canvas and sweep, handled with such command and care by Nickle, that it is a must-read for anyone who wants to know what amazing things can be done with dark historical fantasy."
—Tony Burgess, author of *People Live Still in Cashtown Corners*

"To read David Nickle is to be reminded what the best storytellers can do, and to glory in unbridled imagination released on the page. David's achievements in *Rasputin's Bastards* are innumerable. He reminds me of no one so much than maestro Dan Simmons, another writer unconstrained by the limits of genre. When it comes to narrative, David dances where others plod, and dares where others play it safe. This is all to say, David Nickle takes no prisoners, and leaves a magnificent bruise as a reminder of the encounter."
—Corey Redekop, author of *Husk*

Praise for *EUTOPIA: A NOVEL OF TERRIBLE OPTIMISM*

"Toronto author David Nickle's debut novel, the followup to his brilliantly wicked collection of horror stories *Monstrous Affections*, establishes him as a worthy heir to the mantle of Stephen King."
—*The National Post*

"A dark, complicated and frequently harrowing read . . . *Eutopia* is a compelling exploration of the horror of good intentions."
—*Locus Magazine*

"It's straight-faced, laconic, and quite brilliant."
—*The New York Review of Science Fiction*

"*Eutopia* is the kind of book I'd recommend to literary snobs who badmouth the horror genre while completely ignoring the multitudes of splendid books on the shelves. Nickle comes from a different cut of cloth than a lot of current horror authors. He's created a unique world that's a far cry from any of the current trends in horror fiction. In fact, his style seems generations removed from all the apocalyptic zombie and vampire novels on the market. Thankfully, he understands that the most

important ingredients are strong characters, originality, and a compelling story. That his novel is also dark, frightening, and beautifully written is just icing on the cake."
—Chris Hallock, All Things Horror

Praise for *MONSTROUS AFFECTIONS*

"[L]ike the cover, the stories inside are not what they seem. But also, like the cover, the stories inside are brilliant. . . . You'd think that you were reading a book full of what you had always expected a horror story to be, but Nickle takes a left turn and blindsides you with tales that are not of the norm, but are all the more horrific because of surprise twists, darkness and raw emotion."
—*January Magazine*'s Best Books of 2009

"Bleak, stark and creepy, Stoker-winner Nickle's first collection will delight the literary horror reader. . . . Thirteen terrifying tales of rural settings, complex and reticent characters and unexpected twists that question the fundamentals of reality. All are delivered with a certain grace, creating a sparse yet poetic tour of the horrors that exist just out of sight. . . . This ambitious collection firmly establishes Nickle as a writer to watch."
—*Publishers Weekly* (starred review)

"David Nickle writes 'em damned weird and damned good and damned dark. He is bourbon-rough, poetic and vivid. Don't miss this one."
—Cory Doctorow, author of *Little Brother*

"Rich characters and a love of unique twists top off a captivating and sometimes gruesome collection of nightmares."
—Corey Redekop author of *Husk*

OTHER CZP BOOKS BY DAVID NICKLE

Monstrous Affections

Eutopia: A Novel of Terrible Optimism

Rasputin's Bastards

The 'Geisters

FIRST EDITION

Knife Fight and Other Struggles © 2014 by David Nickle
Cover artwork © 2014 by Erik Mohr
Cover design © 2014 by Vince Haig
Interior design © 2014 by Kailey Lang

Distributed in Canada by
HarperCollins Canada Ltd.
1995 Markham Road
Scarborough, ON M1B 5M8
Toll Free: 1-800-387-0117
e-mail: hcorder@harpercollins.com

Distributed in the U.S. by
Diamond Comic Distributors, Inc.
10150 York Road, Suite 300
Hunt Valley, MD 21030
Phone: (443) 318-8500
e-mail: books@diamondbookdistributors.com

Library and Archives Canada Cataloguing in Publication

Nickle, David, 1964-, author
    Knife fight and other struggles / David Nickle.

Issued in print and electronic formats.
ISBN 978-1-77148-304-9 (pbk.).--ISBN 978-1-77148-305-6 (ebook)

    I. Title.

PS8577.I33K55 2014   C813'.54   C2014-905908-6
                                               C2014-905909-4

CHIZINE PUBLICATIONS
Toronto, Canada
www.chizinepub.com
info@chizinepub.com

Edited by Brett Savory
Proofread by Sandra Kasturi

Canada Council   Conseil des arts
for the Arts   du Canada

We acknowledge the support of the Canada Council for the Arts which last year invested $20.1 million in writing and publishing throughout Canada.

ONTARIO ARTS COUNCIL
CONSEIL DES ARTS DE L'ONTARIO
an Ontario government agency
un organisme du gouvernement de l'Ontario

Published with the generous assistance of the Ontario Arts Council.

Printed in Canada

KNIFE FIGHT

AND OTHER STRUGGLES

DAVID NICKLE

Introduction by Hugo Award-
winning author Peter Watts

ChiZine Publications

For Lawrence Nickle
1931–2014

TABLE OF CONTENTS

DEATH THREATS AND LOVE LETTERS
An Introduction by Peter Watts

I've always been a little jealous of David Nickle.

Actually, scratch "a little." And add a noun: I'm not only jealous, I'm *afraid*—afraid of the inevitable day when word gets out how good a writer the man really is. That day will be as the breaking of a dam: there will come fame, and single-digit rankings on bestseller lists, and movie options with whispers of Guillermo del Toro as director. None of those movies will ever get made—which is just as well because most directors would fail miserably at doing justice to Dave's words—but it won't matter because he'll be rich and famous and I'll still be stuck behind in this midlist genre ghetto where publishers bitch-slap you for the sheer sadistic fun of pulling the wings off flies.

I'm actually a bit mystified as to why this hasn't happened already. After all, the man has three novels, two collections, a TV adaption, and a fistful of awards under his belt[1]. The reviews have been rhapsodic; critics have compared Nickle to Stephen King (*Library Journal, The National Post*), Alice Munro (*Quill & Quire*), Lovecraft *and* Mark Twain (*The New York Review of Science Fiction*). I suspect the reason for his continuing relative obscurity may have something to do with the horror ghetto with which he's associated—a ghetto he quite happily embraces while still acknowledging that he bleeds beyond its boundaries.

Horror gets its fucking tentacles into everything. It's not even a genre, really; it's a state of mind. Its defining characteristic isn't science or romance or the supernatural—horror is, quite simply, any

---

1 A Stoker, an Aurora, and a Black Quill. But who's counting?

literature that hacks the brainstem. Horror can't even be bothered to "transcend genre," as the tweedy elbow-patched literary types like to say when forced to concede the merits of a genre story even though they can't bring themselves to admit that it is one. Horror *subverts* genre. It tunnels underneath the borders, eats the foundations out from wherever you are, be it generation starship or nineteenth-century saloon. The first clue you have is when the floor collapses out from under you and pitches you headlong into a suffocating morass of roots and worms. Horror can sneak up on you *anywhere*.

So it is with David Nickle.

And yet—dammit, the man is *not* just a horror writer. Sure, his debut novel *Eutopia* (and *Volk*, its upcoming sequel) has all the trappings—dark woods, creepy denizens of hidden towns, monsters right out of Lovecraft—but it's pure biology-based science fiction.[2] Wipe the dust off its sepia-tinted 1911 context and you'll see some pretty savvy speculation on genetics, parasite-host interactions, and the origin of the religious impulse. *Rasputin's Bastards* is equal parts Jules Verne, cold-war paranoia, Tony Soprano, and *Bioshock*. And *The 'Geisters*—

Okay, I'll give you *The 'Geisters*. That's pretty much straight-up supernatural horror. But I'm not claiming that Nickle *never* writes horror; I'm just pointing out that that's not *all* he writes, that in fact it might not even be *most* of what he writes. If the CanLit crowd realized that fact—well, he'd still be pretty obscure, because CanLit.

If the *rest* of the world realized it, though . . .

Take the stories in this collection. Sure, some are horror; one creeped me out enough to leave me impotent for a week. (I won't tell you which—but one of Stephen King's seventies-era shorts played around with a similar premise, and Nickle's take bothered me way more than King's did.) "The Exorcist: A Love Story" is a brilliant tale of demonic possession, told by the demon. "The Nothing Book of the Dead" is the ultimate epistolary ghost story. "Black Hen a la Ford," "The Radejestians," "The Summer Worms"—straight-up horror, all of them.

But then there's "Knife Fight," a story which—for all the horrific *feel* of the thing—is an utterly mainstream, entirely plausible and astonishingly prescient tale of municipal politics starring Toronto's most infamous mayor. (Let us take a moment to hope that I have not said anything legally actionable by said mayor—or that if I have,

2 And I shouldn't have to tell you this, but Lovecraft regarded himself as a science fiction writer.

Dave's editor will have caught it.) There's "Love Means Forever," an unholy tongue-in-cheek (please God let it be tongue-in-cheek) love child of *Analog* and *True Romance*. "Oops" is a brief bright nugget of fundamentalist Christian theology, as only Nickle can do it. "Wylde's Kingdom" is giddy epic satiric squid porn. And "Basements"—

Damn, "Basements" almost defies description. It's like reading a dream: languid, arbitrary, beholden to no logic but its own. You watch yourself do things you don't really understand, in environments that grow stranger by such infinitesimal increments that, looking back, you'll never be able to put your finger on just when the reality segued into the nightmare. It's a quiet love letter to the heat death of the universe.

One or two of these stories teeter on the border. "The Summer Worms" doubles as political commentary, perfectly capturing the essential ugliness of nature and presenting a powerful argument for destroying it at all costs. "Drakeela Must Die" might be horror, or it might not—and the latter interpretation is by far the more horrifying of the two.

All this might lead you to conclude that Nickle is a chorus unto himself, that he has narrative *range*, that each of his stories speaks with its own unique voice. That is true. And yet at the same time there's something characteristic about the man's prose. If I had to conjure up a musical analogy I'd point to Jethro Tull: a group whose stylings covered the gamut from Blues to hard rock, folk to electropop, yet whose work remains instantly recognizable thanks to the distinct nasal vocals of front man Ian Anderson (and to his cerebral and frequently vulgar lyrics). Nickle's voice is something like that: there's a certain definitive resonance underscoring every voice he takes. I'm not quite sure how to best describe it. It can be warm and freezing at the same time. It's somehow *humane*, even when speaking through the mouth of a parasite embedded in unwilling flesh. It's evocative: you can smell the stale piss in every dark old house he leads you into, you can *feel* the piercing stare of that cold invertebrate eye, the size of a hubcap, as the thing behind it drags you down into the freezing abyss. If the Group of Seven had worked in prose instead of oils—and if they'd been raised on a diet of Lynch and Cronenberg—they might have come close to what David Nickle fishes from his id for our edification.

If you've read him before, you know this already. If you haven't, then get started; you'll discover soon enough why I fear his breakout success. You'll understand why I may, out of sheer irrational jealous resentment, hunt him down and kill him before that happens.

But probably not. Because then I wouldn't be able to read any more of his stories.

—March 2014

LOOKER

I met her on the beach.

It was one of Len's parties—one of the last he threw, before he had to stop. You were there too. But we didn't speak. I remember watching you talking with Jonathan on the deck, an absurdly large tumbler for such a small splash of Merlot wedged at your elbow as you nodded, eyes fixed on his so as not to meet mine. If you noticed me, I hope you also noticed I didn't linger.

Instead, I took my own wine glass, filled it up properly, climbed down that treacherous wooden staircase, and kicked off my shoes. It was early enough that the sand was still warm from the sun—late enough that the sun was just dabs of pink on the dark ocean and I could imagine I had the beach to myself.

She was, I'm sure, telling herself the same thing. She had brought a pipe and a lighter with her in her jeans, and was perched on a picnic table, surreptitiously puffing away. The pipe disappeared as I neared her. It came back soon enough, when she saw my wineglass, maybe recognized me from the party.

I didn't recognize her. She was a small woman, but wide across the shoulders and the tiniest bit chubby. Hair was dark, pulled back into a ponytail. Pretty, but not pretty enough; she would fade at a party like Len's.

"Yeah, I agree," she said to me and I paused on my slow gambol to the surf.

"It's too bright," she said, and as I took a long pull from my wine, watching her curiously, she added, "Look at him."

"Look at me," I said, and she laughed.

"You on the phone?" I asked, and she dropped her head in extravagant *mea culpa*.

"No," she said. "Just . . ."

"Don't fret. What's the point of insanity if you can't enjoy a little conversation?"

Oh, I am smooth. She laughed again, and motioned me over, and waved the pipe and asked if I'd like to share.

"Sure," I said, and she scooted aside to make room on the table. Her name was Lucy. Lucille, actually, was how she introduced herself but she said Lucy was fine.

I introduced myself. "Tom's a nice name," she said.

The night grew. Lungs filled with smoke and mouths with wine; questions asked, questions answered. *How do you know Len? What do you do? What brings you to the beach when so much is going on inside*? It went both ways.

Lucy knew Len scarcely at all. They'd met through a friend who worked at Len's firm. Through the usual convolutions of dinners and pubs and excursions, she'd insinuated herself onto the cc list of the *ur*-mail by which Len advertised his parties. She worked cash at a bookstore chain in town and didn't really have a lot of ambition past that right now. Which tended to make her feel seriously out of her weight class at Len's parties, or so she said; the beach, therefore, was an attractive option.

She finished my wine for me, and we walked. I'd been on my way to the water's edge and Lucy thought that was a fine idea. The sun was all gone by now and stars were peeking out. One of the things I liked about Len's place—it was just far enough away from town you could make out stars at night. Not like the deep woods, or the mountains. But constellations weren't just theoretical there.

"Hey, Tom," she said as the surf touched our toes, "want to go for a swim? I know we don't have suits, but . . ."

Why not? As you might remember, I've a weakness for the midnight dunk. We both did, as I recall.

I stepped back a few yards to where the sand was dry, set down my glass and stripped off my shirt, my trousers. Lucy unbuttoned her blouse, the top button of her jeans. I cast off my briefs. "Well?" I said, standing *in flagrante delicto* in front of her.

"Get in," she said, "I'll be right behind you."

It didn't occur to me that this might be a trick until I was well out at sea. Wouldn't it be the simplest thing, I thought, as I dove under a breaking wave, to wait until I was out far enough, gather my trousers, find the wallet and the mobile phone, toss the clothes into the surf and run to a waiting car? I'm developing my suspicious mind, really, my dearest—but it still has a time delay on it, even after everything. . . .

I came up, broke my stroke, and turned to look back at the beach.

She waved at me. I was pleased—and relieved—to see that she was naked too. My valuables were safe as they could be. And Lucy had quite a nice figure, as it turned out: fine full breasts—wide, muscular hips—a small bulge at the tummy, true . . . but taken with the whole, far from offensive.

I waved back, took a deep breath and dove again, this time deep enough to touch bottom. My fingers brushed sea-rounded rock and stirred up sand, and I turned and kicked and broke out to the moonless night, and only then it occurred to me—how clearly I'd seen her on the beach, two dozen yards off, maybe farther.

There lay the problem. There wasn't enough light. I shouldn't have seen anything.

I treaded water, thinking back at how I'd seen her . . . glistening, flickering, with tiny points of red, of green . . . winking in and out . . . like stars themselves? Spread across not sky, but flesh?

I began to wonder: Had I seen her at all?

There was no sign of her now. The beach was a line of black, crowned with the lights from Len's place, and above that . . . the stars.

How much had I smoked? I wondered. What had I smoked, for that matter? I hadn't had a lot of wine—I'd quaffed a glass at Len's before venturing outside, and I'd shared the second glass with Lucy. Not even two glasses. . . .

But it *was* Len's wine.

I'd made up my mind to start back in when she emerged from the waves—literally in front of my face.

"You look lost," Lucy said, and splashed me, and dove again. Two feet came up, and scissored, and vanished. Some part of her brushed against my hip.

I took it as my cue and ducked.

The ocean was nearly a perfect black. I dove and turned and dove again, reaching wide in my strokes, fingers spreading in a curious, and yes, hungry grasp. I turned, and came near enough the surface that I felt my foot break it, splashing down again, and spun—

—and I saw her.

Or better, I saw the constellation of Lucy—a dusting of brilliant red points of light, defining her thighs—and then turning, and more along her midriff; a burst of blue stipple, shaping her breasts, the backs of her arms. I kicked toward her as she turned in the water, my own arms held straight ahead, to lay hold of that fine, if I may say, celestial body.

But she anticipated me, and kicked deeper, and I'd reached my lungs' limits so I broke surface, gasping at the night air. She was beside me an instant later, spitting and laughing. No funny lights this time; just Lucy, soaking wet and treading water beside me.

"We don't have towels," she said. "I just thought of that. We're going to freeze."

"We won't freeze," I said.

"It's colder than you think."

"Oh, I know it's cold. We just won't freeze."

She splashed me and laughed again and wondered what I meant by that, but we both knew what I meant by that, and after we'd not-quite tired ourselves out in the surf, we made back for the shore.

I wonder how things went for you, right then? I know that you always fancied Jonathan; I know what happened later. I hope you don't think I'm being bitter or ironic when I say I hope you had a good time with him. If he misbehaved—well, I trust you did too.

Shall I tell you how *we* misbehaved?

Well—

In some ways, it was as you might expect; nothing you haven't seen, nothing you haven't felt, my dear.

In others . . .

Through the whole of it, Lucy muttered.

"He is," she would say as I pressed against her breasts and nibbled on her earlobe; and "Quiet!" as I ran my tongue along the rim of her aureole . . . "I said no," as I thrust into her, and I paused, and then she continued: "Why are you stopping, Tommy?"

This went on through the whole of it. As I buried my face between her legs, and she commented, "Isn't he, though?" I thought again of Lucy on the shore, under the water. "Too bright," she moaned, and I remembered my visions of the sky, on her skin.

And as I thought of these things, my hands went exploring: along her thighs, across her breasts—along her belly. . . .

She gasped and giggled as I ran my thumb across her navel . . . and she said, "Tommy?" as my forefinger touched her navel again . . . and "What are you doing?" as the palm of my hand, making its way along the ridge of her hip-bone . . . found her navel once more.

I lifted my head and moved my hand slowly aside. For an instant, there was a flash of dim red light—reflecting off my palm like a candle-flame. But only an instant. I moved my hand aside and ran the edge of my thumb over the flesh there. It was smooth.

"Tom?" she said sharply, and started on about unfinished business.

"Shh," I said, and lowered my face—to the ridge of her hip-bone, or rather the smooth flesh inward of it. And slowly, paying minute attention, I licked her salted skin.

I would not have found it with my crude, calloused fingertips; my tongue was better attuned to the task. I came upon it first as a small bump in the smooth flesh: like a pimple, a cyst. As I circled it, I sensed movement, as though a hard thing were rolling inside. Running across the tiny peak of it, I sensed a line—like a slit in the flesh, pushed tightly closed. Encouraged, I surrounded it with my lips and began to suck, as I kept probing it with my tongue.

"I'm sorry," she said, and then, "Oh!" as my tongue pushed through. It touched a cool, wet thing—rolling on my tongue like an unripened berry.

And then . . . I was airborne . . . it was as though I were flying up, and falling deep. And I landed hard on my side and it all resolved, the world once more. Icy water lapped against me. And Lucy was swearing at me.

I looked at her, unbelieving. She looked back.

She, and a multitude.

For now I could see that what I'd first thought were star-points, were nothing of the sort. Her flesh was pocked with eyes. They were small, and reflective, like a cat's.

Nocturnal eyes.

In her shoulders—the swell of her breasts—along the line of her throat . . . They blinked—some individually, some in pairs, and on her belly, six points of cobalt blue, formed into a nearly perfect hexagon. Tiny slits of pupils widened to take in the sight of me. The whole of her flesh seemed to writhe with their squinting.

It didn't seem to cause her discomfort. Far from it; Lucy's own eyes—the ones in her head—narrowed to slits, and her mouth perked in a little smile. "He is that," she said, "yes, you're right." And it struck me then: those strange things she was saying weren't intended for me or anyone else.

She was talking to the eyes.

"He can't have known," she continued, her hand creeping down to her groin, "and if he did, well now he knows better."

I drew my legs to my chest and my own hands moved instinctively to my privates, as the implications of all those eyes, of her words, came together.

These weren't her eyes; they were from another creature, or many creatures. And they were all looking upon me: naked, sea-shrivelled, crouching in the dirt.

Turning away from her, I got to my feet, ran up the beach and gathered my shirt and trousers, and clutching them to my chest, fairly bolted for the stairs. I pulled on my clothes, hunted around for my shoes, and made my way up the stairs. At the top, I looked back for the glow of Lucy. But the beach was dark.

The eyes were shut.

———

You and Jonathan were gone by the time I came back to the house.

I wasn't surprised; Len had switched to his Sarah Vaughan/Etta James playlist, and I remember how fond you are of those two. And it was late. The party had waxed and waned during my excursion with Lucy on the beach and those who remained were the die-hards: Ben and Dru, sprawled on the sectional, finishing off a bottle of shiraz; Dennis, holding court in the kitchen with Emile and Prabh and the dates they'd not thought to introduce—at least not to me; maybe a half-dozen others that neither of us would recognize if we met them on the street. Len's party had proceeded without me.

I wasn't surprised, and I wasn't unhappy about it. Skinny dipping in the ocean and fucking on the beach are two activities that hardly leave one presentable to polite company. Best then to wait until the polite company had moved along, leaving only the depraved ones.

I made for the bathroom—the second floor bath, which yes, I know, was a *faux pas* at Len's parties, particularly late into the evening. But there was a small crowd around the two-piece off the kitchen, and I needed to tidy up sooner. So I slipped upstairs and made for the master bath. Which, happily, was vacant. The lights flickered on as I stepped inside and I slid the pocket door shut, and confronted myself in the long mirror opposite the showers.

I didn't think I took that long; just splashed water in my face, ran a wet comb through my hair, shook the sand out of my shirt and tucked it in properly before giving myself another inspection. By my own reckoning, it couldn't have been more than five minutes. But the hammering on the door said otherwise.

It was Kimi, Len's Kimi.

In a week, she'd be on a plane back to New York, done with all of us, gone from Len's circle for good. That party, she was on the verge of it. I slid open the door and apologized. "You shouldn't be up here," she said, "not this time of night," and I agreed.

"Ask forgiveness not permission? That it, Tommy?" she said and brushed past me. She had been spending time in Len's rooms, and it had gone about as badly as it did toward the end. You could tell. Do you remember that time Len had us all on that boat he'd hired for the summer? And she came hammering on our cabin door—with that fishhook stuck in just below the collarbone? And when you opened it, she was so quiet, asking if you knew where they kept the first-aid kit on the boat because "Len isn't sure." You knew something awful had happened, I knew something awful had happened.

We talked about it after we got the hook out and the wound cleaned and bandaged and Kimi, smiling brightly, had excused herself and skipped back to the cabin she and Len were sharing. What did you say? "One day, that armour of hers is going to crack. When it does, she'll either leave or she'll die."

It was a good line; I laughed as hard as you did.

Well, there in the upstairs bath, the armour was cracking. And Kimi wasn't dead. But she wasn't leaving either. She leaned against the vanity, arms crossed over her chest. She was wearing a short black skirt. Her shoulders, arms, and legs were bare. There were no visible bruises. No fishhooks either. She studied me, maybe looking for the same things.

"You go for a swim?" she said finally. "You look like you went for a swim in the ocean."

"Guilty."

Her eyes flickered away a moment as she waved a hand. "Nobody's guilty of taking a fucking swim. And it's a good look for you." Then she looked again, reassessing. "But you didn't just go for a swim."

"You were right. I took a fucking swim," I said, and started to laugh, and she got it and laughed too.

"How's your night going?" I asked. She made a little sneer with her lips—as if she was trying to fish a piece of food out of her teeth. Put her bare feet together on the slate tile floor, made a show of inspecting the nails.

"Len's very tired," she said.

I raised my eyebrows. "Oh dear. That doesn't sound good."

"It's not as bad as that."

"If you say so."

She looked at me. "Are you hitting on me, Tommy?"

I said I wasn't.

"Then why the fuck are you still here?"

There was an answer to that question, but not one I could really articulate—not the way she was looking at me then. I wanted to talk to her about Lucy, about the eyes. . . . I thought—hoped—that she would be able to help me parse the experience somehow. Or failing that, help me put it away, someplace quiet.

But her armour was cracked. She had nothing to offer me. And although I wouldn't know for sure until a week later—she wasn't leaving that night, she stayed the whole time—she was almost certainly planning her escape.

So I left her to it. "I'm very tired too," I said, and stepped into the hall.

That one didn't get a laugh. The bathroom door slid shut behind me, hitting the doorjamb hard enough to quiver in its track.

"You're still thinking about *her*," said Kimi through the wood. "Well, give it up, Tommy. It's obvious to everybody. She's done with you."

Oh, don't worry. I know you're done with me. I'm done with you too.

I joined the conversation in the kitchen, or rather hovered at its edge. Dennis had stepped away, and now Emile was talking about Dubai, which was hardly a new topic for him. But the girls he and Prabh had brought were new. They hung on every word. I leaned against the stove, poured myself the dregs of a Chardonnay into a little plastic cup and swallowed the whole thing. Prabh found me a Malbec from Portugal and poured a refill.

"Yeah, you look like shit," he said. "Bad night?"

"Not exactly bad," I said. "Strange. Not exactly bad."

Prabh nodded and turned back to his girl. She was very pretty, I had to hand it to him: tall, with streaked blonde hair and a dancer's body. Twenty-seven years old, no older. I'd turn back to her too.

So I kept drinking, and Prabh kept filling my cup, and after a while, I'd moved from the periphery of the conversation to the juicy middle. And there, I asked as innocently as I could manage: "Any of you know Lucy?"

Shrugs all around. I showed a level hand to indicate her height. Another to show how long her hair was. "We don't know her, Tom," said Emile, and Prabh poured me another glass.

"Maybe you want to sit down?" asked one of the girls.

It was an excellent suggestion. I made my way to the sectional in the living room with only a little help here and there, as necessary.

Really, I don't think I made *that* much of a spectacle of myself. But I had had too much to drink and I'd had it all too quickly. I was speaking extemporaneously, you might say. So I concluded it best not to speak at all.

I fitted myself into the corner of the sectional. Dru and Ben, a few feet to my left, made a point of staying engrossed in one another— and as soon as it was polite to do so, got up and found spots at the dining room table. And I was left to myself.

By this time it was well past midnight. You know how that is. It's a time when you start asking questions about things that in the light of day you wouldn't consider twice. It's a time . . . well, we both know how it goes, in the dark hour.

I was left to myself.

<hr>

I began to feel badly about leaving Lucy on the beach. I wondered if I might have handled things differently. I worried that I might have impregnated her, or caught a venereal disease. Briefly, I worried that some of those eyes might have migrated from her skin to mine—if I'd caught a case of leaping, burrowing, and uniquely ocular crabs. If I closed my own eyes, would I see a thousand dim refractions of the room from the point of view of my belly?

The notion made me laugh—a little too loudly, I think. Dennis, reeking of weed and vodka cooler, just about turned on his heel at the sight of me and fled back to the deck. But it got me wondering at the nature of Lucy's peculiar disease again, if that's what it was. If not she, then who was looking out through those eyes? And so, in circles, went my thoughts.

The front door opened and closed once, twice, five times. Water ran in the kitchen sink. Lights dimmed in rooms not far from this one.

"Hey, Tom. How you keeping?"

I looked up and blinked.

"Hey, Len," I said. "Haven't seen you all night."

He nodded. "I've been a rotten host."

Len was wearing his kimono, that red one with the lotus design. He'd lost a lot of weight—you couldn't mistake it, the kimono hung so loose on him. His hair was coming back in, but it was still thin, downy. He sat down beside me.

"You met Lucille," he said.

"How did you know?" I asked, but I didn't need to; as I spoke, I saw Kimi over the breakfast bar in the kitchen, putting glasses into the dishwasher. She'd told him about our conversation in the washroom. He'd put it together.

"Yeah," said Len, "you were on the beach. Two of you. Had yourself a time, didn't you, Tom?"

"We had ourselves a time."

Len put a bony hand on my thigh, gave it a squeeze of surprising strength, and nodded.

"Now you're drunk in my living room, when everybody else has had the sense to get out. Too drunk to drive yourself, am I right?"

That was true.

"And you don't have cab fare, do you?"

I didn't have cab fare.

"You're a fucking leech, Tom. You *smell* like a fucking leech."

"It's the ocean," I said.

Kimi turned her back to us, lowered her head and raised her shoulder blades, like wings, as she ran water in the kitchen sink.

"Yeah, we know that's not so," said Len. "You smell of Lucy." He licked his lips, and not looking up, Kimi called out, "That's not nice, Len," and Len chuckled and jacked a thumb in her direction and shrugged.

"Did she leave?" I asked. "Lucy, I mean."

"Miss her too now?" Did I miss her like *you*, he meant, obviously.

"I just didn't see her leave."

"What'd I just say? *Everybody else* had the sense to get out."

A plate clattered loudly in the sink. Len shouted at Kimi to *be fuckin' careful with that*. Then he coughed and turned an eye to me. His expression changed.

"You saw," he said quietly. "Didn't you?"

"I saw."

He looked like he wanted to say more. But he stopped himself, the way he does: tucking his chin down, pursing his lips . . . like he's doing some math, which is maybe close to the mark of what he is doing until he finally speaks.

"Did she tell you how we met?"

"Friend of a friend," I said, then remembered: "Not just a friend; one of your partners. And then you just kept inviting her out."

"Always that simple, isn't it?"

"It's never that simple," I said, "you're going to tell me."

"It is that simple," he said. "Lucille Carroll is a high school friend of Linda James. Linda isn't a partner now and I won't likely live to see the day that she is. But she did work for me. With me. And she used to come out sometimes. And she brought Lucille one day. And not long after, Linda stopped coming around. Lucille still shows up." He sighed. "Simple."

Kimi flipped a switch under the counter and the dishwasher hummed to life. "I'm turning in," she announced, and when Len didn't say anything, she climbed the stairs.

"It's not that simple," I said when Kimi was gone. Now, I thought, was the time when Len would spell it out for me: tell me what had happened, really.

"And she doesn't like to talk about it," was what he said instead. "It's private, Tom."

What came next? Well, I might have handled it better. But you know how I hate it when my friends hide things from me. We both remember the weekend at the lake, with your sister and her boys. Did I ever properly apologize for that? It's difficult to, when all I've spoken is God's truth.

But I could have handled it better.

"It's not private," I said, "it's the opposite. She's the least private person I've met. The eyes . . ."

"Her skin condition, you mean."

"You do know about them." I may have jabbed him in the chest. That may have been unwise. "Maybe you like them? Watching everything you do? Maybe they flatter your vanity. . . ."

Len shook his head. He stopped me.

"You know what, Tom? I'm sick of you. I've been sick of you for a long time. But I'm also sick, and I'll tell you—that clarifies things for a man. So here's what I see:

"You come here to my house—you moon around like some fucking puppy dog—you drink my wine . . . the friends of mine you don't fuck, you bother with your repetitive, self-involved shit. Jesus, Tom. You're a leech."

"I'm sorry," I said, because really—what else do you say to something like that? To someone like Len, for Christ's sake?

"Yeah," he said. "Heard that one before. Lucy's a special girl, Tom. She's helping me in ways you couldn't imagine. And it has nothing to do with my fucking vanity. Not a fucking thing. Lucy's my . . .

assurance. And she's always welcome here."

"I'm sorry."

"I got that. Now are you okay to drive yet, Tom?"

I wasn't. But I said sure.

"Then you get out of my house. Get back to your place. Stay there. I don't think you should come back here again."

———

Yes. That's why you hadn't seen me at Len's after that. He cast me out—into the wilderness—left me to my own devices.

I wasn't avoiding you.

Far from it.

———

Lucy wasn't that hard to find.

She had a Facebook page, and I had enough information to narrow her down from the list of those other Lucy Carrolls who said they were from here. So I sent her a note apologizing for being such an asshole, and she sent me a friend request and I agreed—and she asked me to pick a place, and that's where we met. The Tokyo Grill in the Pier District. I don't think we ever went there, you and I. But at 12:15 on a Tuesday in June, it's very bright.

Lucy wore a rose print dress, not quite as pale as her skin. She had freckles and her hair was more reddish than brunette. Perhaps it was the effect of wearing a dress and not a pair of jeans, but she seemed more svelte on the patio than she did that night on the beach. *Her eyes were hazel.*

Do you remember how I courted you? Did you ever doubt that I was anything but spontaneous? That when I laughed so hard at that joke of yours, it was because I thought it was the funniest thing I'd ever heard?

You didn't? You should have. I'm not good at everything in life, oh that I'll admit. But I am good at this part. I am smooth.

And that's how I was at the Tokyo Grill that Tuesday.

Lucy wasn't sure about me and she made that explicit pretty early. I'd seemed nice at first, but running off like that . . . well, it had been hurtful. It made her feel as though there was something wrong with her, and as she made explicit somewhat later on, there wasn't anything wrong with her.

"It's not you—it's the rest of the world," I said, and when she took offense, I explained I wasn't making fun.

"The world's an evil place. Lots wrong with it. Look at . . . think about Len, as an example."

"What do you mean?"

"Well. How he treats people. How he uses them. Like Kimi."

"He's an important man," she said quickly. "I imagine it takes a toll. All those clients he's got to look after." She sighed. "Clients can be very demanding."

"Clients." I made a little smile. "That's a good word. Len has clients like other people have friends."

Yes, I suppose I was being dramatic. But Lucy didn't think so; she laughed, very hard, and agreed.

"So what about you?" she asked. "Are you client or friend?"

"Something else."

I explained how Lucy wasn't the only one I'd offended with my bad behaviour that night—and again, I layered contrition on top of itself, and doing so took another step to winning her over.

Working through it, I could almost forget that Lucy was a woman containing a multitude—that as she sat here opposite me in the Pier District, the lids up and down her body squinted shut like tiny incision scars against the bright daylight.

Like clients.

I had to forget. Because I couldn't mention them; Len was right— she didn't want to talk about it. She may not have even been capable.

And keeping silent on the subject, and knowing of that alien scrutiny, resting behind translucent lids . . .

I couldn't have done what I had to do.

Lucy's next shift at the bookstore was Wednesday afternoon, so she had the rest of the day to herself, and as we finished our sashimi, she made a point of saying the afternoon shift meant she could stay out as late as she liked.

So we took a walk. We found my car. We drove back to my apartment. And behind drawn blinds, we stripped off our clothes and lay down together on fresh white sheets.

Oh dear. I can tell you're upset—not by anything I've done, but what you think I'm about to do: relay some detailed account of how it was for Lucy and I, rutting on the very same sheets where you and I lolled, those long Sunday mornings, when . . . well, before you came to your senses is how you might put it. . . .

I'll try and be circumspect.

Lucy talked through it all, same as she had on the beach: those half-formed statements: "He's the same," and "The third floor," and "I do not agree." Of course, she was talking to them—fielding questions: *Is he the handsome fellow from the beach? On what floor is this fellow's apartment? Don't you think he's a bit much—being too . . .*

too . . .

To which she answered: *I do not agree.*

I'd drawn the curtains in my rooms, to make it dim enough for the curious eyes to open without being blinded—and sure enough, that is what they did. As I ran my tongue along her shoulder blade, I found myself looking into a tiny blue orb, no bigger than a rat's. It blinked curiously at me as I moved past, to the nape of her neck, and there, in the wispy curls at the base of her skull, I uncovered two yellow eyes, set close together, in the forest of her hair. Were they disapproving? I imagine they must have been, affixed on Lucy's skull, less than an inch from her brain. I winked and moved on.

"Tell them," I whispered into her ear, looking into a squinting, infinitely old eye fixed in her temple, "that I understand."

"He understands," she murmured.

"Tell them I'm not afraid."

"He's not afraid."

"Tell them," I said, before I moved from her ear to her mouth, and rolled her onto her back, and slid atop her, "that I'm ready."

And the rest of it?

Well, I did tell you I'd be circumspect. Suffice it to say . . . just as poor old Len would, not long after . . .

I *entered* her.

You looked good at my funeral. You and Jonathan both. The dress you wore—was it new? Did you buy it especially for the occasion? It would be nice to think that you had.

In any event, I must say that Jonathan was very supportive of you. He held your hand so very tightly through the eulogies. Had you needed it, I'm sure he would have provided a handkerchief; if it had rained at the graveside, he'd have held the umbrella. He seems that sort of upright fellow. A real keeper.

You look great now too. You have a lovely smile, you always have, and the shorter haircut—it suits you. It really frames your face. I can't hear what you're saying, here in Emile's house in town, over the dregs of what I recall as being an acceptable cab franc from Chile.

Still, you're laughing, and that's good. You've left Kimi and poor dying Len behind. You're cementing new friendships . . . with Prabh and Emile and, perhaps, Lucy?

Perhaps.

It's impossible to say of course—I haven't been at this long enough to learn how to read lips, particularly with that damned brooch in the way. I never could guess your mind on this sort of thing. But you seem . . . open to it, to this new friend who works the cash in your favourite bookstore. You are. Aren't you?

Ah well. I must learn patience here in my new place. After all, Lucy will tell me everything—in due time, in a quiet moment, when the lights are low:

She says she misses you. She says she can't believe she let you go. Now that you're gone.

She says that she and I will be great friends.

And then, if all goes well . . . if you and Lucy really do hit it off . . .

I can't promise, other than to say I'll do my best. I'll try not to let my gaze linger.

THE EXORCIST: A LOVE STORY

McGill smoked in the yard. They wouldn't let him smoke inside. There was a baby there after all. McGill said he understood, but he seemed pissed off about it. He stood by the barbecue, squinting at the tree line, calculating the hour, tapping ashes through the grill top. They were pissed off about *that*. The next round of burgers would have a subtle flavour of McGill and probably the round after those too.

But they would put up with it. Oh yes.

They would bloody well put up with it.

———

One of them had gone to high school with McGill. But she didn't know him then. He had a bit of acne trouble, did McGill—quite a bit. A Biblical plague of pimples, one might say. Horrific, seeping boils from his forehead down to his neck. One over his lip, round and gleaming and red, like a billiard ball.

An outgoing personality, some athletic talent, a fancy car—any one of these might have saved him. But McGill had none of that. So there he was.

She had no idea that McGill went to the same school. She got his name through another chain of acquaintances. When she contacted him, he did not offer up any hint of their own acquaintance with one another. He did not let the recognition creep into his voice.

It would be generous to say that McGill handled the interview professionally. Because McGill has never been much of a professional.

I wish I could have heard his side of it. But I could guess—McGill and I go way back.

"We're not Catholic," she'd said, and paused, and laughed nervously. "You're not either." Pause. "Yes, Mr. McGill, I guess that is something we have in common." Another pause. "He's six months old. Born February 12." Pause. "Yes. Aquarius." *What's your sign, baby?* Really? "So explain to me how this non-demon—erm, non-denominational business works." And a long silence, as McGill went through the litany:

First, he must come by and meet the child. What if it's not a child? *It's always a child, dear.* Of course, if it happens to be Gran or Uncle Terry who's afflicted . . . well, McGill would try and adapt. But one way or another, in the course of a conversation, he would try and draw it out. McGill explains this part of his process as very simple—non-invasive—but he's not being completely honest.

He spends a lot of time staring, so intensely that sometimes he brings about tears. He mumbles nonsense words in a made-up language. He takes a photograph using a specially treated lens. And finally, under the parents' supervision, he lays a hand on the child's skull—leaving the impression with their parents that he is reading the aura. He is not. He is looking for a soft spot, a tiny hole in the skull—often no bigger than a baby's thumb. That is really the only thing that he's looking for in that first visit. Because if it's there . . . well, that's how we get in, isn't it?

And that is also how he can tell. If he jams his finger into it—with just the right force—well, even if we're reticent to start it up again with old McGill, we have no choice. It starts the real conversation.

And once that gets going, things become, shall we say, fluid.

————

McGill really needed three cigarettes, given everything—but well-brought-up lad that he is, he cut himself off at just one.

"You finally ready?" Her man was a testy one. He had never met McGill, had attended a different high school, had no earthly reason to suspect. And yet.

"Sure," said McGill. He started to meet his eyes, but didn't get far. McGill looking her man in the eye would have been a challenge. And McGill hadn't the balls for that.

She smiled uneasily, and shared a glance with her man. *Don't fuck this up, darling*, that glance said. He was not easy about bringing McGill, or anyone outside the family physician's circle, in on what he called "the postpartum thing." He didn't entirely buy in to what was going on. And in one sense, he couldn't be blamed. When the door in the basement slammed again and again, seemingly of its own accord, he was already on his way to an early meeting. He had been asleep the whole night, when the business with the hall mirror had transpired. He was at work the day the seven crows got into the nursery, and pecked one another to death as baby laughed.

He was always away, out of earshot, when baby spoke.

"My wife tells me that you're going to go have a conversation now," he said. McGill nodded.

"That's the first part."

He huffed. "Well good luck. Little Simon's not too verbal. Except around Shelly here. That right, babe?"

"I understand," said McGill. "Maybe I'll have better luck."

"Right. Do they all talk to you?"

"Often they do, that's right." McGill stepped toward the nursery. Her man stepped into his way, but didn't stop him either.

"You're for real," he said.

"He's for real," she said. "Please, Dave, just let him do his work."

McGill wanted to say something reassuring—he knew that he should. Couldn't quite muster it, though; he just hunched his shoulders in half a shrug, smiled in what amounted to an ambiguous shrug, and made another try for the nursery. The man put his hand on McGill's shoulder.

"Hang on there, buddy. This is my boy in there. You won't touch him, will you?"

"I'll put my hand on his head," said McGill. "No more than that."

(McGill stammered when he said that. But it's mean to mimic a stammer.)

"No more than that." The man put his hand on McGill's arm—around McGill's arm, really. "You're gonna wash that hand, then, brother."

"Dave!"

"Shelly." He kept hold of McGill. His tone was one that he thought was reasonable, but that she had told him more than once was a tone that was "goddamn scary." Which was all right, she said; it made her feel safe, she said. Protected.

His grip tightened on McGill's arm. "This is bullshit."

McGill drew in a breath. His arm was hurting, and he was doing his best not to show it. But he wasn't doing it very well, because she pointed out that he was hurting McGill and shamed him into letting go.

"It's all right," McGill lied. "Your husband—Dave's right. That is his boy in there, and it's your boy too. If parents are okay with it, it's better if it's just me and the baby. But we can do this with one or both of you in there too. Or I could come back—"

"No!" she said, too loudly, and then, too softly: "Don't go, Mr. McGill."

Did McGill's heart melt then? Did more than a decade of hope, of prayer, of dirty, dirty moments alone in his bed at the break of dawn . . . did all that draw together now, at the broken, pleading tone of her voice? Oh, how could it not? Was this not his dream, here before him, made flesh?

If it didn't melt—might it not soon shatter?

"I'll go in with you," she said. "Dave will wait here in the kitchen. Right, Dave?"

"I don't—"

"Dave. You promised."

And he had, and he knew it, and so that was that.

———

When I arrived, the nursery was a cheery space. She had painted the walls little-boy blue, and dangled a mobile of friendly looking farm animals. The changing table was an antique in a tawdry way; it had been a little sheet-metal desk, just the size for a typewriter, an "In" box and a sheaf of paper. This she had painted a bright yellow, covered in terrycloth and stacked diapers and baby powder and a box of wipes. There was a toy box, filled with bric-a-brac from the baby shower, and a chest of drawers, stuffed with more shower swag: jumpers and bonnets and a little denim jacket for baby to wear, eventually. Adorable.

McGill saw none of that.

They had stripped the place bare, but for the bassinet. Nothing sharp, nothing heavy. Nothing that could suffocate, and nothing flammable.

"That's him," he said, peering in.

"That's my baby." She said it jauntily enough but she finished on the edge of bitter laughter.

All business for the moment, McGill took no notice of it.

He reached into his coat, and pulled out his Pentax, with its smeary lens and etched-in F-stops. He snapped two pictures through that vile instrument, and set it down on the floor. "Don't touch it," he said as she leaned to get it. "Please."

"All right," she said.

He leaned farther over the edge and stared at me. I didn't look away. He shifted down to his knees and calmed his breathing. He blinked when I blinked. He breathed when I breathed. This went on for a while. How long? I can't honestly say; this part of things, it's easy to lose track of time, looking into the pale infinity of McGill's baby-blues. . . .

A girl could lose herself in there, don't you think?

"Aka Manah," he said finally.

"What?" She had been hovering by the door, and now she came closer. He just shook his head and continued—"Vassago . . . Furtur . . . Focalor."—shaking his head again after each name.

"Simon," she said.

"I know," said McGill. "That's the boy's name. Looking for the . . . other one's name."

"Do you just guess?"

"Something like that," said McGill. "Vepar. Mammon . . . Räum?"

"Okay."

"Not that," said McGill, "not him. Are you?"

No, McGill, I'm not Räum.

"Ah," he said, and leaned away from the bassinet. He rubbed his hands together, and blew air out through his cheeks. Just what he was afraid of.

"Gremory."

Aha!

"He snapped his fingers!"

"Did he?" said McGill. He was looking away.

"He did," she said. "Like a little Dean Martin." She thought about that for a second. "Is it Gremory? Is that the right name?"

"Think so."

A long breath. "How'd you guess it so fast?"

"Lucky." McGill came back and looked at me. His lips were drawn thin. His eyelids were too. He reached out with his right hand, fingers spread. They trembled as they rested on the baby's skull.

"What're you going to do?" she asked, and he brought his left forefinger to his lips. "Okay, I'll hush," she said, and his right hand tightened, at the little finger and thumb, like forceps behind the ears. His middle finger danced over the back of the skull, until it stopped, and dithered. It didn't last long, though; like a wedding ring spinning round a sink drain, it soon disappeared inside.

I had him to the second knuckle.

What does McGill see? What I wouldn't give to know. I know what I see; his eyelids, flickering like a hummingbird's wings, his mouth hanging open as he mumbles commands, sweat running down the side of his nose, staining his collar. But him? When he looks on me, does he see an obsidian woman, naked and shining, breasts suckling six crows, wormy cunny dripping amarone-scented menses into the deathly loam of Golgotha? Does he cower at my magnificent obscenity?

Does he wish for his mummy?

I cannot tell. All the times we have met, he has never said.

"You need to leave the baby."

No, McGill. I don't.

He said the baby's name.

That means shit to me, McGill.

"It is the owner of that form."

No. It's nothing. Unbaptized. Belongs to me.

"You got no claim. You are Gremory. You trespass here. Go on back to where you dwell."

I am who I am. I dwell where I am and I am here. You go back.

"I cast you out. I cast you out." He said some of those words that his mummy taught him. I let him go on for a dozen of them before I said anything.

Your heart's not in it, McGill. What's the matter now?

"You got to leave." He uttered another stanza.

You have to want it. You don't want it, do you?

"Git. Go on." He paused. His hand gripped the baby's skull tighter. If it were a baseball, he'd have been making ready to throw a curve. "Fuck out of here, you."

You're in such a hurry, McGill. You're missing steps; really, you're far from your usual professional self. Your mother would never have stood for that kind of thing. Never mind the language.

Oh, that got him. McGill's mother . . . what of her, hey? I hear she has been out of the game for some eight years now. She taught him everything he knows, and now everything she knows rests in McGill's unlovely skull. And she and her knowledge were formidable. Truly: None of us could best her like the Alzheimer's did. Now . . . she wouldn't know herself reflected in a mirror, would she?

He told me to fuck right off and called me hell-spawn. He told me I had "no fucking right." Me? I squirted moist feces into my diaper and chortled.

Mothers get them every time.

Eventually he ran himself down. I waited to make sure before continuing.

You haven't asked me what I want.

"You want to leave."

You haven't asked me why I chose this one.

He paused. "Why did you choose this one?"

The answer to both is the same. McGill, I want you to be happy.

His pause stretched into a silence. I let it sit. I didn't wish to insult McGill's intelligence.

She was so lovely, still; it had been less than a decade since he'd first seen her in Grade 10's History of Europe class. She was a mother now, a wife—but did her skin still not glow with the light of youth? She was a freckle-faced girl then, and those freckles had faded over the years, as they do sometimes. But wasn't her mouth just as thick with girlish eroticism now, as it was as he watched her laugh by her locker in the G-section downstairs—the locker that McGill made a point of passing by, even when his next class was at the far end of the school. . . .

"You knew," he said finally.

I knew. You wear it on your sleeve, McGill.

And of course, that was when he gathered the last of his strength. "You can't tempt me," he said. "Begone!"

Oh, McGill. I know I can't tempt you. That's why I think I'll stay here for now. You begone, for a little while. Think about what I said.

He staggered back, ectoplasm dribbling from his middle finger to make a stain down his pant leg, that had she not been standing there, watching, staring, working it out herself, he would never have been able to explain.

The baby started to cry. I did nothing to calm it.

Its mother looked at it in wonder. Did she think she could tell— that her child was returned to her, that the miraculous laying-on-of-hands by McGill had done the trick? Oh, why even ask the question. Of course she did. A mother can tell when her child is wailing, and when something else—some otherworldly thing, perhaps—is manipulating its tiny larynx, making it gargle out blasphemes that only she can hear. . . .

She scooped the child up in her arms, and held it close. Its tears subsided, and it began to coo. McGill, meanwhile, steadied himself against the doorjamb. He wasn't in a position to do much else; I'd cast him out, good and proper. A man doesn't just walk away from something like that.

She looked at McGill, and he looked back at her. There was something different in her look, and McGill picked up on it. A hint of recognition, perhaps? Gratitude, certainly. Yes, certainly that—McGill could see that it in her eye.

After all, I had put it there.

He drew a shaking breath, and nodded, and might have summoned the will to say something. He scarcely had a chance to, though, because as he straightened, her husband was in the doorway with him. He stood staring at her, hands in unconscious fists—a question in his eye too.

"He's back," she said, wonderingly. "Simon's back, Dave. Whatever he did—worked."

Her husband looked at McGill, at that trouser-stain, at McGill's face, pale and drawn.

"That so, mister?" he asked.

McGill had not yet recovered his words. He gulped air and nodded. Her husband clapped him on the shoulder, and strode into the nursery. He leaned over me—over the baby—and reached out with a tentative finger, to touch its chin. She let him take the baby. It clung to him, as I cooed in his ear.

"It's . . . too soon," said McGill finally, and gasped again, "to say . . . for sure."

———

Eventually, even a specimen like McGill gets his wind back.

When he did, she saw him to the door, while her husband put the baby down. They paused in the kitchen. She put a hand on his arm. This time, McGill didn't try to worm away. She said something softly to him. A question, yes. *Do I know you, from elsewhere? I feel . . . I don't know, it's silly.*

That's the question. I can tell by the way he shuffled, and looked away before looking back.

She glanced away too—to the nursery, where she saw that her husband was properly distracted. Then she looked back, and leaned closer, and whispered something else.

McGill nodded, and looked to the nursery himself where he saw the baby, head at its father's shoulder, looking right back at him.

"Keep in touch, Mrs. Reesor," he said, finally loud enough for all to hear. "In case . . . you know."

She looked at him with such intensity then—turning away only as her husband turned.

"So he's fine?" he said.

McGill nodded, and chin down, headed for the door.

"I gave him the cheque," she said when McGill had left, and her husband tried to look her in the eye.

"As long as you're okay now," he said.

⚬⚬⚬

Oh, she was fine. Better than the day that I arrived in that house, that's for certain. She had been such a melancholic one, that day that I crawled from the dishwater, and slithered on my belly across the kitchen and up and around her leg, to the breast where the infant fussed and suckled. He would not sleep. He kicked and squalled. She was chained to him, that's how she felt. And when I entered him, through the pinhole door in his skull, and had him bite down—he made her shriek. Might she've killed him? Mothers do, sometimes. Their hearts harden. They see the lay of the barren years ahead, serving hand and foot to their child, and its father now grown cold to the touch.

How many times have I been called up by a neglected husband who'd found my name in a grimoire, and begged me on the strength of my reputation, to irrigate the drying slits of their fading brides?

Ah, it would have been the easiest thing for me, to turn her pearl as she looked on her husband—to whisper and suggest—to indicate and to remind her, of what joys the old hunger brings.

But that wasn't why I came to that house. So I held my peace, until McGill came. His aching hunger was nothing I had to tweak.

All I had to do was lay her before him, and reaching into her as McGill reached into me, tweak her heart so, and set her on her course.

⚬⚬⚬

Her husband made her dinner.

It involved shrimp and couscous and dried fruit, some curry flakes and fish stock to round it out. He understood it to be a favourite of hers. She did nothing to correct the misapprehension. She washed up, and saw to the baby, and joined him in bed. When he asked if everything was all right, she said yes. When he touched her, she made a noise that he understood to mean no.

In the deep night, I awoke to find her over my crib.

The next morning, after he left for work, she took me out for the second outdoor excursion since I arrived. As she had that first time, she installed me in a great blue stroller, with thick rubber tires, multiple straps to hold me tight and a pouch behind my head filled with the mysterious tools of the mothering trade. It was warmer out of doors than that first time. She wore a red-and-white cotton dress; I, a tiny blue terrycloth jumper.

We made it quite a way—well past the bank building at the corner of the street where things had gone so badly that last time—along past a filling station—and across another street, to a park with a playground and some benches in the shade of thick, blossoming maple trees. She stopped in front of one of these benches, and looked at me and it, and finally she did sit, and turned the stroller around so that I faced her, and she looked at me again—and it dawned on me that she wasn't looking at me . . . she was searching *for* me, in the empty stare of her little son's eye.

Searching for some pretext, perhaps, to call?

Six days she searched in vain. On the morning of the seventh, she picked up the phone.

I could tell it was not McGill she called by her bright and easy tone. "Hey, you!" she said, and after a pause, "Yeah, things are better now." And another pause, as the phone chirped brightly in her ear. "I know!" And more chirping. "Yeah! Right?" She nodded, her smile brighter than I believe I'd ever seen it. "So it's okay if I come? You sure?"

And finally: "Great!"

She switched off her phone and leaned over the bassinet.

"Guess where we're going, Simon?" she cooed. "Can you say 'Brannigan's'?"

The infant blew a snot bubble out its nose and giggled. I kept my peace.

Brannigan's was a little pub a few blocks past the park. Nice and murky inside, it suited my tastes. But we didn't stay there long. She manoeuvred the stroller around the bar to a door to a back patio. There, in the combined shelter of a maple tree and a great red umbrella, gathered two more strollers, and the mothers who pushed them.

"Hey, Shell!' shouted one of the mothers, standing up with her own baby in one arm and extending the other for a hug. The baby—a big bruiser, flabby and blond like its mother—regarded me with dull hostility from its perch. The other infant—a little girl, judging by the pink—stayed in her stroller seat for the second hug and would not meet my eye. Her mother was a wiry one, with enormous white teeth. She smelled of lawn cuttings.

"How you been?" that one asked, and without leaving time for an answer, turned to me. "Look at him! He's so big!"

"Keep feeding 'em, bound to happen."

The two mothers laughed and laughed, and the flabby one pointed to an empty chair. *She* sat there, after tucking my stroller in between her and the blond baby's stroller. Its mother set the infant back into its seat, and launched into a description of how big it was, and then a long talk about nutrition. I stopped paying attention.

Her baby wouldn't look away.

It sat high in its seat, fidgeting with a little blue pacifier in its hands. It stared at me, an expression that might have been indignation on its face. I looked away, and when I looked back, it hadn't moved.

Did it see what *she* could not? That hidden in the soft skull of this one, was a being older than any here? That McGill's exorcism had failed, and the thing inside was waiting like a barely irradiated tumour to re-emerge?

Did it think there was something it could do about that?

The waitress arrived, and it disappeared for a moment behind her muscular legs and tartan skirt as she took lunch orders. It took longer than it needed to, of course.

"Hey," she said when the waitress finally stepped away, "you remember a kid called McGill?"

"Who?" said the skinny one, but the other waved a hand over the table: "McGill. From high school?" and the skinny one said, "Oh, with the . . ." and waved her hand over her face.

She nodded, reaching down to ruffle my hair. "With the acne," she said, "that's him."

"Weird kid."

"Yeah, wasn't he always wearing black—"

"—kind of goth—"

"—but without the style."

"Right."

"I thought he was going to shoot the school up."

"Columbine our asses."

"Would have served us right."

"Shell!"

"Well, we were total bitches."

"Speak for yourself, Shelly."

"Yeah. Speak for yourself. So what about McGill?"

"He—came back into my life," she said. In spite of myself, I grinned and bounced in my seat. She withdrew her hand, brought it into her lap.

"Ooo," said the flabby one, "that's creepy."

"Not really. We hired him. To help with Simon."

"What, as a babysitter?"

She shook her head. "He's . . . a therapist now. Really, you wouldn't recognize him. From before. His skin's cleared up. He dresses better. And it's like . . . he's found purpose."

"A therapist? For Simon? Shell, is he okay?"

"He's fine now. McGill fixed him right up."

"Wow. McGill. A therapist."

She laughed, a little too lightly. "A behavioural therapist, yeah. Little Simon here . . . he was a handful."

I cooed. Under the table, she crossed her ankles, and uncrossed them. She was fidgeting—the way they do as the feelings take hold. She took a sip from a glass of spring water.

"I gotta say, I'm surprised to hear that about McGill. He was such a mess back then."

"Teenage boys are a mess. They grow out of it."

"He had a lot to grow out of. Did you ever see his mom?"

"I don't remember."

"Yeah, you wouldn't have seen her much. You never went on that trip to Ottawa."

"I had the flu. Did McGill's mother go on that?"

"Not exactly. McGill was going to go. He made it all the way to the bus. He had this suit jacket, and this crazy old trunk with him that was way too big. He got it into the luggage compartment somehow—I think Mr. Evans had to help him with it. And just before we were going to leave, she pulls up."

"His mother?"

"His mother. Bat-shit crazy. She was driving this old Lincoln or something like it. Pulled it up right in front of the bus, so it was blocked in. She got out—huge woman. Not fat—but big like a linebacker. Her hair was white—she wore a big black fake-fur coat like it was winter. She climbed onto the bus, and pointed at McGill, and she yelled: "I Revoke my Permission! Return my Son to me!"

"Jesus."

"Poor McGill."

"Yeah, well he knew what was good for him. He got up and said he couldn't go to Ottawa any more, and got off the bus. Into his mom's car. Didn't even stop to get his trunk out of the luggage area. Had to collect it when we got back."

"That sucks."

"Yeah. But you know something, Shell?" The flabby blonde leaned across the table. "I think he was kind of relieved."

"How's that?"

"You weren't there," she said. "And it was pretty easy to tell . . . McGill was more interested in you than he was in the Houses of Parliament."

Quiet for just a moment, before the three of them broke into a braying round of laughter. The waitress returned with some salads, drinks, and a plate of fried yams. Trickier job this time; she had to sneak in between strollers and the two rattan chairs that'd been displaced to make room for us. She didn't quite pull it off, and several pieces of cutlery slid off her tray. She promised to get more, bent to grab the ones she could find, and hurried off back into the bar.

"I barely knew he was alive," she said.

"Well, he sure knew you were alive."

"Stop fucking—messing with Shelly's head. Stop messing with her head."

"One for the swear jar?"

"No, really. He was a sweet, quiet kid. With, you know, unfortunate skin. If he had a crush on Shelly—well, everybody had a crush on Shelly. Look—" the skinny one with the teeth pointed at her with her fork "—you're making her blush."

She laughed. "Well, he's turned out all right now."

"It's nice to know that boys turn into men, eh?"

"To boys turning into men!" The blonde one raised a glass of spring water, and the others joined the toast. I let myself giggle and clap, and looked right at her as she glanced down. Things were going well, I thought. And at first, I had no idea why her face fell the way it did.

She nearly dropped her glass as she bent and lunged over me, filling my face for a moment with her sweet-smelling tit. To my side, there was a scream—and I looked over just in time to see her pluck a gleaming blade from the big baby's little hand.

He had gotten out of his stroller. He had crawled around beneath the table unseen—by any of us—and he had located a steak-knife the waitress had dropped. And then, the little worm . . . he found his legs.

He had carried the knife three glorious steps, from his mother's feet to the edge of my stroller. It appeared as though the fat little tyke had been about to plunge the knife deep into my left eye.

———

This kind of event is rare; usually, it happens with a family pet . . . dogs, to be sure, but more perilously, cats. They've a fine sense of smell, they do. And that's why, when I arrive in a new vessel, that's the first thing I do.

I make sure the cat is dead.

———

But you know all about that.

The first time McGill and I met after all was over the carcass of a cat.

Remember that place? Squalid little rooms near the very top of a crumbling old apartment building filled with whores and addicts and murderers. Cheap wallpaper peeling off the entry hall. No doors on the kitchen cabinets. No father either. What was it that McGill's mother had said when she first visited the little girl and her overwhelmed, demon-beset mother?

Slattern?

It hadn't gone over well with the mother. I watched from the back of the sofa, where I made the brat I inhabited squat and growl. What, she wanted to know, did McGill's mother have over her, to pass judgement? Could McGill's mother keep a man any better, who didn't want to stay? By the empty divot in her ring finger, she guessed not. That hit a nerve, it did. And so it was that she turned on her heel and strode out of there, and left the poor woman to me.

McGill was the one who finally faced me. His mother had no idea. He came up the next day, on his own, in uniform: a tatty old Nirvana T-shirt, too-loose black jeans and that pustule of a face. He wasn't ready. That was obvious. But for whatever reason, he didn't feel right about disturbing his mother with the contrite phone message, begging her to return because *My God, it's killed the cat!*

I'd done more than that. I'd smashed windows in the bedroom, caved in the ceiling over the door to the balcony, overturned the sofa and caused the television tube to implode. I caused the slattern's neighbour, a man who carried a gun in his trouser-band and dabbled in the narcotics trade to, if not love, then lust for her in an overly solicitous way.

I was, I admit, not pleased when McGill's mother left in such a rage. I wanted her back. To finish things.

McGill found me in the bathtub. The cat, who had been the child's dearest friend, was there too—laid out in the doorframe, its head turned hard back, so it looked at its own tail. I saw to it that it wasn't moved. I wanted McGill's mother to see it. So she'd know who she was dealing with.

It had a different effect on McGill. He didn't know me, then. His mother had left him at home when she met me at the schoolhouse. He'd waited in the car when we danced at the shopping plaza, and she vanquished me again. She obviously didn't tell him about me— about the things I could do, to the world . . . to the hearts and heads of men and women. How formidable I was.

He saw that cat, and he saw me, in the tub smeared with feces and vomit and blood, and there was no fear. All that came up was anger.

"Let that little girl go, you fuckin' cocksucker," he said, and made fists. The camera he'd brought fell to the floor. His eyes filled with tears. And like a stupid, tantruming child, he stepped up to the fight.

＊

That was the first time we met, and the only time I came close to besting McGill. I don't know how his mother taught him . . . what talent he might have simply inherited . . . But even new to the game, blinded by stupid rage . . .

He was a chip off the block.

＊

She was giddy when we got home. She set my stroller in the living room, in front of the TV, and I sat there alone for a time, watching some colourful cartoon show about dinosaurs and science, while she scoured the basement.

She returned with a stack of slim, hard-covered books. Four of them. She settled on the floor in front of the sofa. Opened one of them. The inside flaps were covered in scribbles, notes like a greeting card. She pored over those for a few minutes, then flipped through the pages. It was filled with photographs.

"This is a yearbook, baby," she said, as she noticed me looking over her shoulder. She scudded nearer me, and flipped through it.

"This is mummy when she was a lot younger," she said, stopping at a page filled with faces. Hers grinned out at me. She flipped a few more pages, and there she was, among a crowd of other girls wearing shorts and tank-tops. "This was the girl's track and field team. That's mummy." And finally, she flipped back, to another of those face-filled pages. There, stuck in the middle like a dried piece of chewing gum, was McGill's grinning face.

"And this is the man who brought you back, baby."

I grinned and waved my hands, and she laughed.

"He's our hero," she said, and when I giggled in what I was sure then to be my triumph, she said, "Yes he is. I wish he was here too."

One more day—an awful, interminable day, filled with tears and silences after questions and accusations—and we were in the car.

She had been fiddling around on her computer, looking things up, putting it together in the morning, after he left, silent and stiff-backed. Oh, how it must have stung him, those words: *You didn't do anything to help! McGill saved our baby, and the best you could do was sulk!*

He hadn't said anything to her, but he came to see me in the night, clutching the waistband of his pajama bottoms, damp-eyed and snuffling, declaring his love for me. "I hope you'll remember that, no matter what happens," he said, and touched my cheek.

She strapped me into the child seat behind her. It offered a terrible view, and that made me fussy. After all these years, I must admit that I was acutely curious as to where precisely McGill bedded down at night. In all of our transactions, the McGill family only ever came to me. Never had I had occasion or opportunity to play the visitor.

We sped along blacktop. She braked three times—the last time hard enough to leave skid-marks—before the surface under the wheels grew rougher, and gravel popped up against the underside. The brilliant blue sky above me disappeared behind a canopy of leaves, and soon after that, the car slowed and lurched to one side as she negotiated a narrow turn, onto an even rougher surface. And then we came to a stop and she climbed out.

"Wish me luck," she said, and kissed my forehead before unbuckling me and lifting me out of the seat, and the car.

We were in a small clearing in the middle of the woods. In the middle of that, was a house that I could only guess belonged to McGill.

It was made of wood, its walls shingled in rough, dark cedar, and happily, it had but a single storey to it. The shadow of the trees all around kept grass from growing, but there had been some attempt at a little garden underneath the living room window. The nose of an old Lincoln poked out from underneath a carport. There was a metal shed behind that.

Although it was the middle of summer, the space here had a chill to it. I fussed, and she held me close, and she fussed too, in her way. She took a step toward the house, and another one—then stepped back. She looked back at the car, and shook her head, and said, "damn" in almost a sob. She might have gotten into it, too, if she'd been left to her devices.

But—lucky her—she was rescued.

"Mrs. Reesor?"

McGill stood at the door. He was wearing an old bathrobe. A cigarette dangled between thumb and forefinger, and he flicked ash away onto the steps. His hair stood up on one side—no doubt where he'd slept.

She turned to him, holding me close. "Hey, you," she said.

"How—" he frowned. "How did you find me here?"

"Online," she said. "I looked up your address online."

"It's not under my name."

"It's not. But it is under your mother's."

He didn't say anything to that.

"Look," she said finally. "I'm sorry for coming here like this. I . . . I hoped it would be okay, but maybe it's not."

"It's okay." He dropped the cigarette to the steps, and put it out with the heel of one bare foot. "Is Simon all right?"

She nodded. "He's fine." And she held me up, jiggling me like a carnival prize. I giggled appropriately. "See?"

"He looks good." McGill set his head forward and squinted at her. "Really good. So you're here . . . why?"

She giggled, inappropriately. She let her bangs fall over her eyes. She smiled at him through them. "I remember now," she said softly.

McGill's mouth hung open stupidly for a second. "Mrs. Reesor?"

"Shelly," she said, and with that, found her courage. She strode across the stony yard, and up the steps, and holding me in one arm, wrapped an arm around his neck, and drew him into a kiss.

It wouldn't be as simple as that soon enough. But for the moment, it was.

—

McGill's house stank of old smoke and urine. The living room was a shadowy place. Dishes from a recent meal spread across a coffee table. Random-seeming pieces of clothing, yellowing paperbacks and empty bottles and cans clotted its shadowed corners. A large box of adult diapers sat near the doorway to the kitchen. She noticed none of it, of course—love sees, or smells, only what it wishes—but McGill was still ashamed.

"I . . . apologize for the state of things," he said.

"It's okay," she said. "You probably can't afford a housekeeper. You don't charge enough for what you do."

"It's not right."

"You saved my baby. It's right to charge fairly for that."

Of course, that was not what McGill meant. He meant that this wasn't right, that there was no natural way that she would arrive at his door, and kiss him so . . .

How was it for him these past days? I can only guess. When he watched her sashay past his locker those years ago, didn't he dream of this day? When he could grow into and harness the talents of his mother, and use them to rescue that pale princess—to possess her, even as he drove the demons from her? Then, might he not have slipped his finger into the moist caverns of her mind, and communed with her as does my kind? And in so doing, truly possess her?

Shameful thoughts, for men of McGill's avocation. Shameful, but once entertained, so difficult to dismiss.

"Don't worry," she said, standing near him now. Her heart was pounding—I could feel it as she held me to her breast. "I'm not going to try and give you more *money*. Come on with me."

And she led us all, down a hallway, past a shut door—where the stink of piss seemed strongest—and through an open door.

McGill whispered an apology for the state of his bedroom. She told him she didn't care—that she remembered now . . . that she wished she could undo the years and that she should apologize for not being able to.

There was an ache, she said, a hollowness in her that she had dismissed as ennui, until she saw him again. McGill might have said: that is how it feels, when a demon tweaks a heart, and turns it to another direction. He might have made fists, and turned to me, and said, "Let that woman go, you fuckin' cocksucker."

But our McGill . . . in spite of his vow, in spite of his avocation . . . in spite of his other responsibilities . . . he said nothing.

She took the pillows stacked at one end of his sagging bed, and made a small nest for me on the floor beside the bed.

Then she whispered an apology to me, and set me in it. "Mummy's right here," she said, and turned away.

And McGill . . . precious McGill . . . *your* McGill, he took her in his arms, and ran his hands over the soft skin of her waist, the curve of her buttock. For that moment, he forgot everything . . . transformed forever, by his awful dream made flesh.

———

And so, I crawled.

It was a strain—the infant wasn't really ready for crawling. But such as we know nothing so well as the bending of sinew, the diversion of will. And off I went—out the door, back to the hallway, past the lavatory, and to your door. It opened for me without protest: any wards McGill had ever bothered to place on it had long ago faded.

You smell of piss. I wonder if you know that? I wonder how much you know, locked in that skull of yours? I can see you now, in your old hospital bed.

I can see the leather straps that McGill uses to keep you still . . . to keep you from harming yourself, or burning the place down, or harming him. You could still do a lot of harm—you were always a big girl. I remember how you held down that boy I took, down south, as you slid your thick thumb into his skull and sent me back to hell.

Even then you *stank*.

Are you in hell now? Trapped in that confused swamp of shit that fills your skull these days? Is there any hope you have left?

I'm on your bed now. You can feel me clambering over your fat leg. It's not easy—I'm pushing this little one to its limits to make my way up your torso, over your sagging, spent teats, to your face—your rheumy, drooping eyes.

I want to make sure that you know. McGill is lost. You have no son. Really, as I've proven, you never fully did.

Now, my dear old friend, all the world is only you, and I.

THE RADEJASTIANS

We three ate lunch outside in the springtime. There was a picnic table under a small tree, well out of sight of the loading docks, and it is there we met: Viktor and Ruman and I. We had all come from the old country, the same old country, and I suppose that marked us . . . not in the same way, but as the same, all the same.

Viktor had not been there since he was a child, which was forty years ago, and had worked the warehouse for a decade. The mark was faint on him. Although I had been back more recently—a year earlier—for the solstice festival, I had felt like the alien there, walking the cobbled streets of Radejast alone, among the dancing virgins and the yowling monks in their woven-straw masks . . . the vendors who sold the long, blackened apple dolls of saints I could no longer name.

Ruman, now.

For him, the mark was fresh, for he had just arrived a year and some months ago. His family still lived at home in the smelting town in the southern mountains, waiting for word that he was established enough that they might also make their escape—and profitably join him here.

Maybe he shared his mark; infected us with it too. Maybe that mark pushed the others away from us: or drew us together, and so away from the others.

Maybe this, maybe that. We had a half hour for lunch, and on those fine days that were neither humid nor frigid, the sun only so high at noon, we spent it out of doors. We talked only a little. For truly, we had little in common between us, save our mother tongue and dimming recollections. The conversations we had during that time stand out like horsemen on a plain.

"I am thinking that I am going to be saved," said Ruman one

Tuesday in April. The sky was clouded over us. But Ruman was the greyer.

"What do you mean?" I asked, and Viktor interjected: "He means he's going back to that church."

Ruman shrugged and stirred his soup so the colour of beets deepened in it. "I must think of my soul," he said.

"Shit, Ruman," I said. "Don't do it. Those ones will only rob you."

"No, no," said Viktor, "they will not rob you. When I came here, I tried a church like that one. No one robbed me. What I gave, I gave. How it went, it went. But I don't think it saved me."

Ruman looked up. "You are here, aren't you?"

"Not because it saved me," said Viktor.

"Well this is a different church," said Ruman. "They have a great cross, visible from the motorway. The building is shaped five-sided. And they are all virgins, the women there. The unmarried ones, of course."

"Ha! Now we come to it!" I said, and Ruman's grey flesh went a deep red.

"Wife at home," said Viktor, finger wagging, "wife at home."

"I just think it's time to be saved," said Ruman. And that was the end of that conversation.

━━━

Ruman went back to the church.

Did that place save him? I saw no evidence that it had, as we gathered each day in the growing shade of our tree, at our table. Perhaps that is because he did not speak of it. But that was not the only thing. Ruman brought a little pamphlet that he set out one day—it had a painting of a brown-haired, blue-eyed Jesus, spreading his hands over a multitude of sinners, the light spreading around him as though it had substance.

But he displayed it almost with embarrassment, and when Viktor and I spared it only a glance before setting in to our sandwiches, he pulled it back to his lap with something like shame.

After that, the pamphlet was gone. And so we would eat, and sometimes Viktor would talk, I would answer, and in the end we would return to the shadow of the loading bay doors.

And as the days went by, I found I wondered with rather more urgency: did the church save Ruman?

He came to us a thin man, with the long face and dark brows of our kind, pale of flesh and bent of back. Was his colour any deeper, was there more certainty in his eyes as the days went on? Had he put flesh on in his time there? If anything, he seemed the opposite: thinner, his outer layers honed away.

But could I say? And as I considered that, I considered this: could I say how it was that I wondered so, after the health of Ruman's frail soul?

As the summer deepened, we left the bench to the women from the front office who appreciated the sun more than we. Viktor was so unappreciative that he took the night shift, which he said he preferred in the heat of high summer. As for me—I hefted crates from shelf to belt, and soaked in the heat as it soaked me, and watched Ruman, as he did the same—thin, and bent, and strangely resolute.

And so it was one Thursday afternoon in July that I quietly spoke to Ruman, and the following Sunday, drove with him to church.

Ruman lived in a house in the eastern suburbs, where he rented a room of his own and shared a bathroom and kitchen with five other men. Too many men in the house, and everyone knew it. Ordinarily, he would take a bus from there, after walking ten minutes through twists of the subdivision to the bus stop at the main road—the neighbours' eyes burning his back as he came and went. His very home was an affront to them.

I didn't pity him. Three years ago, I lived in a place just as bad, and these days, I lived in an apartment only a little better. I had a car but it was old and forever breaking down; and I'm not sure my life was much improved by having it. But I could tell he was grateful for the lift.

"I thought you might not come," he said as we pulled away from the house.

"Why not?"

"I thought you were afraid," he said.

"Afraid?"

"Like Viktor," he said. "Men from dark places . . . they fear the Light."

"Men from dark places fear the dark," I said, and he snorted.

The church was fifteen minutes away from Ruman's house, in an industrial park like the one in which we worked. And Ruman was right; you could see the cross from the highway. It climbed over the structure on a steel lattice, and at night you could see it would light up. It would glow blue, Ruman explained as I shifted lanes to get off the highway. Why was it called the Good News Happening Congregation, I wondered as we drove past the driveway, looking for a spot on the road. GOOD NEWS HAPPENING CONGREGATION was stamped out in moveable letters on a sign-board mounted on wheels. Ruman had no proper answer for that.

We crossed a wide parking lot and approached a large bank of glass doors. There were a great many people clustered inside, and more moving in and out. When the doors opened, a burble of music and conversation and laughter drifted out. I speculated that we might be late and worried at the consequences.

"Will the virgins be angry?" I asked, but Ruman straight-facedly reassured me: "This is how it always is."

He took me through the door and led me inside.

There is a cathedral in the middle of Radejast. It addresses the approaching pilgrim as a fist of granite and slate and limestone, lifting black iron bells and arches and gargoyles to touch the dangled teat of the soot-cloud that ever hangs low over the land. Within: a forest of stone pillars, some carved with the likenesses of Radejast's saints, some simply chiselled with the mark of its venerable religion—all surrounding the dome, so high and wide that when emerging from the pillars I stumbled beneath it, madly fearful that gravity might suddenly reverse, fling me from the floor, and smash me against the curved mosaics above the whispering gallery.

The Good News Happening Congregation's hall was larger than Radejast's cathedral by half: a great circular space beneath a peaked roof, lit from high, clear windows on every side. Behind the pulpit stood a crucifix with a painted sculpture of Jesus Christ bound to it, bright lines of blood trickling down his slender limbs from the crown of thorns he wore. Altogether, it was half-again taller than any similar icon in Radejast.

Surrounding the pulpit, curved rows of folding chairs radiated outward across a floor of polished concrete. Ruman craned his neck in a certain direction and waved. When I looked there, I saw a woman with short blonde hair, a deep tan, beckoning us over. We moved to join her and what turned out to be a group of five more.

"That," explained Ruman as we made our way down the aisle, "is Cheryl and her friends. But I do not know all their names still," he added, embarrassed.

"I will introduce myself, then."

"Thank you."

"Are they—?"

Ruman cut in. "Stop talking about the virgins. I don't know."

But Ruman was wrong. I was not set to mock him, make implications about his wandering attentions, remind him of his wife, as Viktor had that day. Stepping into this vast space, breathing the fresh-scrubbed scent of these pilgrims, I only thought to ask: Are they good people? Because looking across their faces, all of their faces—they seemed like good people to me.

"Well hello there, sleepyhead," said Cheryl, as we moved to the seats that she and her friends were saving. "Is this your friend?"

I introduced myself and held out my hand, and Cheryl took it in both of hers. "I am sorry we are late," I said. "My fault."

"Oh goodness," said Cheryl. "You're not late at all. You got Ruman here early."

"Cheryl's just saying that Ruman could use some sleep," said one of the others—black hair and heavyset in a print dress. "Look at the rings under his eyes." Ruman snorted, half-smiled and looked away.

"I'm Rose," she said, and added: "God Bless."

Ruman said "God Bless," and I said so too, and for the first time of many that morning, we all eight of us joined hands and said it again together.

The morning service went on for some hours. There was singing and some talk from the tall, dark-haired pastor of the congregation, and of course some reading from the Bible. And then came a break, wherein everybody else introduced themselves. There was Rose's daughter, Lisa; and Mary and Lottie, sisters to one another; and Carrie, who knew Cheryl from high school and had been married to Cheryl's high school sweetheart until two years ago when he had left Carrie, the city, and the Lord. Both Cheryl and Carrie piously insisted they prayed daily for him. Yet they laughed when I wondered what exactly they prayed their God should do with one such as he.

"You are *bad*," said Carrie, and Cheryl gave my forearm a gentle slap and shifted so her shoulder rested against mine. I felt a pang— for was I not a guest of Ruman, who had introduced me to these women? It is true that he had a wife in the old country, was bound to her in the ways of our people, and so he could lay no claim to any of these women here. Yet in the riot of our lusts, how often do we heed reason and ignore that deeper voice, speaking to us as it does through the ages?

The pang lasted an instant. Looking past Lottie, I noticed that Ruman was gone. Seeing my confusion, Lottie pointed to the pulpit.

"Ah," I said. Ruman had made his way there with some two-dozen others. There was no music playing, but he and they seemed to be dancing, or their shoulders were moving like dancers. The pastor stepped onto the low stage and reached down to help another up: this one an older woman in a long dress, her grey hair tied in a bun. The room dimmed as a cloud drifted past the sun. She held her hands up in the air, waggled her fingers, and began to sway. The pastor said nothing, but held his microphone to his chest, and swayed also. Around me, the congregation began to stand, and Carrie nudged me, and Cheryl tugged my arm as she stood. Beside her, Lottie shut her eyes and began to hum.

A spotlight came on, illuminating the woman on the stage. She leaned her head back as though bathing in it. Then she too began to speak, to shout. She bunched her shoulders, as though coiling a spring there, and released, her arms spreading from her waist, and she did not just shout—she screamed. The pastor stepped back and held his arms out over her head, fingers spread as though he were preparing to catch her, should gravity fling her high.

I remember an impulse then, to wrap my own arms around myself. But I could not. Cheryl and Carrie had taken my hands, one each, and held my arms apart. I suppose I might have pulled away, forcefully drawn my arms in. But the fear passed as fast as it came. And like Cheryl, like Carrie—like Ruman, gyrating and babbling with the crowd in front of the pulpit—

I was swept up.

When it was finished, we all went for lunch at a pancake place on the other side of the motorway. It was crowded and noisy, and there was no hope of finding a table for all of us. We divided ourselves: Cheryl, myself, Lisa, and Lottie took a table near the window; Ruman, Carrie, Mary, and Rose found a booth not too far off. Cheryl thought it important that no one who had come to church in the same car also sit at the same table.

"How else are we going to build community," she asked as we took our places in the sunlight, "if every time we worship, we all sit in our little tribes?"

"Amen," I said. I glanced over at the booth. Ruman's face was obscured by the menu.

"Aw," said Lottie, "you miss your friend?" She patted my arm.

"He seems to like it here," I said. It was true. We didn't speak much in the short drive over, but I had never seen Ruman seem so . . . nourished.

"He does at that," said Cheryl. "How 'bout you? You think you might join us?"

"Perhaps," I said. "I don't know about . . ." I waggled my fingers at my shoulders and swayed a bit in my chair. Lisa concealed a grin. Cheryl didn't bother. She laughed.

We ordered: me, a plate of bacon and scrambled eggs; Lottie, a platter of fresh fruit; Cheryl, an omelette. Lisa asked for a big plate of pancakes topped with stewed apples.

"Did you go to church with Ruman?" asked Lisa, as we waited for our meals. "Back in the old country?"

"No. Ruman came here just recently. I have been here two years more. I did not know Ruman. We have a job together."

"He said he didn't like church in the old country." I could see Lottie trying to shush Lisa, but she made as not to notice and pressed on. "He said he likes this one better. Do you like this one better?"

Cheryl cut in. "Well, I bet there's no dancing back in the old church, not like we have," she said. She waggled her fingers as I had.

"Oh, there can be dancing," I said. "They do all sorts of things in our churches."

"You see?" said Cheryl to Lottie, as though settling a long argument. "There's more we have in common than not, even across the wide ocean."

The food came, but not all at once. First, Lottie got her fruit, which she left untouched in front of her, sipping at her tea until my eggs and bacon arrived along with Cheryl's omelette, whereupon Lisa urged all of us to eat.

"I do like your church better," I said as I scooped egg onto a piece of toast. "But I did not spend much time inside our churches. We have a different . . ." I struggled for the word in the new language.

"Faith?" offered Cheryl, but I shook my head.

"Obligation," I said. "Nearer that. Our God demands different things than yours does."

"It's all one God," said Cheryl, and Lottie added: "Praise Be He."

"It's not all one God," said Lisa, "when you think about the Muslims and the Buddhists and the Hindus . . . the *things* they worship. Can't be. And how can you say God is He?"

"Oh, cut that out. I'll tell your mother." Cheryl wagged her finger and laughed. "It's all one God," she said to me, "when you get right down to it."

"Okay," I said and nodded over Lisa's shoulder. "I think your food is coming."

The plate for pancakes was larger than any of ours, and I had to move aside to make room for it. The waitress smiled as Lottie made an ooh-ing sound, and Cheryl said, "Better you than us, kiddo," to Lisa. "That'd go straight to my thighs."

"Enjoy," said the waitress, and moved off. Lisa just looked at it, hands in her lap.

"What is it, sweetheart?" asked Lottie. "Bigger than you expected?"

Lisa looked up at all of us.

"It's a miracle," she said quietly, and pointed to the top of her pancake stack.

We all looked. Cheryl said she didn't see anything at first, but she was the only one.

"It's the face of Jesus," said Lottie. Cheryl frowned and looked at it, and then at me. I nodded. There was a face, there, in the apples—strong cheekbones over deep-set eyes, brows of apple crescents, and the yellow sauce spilling down the edge of the pancakes in the unmistakable shape of a beard. It was a bright face, a Holy face—formed from apple on a young girl's plate.

Cheryl looked again and gasped.

"You're right, hon. It is a miracle." Cheryl waved at the booth. "Hey! Rose! Come look what the Lord made your daughter!"

Rose came over, and soon everyone from the other table was standing around, bearing witness to the miracle of the apple face on Lisa's plate. The waitress stopped by to see if everything was all right, and when Carrie explained to her, she looked and agreed. Mobile phones emerged from purses and recorded the miracle through their tiny lenses.

Lisa wondered what she should do with it, and it was finally Ruman who settled the matter.

"You should eat it," he said, "for God has delivered your Harvest, and it would be a sin to deny His bounty, yes?"

That made Lisa smile. "Well, I don't want to be sinning," she said, and I suppressed a gasp as she cut into the apparition's cheek with her fork.

I didn't have opportunity to speak with Ruman again that day. As lunch finished, it transpired that Rose had offered to drive Ruman home. The offer created complications, displacing one from that car—either Cheryl or Carrie—and Cheryl wondered if she could take Ruman's place in mine. Of course I agreed.

When in Radejast, I did not only visit the cathedral and walk at night at solstice. I was there for two weeks' time, on my own, and the nights were long. I visited the taverns, and one night, I met a woman. She was no virgin, but not a whore either. I think she may have hoped I would bring her back with me, as my bride. But no words were spoken to that effect as we quit the tavern arm in arm, slipped through a dark alcove and into her rooms. When I left, there were no tears. She kissed me on the cheek and touched her forehead to my shoulder and sent me away.

It was another matter with Cheryl.

She lived on the second floor of a low-rise apartment building that overlooked a deep ravine. When I started to pull toward the front doors where the taxis would come and go, she told me the visitor parking was in back. "If you want to," she said, and put her hand on mine. "It would be okay."

And so I came to Cheryl's apartment. It was not much larger than mine, but she had made it far more pleasant. The television, the sofa, even the pictures on the walls—everything seemed new. The window gave a tantalizing view of the ravine through tree branches, and hid the view of the other high rises that grew from the far bank. It was as though she lived on the edge of a deep forest.

"You like?" she asked from behind me. I said that I did. She reached around and took my hand—and truly, I was not surprised when she placed it on her naked hip. I turned and saw that her dress was abandoned, sloughed off like a skin, on the floor behind her.

"You are very beautiful," I said as she withdrew, and she laughed— softly now—and for an instant turned away.

"You don't believe me?" I said, and she answered, "No. But you're a pretty liar," and the instant passed, and she kissed me once more.

"Oh God, forgive me," she said as she reached down and fumbled with my belt buckle. I reached to help her, but she batted my hand away and finished the work, bent down and yanked my trousers to my knees. I stumbled a bit, and at that she laughed, and pushed, and I fell back, landing hard on my behind just short of the sofa.

Cheryl did not ask for my forgiveness. She laughed, fell to her hands, crawled forward so her face hung over mine, grinning like a mountain cat's. She moaned low. I kicked off my shoes, my trousers. She descended upon me. And in this way we copulated, swaying and growling as if to the rhythms of the old chants, on the thin carpet over her apartment's hard concrete floor.

I wrote down the number of my mobile before I left Cheryl's apartment that afternoon, but she told me not to expect a call.

"You got to go," she said, her voice flat, when she finally came out of the washroom. She had clothed herself in light blue track pants and a sweater. Her feet, still bare, never lifted far off the floor as she led me to the door. I didn't hear her crying, not once that day, but her eyes were red and wet. Perhaps I should have apologized, although for what I could not fathom. So I said all I could think of—

"You are beautiful."

—which only enraged her. She shouted at me to get out, called me names, waved her fists, but I put my hands up in surrender and told her I would leave if that was what she wished. This placated her, and Cheryl stood, huffing and swallowing and glaring, as I gathered myself and hurried into the dim corridor.

I ate lunch with Ruman on Monday but we did not talk about very much. He did thank me for joining him at the congregation, or more properly, for the ride there, but he said he wouldn't need another; he'd made an arrangement with Rose. He didn't, thankfully, ask me if I'd enjoyed myself at the service or afterwards, and I didn't ask him. I made one feeble joke—biting into my apple, peering at the pulp I announced, "No face today." Ruman just shook his head and waved the little blasphemy away with the flat of his hand.

On Tuesday, Ruman brought a Bible with him and made it clear he preferred its company to mine. So I ate quietly, this one last time, at the same table as he, dipping his bread in soup as he thumbed the pages of his book. Did he smile as he read, or was I tricked by the way the overhead fluorescents cast shadows across his lips? I did not stay long enough, or look hard enough, to be sure. On Wednesday, I ate alone.

By Friday, the supervisors had responded to my request to join the evening shift.

In the beginning, the sun set an hour after I started work, and as the nights lengthened, darkness encompassed all my days.

Viktor was glad to see me.

"We should work the night all the time!" he said. "It's cool in the summer, and just as warm as day in the winter. And leaving that aside—it suits us, yes?—this peaceful time."

Viktor was right. There was work to be done, and we saw to it; but the urgency of the place . . . it was muted. When the trucks had pulled away, and one was moving the merchandise to and from its places . . . one might take a moment, listen to the sound of one's footsteps, and stop beneath high lights that only, at best, kept the shadows at bay. One might feel enveloped. Protected.

At home.

We ate together all the time, Viktor and I. And absent Ruman, we found we had things to say to one another. Viktor had once had a wife, and still had a son by her, a boy of fifteen, of whom he was very proud.

"His name is William," Viktor said as he showed me a photograph. William resembled Viktor inasmuch as he resembled any of us: thick black hair, a small mouth with lips bright red, on which formed a small and unpractised smile. The mark was on him too, but fainter than any of ours. "He is a wizard with machinery. And popular with the girls. The most important thing!"

That was the first time I tried to talk with Viktor about that Sunday, the church, Cheryl. But I didn't want to seem boastful, comparing my prowess with that of a teenaged boy.

The second time was during the election that year, when Viktor and two other fellows were talking about one of the candidates—an unworldly woman who professed to have been saved by Jesus Christ, and during a debate had mispronounced the name of our homeland. Had it just been Viktor and I, perhaps I might have spoken of my afternoon with unworldly Christian women. But these other fellows . . . I couldn't even keep their names in my head. I didn't want them smirking at my adventures.

We finally spoke of it much later, when, during a break in late October, my mobile chirped and, answering it, I found myself talking with Cheryl's friend, Carrie. Viktor asked me who calls at such an hour as this, and I shushed him.

"I got this number from Cheryl's kitchen," she said.

"Is Cheryl there now?"

"Cheryl doesn't know I'm calling you. She's . . . no, she's not here now."

Carrie's voice was tight. I didn't know her well enough to be sure, but in another woman I would suspect it indicated tears. Or perhaps anger.

"Where is she? What's wrong?"

"She's . . . she's at Rose's place. With the rest of them." And a pause, and a deep, sobbing breath. And then, sharper: "I just thought you should *know*."

And at that, she disconnected. Viktor raised his eyebrows. "Well," he said. "There is a story behind that."

And so I told Viktor the tale of my visit to the Good News Happening Congregation, and the pancake lunch, and the visit to Cheryl's apartment. He listened quietly the whole time, and sat still a moment when I finished.

"And you fucked," he said finally.

"And then—yes."

He held out his hand, and snapped his fingers. "Give me the phone."

I handed it over. After some fiddling, Viktor extracted Carrie's number. He leaned back in his plastic chair, crossed ankles, and when she picked up, didn't even pause to introduce himself before launching into questions:

"Where is Rose's house? Address please. Hold on." He pulled a pen from his shirt pocket, leaned forward in his chair. "And telephone number?" He scribbled on a napkin. "How long has he been there? . . . How many others? . . . And you? . . . I see . . . No, don't go yourself . . ." And finally, a longer pause, during which Viktor capped the pen, replaced it in his shirt pocket, and stood.

"Pray if you like," he said, and snapped the mobile shut, handing it back to me.

"Carrie asked me to apologize for being angry with you," he said. "She is under some strain. Our friend Ruman has moved into Rose's house, and so has Cheryl now."

I could think of nothing to say.

"So tell me," he finally went on. "Is your terrible death-trap of a car still running well tonight?"

"It is," I said.

"Well." He looked at the break-room clock. "We finish in two hours. It can wait till then, but not much longer."

In Radejast, Viktor explained to me, those who worship do so quietly.

"You can be forgiven for not knowing," said Viktor as we pulled from the parking lot into the deep morning dark, "for you are younger. Your parents . . . they would not have remembered the purges, the reform . . . they themselves would have been only small children, infants perhaps, through the worst of the Copper Revolution."

"They were not even that," I said. "Not even born."

Viktor rubbed his beard and nodded. "It's been many years," he said. "And more than lives were lost, hey?" He chuckled when I didn't answer. "It used to be that *everyone* worshipped. I remember my grandmother told me how at the Harvest, the whole of the land would wait, quiet as mice, as the sun vanished below the western mountains, and the moon, new and dark, rose invisible over the fields. And then, we all would creep from our homes to the churches, and there in the pitch black of night—*whisper* our supplication. And then—and only then—under cover of the blackest piece of the night—would we dare celebrate the invincible shadow of our Lord."

We stopped a moment waiting for a traffic light to turn. Viktor shifted in his seat, so he leaned against the car door.

"What a temptation, though—for any man or woman—to look directly into the brightly lit face of their God. Whatever God that may be. The people here seem to have no difficulty with it, by and by. But us? In the old days at least, we knew our God well enough to know better."

I touched the accelerator and the car lurched into the intersection some seconds before the light turned green. "Whoa, whoa!" shouted Viktor, but it was safe. At this time of night, in this part of the world, we two Radejastians were the only souls in sight.

Rose's house was in a neighbourhood not so different, indeed not so very far, from the one where Ruman had rented his room. The house, however, was larger, newer, and far better kept. The grass had been cut. Leaves were neatly raked and put at the end of the driveway, in a half-dozen orange bags made to look like pumpkins. An enormous spiderweb spread over the front windows, and two figures—one a plastic skeleton, and another, a crude mannequin made from straw—flanked the front door.

Although it was just past three in the morning, the house blazed with light.

"What do you mean for us to do?" I asked as I pulled the car against the curb.

"You have done enough," Viktor said, and opened the car door. "Be prepared to drive off quickly when I return."

I did as I was told, but as Viktor strode up to the front of the house, I began to worry. For as he got out of the car, he had pulled something from his pocket, and I had heard a *click* sound. And as I thought of it, the sound reminded me of the sound a board-cutting knife from the warehouse might make, as the blade extended. And didn't such a blade flash in the porch light as the front door opened and Viktor slipped inside?

So I tapped my fingers on the steering wheel, and thought, and thought again. And I got out of the car, and followed in Viktor's footsteps, up to the house.

The front door was not wide open but had not been properly shut either. I paused a moment, listening, and what I heard put me at ease: women's voices, talking at a reasonable level and even showing some cheer.

And so: inside, I stepped.

First, a vestibule. On one side, a coat rack, and a closet. On the other, a small, dark, wooden table beneath a hat rack.

And there, I saw a thing which made me less at ease: a twelve-inch-high doll swaddled in bright red cloth, its venerable face carved from a dried apple. Tiny black-headed pins were its eyes.

I hurried past, into a high room with a wide staircase curving to the second floor. Past the stairs: a brightly lit kitchen. It was from there that the conversation came, still convivial. Was that Rose's voice? And that, Cheryl's?

I was set to go see, when a door I had not noticed opened at the base of the stairs.

"Trick or treat? It's early for—Oh, it's you!"

It was Lisa. Her black hair was tied in a tight bun behind her head; her pale cheeks flushed red; she wore a bone-white blouse and long red skirt that fell to her calves. She stepped into the vestibule and turned an oddly graceless pirouette.

She recovered her balance and beamed at me.

"You like?" she said, eyes wide, and turned again, this time with more agility. And at the end of it, she was somehow closer, and her eyes were wider—and I could not but think of the forest beyond

Cheryl's balcony, and Cheryl's own eyes as they stared down at me. I took two steps back, and Lisa laughed and raised her arms over her head, and turned and swayed and was at my side again and somehow she was holding both my hands in hers and then we two were turning in the bright light of the entry hall, under the black clouds over Radejast, she stumbling . . . both of us, finding our feet . . . dancing the dance of the virgins.

Lisa flew far from me and drew close, her eyes—so round now they seemed lidless—never leaving mine. She never stood close long. But we were entwined.

Behind her, behind me, figures gathered. First one coming from the kitchen: Rose perhaps? The hair was the right colour, but I remembered the dress too well. In its absence, how would I account this pale naked creature, swaying beneath the stairs, hands in the air, as she came toward us? Or that other, face pinched tight—open hands slapping against her breasts, red hair plastered over swollen cheeks? Who might she be?

Cheryl, now. She was unmistakable. I remembered the curve of her thighs, her breasts . . . her narrow wrists and long fingers, clawing at the air as she swayed. I didn't need to see her face. I couldn't see her face. For she wore a mask of woven straw, its eyes and mouths dark circles, its high crown making a giantess of her.

And we turned, and she was gone.

The women clapped in rhythm, and Lisa drew in close to me, and I bent closer to her, mouth hungry—but she whipped back from my lips, turning so hard and sharply that I feared her neck might have snapped. For an instant, I was looking at the tightly wound bun of hair at the back of her skull, even as her young breasts pressed hard against my ribs. As I wondered at this, her head finished the circle, and those mad, reeling eyes took hold of mine again. She did kiss me then. She tasted of smoke. Of the earth. Of soot.

The clapping stopped. The women looked up, eyes as round as the virgin's. And I felt a jolt—like a tiny tremor of the earth—up my spine.

Lisa let me go. The women were staring past me, and down, and up . . . and I put my hands out, palms up. It seemed as though it were snowing.

But it wasn't snow. Plaster and paint were falling from the high ceiling above us. I half-turned and saw on the floor behind me: Viktor. The hair on his skull was matted with blood and torn scalp. His neck was bent at a deadly angle. His right hand, turned in, gripped in a tight fist. His back was covered in white plaster dust—the same that was falling now, from the long cracks in the high ceiling, where a man might have impacted.

He was not moving. If the first fall had not done the job, then the second had surely finished him.

Lisa knelt down and lifted his hand, unbent his fingers. She drew the box cutter Viktor had brought, and lifted it high, turned to the stairway.

"Ruman," I gasped, unable to take my eyes off the creature that stood on the curving steps, "look at you."

He did not speak. He raised his blackened arms, and lifted off his mask, and began his howling.

Lisa turned to me, but this time I looked away. And alone, I fled the house, and back to the bosom of the early-morning darkness.

I went to work the next evening. The supervisors were uneasy; they could smell the changes, the thickening dark, the same as everyone. Where was Viktor? they asked. He didn't call. Was he sick? Did you drive him home? Drunk perhaps?

I didn't answer their questions, the same way I didn't contact the police. What would I say? What good would it do?

The night after that, Ruman took Viktor's place on the night shift. He found me at the meal break, and grinned as he pulled the chair out, fell into it in a happy exhaustion.

"She's pretty, yes?" he said. "Little girls get big fast."

I didn't look at him. There were so many things I might have said. "You have a wife," was all I finally could muster.

"Several, in fact," he said, and laughed. "Praise Be He."

The next night, and every night thereafter, I stayed home.

As the weeks drew on, the darkness grew over the city. Snow, real snow, swirled in corners, and gathered, covering the smooth pavement and neatly laid brickwork, thickening that darkness.
But sometimes, for hours at a time, the darkness broke, and daylight intervened.

It was at one of these times, three weeks before the solstice, that I ventured out of my apartment, and took my car to the Good News Happening Congregation.

The cross still climbed high over the motorway, but someone

had rolled the sign away. This time, I was able to find a space in the parking lot. Indeed, there were barely a dozen other vehicles there, stopped at the end of wide curves of tire tracks in the snow. All the doors in the wide glass bank of them on the building were locked but one. I slipped inside.

The last time I had been in the Good News Happening Congregation, the hall's wide floor was covered in rows of folding chairs, and those chairs were filled with happy, fervent worshippers.

The Congregation was long gone. As I crossed the vast, dark floor, empty but for scuffed pamphlets and, here and there, shallow puddles, I wondered at where those people had found themselves. Did they gather their money together, flee to somewhere brighter, one or two of them at first, then, once established, slowly draw their kin in tow?

Or were they nearer? Huddled in their homes, blinds drawn, waiting for the shadow to draw over the land, to make it safe to worship?

I stopped at the foot of the pulpit, and looked up at the crucifix, climbing two full storeys high, the cool winter daylight striking the crown of thorns, setting it alight.

But the sun was an interloper here, and soon it too fled. In the ancient Radejastian gloom, the only soul in sight, I danced.

THE SUMMER WORMS

Sharon's hand came away from the tree branch covered in them, but she didn't so much as flinch. She brought the hand to her face, studying them minutely as they crawled between her fingers, inched across her palms. Her brow knitted a little, her mouth opened a crack, and the tip of her tongue curled over the edge of her teeth, straying only an instant. Sharon watched the caterpillars on her hand; Robert watched Sharon watching the caterpillars.

"They don't seem to bother you," Robert said.

"Should they?" Sharon held her hand forward, and as the caterpillars came to him, he did flinch. She withdrew her hand. "I'm sorry, Bob. I'll try and cultivate a phobia too."

She shook her hand, as though she were trying to throw soap suds off after washing the supper dishes, and the worms dropped to the forest floor.

Individually, the tent caterpillars were scarcely more than an inch long, and thin as spaghetti. But in numbers, they seemed huge. Several trunks were entirely covered in them, their tiny mottled bodies making a new layer of bark. Silk hung from the dark branches like torn shrouds.

Robert smiled. "No phobia. But no love for them either." He motioned around them. "By night, the worms will have stripped these trees bare. Turns the bush into a wasteland. Every year they're bad."

"It seems to bounce back," she said mildly. "From where I'm standing, it looks like there's plenty of bush to go around."

He couldn't tell if she was making fun of him. Sharon's eyes had a natural glitter to them, like they were always laughing, at everything they saw.

"The worms don't help it," he maintained, a little too steadfastly.

"Neither does the pesticide," she answered, locking her glittering eyes with Robert's. "Which won't stop you from spraying, will it?"

Robert didn't even answer that. She was laughing—her eyes betrayed her.

She must have seen something in his eyes, though, because as quickly as it came, the mockery passed, her eyes flicking away from his. "They're caterpillars, not worms, you know." She bent for a moment to study a nest, a tapered lozenge of silk filled with a hard black core. "There's a difference. They're butterflies." She smiled a little, and said in an almost affectionate tone: "Baby butterflies."

"Well these butterflies can make a difference between a good season and a bad one."

She looked away then, and nodded, the way she did whenever Robert offered up a fact or observation about his land or the business. It was as though she were filing it away, familiarizing herself as intimately as she could with the life Robert had built here at his campground.

He hoped that was an indication of something. . . . On more than one night back at the cabin, cleaning up after supper or watching her work on her computer or in the afterglow of their nights together, Robert had found himself hoping: This one should stay.

She was younger than most of the women Robert had taken up with over his life. She hadn't said her age exactly, and Robert considered himself too much of a gentleman to ask, but she couldn't have been older than thirty.

Robert had met her in Gravenhurst just over a month ago, at the first of the Sheas' summer barbecues. "She's just separated," Pat Shea had told him as she handed him a dripping can of Ex from the cooler. "Allan—her husband, you remember him?" Robert opened his beer and nodded, although as he thought about it, he could not remember Allan Tefield with any clarity at all. "Allan went back to Toronto last week."

Sharon was perched on the edge of the picnic table under the Sheas' ancient maple tree. Her long, blonde hair was pulled back in a ponytail to reveal a sculpted jawline and what seemed like an impossibly long throat. Robert had been fascinated—everything about Sharon Tefield was elongated, a not-unkind caricature of cover-girl good looks. Although he couldn't recall Allan Tefield's face, Robert was certain he would have remembered if he'd seen Sharon Tefield before, even once.

"Come on, Bob," Pat had said, noticing him noticing. She took him by the arm and directed him to the picnic table. "We'll do introductions."

A month later, Robert and Sharon stood on the southern ridge of the valley that made up the largest part of the Twin Oaks campground. Peering between the trees, the view was pure Muskoka. A dynasty of beavers had dammed up the stream decades ago and made the bowl of the valley into a small lake that reflected the cloud-filtered sunlight in sharp silver flashes.

In better seasons, the lake would be rimmed with fishermen, and this ridge well-travelled by hikers. But the tent caterpillars had started their crawl in June, and by mid-July the campers were staying at home.

"I have to go back to the cottage," said Sharon. "Just for a day or two."

"Trouble with Allan?"

Sharon shook her head, her lips set into a line. "Allan's finished. He's no trouble at all." She turned to Robert then, and the line of her mouth broke into a reassuring grin. "There are just a couple of things I want to pick up. Clean out."

Robert nodded, taking care to keep the flutter tight inside. Words like those often signalled an end—*I just have to go back to the city for a week, a few things to take care of . . . a couple of things I want to pick up.* But until the other shoe fell, there would be nothing to say.

Sharon's arm encircled Robert's waist. "I'm glad," she whispered.

"Glad about what?" he asked. But she didn't answer. They stood still on the ridge-path, while around them the summer worms munched away on leaves and sap and bark, preparing for their long, transforming sleep.

————

Sharon said she would be back not this night but the following, and Robert answered that was fine with him. He would spend the evening reading, he said, then out to work early in the morning. He had some canisters of insecticide in the shed, and while he was loathe to use too much of it, he thought he might spray some of the trees up on the south ridge.

"It's a losing battle," said Sharon. They were standing in front of his cabin, beside her old blue Volvo. She had left her tote bag in the bedroom, and carried her laptop computer under her arm.

"Got to at least put on a brave show for the campers," he replied.

There were only three families staying at Twin Oaks that week, but Sharon was kind enough not to point that out.

"I love you," she said instead. "But I don't want to come back to you stinking of bug spray."

"I'll shower," said Robert.

"Promise?"

Robert just laughed.

So they kissed goodbye and Robert watched the car turn around and start down the long driveway to the highway. He waved as it disappeared in the trees, and turned away. The sky that peeked through the maple branches over his cabin was the dull purple of late-August overcast—any sunset tonight would be lost behind the thickness of the clouds.

Just as well, he thought as he climbed the steps to his cabin. He stopped on the porch, nodded greetings at one of the Torsdale kids who was out playing by the barbecue pit—unlit, he noted sourly: who wants to barbecue this summer?—then let himself in.

Robert had built the cabin in 1970. It was cedar log, a bargain-basement kit house that was more suited to his needs back then than these days: three rooms, all of them miniscule, with heat coming from an old wood stove in the living room. At the time, he'd been inclined to forgo major appliances and a septic system as well, but fortunately had allowed himself to be talked out of it. The flush toilet and electric stove were luxuries that he had since come to appreciate, and as he sank down into the old vinyl recliner, it occurred to him that he—and Sharon, the two of them—could well appreciate a few more.

Over the years since he had come to this country, there had been three other women Robert had invited into his home. None had stayed long: the winters were too cold, the rooms too small. . . . It was a man's house, Lynn MacRae had told him as she packed for Toronto in January of 1983. A bachelor's house.

Lynn had been on the run from a bad marriage, too. She had been a teacher before she married, and within five months of leaving her husband and taking up with Robert, she determined it was time to go back to work. *Thank you, Robert.* She held both his hands and looked him levelly in the eye as she spoke, in that grave, affectionate tone that always marked the end. *I've learned so much from you.*

Robert unscrewed the cap off the bottle of Smirnoff's he kept underneath the end table and poured a finger of vodka into a tumbler. He didn't want to be a lesson for Sharon, any more than he had for

Lynn . . . and Mary, and Laura. . . .

The vodka burned down his throat in a single gulp, and he resisted the urge to pour himself a second. He had been going to spend the evening reading, he remembered.

Robert got up, switched the radio on to CBC, and pulled down the Frederick Forsyth novel he'd been picking at through the summer. He settled down again and, after a moment's consideration, poured himself another splash of vodka. The CBC was playing big band music, just getting into a long set of Woody Herman. Robert heaved back and his chair obligingly reclined.

It's Sharon's life, he reminded himself. *Not Lynn's, or Mary's, or anyone else's. She'll decide.*

It was dark; Robert heard the wind rustling in the maple trees over the house and the jazz show was almost over when the phone rang.

"Hello, Bob." Pat Shea's voice had an uneasy singsong quality to it at the other end of the line. "How's it going with you two?"

Robert smiled: since Sharon had started talking about moving in, it was clear that Pat was more than a little uncomfortable in her role as matchmaker. It would have been easier on her if they'd just gone out on a few dates, maybe kept up an affectionate correspondence between here and Toronto until the divorce was final; then a proper wedding at the nice old Anglican church the Sheas favoured in Gravenhurst. From Pat's point of view, she had created an extra-marital monster by introducing Robert Thacker to Sharon Tefield.

"It's going great," said Robert, then added, to help Pat relax as much as anything, "Sharon's back at the cottage tonight."

"Is she?" There was a measure of change in Pat's voice that Robert couldn't quite place. "That might be just as well. I was actually calling to let you know. Allan phoned here this evening."

Ah, hell. "What did he have to say?" he asked.

"A lot of ugly things. He sounded as though he'd been drinking." Pat paused for a moment—he heard her breaths against the mouthpiece as she decided what to say next. "But he told me he knew about you and Sharon. He asked me if she'd moved in with you yet. I'm afraid . . ."

She'd told him. She was sorry, she didn't know how it slipped out, but there it was. Allan knew that his ex-wife was shacking up with the guy who owned Twin Oaks Campground.

"I'm sorry, Robert."

"It's all right. He was going to find out anyway." In truth, Robert was surprised Sharon hadn't told Allan already.

"We're just worried about you. The two of you. Allan might be calling there later on tonight. That's why I called."

Robert smiled. "To warn me?"

Pat gave a small laugh. "I know you can take care of yourself, Bob. But you might want to screen your calls for the next few days."

"Well I may just do that." Robert didn't remind Pat that his bachelor's cabin didn't have an answering machine or any other means to screen his calls, as she put it. "Thanks for the advance notice."

But Pat went on. "You really don't want to be talking to Allan right now, and when Sharon gets back, she won't either. He sounded so . . ."

Robert held the phone in the crook of his shoulder and uncapped the vodka while Pat searched for the word.

"It was like he was dried out. Like he'd been drinking whisky, straight up, every night. And the things he said . . . about Sharon, you . . . mostly Sharon. Honestly, Bob . . ."

He set the vodka down, uncapped, on the end table. "I wish he'd called here in the first place," he said. "This shouldn't be your problem."

"Do you want us to go out there? To her cottage?" Pat didn't sound as though she wanted him to take her up on the offer, so he didn't.

"No no no. Don't worry; I'll give her a call."

"I just thought I should warn you."

"And you did. Thank you, Pat."

So they said their goodbyes and Robert returned the phone to its cradle. He swore softly. If Allan was in as bad a state as Pat seemed to think he was, Robert was more worried about him calling Sharon at the cottage—or driving there, for that matter—than he was about him calling here. After a moment's thought, he picked up the phone again and dialled the number of Sharon's cottage. It rang five times before she answered—she had been sleeping, he could tell.

He would be brief, he said, and told her about the conversation with Pat. "So you might want to, ah, screen your calls," he said.

"Okay," she mumbled through her sleep-haze. "Go to bed, honey."

"Do you want me to come out there?" he asked.

"No."

"If he shows up and you're alone—"

Sharon made a stretching sound. "He won't come," she said.

"What if he does?"

"Bobby, will you please go to bed? Allan can't do anything to me. Believe me—he's finished."

Finished. That was the second time she'd used that word to describe her ex-husband today.

"I'm just—"

But she cut him off again. "I love you, Bobby. But it's late. Go to bed. You've got a long day ahead of you. And I've got things to do around here in the morning. So get some sleep. Love you," she repeated.

"You too," he said, and hung up.

The phone didn't ring again, but Robert sat up waiting for it all the same. At around midnight, he thought again about calling her, driving out there anyway. But her tone hadn't been welcoming. And she was a big girl, he reminded himself.

Finally, Robert decided to give in to sleep, and stood up to go to the bedroom. It was unnaturally quiet—he couldn't even hear the leaves rustling over the house.

When he opened the window beside his bed, a cool summer breeze teased through his beard. He peered through the screen, out into the dark. A lone caterpillar was curled in an imperfect "S" shape on the outside of the screen. Robert flicked the wire mesh with his forefinger. The worm went tumbling into the night.

"Summer worms," he muttered and pulled off his shirt and blue jeans. He crawled into bed, pulled up the deep green comforter that Sharon had brought over the week before, and settled onto his side. The night was quiet as winter, and through it all Robert slept a fine, dreamless sleep.

The alarm clock jangled Robert awake in darkness, and he fought an inclination to roll over and sleep another hour—if he did, he knew he wouldn't be out of bed until six. It was so quiet in the early morning dark.

With a deliberate groan Robert threw aside the comforter and made his way to the kitchen. The temperature couldn't have dropped too much overnight, but the cabin air was freezing against his bare shoulders and thighs. He measured some instant coffee into a mug and filled the kettle, then went back to the bedroom to get into something warm.

The bedroom was, if anything, worse than the rest of the house. The window, still open from last night, admitted a north breeze that rustled across the two small curtains like flags. They made a faint flapping noise, and that was the only sound Robert heard.

The only sound.

He wrapped the housecoat tight around him and shut the window, but he couldn't stop shivering. Some things, he thought, you only notice by their absence. And with a breeze like that, the rustling of the leaves and branches in the maple tree over his cabin should have been steady, all night long.

"Ah, hell." Doing up the belt of the robe as he went, Robert hurried to the front door and slid his bare feet into an old pair of rubber boots. As an afterthought, he grabbed the flashlight from the hook beside the coat rack—it was still dark outside—and flipping it on, unlatched the front door and went out onto the stoop. He swung the flashlight beam up, to the branches that dangled over his roof.

"Hell," he said again, slack-jawed at the sight.

The branches were white, wrapped in silk thick as cotton candy. Strands of it hung taut between the limbs of the old maple tree, and as Robert played the flashlight beam across the expanse, he saw that it made nearly a perfect wrap; as though an enormous bag had been dropped over the tree, tied snug at the trunk. The leaves, the branches were all caught tight in the fabric, sheltered by it, and the wind left them still in the night. Robert stepped away from his porch and moved around the nest's perimeter, playing the flashlight up and down it. The morning dew glimmered off the nest like spun sugar.

The nest. That's what it is. Robert was awestruck by the immensity of it.

The tent caterpillars had come in the night, and before dawn they had woven a nest around a single tree that must have measured more than forty feet across, maybe half again as high. How many caterpillars would that have taken? Millions? A billion?

As he stood wondering, it occurred to Robert that he had been wrong about the silence. The nest wasn't quiet at all. In the darkness there was a drone of tiny jaws, working steadily at the greenery they had locked inside.

Robert started as another sound came up. It was the whistle from his kettle, high and insistent as the water boiled away. When he went inside to quiet it, his hand was trembling.

The morning went badly.

The Torsdales were the first of the campers to rise, at just before seven, and when Jim, their youngest boy, saw the work the worms had done in the night, he screamed like a girl. The scream got Don and

Jackie Torsdale out of bed—although their daughter Beth slept until they shook her a moment later—and before seven fifteen, Robert figured, the other two families that made up his camp clientele this morning were also wide awake.

When he came out of the shed twenty minutes later with the canister of insecticide over his shoulder and his coveralls, goggles and filter mask on, he noted wryly that those two trailers were in the process of packing up.

"Hey! That stuff's harmful!" shouted Mrs. Poole, setting her fists on her wide hips and glaring across the nearly empty campground while her husband disassembled the canopy on their trailer behind her. "Don't you go sprayin' it while there's people here!"

No danger of that, he thought, not for much longer. Then he pulled aside his filter mask to answer: "Don't worry, Mrs. Poole. I'm following the instructions."

"They don't mean nothin'!" she snapped before turning to her husband. "Hurry up! I don't wanna stay here no longer than I got to!"

Robert slipped the mask back over his face and walked over to the spot where the branches hung lowest. The weave was thick here, hanging deep over the wood pile and casting a uniform grey shadow over the sandy soil. If Robert reached up, he could touch the silk with his hand, and even through the blur of the goggles he saw the dark mass of the caterpillars. They crawled outside the nest too, and as he stood there, they dropped in twos and threes, landing to die in the sand or insinuate themselves into the crannies of the wood pile. Absently, Robert brushed at his shoulder.

Robert unhooked the hose on the end of the canister. It had a long metal nozzle, and he lifted it to the fabric of the nest. The silk felt rough on the end of the nozzle, and Robert hesitated a moment before pushing it through—he was struck by an image of the entire nest bursting, the nozzle a sharp pin to the tree's balloon, and him trapped, exposed under the weight of a million summer worms.

But the other option was fire. More than a few landowners in this part of Muskoka used that option readily, and Robert had in the past: just hold a lighter to the silk, watch it catch in gossamer embers and black curls of ash. Nature takes care of itself.

But he wasn't about to burn a nest this big. Any fire that could destroy this nest would take the maple tree, his cabin, maybe even the rest of the campground as well.

The nozzle slid into the nest like a syringe, and Robert squeezed the valve lever. He did it in seven more spots around the tree, until the canister was empty, leaving ragged holes of a size that bullets might make. Finally, he stood back, squinted at his work.

There was nothing he could see, of course—the silk wrapped it, and even in the harsh morning sunlight, the blackness underneath still clung.

Robert pulled the goggles off, wiped the condensation from the inside. He skirted around the tree's perimeter and hurried up the steps into his cabin.

Robert stripped his coveralls off in the living room, leaving them draped over the sofa, and he ran the water in the shower until it steamed before getting in.

Robert drove into Gravenhurst white-knuckled. As he turned onto Bethune Drive from the highway, he had to resist the urge to yank down his collar, pull out the worms. His stop at the Beer Store was quick, and the girl who worked at the counter looked at him funny— just for a second, as his twelve-pack of Ex rumbled down the rollers from the storeroom—and once again, he was tempted to brush his shoulders: what had she seen to make her look at him so? He hurried back to his truck, bottles jangling in their case.

He parked on Muskoka Street and walked to the A&P, where he gathered his groceries like an automaton, filling up the little arm basket by rote: extra-large eggs, butter, bread, a two-litre carton of two percent, a package of bacon, a three-dollar pepper steak from the meat department. Some days, walking the aisles of the A&P, Robert would actually meet three or four people whom he knew by name. Back in '69, when he came up from Kentucky and started Twin Oaks, he could count on doing so nearly every time he came to town. But Gravenhurst had grown over the past two decades, filled up with too many well-heeled strangers. Retired doctors and lawyers moving up to the brand-new subdivisions by the lakes. Younger families trying to beat the high cost of houses in Toronto. They were transitory, though, just like the summer people.

Just like the women who passed through Robert's home from time to time: summer women. Robert had to wait until the light changed behind him before he could pull onto the street, and he thought about it.

Was Sharon another summer woman? She had escaped her marriage without the obvious damage that some of the others had brought with them; hell, Mary's husband used to beat her up, and the asshole Lynn had married was cheating with her cousin before she left. They had been on the run, and in retrospect Robert knew he probably should have expected that anyplace they stopped was just a way station.

But Sharon . . . Where was the damage, what was it in Allan Tefield that she really had to flee? She had said it herself: He's finished.

Then he remembered Pat, and her warning phone call.

The light at Bay Street turned from yellow to red, and Robert put the truck into gear. He gassed it too hard, though, and it lurched as he swung onto the road.

There was no evidence of the caterpillars in downtown Gravenhurst. But it didn't seem to matter. At the Canadian Tire, Robert went straight to the men's room, locked himself in a stall and stripped off his shirt. The raw pungency of his sweat hit his nostrils like belly-gas from road kill. With shaking hands, Robert pulled the sleeves of his shirt inside out, and when he found nothing in its lining, he threw it to the floor. He ran his fingers around his belt-line, reached inside—he was sure he felt something down there, nestling in the warmth—and snapped the elastic of his briefs hard enough to leave a sting. Then he sat down on the edge of the toilet, pants still up, and exhaled a long, jagged sigh.

The nest was as big as a house. It was bigger than his own house; it would hold a two-storey townhouse and its basement, easy, and still have room for the worms that had spun it.

Jesus.

Finally, Robert reached down beside the toilet and pulled on his shirt.

"Ah, Christ," he said aloud, fingers fumbling as he did up his buttons.

He stood then, tucked in his shirttails and left the stall. At the garden section, he picked up five more canisters of insecticide—as many as were left on the barren metal shelf. He paid for them from a roll of Canadian Tire money, and when he got them outside he put the canisters in the back of the pickup. He paused for a moment before getting behind the wheel again, to steady himself.

"To hell with it," he said aloud and climbed into the cab. The tent caterpillars had made him twitchy, and it was getting worse the longer he sat and stewed on them.

When he got to Bay Street, he made a quick right and started off along the winding lake road in the direction of the Tefield cottage. If Sharon had a couple of things to do there, well she could damn well do them with him hanging around. If she didn't need anything right now, he sure as hell did.

The late-morning sun played across the ripples on Lake Muskoka like cascading jewellery as the road dipped past it. In the distance, a single motorboat hauled a water-skier in wide loops with a noise that, from this distance, sounded like a model airplane engine, a giant mosquito. Robert barely gave it a glance before the lake and the skier vanished behind a high tongue of bedrock.

If the summer worms had left the Canadian Tire alone, they'd been more conscientious diners along the road to Parker's Point—hell, by the time he got to the turnoff to their driveway, it looked as though they'd finished every last pea on their plate.

The trees around here looked dead. Leaves dangled like tattered doilies, and silk strands drifted across the narrow dirt road to catch on the truck's antenna, flying behind it like spectral pennants.

The driveway was narrower still, barely wide enough for Robert's pickup. It should have been a deep green tunnel this time of year, buried under the overhang of stands of mature maple and oak. But the light that filtered through the branches was grey, only occasionally broken by the shadow of one of the few fir trees. The rest were utterly denuded, not a speck of greenery left.

And the summer worms themselves were nowhere to be seen. Robert couldn't see a single caterpillar through the entire desolate bramble. They had finished the forest, and then they were gone.

Robert pulled the truck up behind the Tefield cottage and got out of the cab.

The packed-earth turnaround behind the cottage was empty, and at first Robert thought Sharon had parked her Volvo around the far side of the cottage, near the boathouse.

But when he tromped down the steep driveway, what he first took to be her car wasn't hers at all. It was a yellow Porsche. Its driver's window was half down, and it was parked just outside the doors to the boathouse, at the far end of the driveway.

Robert didn't know what kind of car Allan drove—Sharon didn't talk about him enough for details like that to stick in Robert's mind—but from what he'd gathered over the past month, the Porsche was completely in character.

Which meant, if Pat Shea were any judge of character, he had stumbled into what would at best be a very awkward situation.

And at worst . . .

The damage Sharon Tefield would finally bring from her marriage was only starting.

Robert turned back to the cottage. It was built high on a ridge so that the lakefront deck stuck out about three feet higher than Robert's head. The branches rustled in a sudden breeze off the lake. The reflection of those dry branches, the electric sky, jiggled as the wind caressed the panes of the cottage's immense picture window. Robert couldn't tell if anyone was up there or not.

"Hello?" he called, cupping his hands around his mouth.

The cottage was silent.

"Everything okay in there?" Robert dropped his hands to his sides and started up the path to the steps onto the deck. "Anyone there?"

When there was still no answer, Robert started to run.

"I'm coming up!" he shouted, taking the steps two at a time. He should have driven out last night, he told himself. No matter what Sharon had said.

He stopped at the top of the stairs, nearly reeling backward off the deck at the sight before him. He grabbed the railing, righted himself and stepped forward.

"Sharon!"

She wasn't anywhere amid the detritus on the deck, and he couldn't see any movement in the dark beyond the picture windows, but Robert was filled with a sudden dread that she was still here— maybe in the bathroom, maybe locked up in the bedroom. Left there by her crazy ex-husband to rot and die. After he'd worked her over. And maybe after he'd done this to their deck.

Robert stepped gingerly around the shattered glass that had once been the top of their patio table, through the torn strips of cushion fabric, the thick chunks of foam rubber scattered across the wood.

Allan must have taken a butcher knife to this, Robert thought. *He must have been crazy—completely Goddamn crazy.*

"Who's that?"

Robert looked back at the window in time to see a blur of motion—a flash of white flesh, quick across the darkness of the living room and blurred by Robert's own reflection. The voice had been a man's, muffled by glass and curtains. It had sounded rough, uncertain.

"Bob Thacker." He stepped over to the screen door, which was ajar. He pulled it open, then lifted his hands, palms outward, in a belated gesture of truce. The cottage stank, of liquor and spoiled milk, but he resisted the urge to cover his face. "I'm Robert Thacker," he said again, squinting around the dim living room. "No trouble, okay?"

It was a mess in here too. As Robert's eyes adjusted to the dimness, he could make out more victims of Allan's knife. There was a set of pine furniture—sofa, loveseat, and armchair—that had all been overturned. The pillows were sliced to ribbons, and the stuffing was spread across the floor in a way that reminded Robert of the caterpillar nests. There was a large picture on the wall—Robert recognized it as the work of one of the local artists, a watercolour painting of this very cottage, maybe as seen from the boathouse. The glass fronting it had been smashed and lay on the rug in a glittering jumble. A floor lamp with a stem of lacquered birch lay on its side, bulb smashed, and the ceiling fan had been knocked askew. The floor was also dotted with bottles. He bent to pick up a plastic mickey of Captain Morgan's from a sticky puddle of rum at his feet.

There was a sudden movement in the room's far corner, behind the fireplace—like an animal, scrambling back into its hole. Cautiously, Robert crossed the floor to the fireplace.

"Is that bitch with you?" The fireplace made a bong, a hiss of flesh on metal, as weight shifted against it.

"I'm alone," said Robert. Now that he was closer, he saw a single foot protruding from behind the fireplace. The tips of its toes were scabbed black where the nails had been chewed down to nubs. As fast as Robert had seen it, the foot withdrew.

"Bullshit."

Robert stopped, shrugged. "Think what you like," he said. "It's just me. Where's Sharon, Allan?"

"How should I know?" Pat had been right about his voice, thought Robert—it sounded dried-out, whiskey-cured. "I'm not her keeper."

"Did she leave already?" Robert inched forward—he didn't want to startle Allan, bring on another outburst. "Has she gone?"

No answer.

Robert tensed, kept his eye on the corner.

"Did you do anything to her, Allan?" he asked, struggling to hold the tremor out of his voice.

"Do anything to her?" A dry chuckle. "No."

Robert stepped around the fireplace.

"I'd like to, I have to admit that. But I don't really think I could," he said, reasonably. "Do you?"

Robert couldn't answer.

Nothing in Allan's voice could have prepared Robert for the sight of him. He was completely naked, and his entire body was freckled with black scabs—including his scalp, which was nearly hairless. From his conversations with Sharon, Robert had placed Allan in his mid-thirties, but the emaciated creature behind the stove might have been in his seventies. His eyes were round and wet under naked brows, and his hollow chest trembled as he breathed. As though he were sobbing.

"Sucks it out of you," said Allan Tefield. "Sucks it right out of you."

Robert crouched down, reached out to Allan, but he scrambled backward. His hands flashed for an instant, and Robert saw the same thick scabs at their tips as on Allan's toes.

"No! Don't touch!"

"All right, all right," said Robert, raising his hands again. "I'm not moving."

"Everything hurts."

"I know," said Robert, although he knew he could only imagine. What had done this to him?

"I'm sorry things have gone this way for you," he said. "I truly am."

Allan looked up, his round eyes narrowing. "You're sorry that you're shacked up with my wife?"

Robert didn't know what to say to that one—he wasn't sorry, wasn't sorry at all—so he didn't even try. "How—how did this happen?" He gestured to the mess of the house, to Allan's own ruined flesh.

"The worms," said Allan, a narrow, crazy smile growing on his face. "They're crawling this year, aren't they?"

"They are," said Robert. He felt goose flesh rising on his arms.

"Well. They're almost finished." Allan's peeled lips broke into a full grin, revealing incongruously clean and even teeth. "She's almost finished."

Robert let those words sink in. "She's almost—" he repeated, then: "You finished her?"

Allan's eyes were gimlets over his grin.

The pity dissolved into fear, then reconstituted as anger, and Robert rushed forward. He bent into the space behind the fireplace and took Allan by the shoulders. Allan squealed as Robert's hands closed around his clammy, prickly shoulders, and lifted him from the dirt.

"Where is Sharon? You done anything to her?"

"Nothing!" Now Allan was sobbing, tears streaming down his cheeks, streaking red where they crossed the scabs along his chin.

"Nothing nothing nothing! Let me go! Please, please please, lemmego! It hurts!"

Robert let go, and Allan stumbled backward, nearly falling in the mess at his feet. The scabs had broken where Robert had grabbed him, and had left a sweaty sheen of old blood on Robert's palms. He raised his hand to slap Allan, but stopped as the other man fell to his knees, put up his hands.

"Don't!" he whimpered, his eyes pleading as he spoke: "She went back. Back to your place. Half hour ago."

"I'm calling the campground," Robert finally muttered. "She better be there. And she better be okay."

Then he turned and picked his way through the detritus to the kitchen, where the telephone was, miraculously, still intact. As he dialled the number, Allan's sobs turned into a wail.

Waiting for an answer, Robert glanced around the kitchen. It was worse than the living room: a thick steak, going grey in a bed of Styrofoam and cellophane; puddles of liquor and milk, mixing into a pale oil slick on the counter; an overturned pot, spilling burned rice and vegetables into the dish-clogged sink; and everywhere, broken glass, smashed bottles and glasses and plates, jagged metal cans.

Through the doorway to the living room, Robert saw Allan fidgeting nervously with his hands, rocking from one foot to the other, watching him watching. From a distance, the scabs on his flesh seemed to bundle around where his hair would grow. As though he'd actually ripped his own hair out by the roots. Maybe that's what he'd done.

After the tenth ring, Robert set the phone back in its cradle.

"She's not answering, Allan," he said, in as reasonable a tone as he could manage. "Where's Sharon?"

"I told you. She's gone." Allan smiled.

Robert was trembling again—worse than at Canadian Tire, worse than he was after the worms.

"I'm going to find her," he muttered, and pushed past Allan into the living room. "If she's here . . ." He turned and glared back at Allan.

But Allan just shrugged. "Go look," he said. "I'm not going anywhere."

Robert swore, and hurried down the short hallway to the rest of the cottage. There were only three other rooms—two bedrooms and a washroom—and it didn't take Robert more than five minutes going through them to confirm Allan's story.

Sharon was gone.

"I know all about you," said Allan as Robert came back into the living room.

"Is that so?" said Robert.

"I called around." Allan had an almost comically smug expression on his face. "I thought about helping you, at first."

I'm not the one who needs help, thought Robert. But he kept quiet.

"People say you were a draft dodger. Didn't want to go to Viet Nam, so picked Muskoka instead." Allan's hands trembled as he brought them up to his chin. "That true?"

"I came up here from the States," said Robert.

"It is true, isn't it?" Blood smeared across his chin, over his lips, as Allan's hands drew circles on his face.

"Where is Sharon, Allan?" Robert felt his fists bunching, and willed them open again.

Allan snorted derisively. "Oh for Christ's sake, Robert, work it out." He gestured around him with bloody hands. "You saw for yourself that she's not in the house. Did you see her car out there? What, do you think I drove it into the lake? Think about it. She went back to your cabin, like I told you."

Robert didn't answer at first, but Allan had a point. The car was gone, and Allan was really in no shape to have disposed of it with any efficiency.

"I'll call again before we leave," said Robert finally. "Look, Allan . . ." He stepped forward.

But Allan put up his hand. "So you bought a plot of land, put up a sign and cleared the driveway. Built yourself a shack. Then you just stayed on. I guess you put down roots pretty firm here."

Robert stopped. "It's a good place," he said.

"It's a shitty place." Allan leaned against the windows, the skin of his shoulders making a rubber noise on the glass. "Sharon wanted to buy up here. But it's shitty. Mosquitoes every summer, snow up to your ass every winter, two fucking days in the fall when the colours change, and then it rains until November. And this!" He gestured outside to the naked trees, their twisting branches a caricature of Allan's own twig-thin arms. "*The fucking worm!*"

"It's where I am," said Robert reasonably.

"It's where your *roots* are, Thacker." Allan grinned. "These trees have roots too. And from the looks of them, I think they'll have to come down next year." He leaned forward, bare ass squealing obscenely along the pane. "Dead wood."

Robert regarded Allan, and it occurred to him: Sharon was fine. The only person who had come out of this relationship with any damage was Allan Tefield.

"You've really screwed up," he said. "You know that, don't you, Allan?"

"Go back to Sharon, you asshole." Allan sneered, showing his white, perfect teeth. "That's what you're here for, isn't it? Go back to Sharon. That's where you belong."

"All right," said Robert. "But before I go—tell me what happened to you."

"The worms."

"The worms didn't do this. What happened, Allan?"

"Eaten," he said, eyes down. "Eaten by the worm."

At that, Robert made up his mind: Sharon could wait. Right now, it was Allan who needed his help.

"Come on," said Robert. "Let's find your clothes."

"No clothes."

He wasn't going to argue—Allan was beyond reasoning, and Robert wanted them both out of there as fast as possible. "All right. Then I'll get a blanket from the truck to cover you up. We're going to Bracebridge. I'm taking you to a hospital."

"Hospital?"

"I think we'd better," said Robert. "Don't you, Allan?"

The emergency room at South Muskoka Memorial was busy. There had been a pileup on Highway 11 just north of Gravenhurst, and the waiting room and the hallways leading off it were a conduit for paramedics and their patients. The early afternoon heat was filled with the sounds of sirens as more ambulances pulled in.

Robert waited until the latest ambulance had cleared the entrance, then led Allan to the admitting desk. The nurse there was young, barely out of her teens. She looked first at him, and then at Allan. Her eyes betrayed only a little of what she must have felt seeing him.

"I found him like this," explained Robert. "In his cottage. He's in pretty bad shape."

"I can see," she said. Allan was wearing the cotton blanket from the truck's seat, clutched around him like a poncho against the ER ward's air-conditioned cool. His scalp was beginning to bleed again, and it covered his face in a deep pink sheen. "What happened to him?"

"I don't know, exactly." Robert leaned closer to the nurse, and whispered: "I think it may be self-inflicted."

"Like hell." Allan sat down in one of the chairs, glared across the desk at the nurse.

"I didn't think he should be left like that," said Robert.

The nurse looked at Robert suspiciously. She was about to say something when an older nurse came up behind her with a stack of papers. She set the stack down on a bare spot on the desk.

"Is it life-threatening?" she asked Robert, and when he said no, sent the two of them over to a vacant row of chairs, along with a set of forms to fill out.

They didn't wait for as long as Robert feared. Three more stretchers came in from the pileup—from what Robert could overhear, there had been eight cars involved—and once the paperwork was out of the way from those, an orderly came with a wheelchair to take Allan away. He was as young as the nurse behind the admissions desk, his blond hair spiked like a hockey player's. He gave Robert an apologetic smile as they helped Allan up and into the chair.

"What happened to you?" he asked as Allan settled.

"The worm," Allan said, staring into his lap.

The orderly looked at Robert, and he shrugged.

"Tent caterpillars," said Robert. "Thinks they did it to him. They're enough to make anyone buggy, I guess."

"It's bad this year," said the orderly, pushing the wheelchair along the corridor. "Did you hear about the pileup?"

Robert made a non-committal noise.

"I hear it's caterpillars that caused it."

"Come again?" Robert slipped behind the orderly as they passed the stretcher of what might have been one of the pileup's victims: a middle-aged man in a blood-stained Blue Jays shirt. He had a compression bandage on his scalp, a plasma bag hooked up on the IV tower, and he stared glassily at the ceiling.

"A truck hit a slick of them, crossing the highway." Once past the stretcher, the orderly slowed to let Robert catch up. "Tried to brake, but the tires couldn't get any traction. They were like an oil slick. So the truck jackknifed, and the cars behind couldn't stop." He gave Robert a secretive little smile. "Weird shit."

Robert didn't know whether to laugh. It sounded like another wives' tale—When the summer worms crossed the highway, they'd pile so thick you couldn't drive. It was ridiculous: almost as ridiculous as . . .

As a nest of summer worms the size of a house.

The orderly stopped outside a pair of double doors. "I'm afraid this is where we get off, sir. You can wait in the lounge, if you like."

"All right." Robert's throat was dry, and he cleared it. "I'll do that."

Before he could leave, Allan's head twisted to face him. "It was just two years!" he snarled. "That's all we were together!"

"Goodbye, Allan."

"Two years!" he called as the orderly wheeled him through the doors.

Robert went back to the waiting room, fumbling in his pockets for a quarter for the pay phone. By the time he finished dialling his number, his hands were shaking.

Sharon answered the phone on the fourth ring, and when she spoke, Robert nearly collapsed with relief.

"Are you all right, Bobby?" Her voice was smooth, the worry in it no more than a vague undercurrent.

"I was at your cottage," he replied. "I'm all right. I don't know about your ex, though."

"He's there?" The worry turned into a rising alarm. "Bobby, you've got to come home."

Robert cupped the mouthpiece close. "He's in pretty bad shape," he said. "I've got him at the hospital in Bracebridge."

"I know," said Sharon quickly. "I was at the cottage today. Look, just come home, okay? Don't make it worse."

"I should stick around," said Robert. "Make sure everything's okay."

Now Sharon's voice grew sharp.

"Don't bother. I've already called his parents in Toronto. I'll call them now, tell them where he is."

"Sharon, will you please tell me what—"

"Just come home!"

Then Sharon said something softly, and when Robert didn't hear, she repeated:

"I need you, Bobby. I need you here."

And she hung up.

＊

Robert nearly missed his turn-off, and when he saw it, he braked so hard he thought he was going to spin out. He wheeled the car around, barely checking the oncoming traffic, and his tires spun on the gravel of the side road. He passed the TWIN OAKS CAMPGROUND-1/4 MILE sign at what must have been double the speed limit, and only slowed when he hit the first steep bend in the road.

The caterpillars had caused the pileup. And the maple tree over Robert's house was so enshrouded in caterpillar silk, it looked like rolls of cotton candy. And Allan Tefield had no hair, and when Robert asked him why, he blamed the worm. And Sharon was alone at Twin Oaks.

And she had wanted him back there. She had insisted: I need you here, she said.

Robert didn't even look at the trees until he was almost at home.

Robert stopped the truck at the foot of his driveway. He felt his heart racing, his breath raw in his throat.

The sign at the entrance was nearly illegible, the silk had covered it so thickly. All the trees facing the road were draped with silk, and the driveway was obstructed by wide, worm-mottled curtains that caught shafts of afternoon sun like columns of dust. Robert heard the noise of the summer worms' mouths over the pickup's idling engine.

They had sealed the campground off—nearly as effectively as they had the maple tree this morning.

Robert threw the truck into low gear, and gravel crunched under his tires as he crept up the driveway.

The first curtain of summer worms stretched like nylon hose where the grille pushed against it. Finally, the curtain came unmoored and the silk descended on the front windshield, like a sheet thrown over a fresh bed. Robert had to stop himself from flicking on the windshield wipers: there were too many worms; they would smear. He kept his foot steady on the accelerator, and the truck lumbered forward into the next curtain. His hands trembled on the steering wheel as another layer of silk fell in front of him, and another.

By the fifth curtain, he had to stop. The windshield was completely opaque, and even the back and side windows were so thickly plastered that he couldn't make out anything beyond the vaguest of shapes. He guessed that he was maybe a third of the way up, but it was hard to tell: even in winter he wouldn't have taken the driveway this slowly.

Robert turned off the engine. There were no two ways about it: he'd have to walk it from here. He opened the door and pushed the membranes of silk aside. It made a sound like tearing cotton batten, and maybe a half-dozen worms fell lightly on his arm.

He resisted the urge to draw back, shake them away. If he were going to make the walk, Robert would have to get used to the feeling of worms on his skin. He opened the door the rest of the way and climbed out of the truck.

The worms had made his driveway into a tunnel of white. Every tree was enshrouded with them, and the silk extended through the branches overhead to make a thick ceiling. The bright afternoon seemed overcast in here, under their shadow. Looking back through the tunnel his truck had made, Robert thought he could almost see the clean sunlight on the road. But the shrouds distorted distance, and it was hard to tell for sure.

The truck itself was nearly as well-disguised. The silk draped across it from back to front, and the caterpillars moved across it in thick clusters.

Arm in front of him to ward off the caterpillars that dangled from threads every few feet, Robert walked around to the back of the pickup. The bag containing the canisters of insecticide were packed back near the cab, barely visible through the mess of worms and silk. Robert reached into it, his hand gathering more worms as he did so, and pulled out the bag.

Robert shut his eyes for a moment, then turned away from the road he imagined he could see and walked toward the next wall of worms.

They gathered on him as he moved. His hands always touched the webbing first, and were sometimes black with the worms up past the wrists. But there were enough worms for all of him. They burrowed into his hair, and he was certain he felt them under his collar, moving down his back, among the copse of thick hairs that grew on his shoulders. When he looked down, he saw them all over his jeans, clustering by the hundreds around his knees and thighs, the tops of his boots. He kept his mouth shut and snorted whenever he exhaled to blow away the ones on his lip.

But he didn't brush them off. To do so would be to admit to the spiralling terror in his belly, and such an admission would paralyze him—or worse, send him crashing into the trees, running blind.

He was nearly blind now. The farther along the driveway he got, the more intricate the weave became. Every few feet he had to clear another shift of silk, and at times it was only the feeling of gravel under his feet that reassured him he was still on the driveway at all.

He stopped once, to bend over and breathe, shake the sweat from his hair. It was greenhouse-hot here, but the air seemed to hold little oxygen. Worms fell to the ground as he straightened and pushed forward.

He knew the campground was getting closer as the silk in front of him began to glow with the yellow of the afternoon sun. At first it was just a dim hue, like the sun through a thinning patch of cloud on an overcast day. As Robert went on, the light grew, making each sheet of silk more luminescent than the last. Finally, with scarcely more than a sheet to go, Robert saw the bright shapes of his campground through the glowing threads of silk.

He ran forward, nearly dropping the insecticide as he went, and burst from the wall of the nest, trailing silk like a bridal train. He shook off his hand, wiped the worms from his lips and opened his mouth to shout:

"Sharon!"

The campground was silent. The silk from the maple over his house now extended over all the trees. The canopy sloped down in places to touch the shrubs and saplings nearer the ground, in the clean parabolas of circus-tent roofs. There was a clearing in the trees maybe a hundred feet in diameter, which Robert used mostly as a cul-de-sac and parking lot for the day-trippers. The worms had left it a barren oasis of gravel and scrub grass.

"Sharon!" he shouted again. "You there? You all right?"

His cabin was nearly invisible under the silk, a peaked cube of shadow. No sound came from inside.

Almost absently, Robert peeled the silk from his shoulders and strode across the clearing to the far edge. He tried to imagine how Sharon must feel in there—cocooned inside his already-too-small cabin, choking on what must be stifling heat. The worms hadn't bothered her the day before; she'd barely given them a second glance these past few weeks. But this . . .

The cabin was too quiet. Christ, he thought, what's happened to Sharon while I've been gone?

I need you here.

Robert started toward the cabin. If he'd made it up the driveway on his own, he surely wouldn't have a problem making it through a few layers of silk into his cabin.

But the silk was tougher here. Robert had to use his jackknife to cut through it, and the sound of his passage was like ripping fabric.

There were fewer worms on the curtains, but the task was no easier for that: in the worms' place were row upon row of hard cocoons, brittle like plastic and some as large as Robert's thumb.

He groped on, cutting and advancing, until he found his cabin—not by sight, but by touch. He had come through at a point in the middle of the south wall, underneath the kitchen window. His hand glided up to confirm the glass, the rough metal screen. But before he could withdraw, worms tumbled down onto his head, and he shook them away. Dim yellow light shone out from the kitchen, in the spaces where his hand had cleared the screen of caterpillars.

"Sharon!" His voice was weak, gasping.

She didn't answer, but Robert thought he heard movement inside.

Robert inched along the dry timbers until he reached the stoop to his front door. The overhang kept the space of his vestibule clear of silk, so Robert didn't have to do much more cutting. He stumbled up the stairs and grabbed the door handle.

"I'm here, Sharon," he whispered. The door wasn't locked—it wasn't even closed properly—and Robert yanked it open. It banged against the wall with an oddly muffled crunch. "I'm—"

He couldn't finish.

The walls, the floor, the ceiling of the living room were blanketed in them. They crawled over the floor lamp, tiny bodies making an uneven pattern of curling silhouettes on the shade. They blacked out the three oil paintings on the wall over the Coleman, and they utterly covered his leather recliner, like a new, writhing layer of upholstery. The sofa's stuffing was laid bare, and more worms burrowed into it.

Robert began to tremble. His mouth opened, and he shut it again as quickly: the idea that the worms might get in *there*, too . . .

Oh Jesus, oh God. Robert felt himself unravelling.

Robert's eyes widened, and the scream that should have come through his mouth forced its way instead through his nostrils. The canisters of insecticide fell to the floor, and Robert's hands grasped at the lapels of his own shirt, and tore.

The shirt came away in a cascade of buttons. He threw it across the room. He yanked his belt undone next, and stripped off his jeans—they were filled with worms, as bad as the shirt, and when they hitched over his boots he nearly screamed again, fell into the worms at his feet. But somehow he managed to stay upright and, jeans at his ankles, kicked the boots free. Then he kicked clear of the jeans as well, and bent to pick up one of the insecticide canisters from the bag at his feet.

Robert dug his thumb into the nozzle and found the pin. *The Contents* were *Under Pressure*—that was only the first in the long list of fine-print warnings that ran down the side of the insecticide canister. When Robert pushed the pin in, the insecticide came out in a cool, spreading vapour that made Robert's eyes sting. He coughed only once, and turned the spray onto the summer worms.

By degree, the cabin's living room and kitchen filled with billowing, stinking white mist. It settled on the glass of the mirror on the bathroom door like a frost, hung in the air like a stratum of cigarette smoke at an all-night poker game. Robert coughed again, three times. His thumb was getting cold, and he felt the stinging spread to the quick under his nail. Snot dribbled from his nostrils, running fast over his thin, clamped lips. He kept up the pressure.

The spray got to the ceiling worms first, and they began to fall. Robert felt them land on his shoulders, in his hair, but he resisted the urge to scrape them away. He'd have to let go of the insecticide for that, and it was still heavy with product.

He moved forward into the living room, spraying as he went. His vision was beginning to blur, but he could hear well enough. And the sound that he heard was the pitter-pat of worms, falling all around him in a solidified rain. Robert wanted to laugh. If only he could open his mouth . . . He giggled through his nose instead, and thick strings of snot fell onto the backs of his forearms.

This was *his* land. *His* home.

My roots, Robert said to himself, and noted with satisfaction that the worms were coming down from the walls now too.

"Stop it."

The voice was quiet, pained, and it was only after it came three times that Robert remembered Sharon.

He still had to struggle to make himself lift his thumb.

———

The voice came from the bedroom. Robert was dizzy from the fumes, and his ears had started to ring now as well, but he could tell that much.

"Stop."

Robert had a hard time staying upright—*I should open a window, that would air the place out*. He coughed some more, tasted salt and copper in the mucous this time. The bedroom doorframe came up under his outstretched hand as the house lurched, and took his weight. He guided himself past it, into the cabin's other room.

"Sharon." The word came like a bark. It hurt in his chest, but he said it again.

"Sharon."

He couldn't see a thing in the bedroom. The light was out, and his eyes felt like they were going to burn out of his head.

Robert stumbled through something on the floor and stopped the spinning house again, this time grabbing the bedside lamp as it passed. He flicked it on with his insecticide thumb.

Sharon lay curled on the bed, underneath the comforter she'd brought with her. Robert blinked, tried to focus his eyes on her—it seemed as though she lay in a mist, thicker even than the vapours he'd sprayed in the living room. Christ. How much had he sprayed? Robert felt normalcy returning to him, and with it, a sickening realization of exactly what he'd done. The poison must be everywhere by now. The worms fell here too, landing on him, the comforter. On the mist over Sharon's face, suspended . . .

"Oh Sharon, honey." He set the insecticide down on the night table. As he reached down to touch her, the realization chilled him:

Sharon was enshrouded in silk. As his fingers pushed through it, Sharon's eyelids fluttered, and she shifted slightly under the comforter.

More deliberately this time, Robert set about pulling away the silk. Sharon blinked her eyes open, and as her lips parted, he stopped pulling.

"Bobby." Her voice was gummy, and it had a sleepy drawl to it. "Stinks in here."

Robert yanked the remainder of the threads clear. His vision started to double, but he could make out Sharon's arm as it came up to him. It was so thin, he thought. In his doubling vision, it seemed to undulate, as though boneless. Silk wrapped it like the lace sleeve of a bridal gown.

"I'm glad you came back," she said. "I was almost ready to go to sleep without you."

"I'll always come home," said Robert. Her fingertips felt rough as they brushed the back of his neck, and her touch left a sting behind on his sensitized skin.

"You're late, though." Sharon's eyes glittered, and Robert thought: *I'm an idiot with this woman; she makes me slow.*

"I took Allan to the hospital," he said. Sharon's hand moved up through his hair, drew him down onto the bed. "I know you wanted me back soon. I'm sorry."

"You should have come," said Sharon. Her hand came over his scalp, leaving it cool where she passed. "Time for bed."

"Honey—"

—*we have to get you out of here*, Robert would have said. But at that instant, her hand appeared over his forehead. Clutched in its fist were clumps of brown hair. They were bloody at their roots.

"Jesus!" Robert's scream sounded high, distant in his own head.

He pulled back, but he wasn't quick enough: Sharon's other hand shot out and grabbed his left wrist. She smiled and her lips collapsed inward. As they parted he confirmed it: her mouth was a pink and black pit, toothless. She pushed his bloody hair inside.

Robert yanked at his wrist, but her fingers dug into the flesh there like a tightening noose. He felt his pulse quicken, even as his vision started to grey. The lump of hair and blood travelled down Sharon's elongated throat like a rat through a python.

The worm, Allan had said when Robert asked what had done this to him. Not the worms, not the tent caterpillars, but a singular creature. He said he had been eaten by the worm.

Sharon's free arm lashed at him again, but Robert wheeled back fast enough to avoid it. The arm cracked like a whip in empty air, boneless. His hand was going purple in her grip, but he pulled back anyway. With his free hand, he grabbed the insecticide from the night-table.

"You drew them here, didn't you?" he asked.

She mumbled something—butterfly?—but her mouth had taken on an odd "O" shape, and the word mushed.

Robert hoisted the insecticide canister onto his hip, and pointed the nozzle at the bed. His heartbeat thundered in his ears, and the hand that she still held felt thick, numb. He moved his thumb over the nozzle.

"Allan warned me," Robert said, and pressed the pin.

The mist spread before him. Her fingers unravelled from his wrist, and Robert stumbled backward under the force of his own weight. She reared out of her bed. She was naked under the covers, although her body was growing indistinct—her breasts, small to begin with, had shrunk to boyish proportions, and her hips had disappeared in the sinuous curl of her torso.

Robert shook the blood back into his hand then gripped the bottle two-handed. He felt the chemical as it settled on his bare scalp—certainly, he could remember that one of the cautions on the packaging was to *Avoid Contact With Open Wounds*. The manufacturers were right—it stung like battery acid where his scalp bled.

The effect on the thing in the bed was similar. The "O" of her mouth expanded like an iris, and her eyes glittered black. Her mouth made a sound like *stop*, but Robert kept spraying. She stretched back, her hands touching the wall behind her, and with a quick undulation, she was pressed entirely against the wall. Robert's thumb slipped as he watched her crawl up the sheer surface, toward the ceiling, but he found it again and the spray resumed. He coughed and spat bloody phlegm onto the bedspread.

The creature hung over him, face to the ceiling, and Robert lifted the canister over his head. The chemical rained down on him, and the mist grew, and his hands became numb, and by quick degree the room darkened.

Sharon's hands slipped from the ceiling then, and for a moment she dangled by her knees alone. At first he thought she was going to fall—a great worm, dying in the spray.

But she surprised him. Her arms flew forward, and in a single motion knocked the insecticide from his grasp and wrapped around his chest. She descended, round mouth wide, as the darkness finally overtook him.

———

Robert woke in blackness. He was on the bed—he felt the comforter, the pillow beneath his bare scalp. But the room was utterly dark, more so than he had ever experienced. Hand trembling, he reached for the lamp. He found the switch, but when he pressed it, the darkness remained. He pulled his hand back quickly. The pain of that simple movement was excruciating; his fingernails were gone, and the raw nerves underneath howled. The skin of his arm felt like it had been scraped along asphalt. He opened his mouth, and when he spoke his voice sounded like an old man's.

"Hello?"

The house was silent—even the sound of the caterpillars was absent. Robert repeated: "Hello? Who's there?" but got no better results.

He was alone.

He chuckled at the thought. Lynn, and Mary, and Laura, and now Sharon—they'd all taken what they needed. The chuckle turned into a snorting guffaw. They'd all stripped him bare, left him in his cabin, on his land. Here where his roots were.

Robert got himself under control and tried to sit up in bed. The effort it took was Herculean, and he had to sit for a minute after that to get his wind back. Lynn had gone back to the city, Mary had gone back to the States, and Laura . . . she had just gone. Where would Sharon go? Where would she fly?

Gingerly, Robert lowered his feet to the floor. He sat there for some time in his new, silent night, straining to hear the beating of her wings.

KNIFE FIGHT

Not many outside the confines of the political wing at City Hall would guess it, but our new mayor is an expert with a knife.

He has been practising since he was a boy—from the day he first laid eyes on the eleven-inch bowie knife jammed hilt-deep into a tree stump in the family's ancestral woodlot, and withdrew it, claiming it as his own then and forever.

The concrete of his father's basement workshop floor is still flecked with tiny, reddish-brown dots, a Jackson Pollock record of the young mayor's apprenticeship, those nights when he was too slow, or worse . . . too quick. Those days are long past, and now the mayor is neither. He is merely bold. He is an expert.

Since the hour of his swearing-in, the mayor has kept the knife in the desk drawer next to his chain of office, wrapped in an oilcloth tied with thin leather straps. There it slumbers, six nights a week. The seventh—Thursday—the mayor carefully unwraps it, holds it to the fading afternoon light to see that its edge remains keen and, in the company of his older cousin—the one who oversees road repairs in the west district—the mayor steps into the elevator that takes him straight to the parking garage.

And so it begins.

In the beginning, the waiting crowd had been small indeed—comprised of a handful of senior staff and five city councillors, each hoping to become the mayor's deputy and thereby enjoy the attendant perquisites and honours. They had been there since three p.m., stripped to the waist and greased with goose fat, not daring to speak, barely breathing. The mayor's cousin had reviewed the rules with each of them, which he called "Robert's Rules of Knife Fight." It is said that the city clerk, leaning against the planning commissioner's SUV, snickered at the procedure, and that this—not political differences—was the reason for her dismissal at the next meeting of council.

The mayor's cousin explained the rules then, as he has at each subsequent Thursday.

> 1. There are only ever two combatants in a knife fight, and each combatant is allowed a knife.
> 2. The knives are to be provided by the combatants, in a keen, clean condition free of rust. Other objects— scissors, hammers, axes, surgical instruments—shall not be considered knives for the purposes of the knife fight.
> 3. Combatants shall arrive stripped to the waist, and well-lubricated so as to keep the knife fight from becoming a wrestling match, which is unseemly.
> 4. Goose fat is considered an acceptable lubricant for the purposes of a knife fight.
> 5. Victory in the knife fight is usually decided by the drawing of first blood.
> 6. Combatants shall avoid their opponents' faces, hands, and throats, confining their strikes to parts of the body usually covered by appropriate business attire.
> 7. In the event that both combatants draw blood from one another in the same instant, the knife fight shall be considered a draw and entered into the Records as such.
> 8. To the victor go the spoils.

The knife fight remained a well-kept secret for many months. It is true, we wondered at the selection of the new deputy mayor—a stocky, dull-witted rookie councillor from the slaughterhouse district who was unable to finish a sentence without uttering a profanity and crumpled his briefing notes without reading them. And more than once we had seen a blossom of red erupt on the white blouses that the new budget chief wore to the committee meetings regarding capital allocations for the coming fiscal year. And we had wondered at the propensity of the new chair of the Transit Commission to press a fist to his mouth and shut his eyes during breaks in meetings—as though holding back tears at some awful recollection.

But who cared about such things in the larger scheme? Not us, not at first.

The first year of the mayor's first term was successful by any account. The budget chief not only balanced the books but was able to deliver a modest property tax reduction for the elderly and lay down plans for a swimming pool and target range, creating the first two-thirds of a much-needed triathlete program in the underprivileged slums lining the west riverbank. Our editors wrote supportive editorials as the deputy mayor announced that the Association of Suburban Golf Courses would open up in the winter months, for the final third. The new light rail line servicing the old, blue-collar municipality of Smelt received all the funding it needed from a new federal grant program, announced by the Transit Commission chair in tremulous tones.

So we filled our newspapers and broadcasts and blogs with triumphant stories of the mayor's success. We remained silent on the price that his council seemed to be paying for that success. Perhaps we intuited the truth: getting too close to the story might mean crawling too close to an edge.

A knife edge.

⚊⚊▬▬

Tabloid reporter Stan Bollixer broke the story. Nobody should have been surprised, yet we all were. For few outside the jungles of El Salvador knew it at the time . . . but Stan also was an expert with a knife.

The carbon-steel butterfly knife Stan keeps in the pocket of his jeans has been with him nearly as long as the mayor has possessed his bowie knife. But Stan was a grown man when he first wielded his blade; when we asked him later why he kept it so close, he would say only that it had saved his life enough times that he owed it a good home.

No doubt: Stan was an old hand, with sound instincts. He'd come to City Hall during the election and had watched our mayor from the start of the campaign. In the newsroom, he'd predicted that the mayor would prevail, even when the polls placed him a distant fourth. Stan recognized something in the man's eye, in the way he handled metaphor in his speech . . . in the way he moved.

He recognized a predator, and he recognized prey.

So Stan went to work on the mayor, the way a reporter does. He started asking around with his police contacts and located an arrest report from twenty years earlier, when the candidate, then just a lad, was caught knocking over tombstones in the nearby town of Reamington. The story made the front page and sent the future mayor's campaign into a flurry of damage control that proved unnecessary: for who among us has not, in the naïveté of youth, mocked death with a well-placed boot and a war cry?

Stan pressed on. The mayor was but a lowly school trustee prior to his ascendency. Stan dug up the mayor's voting record and discovered he had voted to ban several well-regarded texts from public school libraries, that he had voted for his own salary increase—not once, but three times. Stan discovered a formal complaint, alleging that the mayor had arrived inebriated and used salty language during a Parent-Teacher Association meeting to discuss the refurbishment of playground equipment.

None of it stuck. With each article, the mayor's public approval rose. The campaign stopped even responding to Stan's reportage, and the week before the election the campaign manager sent Stan a thank-you note on gilt-edged, embossed stationary that seemed very expensive, in gratitude for all his support. Stan wrote another story based on the note, questioning whether the mayor was operating within campaign spending guidelines, given the opulence of the gesture. Three days later, the mayor was elected.

Thus did Stan's permanent assignment to the press gallery at City Hall become an inevitability.

We liked Stan very much from the start. He was soft-spoken in scrums, but attentive. When he did ask a question, it would be the question that pierced the heart of the matter. When he filed his story, it would be the one that, if we were all to be honest, best described the nuance of the issue at hand.

When he watched something, before too long, he saw what it was about.

So it was that on the Tuesday after the announcement of the new light rail line to Smelt, he requested a personal, one-on-one interview with the mayor. No one thought he'd receive it. Our mayor, as everyone well knows by now, is not a friend of the media. He prefers to speak to constituents directly, over the public address system on the subway or via skywritten aphorisms—or in person, descending upon the backyard barbecues, garage sales, and weddings of leading citizens for impromptu moments of bonhomie. He does not grant many interviews.

But he made an exception for Stan. The interview was scheduled for 12:05 p.m. and expected to last fifteen minutes. The subject was to be a retrospective of the mayor's first hundred days in office. The Mayor's Office was suspicious, for they had a sense that Stan was up to something. So the mayor didn't face Stan alone; his second-floor office was crowded with his press secretary, his deputy mayor, and his cousin in the Transportation Department, who had taken a lunch break from road repair to see what Stan Bollixer truly wanted.

Stan was not dissuaded. He smiled, sat down across the desk from the mayor, and reached into his pocket, as if to produce a digital voice recorder.

There was no recorder.

"This can be off the record," he said, as he flipped open his butterfly knife, turned it so it gleamed in the noonday light, and with a sudden, savage plunge drove its point deep into the mahogany top of the mayor's desk.

***

Tuesday comes but two days before Thursday, and there was much to be done. The mayor's chief of staff and communications director tried to talk the mayor out of it, but he was determined. So they set about devising political strategies, anticipating the worst possible outcomes. The mayor's cousin attempted to arrange to have coffee with Stan to see if he might be dissuaded, but Stan refused even to take his calls. Stan meanwhile whispered, to those few of us he'd come to trust, about the thing that he had begun. He spent time in his office, honing his blade with a whetted stone and recalling, again and again, the night in San Salvador—August, hot as a sauna, smelling strangely of cinnamon—when the one-eyed man from the jungle had appeared at his room and tried to kill him.

One thing he did not do was inform his editor. Neither did any of us.

***

Our mayor is a man of chiselled granite. This is not apparent when he appears in public, bedecked in his checkered blazers and generously cut trousers, the novelty ties that light up with strategically placed LEDs. Were his constituents to see him shirtless, the goose fat sliding down his torso in thick rivulets, highlighting tendons and veins and ropey, hard-won scars, they would not recognize him—and, worse, they would no longer recognize themselves. They might recoil, as we did, seeing him step off the elevator in the parking garage reserved for city councillors and senior staff, watching him meet each of our eyes in turn with his hard and fearsome stare.

The mayor's cousin allowed three of us to accompany Stan—on the condition that we left all recording devices, including pens and notepads, in a small organic recycling bin left over from the previous administration. The mayor was accompanied by his cousin, and his deputy mayor, and his budget chief. The interim city clerk sat in the passenger seat of his Citroen, an ancient portable typewriter in his lap, a stack of carbon paper by his side.

The interim clerk squinted at Stan as he came out from the stairwell, and in his lap the typewriter keys began to clack out a description.

Stan Bollixer glistened. He was stripped naked to the waist, polished with a thin slick of goose fat, which stained the beltline of his old cut-off jeans. His eyes were wide, and seemed a little crazed, and the interim clerk noted for the record that Stan might be under the influence of a performance-enhancing stimulant. This was true, in a way: he had downed a room-temperature extra-large cup of Colombian coffee from the commissary just prior to coming downstairs. The butterfly knife rested, closed, in his left hand as he walked out past the Works Committee chairman's Harley Davidson, and faced the mayor.

The rules were read then—the mayor's cousin declaiming them in a slow drawl that was almost a song. When he finished, "To the victor go the spoils," the deputy mayor knelt beside his Subaru, lifted the mayor's knife, and put it in the mayor's extended hand. Stan made a whiplash motion with his wrist, and the blade of the butterfly knife—less than a quarter the length of the bowie knife—flashed silver in the pallid light of the garage.

We all withdrew to a more than respectful distance. For the knife fight between Stan Bollixer and the mayor was on—and no one wanted to be caught in the middle of it.

There are rules for the knife fight, and those are written down. But there are also customs. The mayor knows them instinctively, for many are his own, but most of his opponents do not. We suspect that inwardly the mayor is saddened by these vulgar bumpkins, who enter combat with thin-lipped, badly feigned rage and leap directly for the mayor's midsection to end things at once with a slash to the nipple or a stab at the collarbone. The mayor finishes these opponents quickly.

Stan Bollixer was not one of those.

Eyes never leaving the mayor's, Stan drew a long, slow circle in the air using the point of his knife; and again, marginally faster—and so on, until he was looking through a circular blur of steel and arm, spinning as fast as a propeller on a biplane. Did we hear the crick-crack of a shoulder dislocating, the creak of sinew bending? Could any of us mark the precise instant that the knife shifted from Stan's whirling left hand to his right? Did any of us truly see admiration, respect, and perhaps a soupçon of fear, cross the mayor's implacable brow?

No, not truly.

But we did hear the mayor emit a long, low growl—the only appropriate response to such a fundamental challenge . . . an alpha-male warning cry that came from the depths of our ancestry. The mayor bent down, pulled a dollop of goose fat from the fold beneath his arm, and dipped it into the dust of the garage floor. As he stood, he smeared the filthy grease in long black lines under his eyes, and over each brow, and then again at the edge of his jaw. Weapon clutched in his left hand, he raised both arms over his head like wings, the tip of his knife scoring the bottom of the blood-red EXIT sign. The effect was fearsome: no one would leave without going through him.

Stan flexed his arm and spun the butterfly knife, handle clicking open and closed, and bent his neck first to the left, then the right.

The mayor drew his breath over his teeth in a serpentine hiss.

The butterfly knife solidified in Stan's fist.

The mayor bellowed, and the knife swung in a crescent of steel that shimmered in the fluorescent afternoon. It might have slashed Stan's left pectoral in two, but his own blade met the mayor's as Stan ducked low and drove his opposite shoulder into the mayor's stomach. Stan let out a cry and drew his blade down in a slice that might, on another day, have relieved the mayor of a kidney. The mayor skipped aside instead, then retreated and swung his free arm contraclockwise to create a deadly momentum. The knife plunged, and Stan shifted, and the blade squealed across the windshield of the mayor's truck as Stan whirled in a failed attempt to slice a piece from the mayor's shoulder. It was too much—Stan's shifting and whirling—and the mayor caught Stan with his free arm, hard in the chest, and Stan doubled over. The butterfly knife would have been airborne had Stan not hooked his pinkie through the handle. The mayor might have had it then—he brought his own knife about, holding it an inch above Stan's shoulder. It hovered there as Stan wheezed, then withdrew. The mayor stepped back, knife at his side, fixing Stan with an expression that may have been a grin of triumph, or simply a mask of exhaustion. The parking garage fell silent but for the increasingly frenzied clacking of typewriter keys from the Citroen's front seat.

By degrees, Stan Bollixer stood. The mayor raised his knife, and pointed it at Stan like a deadly forefinger.

"Next week. Same time," he said. "Same place."

It is rumoured that one of us—a new reporter with something to prove—filed a news bit about the battle. But her piece never saw print, nor appeared on the internet. Before a week had run out she had been transferred to the radio room where, it was said, she spent her nights listening to the police scanner for word of fires, and crimes, and other nocturnal catastrophes.

The rest of us kept to the pact, and the mayor kept to a busy public schedule. Stan joined us in following him—how could he do otherwise? Following the mayor through the wards of his city was Stan's job as much as it was any of ours. When time came for the mayor to declaim, Stan Bolixer's microphone had its place: in front of the podium.

Stan was a professional. If his eyes ever met the mayor's through the scrum, and if he ever felt the mayor taking his measure . . . well, he didn't let it show. Nor did the mayor. At least not in those moments.

But we wondered: did the mayor's frenetic activity that week—shielding him in the midst of the children of the Smelt Community Centre, Pool's Summer Fun Day Camp, or the Cannery District Seniors Snooker Club—indicate that his nerve was slipping? Or perhaps he was using the business and ceremony of his office as a kind of extended display, a demonstration that he, and not this cocksure pretender, was the leader of this tribe?

But if he was so shaken, we wondered, why hadn't he simply ended the knife fight the previous Thursday—taken his slice from Stan Bollixer's greasy shoulder, and called victory?

On the following Thursday morning, several of us came in late to work. We'd been called from our beds by frantic city editors to join the night team in covering an atrocity unfolding in the food court at Old Town Abattoir Mall. It was a terrible crime, a tragedy, but so immense that in those early hours—days, really—no one could reliably determine what precisely had happened.

Early reports indicated a hail of gunfire, erupting from the rendering gallery, perhaps. But injuries did not bear this out, and the theory did not explain the smashed masonry at the base of the fountain, or the size of the holes in the ductwork. Although many had been knocked unconscious in the event, no one was treated for bullet wounds. Descriptions of the perpetrators were similarly vague and contradictory: giant men, possibly of African descent, faces covered in cheap fabric, heads shaven, teeth emerging like tusks from their jaws. . . .

The Abattoir Atrocity, as our editors dubbed it, was an impossible story to tell; it would not make sense of itself. Those of us called upon to help wrestle it into a narrative came in late, exhausted and dispirited. The only thing that kept us going was the resumption of the struggle between Stan Bollixer and the mayor.

Although we knew we could never tell it, that was a story that at least we could understand.

———

The knives flashed ribbons of steel through the air as the combatants danced across the concrete floor of the garage where it was not smeared with long slides of goose fat and back hair. A fluorescent tube sent a snowfall of shattered glass as the bowie knife cut through it; the director of Community Services spent the second part of the fight huddled behind a Subaru, applying pressure to an accidental slash across his arm from the fine-honed blade of the butterfly knife. Although it was warm in the parking garage, the city clerk rolled up the windows on his Citroen and kept low as he clacked away on the minutes of the second installment of the knife fight.

This one lasted longer than the first—the mayor's cousin called it at twenty-seven minutes, fifty-three seconds, standing over the mayor collapsed on his back, while Stan, similarly exhausted, propped himself against a cement pillar. The two may have been invulnerable that afternoon to mere steel—but middle age and the hot, dry, carbon-monoxide-rich air of the VIP parking garage were another matter.

"Why don't you call it a draw?" cried the director of Community Services, blood staining his fingers and necktie where he held it against his arm. "Haven't you proved enough?"

The mayor drew a wheezing breath and fixed narrow eyes on the bureaucrat, who looked away. The mayor turned back to Stan, who was coming out the other side of a long coughing fit.

"These are the end times," the mayor said, and sat still a moment, before gathering himself up and quitting the ring.

———

The words were prophetic. The following week's monthly city council meeting was attended by not only the mayor and all his councillors, but also the senior staff and their assistants, all of us, and delegations from wards across the city. This meeting had been scheduled to go long. Merchants from Abattoir Mall had come with a petition demanding greater police presence and the installation of video cameras. There was to be discussion of a cost overrun on the light rail line into Smelt, and a committee of residents were asking for additional stops to better service the rehabilitation hospital. The city's poet laureate had composed three new stanzas of an epic retelling of our amalgamation fifteen years ago, and there was to be a presentation no later than three p.m.

These things, combined with several dozen routine items, ought to have added up to a sometimes vigorous but relatively straightforward session, finishing no later than seven; meetings under the mayor were famous for running with brutal efficiency.

It was not to be.

The merchants were joined by a local civil liberties group shouting down the Abattoir Mall manager's deputation, requiring the services of the City Hall security squad and a recess to clear the chambers and restore calm. The debate continued for three solid hours after that, the matter becoming so confused with amendments that, on the clerk's advice, council finally deferred the item until the Christmas session.

Through all this, the denizens of Smelt hovered at the back, stoking their grievances one upon the other until their matter came up, and as a group they demanded that the light rail line be ripped out altogether and the remaining funds be reallocated to the restoration of the Smelt Arms Bijou—a cinema that had been derelict since the war, but held many fond memories for the elder Smelters. Despite vigorous lobbying by the mayor's staff, council sided with the deputants, and narrowly voted to kill the rail plan.

The poet laureate, meantime, had grown bored early in the meeting and, as poet laureates do, comforted himself with the contents of his hip flask throughout the afternoon. When his time came, he'd drunk himself into sufficient belligerence to substitute an obscene limerick in place of his more sublime stanzas. While some of us might have commented that the limerick was an improvement overall, the mayor obviously did not agree.

"This city is swirling into the toilet," he was heard to mutter, unaware, momentarily, that his microphone was still on.

The third time nearly finished it.

Mayor and reporter went at one another savagely from the outset, crashing together, each wrestling the other's knife-arm with his free hand. The mayor smashed his forehead into Stan's, twice, and Stan at a point managed to loop his arm between the mayor's legs and so hoist him above his head, slamming the city's chief magistrate hard onto the hood of a midsized sedan. Had this been a wrestling match and not a knife fight, Stan would have won it.

The savagery grew. The parking garage onlookers gasped as one when the mayor missed slashing Stan's throat by scant inches—and again seconds later, as the tip of Stan's blade hovered an instant over the mayor's right eyeball.

In the third round, it seemed, the knife fight had transformed into a killing fight.

Yet, for the third time, not a drop of blood was shed.

On Friday morning, the Doucette Greeting Card Company held a press conference at which their president, Wallace Doucette, announced that they would be ceasing production by November; by year's end, they planned to have moved all remaining operations south of the border, where a more favourable tax regime combined with a more eager labour market in a city more attractive to executives and their families would ensure the company's survival. The workers received their layoff notices at the beginning of the morning shift.

The mayor spoke to reporters afterward, attempting to downplay the impact of Doucette's departure and deflect the suggestion that our city was no place an executive would want to raise a family. But he could carry it only so far; the Doucette family was the third-largest employer in the city, and as a boy the mayor had played Lacrosse with Wallace. The betrayal was both civic and personal.

On the weekend, it rained. The rains started early Saturday, coming down in thick, grey sheets reminiscent of flying knives, and did not relent until early Sunday. Creeks overflowed; storm sewers clogged; and unlucky householders found their basements filling with sludge as the sewer system overflowed. Three footbridges washed away in parks, and a great sinkhole opened at an intersection to the east of the downtown, all but devouring one of the city's two dozen new ecofriendly buses.

The mayor did not immediately respond to calls from our weekend reporters.

How could he? He had other things with which to occupy himself.

He had to become better.

On Monday evening, Stan joined us for drinks after deadline. The storm had given way to awful humidity, and so we gathered in the pier district in the back room of a Czech pub well known to reporters.

As he had been since the fights began, Stan was quiet. Fortunately, drawing information from a quiet man is a hallmark of our profession. So we speculated—making note of the fact that the mayor's fortunes seem to have turned over the course of the long, stalemated battle between himself and Stan. We supposed that the stalemate may simply have sapped the mayor's confidence, although that, as we thought about it, didn't explain the rainstorm, or the drunken limericks, or the perversity of the men and women of Smelt on matters of public transit.

Stan smiled at that, and shook his head, and concentrated on the shape the foam took atop his ale.

And so we wondered: how was it that there wasn't any blood in the fights? How was it that Stan Bollixer and the mayor, both experts with the blade, could not land so much as a nick as they battled so energetically? The blades had cut cars, light fixtures, even a senior bureaucrat; what unknown agent so thickened the hides of the mayor and of Stan Bollixer?

Would this battle of titans ever end? To the victor went the spoils, said the rules. What if there was no victor?

And Stan shrugged, and smiled, and downed his beer in a single, long swallow. "Good question," he said.

We persisted. What if there was no victor?

"What if it stopped, you mean?" said Stan. He slid his glass across the bar and signalled for the cheque. "What if the long fight that has shaped the mayor—shaped the city—just came to an end?"

Yes, we said—what if no one took the spoils?

"Well," he said, grinning a little, "I guess this city wouldn't go to anyone. I guess it would be on its own. I guess it might be *free*."

The budget committee began deliberations three weeks later. This time it did not go smoothly. The city's treasurer had underestimated revenues, putting the city tens of millions of dollars in the red for the coming year. Flooding from the rainstorms had created an emergency liability that the city would have to cover through tax revenues, and the collapse of the greeting card sector meant a precipitous drop in assessments. While no one spoke the words aloud, several of us found well-placed sources who hinted that the city could be on the verge of bankruptcy by Christmas.

Meanwhile, council members and senior bureaucrats quietly found other places to park their vehicles than the VIP parking lot—at least on Thursdays. For who, really, wants to leave their cars unattended on a battlefield?

Guided by the same principle, the audience grew smaller each Thursday—some nursing wounds from errant slashings; others sensibly retreating to their offices, or their homes, while the mayor fought his nemesis to a standstill, week after week after week.

Some of us stopped attending as well. Partly it was self-preservation, but also something more fundamental: work.

Termites rose up from the earth in the fashionable Palm District, devouring the stout oak-trimmed homes of our leading citizens. The garbage workers went on strike just before Halloween, and the bus drivers joined them in solidarity a week later. Three more atrocities followed the Abattoir Atrocity in quick succession, each incident delivering more mayhem and making less sense than the last, causing our editors to deem this The Year of the Atrocity.

On the Thursday before Christmas, none of us attended. How could we? The city was bankrupt, its homes crumbling to sawdust, the busways silent but for swirling snow, and garbage piled up in mountains outside the shooting range by the river. . . .

We had our hands full.

And then it was Christmas.

City Hall was not entirely empty, but near to it. Only a few of us came in to check on the place. Janitors and security guards patrolled the halls, and a handful of councillors wandered the political wing. But there were not many of those; most huddled in their homes, dreading the new year when, almost assuredly, the city would not be able to make its payroll.

Calls to the Mayor's Office went unanswered. Stan Bollixer's office was dark, the door locked. In the quiet of the Yule, we began to wonder: had there been a final battle? Had the mayor prevailed? Had Stan?

Had one or the other died? Had they slain one another?

"We ought to go see."

"What—you mean . . . ?"

"The garage. We ought to see."

"It's locked up."

"We ought to go see."

The conversation went in circles like that, and might have gone on forever had not the budget chief happened by. Unlike the mayor, she was a great friend of the media and sought us out as often as she could. After handing out her annual stash of candy canes, she asked us if we would join her on a tour of the VIP parking garage. Her pass card, so far as she knew, still worked.

———

The garage was empty but for an old convertible covered in a canvas cloth, rumoured to belong to the Works Committee chair. The floor had been swept; there was not so much as a smudge of goose fat on the ground, or along the walls. It was as though the knife fight had never happened here.

We asked the budget chief if she had seen the mayor recently. She said that she had not, but that wasn't unusual. "He seems preoccupied," said the budget chief, "and who can blame him?"

"What do you mean?"

The budget chief shrugged as we walked the wide circle of the garage. "It's tough times. You guys were all calling him on it; he couldn't miss it. And that's got to weigh heavy on him. I mean, a mayor's supposed to keep a handle on things. He let go."

And to no one, we realized, went the spoils. We stood near to one another in the cold, empty parking garage, considering the implications of that. How had Stan Bollixer put it?

We would be on our own.

We would be *free.*

One of us wondered aloud if the budget chief thought the mayor's time might have come; if she might have thought that she, the budget chief, could do a better job of it.

But the budget chief didn't answer. She stopped, looking down at the base of one of the pillars—where a glint of steel emerged, below a hilt bound in old leather. The blade had been driven into the concrete, tiny cracks like capillaries branching off from it.

"Look at that," she said, and wrapped her fingers around the hilt.

BASEMENTS

Mr. Nu was in the basement of his small workman's house on Larchmount when our firm's team came for him, and at first they thought he was barricaded down there—possibly sitting on a cache of weapons, or explosives, or biological agents. Possibly, on something worse.

They had swept the two above-ground floors and found nothing there, almost literally.

This by itself put the team on guard—even without the incriminating weight of our firm's considerable file on him, the paucity of personal effects in Mr. Nu's dwelling was suggestive of a life led to a particular end, of a particularly quiet march . . . to a *particular* end.

The basement was only accessible by one staircase, off the kitchen. Marisse, the team leader, was confident that he would not flee. But that was not a comfort, either. If Mr. Nu were of a desperate frame of mind—if he were under instructions to avoid capture at all cost, let us say—being cornered in the basement with no exit but one might lead to acts similarly desperate.

These were thoughts upon which Marisse did not wish to dwell.

Later, before an ad-hoc panel of her superiors in the Peel Room at the Marriott, she would face the question: why did you not send a team to the basement immediately? Why did you search the remainder of the house when the infrared imaging indicated with some certainty that Mr. Nu was not in the kitchen or the bedroom or the upstairs bath?

Marisse had no satisfactory answer to these questions. She grew quiet, almost sullen. On the hotel notepad, she doodled images of cubes, stacked upon one another in such a way as to make it impossible to tell whether the boxes were stacked as the stepped wall of a giant pyramid, or a precarious overhang of packing crates. Benoit demanded that she respond as a professional, and she mumbled something softly, then leaned toward the microphone in the middle of the table, reached across and turned it away from her, and to Benoit. "You respond," she said, and Benoit became angry enough that I had to intervene.

"Marisse completed the mission," I said, sliding the note pad from Marisse and underneath my laptop. "Don't forget that, Bennie."

I caught her eye a moment, attempting to draw out some connection and put her at ease; we had known each other for many years at that point, and sometimes confided in one another on matters personal and professional. But not tonight.

Tonight, nothing.

The apprehension, when it came, occurred without serious incident. This much, we confirmed during the meetings at the Marriott. Marisse, her team, did complete the mission. No one was injured, not agent, nor civilian, nor the target: Mr. Nu.

Mr. Nu arrived at Sandhurst Circle with just the clothing he wore: a dark brown T-shirt, a pair of greenish cotton briefs and low white socks made from a material designed to transmit perspiration during exercise.

He had been there only a month when I attended the Marriott; a month and a day, when I made my way up the highway to Sandhurst itself. To see Mr. Nu's new home.

Twenty-three square kilometres, and Sandhurst in the middle of it—specifically, at the municipal address of 12 Sandhurst Circle.

There: Seven hundred and fifty square metres on main floor and second. Granite countertop in the kitchen, matching those in the three baths, except the master bedroom's en suite, which was a deep pink marble. Dark hardwood floors throughout, matching the bevelled trim around doors and other openings. It was, as the brochure stated, ducal.

The yard, now—that was incomplete. A swimming pool, defined by stakes and string in tamped-down topsoil, waiting for the builder to come and finish the job with landscaping and excavation.

The basement, although large, was not considered in the real estate listing for this or any other home when the subdivision was, briefly, on the market. Before the developer went bankrupt, and his assets were spread among an ad-hoc group of companies and funds that together formed something more useful.

Before we moved in.

"That's where we keep the cells," said Stephan as he sipped the espresso he'd made in the identical granite-countered kitchen in 42 Cathedral Crescent. There we sat, waiting for the driver to take me to Sandhurst. Stephan took the time to bring me up to date. I ran my finger along the lip of the counter-top.

"There are seven altogether." Stephan set down the tiny cup with a click, then counted fingers as he continued: "Seven cells. An interrogation room. Laundry room. Three-piece bath." Stephan allowed himself a smile. "Italian tile. Etruscan fixtures."

Mr. Nu's basement on Larchmount, now: no comparison. That one is small, barely six feet of clearance, the floor made of uneven concrete sloping too steep to a drain in the middle. Light comes from bare bulbs, two of them, one at either end of the long space. Under one bulb, the canvas lawn chair, where the team found Mr. Nu, one pale thigh crossed over the other, hands folded over brown-shirted belly as Marisse and team finally—finally!— crept down the stairs, their laser sights tracing jittering nonsense script across his wide chest.

"Some of us were thinking slate." Stephan's smile faltered and his eyes strayed to the French doors, beyond which subterranean sprinkler systems flicked water across the newly laid sod of #42. "But really. For a three-piece it was overkill. And the tile we chose—two kinds; big octagonal pieces, the colour of cream, and the palest blue in square . . . you know, to fill the spaces."

I didn't interrupt him as he continued, outlining the pattern on the countertop with his fingertip. I had not known Stephan for as long as Marisse; he was relatively new to the firm. I had, indeed, only met Stephan once before, at a conference in Las Vegas wherein he and I shared a panel discussing covert logistics opportunities. I think we had impressed one another but that was as far as it went. I was even more at a loss here than I was with Marisse. So I waited for Stephan to exhaust his renovation stories, refill his espresso cup, and fall silent, staring into the foaming murk, before saying it, as gently as I could:

"There is no driver, is there?"

He looked at me, naked apology in his eye. "I'm sorry, sir. You're on your own."

It should not have been a long walk, but it took more than an hour to cross the distance between Cathedral and Sandhurst. The subdivision was constructed at the crest of a gentle hill, foundations sunk in land that had until very recently anchored nothing more than rows of corn. It was the highest farm in the area, between a low marsh to the north of it, and the city and the river it sat on to the south. Standing amid those cornstalks, how intoxicating it must have been to turn and turn, and everywhere see the world beneath you.

The walk was quiet. Most of the houses we kept in the compound were vacant, but not perpetually. When we acquired the real estate, we determined that maintaining a population equivalent to one-tenth of the subdivision's population capacity was adequate both to cover, and to staffing needs. And so our sub-contracted staff moved about—from one structure to another, clearing driveways and cutting grass, paying taxes. Keeping up appearances.

It was a hollow facade, and could not be anything else, given the limitations of our contractors . . . hard men . . . hard women. . . .

Comparing it to Larchmount, now: a straight street, and short, with tight-packed houses many of which do not have driveways—all of which have front porches. So cars jam the curb, even at eleven in the morning. From dawn, elderly men sit on porches, in their plaid shirts and baseball hats, having seen it all, still watching; pleased young mothers with baby carriages make their way down to the coffee shop at the bottom of the street. On such a street, in such a house as his, Mr. Nu might hide forever, ensconced in his basement beneath his lightbulb, wearing his brown T-shirt and greenish shorts, his socks . . .

. . . of a fabric, to carry perspiration, from flesh.

The subdivision surrounding 12 Sandhurst was intended for wealthy families with good credit. So even the smallest home is over-large, more dramatic than practical, and the houses grow as they reach the centre. Number 12 Sandhurst, near that centre, is of course one of the very largest. Sheathed in limestone or something very like it, the building presses against the lot's edge. It has a square tower at one end that resembles somewhat a steeple, a clock tower. Although no higher than its neighbours, the elevation of the ground on which it was built grants it a subtle dominance. It might be approached from two directions—but from either, doing so is an ascent.

It must have been a warm day, because I was perspiring heavily. Itching, too; Sandhurst Circle was the last portion of the subdivision scheduled to be finished, and the collapsing banking industry—the sudden extinction of wealthy families with good credit—did not wait for the developer to complete the landscaping.

So the hot breeze blew clay dust up in miniature sandstorms, eddies that swept across the front walk and driveway, frosted the tall, dark windows grey. The dust coated my throat and stung at my eyes. I approached the front door. It ought to have opened—12 Sandhurst is equipped with well-hidden cameras and security with access to face- and gait-recognition software, and I was in the database. But it was left to me to shift the door-knocker aside and enter the access key. The double oak doors swung inward, and I stepped inside, into the front hall.

The room climbed two tall storeys, with the sweep of a staircase following a curved wall upstairs. The only light came from the tall windows behind me, zebra-ing the dark-trimmed doorways and gleaming dark floor. Somewhere within, the pulsating whine of a vacuum cleaner. It seemed to be moving from surface to surface; first the muffled draw of thick-pile carpet, then a click and the rattle of crossing hardwood.

How near was it? I couldn't tell at first. While I had some idea of the lay of 12 Sandhurst, I had not studied floor plans in great detail. Whatever the trouble with Stephan and the driver, I was expecting that I would arrive here and be greeted by the duty officer, then ushered through the appropriate hallways and staircases. Not standing alone, attempting to triangulate the location of a housekeeper, while work waited to be done.

There were five exits from this space, counting the stairs and the door that I had come in: two on either side of me, and another in an archway beneath the stairs itself. Pale, dust-coloured light hinted from all of them. As the vacuum cleaner shifted from pile to board, some of that light flickered—as though the cleaner passed before a window—then seemed to pulse brighter—as if perhaps that cleaner, or another, drew back a curtain. The bannister from the staircase cast a sharp shadow at one point, the wall behind it glowing a dusky orange. The light of the setting sun? Perhaps. The shadow moved as I watched, growing and climbing to touch the ceiling before fading again. It was as though time were accelerating, and I was left behind, here in this dark vestibule, watching it Doppler ahead.

I blinked, and my eyes stung ferociously, so I blinked again.

In front of me stood a tall man, hair close-cropped in the Marine style. He wore an olive-green T-shirt that showcased a powerful physique—black trousers that tucked into high military boots. His fists were clenched at his side. Jaw clenched too, with tendons swelling and subsiding up and down his neck. His eyes were wide. Brimming with tears.

And again, I blinked.

Behind him, on the staircase, was an upright vacuum cleaner, a dozen steps up, unattended, abandoned—the power cord descending taut from the dark of the second floor, like a single, black marionette string. At the very end of its reach.

Once more: the blink. With a grandiose leisure now, as though the passage of time had slowed . . . was readying itself to stop here, in the infinite silence of the instant between heartbeats.

I couldn't let it. I didn't let it. I took a shuddering breath—and shouted, and so did he, and then we both screamed, yowled like animals, into the dark chambers of 12 Sandhurst Circle.

And it was only then I turned from him—and fled out the front door, into the deepening night.

<hr>

His name was Scott Neeson, and the haircut did not lie. He was a former U.S. Marine Sergeant, recruited after three tours in Iraq. He was living just now at 84 Twilling Row, and there he would stay until he could finish building a vast wooden deck with an installed hot tub and a covered grill-house.

He came over with a twelve-pack of beer and a pair of sirloins, the day after I settled in to 37 Ridgeway. So named because the houses scattered along the northern edge, their yards edging on a drop that looked down on woodlots and farmlands in the old marsh. A ridge-way. In moving in to #37, I had inherited an immense barbecue grill, five burners on the grill itself, with a small gas range attached. The cover was fire-engine red, with a round brass thermometer dial in the middle that looked like a device from a Jules Verne novel. Neeson, sporting a pale blue Hawaiian shirt and long brown cargo shorts, came around the back of the house in the late afternoon, set down the clinking case of beer and fired the beast up.

"You're joining us," he said, bending to pull bottles from the case. He handed me one.

"Something like that." I twisted the bottleneck and set the cap down on the deck-railing.

"Good. We can use good people here. And it's a nice place."

"Is it?"

"It is. Nice big houses, and the money's good when you don't have to pay for them. Nobody bothers you." Neeson turned to the grill, examined the dial. "Pretty light lifting, is what. You come from the Service?"

"You think I'm a Marine?"

"I thought you were a Marine, I'd have said the corps. But service isn't the word I was looking for, either." He snapped his fingers as he spoke.

"You're thinking about Company?"

He nodded. I shook my head.

"Does that even mean anything?" he asked. "You saying no?"

I smiled. "I told you, I'd have to kill you." And although that is what I always said, and that is what most of us always said when we could not think of a proper joke, Neeson laughed as though he'd just heard it.

"But you're from up the chain," he said, turning serious, "aren't you?"

"I am."

"You came here to check out what was happening with . . ."

"Nu."

"With him." Neeson lifted the grill and peered into the dark, hot space. "We met in Sandhurst, you and I."

"We did."

He let the grill cover down.

"And now, you're moving in."

I took a long pull of my beer. It was a dark-coloured ale from a local brewery. I thought I might remember the brand, for later.

"Word gets around," I said. "I'm moving in."

"That's some inquisition you must be planning. How long do you think?"

I sipped my beer. Stephan had told me I could have Ridgeway as long as I needed it, so long as I kept up the lawn and did the same for four other houses, two to either side of mine. By the book, I would rotate out of it after a month. But that could be extended, he explained, if I were engaged in some special project, one that only I could properly finish—like Neeson's deck.

Neeson leaned back against the railing, crossed his arms. "So you have any questions? Figured I'd come here, save you another trip out."

"In."

"Yeah. It is 'in' from here, isn't it?"

We looked at each other for a moment. In the sunlight, Neeson's face took on a harder quality than it had in the shadowy foyer of Sandhurst. No tears, that was one thing. But the late afternoon tempered him in other ways. Lines at the corners of his eyes, a droop in the corner of his mouth, flesh beneath his eyes folded like lava-flow. It made him a hard statue that the years had eroded as much as they ever would. He was a man who knew about car batteries and pliers.

"What have you learned?" I asked.

Neeson opened the top again, and the heat hit us like a wind. He nodded, lifted the sirloins from their wrapping, and draped them over the grill. There was a ferocious sizzling and a great cloud of smoke came up.

"Better get a spray-bottle," said Neeson. "There'll be flare-ups, and we don't want to turn this fine meat to shoe-leather."

I found a tall plastic spray bottle beside the sink, filled it with tap water, and hurried back. Sure enough, he was right—fat from the steaks had dripped down to the steel plates that stood in for the rocks you'd find in older models, and it was burning furiously. We sprayed and sprayed, but the flames never quite went out.

The subdivision is fairly remote from major shopping districts. The nearest is a forty-minute drive through farm country, past cornfields and finally across a great, near-empty parking lot, to the massive building supply store that had once been a continent-spanning chain.

The road is never very busy, but it is a particularly pleasant drive on a Sunday, in the dark green minivan from Ridgeway's garage. It is a drive that I have done more than once—gathering paint and lumber and what exotic power tools as are not already in the well-equipped workshop in Ridgeway's basement.

Some days, I recognized my neighbours in the aisles: Scott Neeson on more than one occasion, hauling sheets of plywood as big as flags and bags of concrete on orange-painted dollies; Stephan and Lynette, a slender south-Asian woman some years older than he, looking speculatively at kitchen cabinetry; Luis, a small and swarthy man with black hair to his shoulders, a thin and patchy beard and an unstoppably cheerful grin, who one Sunday afternoon admitted to me that he is flirting with the idea of building a sauna, but mostly shops for floor lamps and fine art prints. "There are so many *rooms*," he explained.

One day, I met Benoit there.

"It has been months," he said. We were loitering in the aisle for drop-ceilings, me in my Chinos and golf shirt, Benoit in a white starched shirt and tie, his navy blazer slung over his shoulder.

"I know. I'm sorry."

"Sorry." Benoit snorted. "I hear that you have taken a house there. You are doing—what?"

"It's a complex enterprise. I cannot complete it in a day."

"Months," he repeated and glared up at me. Benoit was a head shorter than me, and heavy in the gut. If he was higher on the chain than me, it was not by much—and although I don't think he was much lower, either, I have taken it as a matter of pride that he has never had the capacity to intimidate me. But when our gazes broke, it was I, not he, who looked away.

"I haven't reported much, I know," I said.

"You haven't reported at all. We received word of your arrival from the Superintendent. But from you? *Rien*."

Benoit led us to the end of the aisle as a couple pushing a big orange cart appeared at the other.

"What is your impression of Mr. Nu?" he asked. "From the meetings you have no doubt had by now?"

I didn't answer, and Benoit nodded.

"No meeting, hmm?"

We rounded the end of the tandem, and stepped into an aisle filled with exterior siding materials and window frames. Benoit smiled gently.

"You think that I will be shocked now, and angry—don't you?"

"You would have the right."

He shrugged. "I, the right. Do you know that there was a time that I actually feared you? Now—*you* tell *me* I have the right to be angry with you. I wonder: is it because I have become so much more impressive?"

"I'm not afraid of you," I said, and he nodded knowingly.

"Marisse," he said. "What was your impression of her, after our interview at the Marriott?"

"You have my report—"

"I do," he said. "Now tell me. Do you still think that she suffers from a 'simple dissociative disorder resulting from mission-related trauma'?"

"That's what I wrote?"

"It is." Benoit looked down. "Two weeks ago, she killed herself. Shot herself through the eye with a semi-automatic pistol. Her customary sidearm. You'll forgive me if I cannot summon the precise make—"

"A Glock," I said. "Lately. She also has a Desert Eagle."

"Not the Desert Eagle. Absurd. No. The Glock. Yes. She was the fourth member of the team that assailed Larchmount to attempt suicide, the second to succeed."

I put my hand on the shelving and leaned hard. It had been built for siding and window frames and, on the other side, ceiling tiles, and it didn't so much as quaver.

"Her family?"

"Grieving, I imagine. I have not had opportunity to inquire in detail. We are concerned now with the examination of other links in the chain."

We hurried from window frames and siding, and moved into gardening supplies. There, Benoit expounded on the fate of the transfer team, whose leader had simply vanished three weeks before; on the firm's government contact, a small former FBI woman named Lester, who had spent ten minutes with Mr. Nu, the two of them on either side of a glass barrier . . . suddenly and inexplicably replaced by an older man—because, the firm's intelligence indicated, she had gouged her eyes out and attempted to disembowel herself with an X-Acto knife during a debriefing.

And then . . . the matter of Sandhurst, and the changes that had wrought themselves there.

"You have noticed," said Benoit, "or perhaps you have not—that we have suspended prisoner intake at Sandhurst these past few months. We are making other arrangements."

I had not.

"You must have noticed," said Benoit, "that in spite of your obvious failure to resolve matters—we have not taken steps to replace, or indeed even supervise you."

That, I had.

"Don't worry. I am not doing so now. You can continue where you are—as long as you wish—to do what you wish. You will be compensated. You may leave. Or stay. You may also, of course, do the thing you went to do. But I will remind you, my friend . . ."

And we made it through gardening supplies, and stood by the tall glass doors that were wide enough to haul a house frame through, and Benoit extended his hand.

". . . Marisse shot herself in the eye."

And with that, he turned and stepped into the brilliant Sunday afternoon sunlight. And that was the last I ever saw or heard of Benoit.

One evening not long after, Scott Neeson stopped by Ridgeway. No beer this time. He came with a single bottle of red wine. It had no label and he bashfully admitted that was because he had made it himself, using a kit he'd obtained from the wine-making outlet next to the building supply store. He suspected that it might not be adequate. I suggested we try it and see.

We took it to the back deck and sat beside the barbecue, now hidden by a form-fitted cover I'd found in the garage. Scott drew a breath at the view of the woodlot, orange and red over a carpet of pale yellow and dark brown leaves that had fallen the past week, all set alight as the sun set over the rooftop of #37.

I poured wine into stemware, and sat beside him. He didn't speak for a long time, and I didn't prompt him. He finished his wine. I poured him another and topped up my own. As the light faded, so did the hard lines of his face, the slack flesh beneath his eyes. The shadow of 37 Ridgeway erased years. I watched them vanish, one by one, until finally he was ready.

"I used to know what to do," he said in a voice that trembled, looking me with eyes that were wide and wet. "I used to be sure."

I put my hand on his arm.

"Not now, though," he said. "Now, I have no fucking idea. Whether I'm coming or going."

We spent time deciding which of the houses to inhabit next. Scott Neeson had not put all the touches on Twilling Row's elaborate rear deck; the plumbing and electrics for the hot tub installation were barely roughed-in, and the covering for the grill area was up but needed shingling. We talked about remaining there; the winter would not treat the unstained decking kindly, and he'd done so much work already, it seemed a shame to abandon it now. But he insisted he didn't care anymore. He wanted to be away. So we tried a few nights at Ridgeway, and that worked well enough, at first. We slept curled together on the king-sized bed in the cavernous master bedroom; took turns cooking and clearing dishes in the bright kitchen; in the sitting room, we watched the classic western and noir and science fiction films that were shelved under the entertainment console.

But that didn't last either. I woke up on more than one occasion suddenly shivering, alone in the bed, to find Scott, standing by the open bedroom window, naked, arms wrapped tight around himself as he looked north, up the gentle slope to Sandhurst, and wept. Or once, finally, in the bathroom, looking blankly at the open medicine cabinet—filled with razors and sleep-aid medications—hands on either side of the sink, muscles in his forearms tensing, as though he were readying himself to leap into it. That night, I went to him, put my arms on his shoulders, and gently, I hope, drew him back to the bed—thinking all the while of Marisse, and the bullet that Benoit said she had put through her eye.

And so in the end, with Stephan's help, we found a new house: a genuinely new one this time, near the southern part of the subdivision—60 Wyatt End. So new the drywall in the family room was still unpainted. The basement bath was only roughed in. The tiling for the floor in the laundry was stacked neatly in boxes, waiting for a tradesman whose arrival was forever delayed by bankruptcy.

No one had lived there since the firm moved in. It was a blank slate.

At Christmas, we had a party there. I invited Stephan and Lynette and some others I'd met over the months; and Scott invited some of the others who worked with him—the Sandhurst Crew, they called themselves. They all brought bottles, and threw them in with Scott's batch of home-brewed wine, and we carried on through the night.

I had too much to drink, I have to admit. Stephan and Scott had to help me up to bed. Early Christmas Day awakened by stale wine in my gut and off-key carolling a floor below, I found myself standing naked by the window, looking through thin snowfall to the few dim lights in the city many kilometres to the south.

Thinking of Larchmount.

Children. That's what was missing.

Larchmount was the kind of street that was lousy with them: infants and toddlers and teenagers, sullen and giddy and beautiful and awkward; fat moms and dads, going to work and coming home again, where they chased diaper-clad little fatties from room to room, catching sleep in precious moments until they did it again. If Mr. Nu sat next door, in a chair beneath a lightbulb in a house nearly empty . . .

Well, the people of Larchmount had other things to bother about.

There were no children on Wyatt, or Cathedral, or Twilling, or any of the others here. Nothing came from Stephan's friendship with Lynette—nor, obviously, Scott's and mine—nor any of the other half-dozen couples who'd coalesced around Sandhurst over the days . . . the months . . .

The years.

Even without children, we got fat.

It happens. All you have to do is sit still for long enough. And that is what we did. Trips to the building supply store grew less frequent—a combination of its diminishing stocks, and our own waning interest, the growing complacency of our house-pride. Power wasn't reliable enough to keep watching DVDs, but we enjoyed reading. Anything to sit still.

It's not always a bad thing, fat. The roundness of it smoothed Scott's skin, took the worry from his eyes, the knowledge from his mouth. Combined with his less-and-less-frequent visits to Sandhurst, it allowed a measure of innocence to return, or perhaps just emerge. He smiled so easily, and I envied him. I was the ugly fat man, a furtive grey toad that couldn't even meet its own eye in the bathroom mirror.

But I don't blame the fat.

We kept having parties. Smaller parties, but more of them.

Smaller, because of the subdivision's shrinking complement. Early on, it was simple departures. The medical station in 4 Battleford Avenue lost a surgeon; Linguistics in 52 Burling Street lost their Russian and Farsi specialist—a serious blow, that one; and at least two cleaners. . . .

The flow was finally stemmed when Stephan announced that the firm had established a covert perimeter around the subdivision. He went in to no further detail about what that perimeter entailed, but enough understood the implied threat to need no further encouragement to stay put.

Yet still, we diminished. There were some suicides, three of them among Scott's former teammates at Sandhurst. Some didn't die, but locked themselves in their houses and refused to communicate or co-operate when Stephan sent in rescue and medical teams. They remained in flesh, but truly, were no longer present in the subdivision.

Smaller parties. But far more frequent.

Never properly sodded, our yard was soon taken over by tall wildflowers and thistles, vines that could tear flesh. So we limited our celebrations to the concrete-tiled back deck, where perhaps a dozen of us would sit on resin chairs, heads tilted back to look up at the froth of stars that gathered into prominence over the ever-diminishing glow from the city, a hundred more stars each year than the last. We would drink Scott's wine and talk and stare at outer space.

Enough wine in me, I would bring myself to wonder—would tilt my head from the Heavens down, to the top of the subdivision's hill, and Sandhurst.

One night, helping Scott up to our bed, I posed a question:

"Who is looking out for Mr. Nu now? Is he even still alive?"

"Nu." Scott lowered himself to his bed, and let out a long, laboured sigh. We were both drunk—drunk, fat old men. "You asked me a question, a long time ago."

"Okay."

"When we first met. When we second met."

"When we second met. In my yard. With that beer."

"And steaks. What did I learn, you asked me."

"And what did you learn?"

He looked at me in the dim candlelight of our bedroom, my happy old fat man.

"When you go into a dude's house—make sure you're invited," he said. "Make sure dude knows you're coming, and is cool with it, and has taken the steps. Steps not to show himself. And if he's in the basement—" and in his slurry, drunk, *innocent* voice, Scott whispered:

"Leave him be."

—————

What did you learn?

The question doesn't come easily. I don't think it can come easily.

When I can't sleep, I take out Marisse's notepad, and look at that doodle she did in the meeting room in the Marriott, in her last debrief—a stack of cubes, either made sturdy like a pyramid, or impossible, precarious, boxes stacked on ceilings. Ball-point perspective makes both true. Both a lie.

And both a lousy answer to the question: why would you search every room but the one you knew that Mr. Nu was in? Lousy answers, but as it happened, the only answer forthcoming.

＊

Not everybody puts a bullet through their eye, but everybody dies.

Stephan's Lynette, for instance. Dead. Cancer, started in her left breast. Undiagnosed. Spread all over. And so. Dead.

Stephan took it hard. The two had been together for decades when it came, and as Stephan told me: "There's no one now, forever." He was right, and I gave him a long hug—although silently, I thought (perhaps unkindly) he ought to have prepared himself, she being so much older than he. But I didn't argue when he announced he wanted to turn the faux-Tudor mansion on Wellington Way into a mausoleum, for "the beloved departed"—Stephan's code for those who died not from suicide or escape attempts, but simply in the course of things. So we worked to seal off some rooms in the basement as crypts. And into the first of those, we bore Lynette— her boney cadaver wrapped in 600-thread sheets from an upstairs linen closet—and by the light of a dozen candles, listened to Stephan as he sang her praises, and wept, and said a prayer. Then Luis, who'd volunteered, stayed downstairs with trowel and cement and bricked in the crypt.

Stephan could have expected to bury Lynette. Burying Scott, now . . .

Yes. Scott Neeson. Heart attack. Too fat. Too drunk, maybe. So a massive coronary, while I snored beside him. And yes.

Dead.

I took it hard too. But who would have thought? I'm a fat old man. Fatter, older, and I never was a Marine, and I never was strong. Scott should have been burying me. But there he lay, eyes wide and wet and empty in the morning light. Soon to be the second resident of the crypts, the catacombs, beneath Wellington Way.

＊

I could leave. I could stay. I could do the thing that I came to do.

I put on my parka, a pair of boots. I fished around in back of the china cabinet until I found the latch, and opened it, and from there pulled out the little Russian automatic pistol that Scott favoured, and a clip of ammunition. The kitchen, where I found an LED wind-up flashlight. Then I went upstairs one more time, to look at Scott, make sure I wasn't tricking myself with ball-point perspective, then as fast as I could to the front door, and into the street.

It was tough going. A week ago there'd been a heavy snowfall, and then it had been cold since, so the road was rutted and icy. And uphill, around and around, in a gentle and exhausting slope. It took me until the noon-hour to reach Sandhurst Circle.

I nearly turned back. The whole street was choked with high drifts of snow, rising in places to the tops of first-storey windows. There was, simply, no path to or from #12. I couldn't see how I could make it to the front doors, which were buried in snow up to the handles. But I thought: I could do the thing that I came to do. And: there's no one now. Forever.

I pushed through the snow, nearly fell as I climbed over and through the drift to the door. Pulled aside the knocker, and spent some time recalling the access code before entering it. The doors swung inward, and the snow fell inside along with me.

There: the same vestibule. Dark, but for what light filtered in through snow-covered windows.

No one was vacuuming. The house was icy cold. But there was the sound of running water. A burst pipe? That's what I thought too.

I might have stood there again, for hours, guessing at where the sound came from, losing myself in the rhythm of this place. I might have just fled. But finally, I was done with guessing, done with fleeing, just so far. My thumb found the switch on the flashlight, and soon the three blue LEDs cast a circle on the floor ahead of me. I thought only a minute about looking upstairs first—and thought about Marisse—and thought: No. And so I stepped through an archway, wallpaper peeling from it in wide strips. From there, I passed through a high living room, floorboards creaking underfoot. At one time, this room had been used for conferences; there was a long table in here, and at one end a projector with a bay for a laptop computer. Chairs everywhere.

"Mr. Nu," I shouted. "What are you up to?"

The water—perhaps just a tap left on in one of the bathrooms? No. I passed into a wide, short hallway, made to look grander with art-deco wall sconces that would send light to the ceiling and back. Through the archway beyond, one might expect a kitchen, but over the decades I had become savvy to the architecture of the subdivision, and didn't get my hopes up.

"You have associates," I said, "isn't that so? Tell me who they are, and we'll give you back your clothes."

I was right. The next room had a sunken floor, high shelves on every wall but one, and where the floor dropped, a big metal fireplace, open at every side. That fourth wall: tall windows of leaded glass. Mostly snow-covered now, so what light came in was a creamy grey. Some of the shelves had books on them.

"No one's coming for you," I said, in a threatening tone. "I'm your only hope. Now tell me: What are you up to, Mr. Nu?"

Not a tap, not a broken main. The water sounded nearer now, and more . . . elemental. It made me think of times long ago, sitting on rocks on a hot summer day, by rapids, mist making my breath cool.

"Our operative—never mind what her name was, you don't need to know that—she shot herself in the eye. Dead. Why did you make her do that?"

Next to this room was the kitchen. A fine kitchen, but not the finest in the subdivision. Wellington Way's was nicer, for one. But still. The countertops gleamed. The appliances—huge; the cabinetry, fine dark cherry wood, stretching high and for miles. I reached into my parka's pocket, and pulled out Scott's gun. I stood there I don't know how long. Then I lifted it high, flipped the safety off and shot the refrigerator.

"You think I put that bullet in my eye? You are wrong, Mr. Nu. That was your friend. He wouldn't talk to us. Now he's dead too."

Beside the refrigerator—a doorway. Not as grand as the others, but why should it be? It only led down to the basement. Basement doors should not be grand. I put Scott's gun down a moment on the butcher block, gave the flashlight another cranking and picked it up again, and opened the door.

"Why do I want to go upstairs right now, Mr. Nu, not down? Is it you?" I asked, as I shone the light down the long flight of metal stairs. The light caught rust like moss growing on the edges where the paint had scraped away, a rime of frost that coated the bannister. The beam hung ahead of me in thick, icy mist. The sound of running water turned into a racket; it was close by now. It sounded like a river.

The stairway was long—so long it switched back on itself once and then bent out at ninety degrees for the last five steps. Slow going too; the mist and the frost made the metal treacherous for a young man. Fat old men carrying guns and flashlights had to take particular care.

I passed the time asking more questions. Some were questions I'd come to ask: more about Marisse and her team, and as it followed the things that might have happened to the transport team, and to the firm's government liaison. And more that had occurred to me in the months and years that followed: What of Scott? Of me? Of the world? What have you done, Mr. Nu, Mr. Nothing, Mr. Null—to cause us all to so badly recede? Is it you, now, you and your *associates*, that walk the world you persuaded us all to so easily abandon?

Why us? Why not Larchmount?

Questions along those lines.

I stood alone, finally, in the basement of 12 Sandhurst, playing the flashlight beam across the wet, icy stone—looking for some sign of the interrogation room; the three-piece bath, with the Italian tile that had so pleased Stephan. Were there any remains of the seven cells in this cavern? Would Mr. Nu somehow still be in one of them? Alive? After so long?

There was nothing that I could see. The place was all ice and rock, flickering in dim reflected light.

I took care as I moved along, but it was no good. I slipped, and pinwheeled, and landed hard on my behind. Nothing was broken, but in the fuss of it all, I let go of the light and the gun. I listened to them both, skittering down rocks as might lead to a fast-moving stream on a summer's afternoon. There was a splash, and then another.

A stream. Was that what had happened here? An underground stream, an aquifer, broken through the thin layer of concrete that the bankrupt builder had spread over the ground, and flooded the basement, over years perhaps corroded the foundations; swept away the neat, levelled chamber here, the seven cells and the interrogation room and the three-piece bath . . . leaving . . . only this cavern?

This cavern . . . where a man might sit, under a single lightbulb, on a canvas lawn chair, in a brown T-shirt, pale green underpants and socks of a material that drew moisture away from flesh. Looking with a hollow, knowing eye at another: this one an old man, fat, blind, freezing cold, looking for purchase on the slippery stone . . .

—

. . . finding some, finally, on a ledge of concrete, just inches above the icy, flowing earth-water. I might have stood; there seemed enough space. But I tucked my feet close under my knees instead, stayed low, because I knew if I stood up, I would turn, and try and scramble away, flailing in the dark until I found the base of the stairs. Then, I would haul myself up those stairs, fast as I could, and run. Flee.

I wrapped my arms around my knees, and looked, and checked against the data from his file, some of which (not all, not all) I had committed to memory. Might he have lost weight, over time? It didn't seem so. He was, if anything, a little chubby. His dark hair seemed long for the style he'd cut it in, but it was hard to say whether that was a result of inattentive incarceration. His clothing seemed fresh though. And he was clean-shaven.

He leaned forward in his chair—looking straight at me, frowning, as if deciding whether to say anything; whether after all these years, this time, he had any answers for me. Whether he'd thought of any questions, for that matter.

Then, both hands on his knees, he stood. His head came near the 200-watt bulb that dangled over his chair, and he shifted from the hot brilliance, of a kind that had not come to light the night at Sandhurst in decades.

And he looked down—down at me—and yanked his briefs from the crack in his behind, adjusted the waistband so it cradled his gut. Fattened on stillness.

Head still bent under the low beams of Larchmount, he eyed me once more.

No. No questions worth asking of one such as I.

And with that, Mr. Nu made his way to the narrow wooden stairway and climbed, to the kitchen at Larchmount. To the world, which he now inhabited; which he had, in his agreeable solitude there, spared. Which I had abandoned.

Mr. Nu reached the top. He stopped there an instant, as though considering one more time, then flipped a switch, and so. The bright yellow light vanished. Larchmount, forever gone.

In its place, nothing.

LOVES MEANS FOREVER

Suki Shannahan felt like she was the luckiest girl in a million light years.

The starship *Gwendolyn* had a staff of more than fifteen cryosurgeons, a payload of three thousand, two hundred and twenty-four crew and colonists, and a nursing staff of thirty-four. The first person she saw when she revived could have been *anyone*.

It could have been that hateful Chief of Nursing Staff, Helen Rockholme, who had broken Suki's heart back on Luna when she signed Suki on as a Candy Striper Second Class, even though Suki'd passed the exams at the top of her class and everybody *knew* she was more qualified for the rN-5 position than that horrible *pill* of a former best friend, Betty-Anne Tilley.

For that matter, it could have been Betty-Anne Tilley that Suki'd seen first—she'd studied all the procedural manuals until it seemed like her brain was ready to burst, and Suki knew that registered nurses often monitored the routine revivifications without any supervision at all. It was part of the job.

Betty-Anne Tilley at the console of my *cryo-unit*. The very thought was enough to make Suki's still-frosty cheeks flush hot with anger.

But as she lay back in the recovery room on the outside rim of Torus 3, Suki couldn't stay mad long. Because when her eyelids peeled open like the paper off a Popsicle, the first thing she saw wasn't the stern glare of Nursing Chief Rockholme, and it certainly wasn't the smug little face of Nurse—*Nurse!*—Betty-Anne Tilley.

It was Doctor Neil Webley. And after seventeen years of waiting in the residential arcology of Torus 2, seventeen long years spent in the dark spaces between Earth and this star that shone outside the viewport now like a glowing red beacon of their love, Doctor

Webley—Neil Webley, *her* Neil—was every bit as gorgeous as the day they'd first kissed.

When they'd first met on the shuttle up from Luna, Neil had only been five years older than Suki, and had just completed his residency on both legs of the Earth-Mars comet run. The old Russian-built ship that ran the loop between the two worlds had been constructed without a torus, so Neil had spent the entire year and a half in zero gravity. Which, he'd told her, was one of the reasons he'd signed on to the *Gwendolyn*. He'd been engaged to a girl in the Free Principality of Greater Seattle, but the eighteen months he'd spent in freefall had done such damage to the calcium in his bones that he'd never be able to return to a full-gravity environment.

"She broke off the engagement the moment I told her," Neil had explained as they sat together watching the *Gwendolyn* grow from just another star in the forward porthole to the two-mile long chain of rings and cylinders and star drives that was to become their new home. "Judith always hated space travel—I suppose I should have known."

"That's no excuse," Suki answered, without even thinking. "I know that I'd follow the man that I was going to marry to the bottom of the ocean if that's where he wanted to go. Love is supposed to mean forever, Neil."

There had been an uneasy silence then, and Suki was sure that she'd put her foot in it.

"I'm sorry," she finally said. "I didn't mean to suggest—"

But Neil had put her at ease with one of his patented grins, and patted her arm with his still-strong surgeon's hand. "What? That Judith didn't truly love me? There's no need to apologize for being perceptive, Suki."

Neil's hand lingered for a moment on the bare skin of her arm, and Suki felt gooseflesh rising. From across the lounge, she was sure she felt Betty-Anne's envious glare boring into the backs of their seats. At another time, she might have taken a little guilty pleasure in it—but Neil Webley consumed her attention like a flame.

"It's possible to marry for other things than love," Neil had continued. "On Earth it is, anyway. You can marry for status, for wealth . . . for trophies like lawyers or engineers. . . . Or, I suppose, for doctors." His grin turned wry, for just an instant. "In space, though—"

And then his impossibly blue eyes had met hers—their eyes had truly *met*—for the very first time.

"—in space, the trophies are different. And when we marry, true love may be the only thing we have that can keep us together."

And finally, as much to his amazement as hers—or so he later claimed—Doctor Neil Webley had leaned in closer, and the gooseflesh vanished in the tide of Suki's quickening pulse, and the two had kissed. It had been their first kiss—and in many ways, Suki later decided that it had been *her* first kiss. The first kiss that had mattered, in all her eighteen years.

True love, thought Suki as she lay alone in the immense recovery ward of Torus 3, waiting for the pins and needles in her arms and legs that were the last stage of revivification to subside. *It really is forever.*

<hr/>

"How's my Suki?"

Wonderful, she mouthed—it was still too soon for her to talk, even twelve hours after they'd pulled the tube from her throat. But Neil understood. He leaned over her bed and delicately brushed away a strand of hair that had fallen across her eyes.

This was only the second time she'd seen him since revivification. The first time she had been unable to even breathe unassisted, let alone speak. There had been his face, that strong, even jawline, that wide, sensuous mouth that always seemed about to smile. The only sign of the intervening seventeen years had been a slight thinning in his luxuriant mane of brown hair, and the appearance of thin laugh-lines around those wonderful blue eyes. And then the face was gone, and she had slipped back into sleep, while her beautiful doctor went back to work.

Now, in the recovery ward, she was able to give him a more appraising look. And Suki had to admit that she liked what she saw. In spite of his weakened bones, Doctor Neil Webley had kept himself in top form. It had been seventeen years, after all—*goodness, that meant he'd be nearly forty!* Suki realized. And if anything, his shoulders were broader, his stomach flatter, his demeanour more assured than the young man that Suki had left when she went into the cold sleep vaults with the other colonists.

Neil patted her shoulder and blinked up Suki's charts. The projection hung between them, reversed to Suki's eyes so that the strings of numbers and charts were all but unreadable. But she could tell by the reassuring green of the status bars and the steady jags across the EKG window that there wasn't anything serious to worry about. As if to reassure her even further, Neil called up quick views from the nanocameras in her aorta, at the base of her cerebellum, in the cilia of her lungs. All showed healthy tissue, every sign of business as usual for a by-the-books cryogenic revivification. Neil blinked, and the air between them was clear once more.

"You're doing great, Suki. Everything's proceeding on schedule; we should have you up and around by tomorrow, Thursday at the latest."

Suki opened her mouth to try and speak. He shushed her with a finger on her lips.

"No talk. We'll have plenty of time for that later. Right now, I want you to collect your strength. We have a lot of work to do in the next few weeks."

Suki found that she could nod her head, ever so slightly, so she contented herself with that. Neil nodded back, leaned forward, and Suki lifted her chin, waiting for the life-giving warmth of his kiss.

It didn't come.

"I have to go," he whispered, his eyes strangely avoiding hers in their new proximity. "I can't spend too much time here. I'll—" Neil only pulled back a few inches, but it seemed to Suki like a gulf of a million miles had arisen between them "—I'll talk to you about it later."

If Suki hadn't known better, she would have thought that the temperature in the torus dropped by ten degrees then. Neil's knees cracked as he stood up from the bedside.

"Try and get some sleep," he said. "I'll be back to see how you're doing in a few hours."

And then, with a thin smile that was a shadow of the smile that Suki knew, he was off. As Suki watched him climb the gentle slope of the torus floor, she felt her eyes brimming with slushy tears.

What had just happened here? Where was the Neil Webley that Suki Shannahan had known and loved? Wasn't love supposed to mean forever? Suki didn't know how long forever was, but she had always assumed the word meant a time span longer than seventeen years!

Suki felt a sob, the first sound she had uttered in those seventeen years, rise up in her throat. It came out as a horrible croak, the sound a frog might make—if that frog's heart had just been sliced in two, on the cold steel dissection table of thwarted romance.

By degree over the next six hours, the recovery rooms of Torus 3 filled up. From the manuals that Suki had committed to memory those seventeen years ago, she knew that these ghost-white forms who nested in complicated tangles of thick tubes and wires would count few if any colonists among their number. Phase One of the revivification would include only the crew, scientific teams and medical technicians absolutely essential to the task of preparing for the colonization drops. It would only be after the *Gwendolyn* was installed in orbit; the planet below thoroughly explored and charted; the livestock embryos grown and modified for survival in the new ecosystem; and the landers assembled, fuelled and tethered into their drop positions; only then that Phase Two, the truly monumental task of reviving more than three thousand colonists, would begin.

In a way, Suki envied those colonists, sleeping in the long tunnel of freezers along the *Gwendolyn*'s core. They would wake up to a new world, made up like a brand new subdivision complete with high schools and strip malls and cineplexes, there waiting for them to begin their new lives. And in the meantime, they slept insulated from the hardships of construction, of exploration. From the simple heartbreak of waking . . .

"Well, well, well," said a voice that was at once familiar and strangely unknowable. "Look who's rejoined the living."

Suki looked up from the novel she'd been trying to start for the past hour, and almost instantly found she had to supress the urge to gloat.

"Betty-Anne Tilley," she said, as sweetly as she could manage. "Look at you."

After seventeen years, there was little left of the petite, strawberry blonde beauty that had taken Suki's job away and thereby sentenced her to the freezers and the lowly status of a candy striper. Years in low gravity had lengthened Betty-Anne's bones and drawn lines across her face that gave her a hard, spinsterish look. Although she was, like Suki, fully five years younger than Neil, this day standing beside Suki's bed with her pharmaceutical pallet tucked under her arm, she seemed almost elderly. Betty-Anne smiled, and Suki was struck by how similar that smile was to the one Neil had given her before he had left her bedside—cool, professional, and more than a little heartless.

"It's been longer for me than it has for you," said Betty-Anne, as though she were reading Suki's mind. "You haven't changed a bit—I guess the freezers really are the ultimate beauty sleep."

Betty-Anne laughed then, the way she always laughed after she made a joke, and in that instant the years fell away and Suki saw the girl that had been her best friend in the whole world, all through nursing academy. Suki felt a smile, a genuine smile this time, creep across her face.

"It's good to see you," said Betty-Anne as the years ebbed back into her face. "Really, it's been too long. You're going to have a lot to catch up on." The corners of her mouth turned up again in that same cruel parody of a smile she'd shown a moment before. "Particularly, I think, with our mutual friend Doctor Webley."

Mutual? What did she mean by that?

"We've already spoken," said Suki coolly.

"Have you?" Betty-Anne regarded Suki speculatively. "Then you already know about the Arrangement? I must say, you're taking it all rather well. You two had quite a thing going before we launched, didn't you?"

Now Suki was angry. She sat up in bed, and as she did, long knitting needles of pain and jealousy pierced through her nerves. She was about to ask the obvious questions—*what Arrangement? With who?* and its chillingly obvious follow-up, *How could you steal the man I loved, Betty-Anne Tilley?*—but Suki wasn't about to give Betty-Anne the satisfaction. She set her bare feet down on the warm, carpeted curve of the recovery room floor and teetered to her feet.

Betty-Anne reached out to take Suki's arm. "Now, now, girl. Let's crawl before we can walk."

Suki pulled away.

"You crawl, I'll walk," she snapped, stalking off to the lockers where she knew she'd find a change of clothes. Before she stepped through the door, she turned back to see Betty-Anne standing in a shocked silence beside the empty bed.

"And one more thing, *Nurse Tilley!*" she shouted across the curving floor of the torus. "My name's Suki Shannahan! Don't call me girl!"

Arrangement? What in goodness' name was this Arrangement that Neil had gotten himself involved in? Was he married? If so, then why didn't Betty-Anne just call it that? Was he—Suki shuddered at the thought—living *common-law*? She supposed that living common-law was something of an Arrangement. But that didn't seem right either, somehow. Everything was suddenly so confusing.

No one had tried to stop her as she came out of the locker room, velcroing closed the last few tabs on her red-and-white candy-striper jumpsuit. Strictly speaking, there was no reason to; her revivification had been routine, and there was no medical reason for her to stay in bed any longer than she felt she needed to.

Right now, the thing that Suki needed most was information.

Each of the six tori along the length of the *Gwendolyn* were connected to the core via three equidistantly spaced tubes, and Suki rode the climbing chain up the centre of the C-tube. Occasionally, she rode past a porthole, and caught a glimpse of the long, gleaming core of the *Gwendolyn*. From her slowly rotating perspective, it was as though it were nothing more than a gigantic barbecue spit, slow-cooking over the distant flames of their new sun. The starship wasn't much different today than it was before she'd gone to sleep—if it weren't for the red star's peculiar light, they might have still been accelerating away from the Earth, barely past the beginning of their journey. At least, Suki reflected, the enormous wheels and gantries of the *Gwendolyn* remained a constant for her.

And hopefully, the operating system they'd installed on the *Gwendolyn*'s holographic-memory computer net had remained a constant, too.

Suki reached the top of the C-tube just as the hatch irised open and a pair of nurses she didn't recognize guided a stretcher into a controlled descent on the tube's opposite side. One of them, a balding Japanese man, nodded a greeting at her while his partner, a heavyset red-haired woman still wearing her surgical mask and HUD goggles bouncing in wide loops around her neck, hooked up the stretcher to a link in the down chain.

"Just woke up?" the balding nurse inquired politely.

"You could say that," said Suki. Before he could say anything else, she pushed past him into the core of the starship. By the time the hatch irised shut, she had already strapped herself into the interface couch outside the cryosurgery theatre, and was tightening the headset.

You could say that again, in fact, she said to herself as the bright, friendly colours of her personal interface came to life in front of her.

"I'm just waking up now."

━━━

When she signed on with the company's medical corps for deep-space work, Suki Shannahan had been offered a personalized interface as part of the package. And like many of her fellow volunteers, she had chosen an interface that would remind her of home: in her case, her family and their spacious estate home in the Richmond Hill Enclave. In those days, she had thought that such reminders would be a comfort in the coldness of space—now, she realized the decision was a mistake. The clean, white vestibule of the house on Fir-Spiralway, with the sounds of her brothers tussling upstairs and her mother on the phone in the kitchen and the TV in the living room replaying old CFL games as background noise were nearly perfect simulations, much more than reminders. But here and now, on board a strange starship orbiting a distant star, those memories were no comfort at all. Indeed, it was all she could do to hold back the tears and assign herself to the task at hand.

"Mom," she said aloud, and waited dutifully while the simulacrum of her mother went through the standard exclamation into the telephone:

"Oh, look who's come home for a visit! Sherry, I have to call you back—Suki's here!"

And from the living room, her father hit the mute button on the CFL commentary, and called over his shoulder, "How's Daddy's little girl!?" and, before she could even consider the question, flicked the volume back up to twice again as loud and turned back to the television.

It really was just like home.

"Tell me about the Arrangement, Mom," said Suki.

Her mother appeared in the doorway to the kitchen. Sunlight streamed in behind her through the French door to their minuscule back yard, throwing her into silhouette.

"The Arrangement," said Suki's mother. Her index finger went to her chin, as though she were contemplating how to explain something far too grown-up for her little Suki to understand. "Well, dear. The Arrangement was a plan that the medical crew of the *Gwendolyn* implemented amongst themselves on Day 689 following a 214-day review of crew family counselling records. The Arrangement has remained in force until this day."

"More," said Suki. "Text."

"Well, dear. Come into the living room. I'll have to show you the rest on television."

Suki followed her mother into the living room and sat down on the couch. Her father lifted the remote and switched the channel from the CFL to a screen that was filled, according to Suki's request, with nothing more than text. At the top was the heading,

HORMONAL SUPPRESSION THERAPY AND THE NORMALIZATION OF SEXUAL/AGGRESSION RESPONSES IN HIGHER PRIMATES

and underneath that,

HELEN ROCKHOLME,
BSc MA

and below that, more than thirty-three screens of densely packed dissertation and equations, appended with charts, tables, and a hypertext index that Suki didn't even need.

After cramming all those cryogenics manuals back on Luna, Nursing Chief Rockholme's slim research paper was an absolute piece of cake. When she was finished, she took the remote from her father and used it to check on a few other things in the system, accessing the nano-surgery databank, before she switched the CFL game back on.

"Would you like something to eat?" asked Suki's mother.

"No, thanks, Mom," said Suki, giving her mother a perfunctory hug.

"We always love you, dear," said her mother.

"Exit," said Suki. Her voice was trembling, but it was clear enough for the interface—her mother and everything she came with vanished in a flash of phosphor.

"Love me," said Suki as she took the headset off and rolled off the interface couch. "I'm glad somebody still does."

She found Neil in his apartments in the residential torus. The ship's engineers had done all they could to make the torus seem like an Earthly garden, but aside from planting shrubs and trees and vegetable plots every few metres, there was only so much they could do. It was still nice, Suki had to admit it—nicer than the recovery rooms, nicer than the core shafts, nicer than the cryosurgery theatres.

But without someone to share it with, let's face it, Suki thought. *A shrub's just something else in the path. Something else to trip over.*

Neil answered his door on the second chime. To Suki's surprise, he didn't seem particularly surprised to see her.

"Come inside," he said, ushering her into the narrow space that made up a second-class cryosurgeon's living room. "You're looking well." He said it without looking at her, Suki noted bitterly.

"Why did you do it?" she asked him.

Neil just looked at her. Seeing him this third time caused her to revise her assessment of the effects of his aging once more. It wasn't as though the years had made him stronger, or more assured, or better looking. They had only emptied him, she realized, made him simple and streamlined.

"What are you talking about?" he finally said.

"You know," said Suki. "You know what I'm talking about."

Neil sat down on the sofa, shrugged his confusion. He really didn't get it, Suki saw. He really had no idea!

"The Arrangement!" Suki was shouting, and she didn't want to be shouting, but she couldn't control herself. "I know about the Arrangement!"

"Ah."

Neil folded his hands on his lap, and sat staring at them. Suki folded her arms across her chest, glaring across the tiny room at the man she had thought she had loved more than anything in the world. Finally, Neil looked up. His perfect blue eyes were rimmed with red, although his face otherwise betrayed no emotion.

"Would you have rather that I'd married?" It came out as nearly a whisper.

"That was the only other choice?"

Neil tried to smile, but perhaps seeing Suki's reaction, he abandoned the attempt.

"That was the only other choice?" she said again. "Let Nurse Rockholme inject you with her nano-machines that you knew would shut you down for good, or go off and get married . . . to some . . . to some . . ." Suki was so angry she could barely speak.

"Some bimbo?" Neil finished it for her.

"Your word," said Suki. "But yes. That's the general idea."

"Oh, Suki." Neil stood up and stepped over to her. "You went to sleep so early. You have no idea how bad things got."

"I read the reports," said Suki, stepping away from him. "I know what happened."

"You did." Neil stepped back too, crossed his own arms. "Well, you know what happened. But you still don't know how bad things got. Seventeen years—that's how long we all had ahead of us. We'd all signed on to spend the prime of our lives in the dark, between the stars. Nothing to do but monitor the life signs of all those colonists. And when we had to, intervene. And I don't have to tell you, Suki—

when a body's down to six degrees Celsius, there are precious few medical emergencies that can't wait a day or a week or a month."

"So you got bored."

"More than bored," said Neil. "Do you remember what I told you about space, back on the shuttle? About love?"

"Like yesterday," she answered wryly.

"Well, I was wrong," he said. "Love didn't keep us together. Not when it went sour. It divided us, started feuds. Simon LeFauvre nearly died—"

"The knife fight. I read about it."

"It was scalpels—not knives. And it would have gotten a lot worse—someone *would* have died—if we hadn't nipped it all in the bud."

"With the help of Helen Rockholme's research project." Suki felt fingernails digging into her elbows. They were, she realized belatedly, her own. "What about *us*?" she demanded. "Didn't you ever think about *us*? As something other than some kind of . . . of sickness?"

His shoulders slumped, and Neil turned away at that.

"It made us crazy," he repeated. "You don't know. You weren't there."

Suki felt something in herself soften at that. What if she had been there, she wondered? Would she have fallen into the same morass of promiscuity and licentiousness that overtook the medical crew of the *Gwendolyn* over the first two years of its voyage? Would her love for Neil have grown pale, the way so many of the others had for one another, and finally transformed into something darker, something like hate? Would she have volunteered, like the rest of the crew, to take Nurse Rockholme's little machines into her bloodstream, and shed that part of her forever?

Suki's love had been preserved, after all, a perfect flower pressed between the frozen pages of her hibernation. It had never thus far faced a true test.

Until now, that is.

"Do you love me?" she asked softly.

"They've found a habitable planet here," said Neil. "Really that's an understatement; it's quite a paradise. Lots of free-standing water, an oxygen/nitrogen atmosphere, average mean temperature of fifteen degrees Celsius, even some native plant life. Just like Earth. Except . . ." he paused.

"I asked you a question," she said.

"Except," he continued, "it's a bit more massive. One and a half gees, I'm told. I'd never survive there."

"Do you?"

"My place," said Neil, "is going to be up here—I'm afraid for the rest of my life."

"Love me?"

"You deserve better," was all he would say.

Suki left then. She considered his face—how it had betrayed nothing, the entire time he had spoken.

She took the hypo out of her pocket, and turned it in her fingers as she thought:

Everything is so easy, every pathway is so clear—once you remove love from the equation.

—————

By the time they were ready for the first drop, Nurse Suki Shannahan had overseen a grand total of seven hundred and sixty-two revivifications—two-hundred and twelve of them unsupervised. That was part of the job, after all, and Suki was good at it; even Nurse Rockholme, who had overruled the recommendations of the examinations board and denied Suki entry into the *Gwendolyn*'s nursing team, even she had to admit it. Nurse Rockholme had watched Suki's progress from the day of her revivification, with perhaps an unusual and some would say unwarranted degree of interest.

Suki had been such a silly girl in the early days at Luna—a Barbie Doll, that had been Nurse Rockholme's word for her. Pretty, too pretty for her own good, inside as well as out. Space, Nurse Rockholme had concluded, would kill that pretty girl if she ventured very far into it.

And yet . . .

Nurse Rockholme turned in her vat in the forward core, watching and listening and tasting as Suki Shannahan finished her seven hundred and sixty-seventh revivification. Her hands caressed the pharmaceutical pallet like an artist's—entirely confident, uncompromised by pity or anger. . . .

Or by love. Suki's seven hundred and sixty-seventh colonist twitched as the electric current ran through his nerves, exciting his heart into what would have to become its regular rhythm and shocking his brain-stem out of its low-frequency funk, and as Suki worked those nerves, she smiled. It was a cool smile, thin and professional and entirely heartless.

She has come along, Nurse Rockholme burbled to herself. *She has turned into a fine young nurse.*

The night after Suki Shannahan's last revivification, she joined Doctor Neil Webley for dinner at his apartment. He opened the cover over his porthole, affording them a slowly rotating view of the landers, which floated assembled and tethered and fuelled over the vast blue and white expanse of the new world below them.

"You could go," said Neil. "There's nothing more for you up here."

Suki shook her head. "I've made my choice," she said, her voice flat.

Neil said nothing more. The two seldom had words for each other these days, but that was fine with Suki. The nanotech in Nurse Rockholme's serum brought a kind of quiet to her heart, a cool passionlessness that was best served by external silences as well.

Neil put his hand on top of Suki's. She remembered how it had moved her before, when he touched her like this. It was that touch that had moved her to follow him—*to follow the man she loved to the bottom of the ocean, if that was where he wanted to go.*

Now, as they sat together high above the new world's ocean, where both of them would spend their remaining days together, she knew it was only a touch; only flesh.

He could keep his hand there forever, she knew. And it wouldn't change a thing.

WYLDE'S KINGDOM

PILOT:
LOOK OUT FOR JIM!

Max first spied the two fanboys through the mosquito netting surrounding the bed in his nearly submerged Brazilian apartment. He was sure he had them pegged: just another couple of bottom-feeders churned up from the silt by Atlantica, who'd tracked down their hero, Jim, to his dank retirement here at Serra Do Mar Bay. They'd kicked in the door, true. But Jim fans had done far weirder things in Max's experience.

One fanboy had an acoustic-guitar case slung over his shoulder. "Either of you know 'Girl from Ipanema'?" Max asked. Although it wasn't what he was going for, they both laughed appreciatively.

The two introduced themselves as Dan and James and, as James pointed out, *James* was another name for *Jim*. James was the one carrying the guitar case, and he set it down on the floor and opened it while Dan explained in detail just how much Max's work as Jim on *Wylde's Kingdom* had meant to him. Trying to be polite, Max noted he had put on a little weight since then and didn't think he could do the stuff Jim had done anymore. Just as politely, James pointed out that was one of the reasons they were here.

"You have put on a few pounds there, Jim," agreed Dan.

Then Max heard a click, followed by a whine that sounded like a vacuum cleaner cycling up. James raised his head. He was holding a narrow plastic hose that ended in a gleaming steel needle. A hissing whistle came from its tip, and Max realized what his dormant survival instinct had been trying to tell him since they showed: these guys weren't fanboys at all—or, at least, not just fanboys. They were professionals: barrio cosmetic surgeons, the very worst kind.

Max stirred, trembling toward thoughts of escape.

Years ago, back when he was a regular on *Wylde's Kingdom*, and his day consisted of garrotting gorillas and chainsawing rampaging elephants, that instinct would have seen him clear. It would have thrown Max out of bed and had him halfway to the door before the fanboy-surgeons had a chance to react. If one of them had managed to grab him, he probably could have wrestled the needle of the AbSucker 2020 away from him and jammed it into one fannish orifice or another to break the hold and made it to the door and dived off the balcony into the bay in the span of a dozen heartbeats.

But not these days. Max *had* put on a lot of weight —two-fifty sounded about right, and three hundred wouldn't really have surprised him—and he hadn't exactly been physically active during his voluntary convalescence here. So when he grabbed at the needle, the fan pulled it out of the way easily, and speckles of dizziness darkened Max's vision before he could do anything about it.

"Don't stress yourself," said Dan, who was holding the second hose-and-needle assembly from the AbSucker in one hand. It was hissing too. Before Max could do anything more, he felt a sharp pain on his left side, and he realized James had managed to skewer him in the love handle. Max felt another prick on his right handle. The AbSucker's motor whined as it worked on both sides of him, siphoning off eight months of accumulated lipids like they were a milkshake.

James tried to be apologetic. He explained that, usually, they'd have him onto their boat in Rio, and if he wanted he could even have had a general anaesthetic and in just under an hour woken up eight months younger, with none of this painful and clearly disturbing fuss. They would have given him a mint.

"But we were under instructions," said Dan.

"Just doing what our boss tells us," said James.

"Your boss?" gasped Max.

James looked down at his own T-shirt, which was emblazoned with a scan of Jerry Wylde, ubiquitous pith helmet covering his hairless scalp and his antique Sharps hunting rifle slung over one narrow shoulder. Dan looked over at it, too, then back at Max. Dan nodded, his open-mouthed grin an eerie parody of the one Wylde sported on the shirt.

"Our boss and yours," said Dan.

The AbSucker made an ugly *whup!* sound as something thick

passed through the orifice. The way Max was feeling, he thought it might be a testicle.

"Mr. Wylde wanted everything to be just right," explained James. "He wanted you to 'recontextualize.'"

"And he said you needed to have an 'adequate sense of danger,'" said Dan.

"Yeah," agreed James. "Those were his exact words. 'Recontextualize.' 'An adequate sense of danger.' Mr. Wylde says that's when you're at your best."

The three of them were quiet for a moment—James and Dan contemplating the words of the master, Max contemplating the sagging flesh below his ribcage. The noise from the guitar case shifted from suck to slurp, like the milkshake was finished, and James snapped out of it.

"Shit!" he yelled, and reached down and flipped off the machine. "Almost got your liver," he said as the sucker cycled down. When Max didn't laugh, Dan patted him on the shoulder.

"Joke, Jim," he said.

The wind picked up then, and the broken door swung open. Dan hurried to close the door against the returning rage of Atlantica, and Max shut his eyes.

"I'm not Jim," he whispered.

———

But that wasn't entirely true. Max was Jim—and Jerry Wylde had made him that way.

Jerry Wylde and Max had hooked up the year the first hurricane cluster of Atlantica had been tracked. Jerry Wylde was still with Disney, exec-producing a now-defunct celebrity arena show called *Let the Games Begin*. Max had been working in a string of middling-successful Bollywood sitcoms, the latest of which was an extended-family urban musical actioner called *Look Out for Shoorsen!*

With *Shoorsen!*, Max had managed to achieve just the level of celebrity *Let the Games Begin* liked best: sufficiently known to pull in a few ratings points, but not so famous their agent could alter even a semicolon on the standard Disney contract.

Legend had it Jerry had been the one to pick Max, over the objections of some of the execs who were worried about how Max's recent, well-publicized bout in rehab would play. But that was crap—Jerry didn't have anything to do with the decision to make Max a centre-forward in the East-versus-West Five-Ball Sudden-

Death Australian-Rules Soccer match. In those days, Jerry Wylde didn't soil his hands with booking decisions. When the two met in the dressing room, Jerry mistook Max for a member of the camera crew, then once corrected, faked his way through an embarrassingly inaccurate appreciation of this season's *Shoorsen!* and got Max's name wrong.

Even in those early days, the one thing Jerry Wylde was not was a detail man: he spent his days pushing the envelope, articulating vision, and that day he had such immense envelope-pushing, vision-articulating plans that he was more preoccupied than usual.

In his ghostwritten autobiography, Jerry would take an entire chapter to carefully explain how Disney was poised to drop the metaphorical ball on *Games*, that after just three years in circulation, it was headed for a ratings nosedive, and that what would later become known as the Five-Ball Bloodbath was his honest attempt to inject some life into the ailing property.

━━━

From Jerry's ghostwritten autobiography, *I, Jerry*:

Disney's problem with *Games* was the same problem they'd been having since "Steamboat Willie." They settled into a safe spot that only *seemed* dangerous, and their Five-Ball Sudden-Death Australian-Rules Soccer spot was a perfect example: divide a pack of mid-level television actors into teams, throw down five balls instead of one, and tell them they can do anything they want to get as many of those balls between the goalposts as they can before the commercial. Ooh, they do sound extreme, those rules: *Do anything you want*.

Well I tell you something: to an actor, doing anything he wants means driving his convertible to his beach house where he'll screw his actor girlfriend while his agent is signing him for a movie deal that'll let him take a different actor girlfriend to the Oscars and screw her in a different way when he wins, all of which he regards as nothing more than his God-given *due*. Kicking a ball into a net in Five-Ball Sudden-Death Australian-Rules Soccer? I don't care how good actors these guys are; there's no motivation, and the audience can smell that.

I could sure smell it—and that's why I made sure their uniforms were scented a little differently: with what I like to call *Eau de Jerry*.

━━━

Eau de Jerry was Wylde's affectionate name for a pheromone soup tailored to drive the five African rhinos Jerry had managed to hide on-set into a mating frenzy.

None of the actors, of course, had any idea. Billy Kaye, the surgically stunted twenty-six-year-old who'd been playing the same precocious eight-year-old on *Ungrateful Bastard* for the past eighteen years, did complain in the dressing room that the uniforms had a funny smell to them. But the rest of the team wrote the observation off as more of the overpaid dwarf's well-documented backstage whining. It was ironic: when the balls dropped and the rhinos charged out, Kaye was one of the first to go down—or up, rather, gored on one of the great beasts' horns and tossed into the air like a discarded action figure. The Man-Boy Who Cried Rhino, Jerry later dubbed him.

Seven other celebrities died in the televised bloodbath that followed. Another eleven were maimed, and the rest suffered more minor injuries. Or most of the rest did.

Live on television, Max Fiddler—and only Max Fiddler—came through the ordeal unscathed.

Emerging from his Serra Do Mar Bay apartment and struggling through the rain toward his psychopathic fans' limousine, Max still wasn't sure how he'd survived that bloodbath. He'd seen the tapes enough times: watched himself leap out of the path of a charging rhino, bolt across the pitch to the opposing team's goalposts, and shimmy up to the top, then jump again when a couple of smitten rhinos rammed into the posts hard enough to knock them down. He saw himself grab onto the bottom of the camera crane that was even then pulling in for the close-up on what could have, should have been his death scene. Max watched as he swung overtop and wrestled the camera operator like he was the last Nazi guard on the truck with the Ark of the Covenant in the back. Max did remember that fight, or at least the feelings it had brought out in him—a strange mix of terror, elation, and vestigial guilt as he finally managed to unstrap the operator from his seat and knock him twenty-five feet down to the Astroturf below. The feelings were there, but the particulars were lost forever. Something within him had taken over and guided him to safety. Max chose to simply call it his survival instinct, but in Wylde's autobiography, the ghostwriter found a better name: "Max Fiddler's Inner Jim."

The ghostwriter hadn't needed to embellish the events that followed. Jerry had indeed been the first one onto the pitch, before the rhinos were subdued, and he had stood directly underneath the crane smoking a locally banned cigarette, gazing wordlessly up at Max for almost a minute before the floor director, surrounded by three terrified PAs brandishing cattle prods and cellphones, came out to take Wylde off-set and bundle up the camera operator.

Transcript of the subsequent meeting between Jerry and Max in the Disney World Trauma Center, from *I, Jerry* (pretty much how Max remembered it too):

JERRY: Hello, there. I'm Jerry Wylde.

JIM: Yes, I believe we have met. Just this afternoon.

JERRY: And I'm sorry—you are . . . ?

JIM: Max Fiddler. *Look Out for Shoorsen!*? Didn't we have this conversation?

JERRY: Max Fiddler. Ah, no. You're Jim. Right?

JIM: Max Fiddler. I am an actor.

JERRY: An actor. Listen, Jim—I don't want you to take this the wrong way, but the one thing you are *not* is an actor. You have more *cojones* 'tween those gams than half of those bozos on the pitch showed today.

JIM: That is only because your triceratops spread their cojones across the pitch, Mr. Wylde.

JERRY: You exaggerate. And they are rhinos. Triceratops are dinosaurs, and dinosaurs are extinct. Rhinos are alive and kicking. Where'd you go to school, Jim?

JIM: Idaho. Why are you calling me Jim? I keep telling you my name is Max Fiddler, that is the name on the contract I signed, which by the way I also read all the way through, and I did not see any mention of rhinos in the—

JERRY: Whoa, Jim. Settle down. I don't handle the contracts, and we don't have a lot of time for me to look into it for you anyway. But listen—let's cut to the chase. I've got some new projects on the horizon—big projects. Stuff that's going to turn Disney and Fox and the whole goddamn planet on its ear. Hey, riddle me this, Jim: what do you get when you cross a nature show with a fishing show?

JIM: That would be . . .

JERRY: A hunting show! Ex-actly! Do you remember the last time you went hunting—sat in the scrub for hours with your dad's old M16 and a box of hand grenades, waiting until the moment—the precious, perfect *moment*—that deer shows up in your sights?

JIM: I've never been—

JERRY: Never been hunting! Of course you haven't! Who hunts deer these days? *I* can't afford the price of a license, and I'm loaded! Okay, how about this: you ever shove firecrackers up a frog's asshole? Watch that little bastard *hop*? No? Stick an aerosol can and a cigarette lighter under a wasp's nest? Hold a magnifying glass over an anthill on a sunny day?

JIM: Actually, not—

JERRY: Gahh, you're shitting me, Jim. I saw you out on that pitch today. That was not a prissy little rhino-hugging second banana from the subcontinent I saw climbing that goalpost. Oh, no. You're one cold-blooded survivor, Jim. You're a survivor, and you're more.

JIM: You tried to kill me.

JERRY: Yeah, Jim. I guess I did. (Pausing sheepishly) And you know what? I think I succeeded.

JIM: Huh?

JERRY: Yeah. I look at you, and I don't see any trace of that Max Fiddlehead—

JIM: Fiddler. Max *Fiddler.*

JERRY: —Fiddle. Whoever. I don't see any trace of that guy in you. You're Jim—the guy that faces five sex-starved African bull rhinos, scales a sheer goal post then leaps—*leaps* through the air and knocks the camera op out of his seat to dominate the whole show! Forget *Look Out for Shoorsen!*—from now on, it's Look Out for Jim, world! *Look Out for Fuckin' Jim*!

At that point, a phalanx of Disney cast members had burst into the room, fired off a Taser into Jerry's ass and, with nothing but that and a commandeered restraining wheelchair, effectively ended the meeting.

But the meeting had lasted long enough for Jerry Wylde to leave his mark. As Max lay alone in the dark room, halfway down the biggest adrenaline crash of his life, he played Jerry's words over and over in his head: *Look out for Jim.* Jerry Wylde was a lunatic, thought Max, and not a particularly unique one either. *Look out for Jim,* he'd said. The trouble with guys like Jerry Wylde, thought Max, was they figured they could motivate you with nothing more than some meaningless catchphrase—*Look out for Jim,* for Christ's sake—and make you dive off a cliff with it. Like that was all it took.

Max got out of bed. The linoleum floor was cold under his bare feet. They kept these rooms too cool—after three years in New Delhi,

Max was used to the heat, and he could have stood a little Florida sunshine. Right now, the only light came through the drawn blinds of a single window, and it cast only the faintest, greenish glow over everything.

"Look out for Jim," whispered Max. He shuffled over to the window, put his hand on the blind.

As he did so, there was a terrible *crunch!* sound, as of breaking glass, followed by the escalating moan of spreading cracks. There was another sound as well, somewhat more distant, and for Max the room got even cooler.

It was the sound of wind. Big wind. Max inched the curtain back, looked out through the spiderweb cracks of the window, and saw just how big a wind could get.

Three thick-waisted tornadoes were dancing across the Magic Kingdom under a sky green as a frog's ass. The infirmary was second-storey, and most of his view was blocked by a grass-covered berm, but Max could see the top spires of Cinderella's Castle as one of the tornadoes brushed against it. For an instant, it seemed as though the wind was working like a lathe on the fantasy parapet, sending bits of it flying off like woodchips, but then the funnel shifted maybe three dozen feet the wrong way, and the tower disappeared inside it.

"Look out for Jim," said Max, as one of the other tornadoes began to grow and moved away, the castle now erased from the skyline. Then something else slammed into the window, shattering it—and once again Max was running, slamming open the door to the hallway, which was already filling up with patients and orderlies and security guards. No one seemed to notice him as the adrenaline started pumping and his survival instinct—his "inner Jim"—took over.

"Look out for Jim!" he yelled, and pushed his way into the first stairwell he saw. In no time at all, he was safe in the tunnels under the studio theme park. He would be stuck there for seven and a half days, while Atlantica's first-ever foray onto the mainland United States reduced eighty percent of Walt Disney World to the swamp and scrub and mud from which it had sprung.

By the time the job was done on Disney, Max's agent had done pretty much the same thing to his contract with *Shoorsen*'s producers in New Delhi. Against his agent's advice, Max handled the talks with Jerry Wylde himself.

EPISODE 1:
THE PASSION OF THE VOLE

Max took advantage of the screen and mini-bar in the wide seating in back as the two fan-surgeons up front found some dry highway and hauled inland to Rio. The weather was the shits, and Max didn't want to know about it. So rum cooler in hand, he shut the Weath-Net scribe—which was tracking a tentacular offshoot of Atlantica scraping its way down the coast—and settled on one of the Argentinian sitcom feeds. They were showing the first season of *Happy Days*, when Joanie was a kid, Fonzie was still a greaser more threatening than lovable, and Ron Howard at least superficially resembled the mid-twentieth-century teenager he was supposed to be playing. It was the only season of the show with any artistic integrity as far as Max was concerned. Although it had been dubbed in Portuguese, he watched it raptly as Dan steered the amphibian over and around the remains of the highway into Rio. He suspected both of the fans were glad he'd found something on the screen. Like most fans Max had encountered through his career, these two ran out of conversation after the first hello.

Max was glad for the distraction of the screen himself. He hadn't seen Jerry Wylde—even onscreen—for something like three years. *Wylde's Kingdom* had enjoyed a good seven years at the top of the ratings, but now it was faltering and most networks had shunted it to the bottom of the schedule. "I'll show you an endangered species," Wylde had said in one of the early promos, in front of a loop of Jim lobbing hand grenades into what Wylde's team of researchers believed was the last African mountain-gorilla nest in existence. "Now *that's* endangered!"

———

The limousine crawled up the highway into the suburbs of Rio and finally stopped behind the ruins of a shopping mall. There was a sleek yellow VTOL executive shuttle waiting for them when they arrived. The flight crew were huddled in the lee of a little Quonset shelter, arguing in Italian.

James and Dan jumped out of the limo, opened the door, and hauled Max out. The rain was coming down so hard now that, when Max turned his face toward it, he felt like he was drowning. He was only able to make it across the dozen feet to the hatch of the shuttle because his two abductors-fans-surgeons-whatever-the-hell-they-were helped him.

"This is where we get off," said James.

"Take it easy, Jim," said Dan, smiling through the downpour. Max thought both fans looked relieved to be rid of him, and he didn't blame them. Max sighed and turned to climb into the relative dark of the cabin.

"Max Fiddler," said a voice he recognized instantly.

"Mimi?"

The shuttle's cabin was a reinforced bubble affair, with round windows spread polka-dot across the walls and ceiling. The woman sitting inside was just a shadow against a rainy circle of slate-dark sky. "None other," she said. "You look great."

"Thank you," said Max. "I feel like a drowned vole whose balls were cut off with rusty nail clippers."

"From what I hear about you lately, that's got to be an improvement." Although her face was still obscured in silhouette, there was a familiar smile in Mimi's voice. It was a familiarity that chilled Max; he should never have gotten to know this woman so well. She patted the seat beside her. "Come sit by me," she said.

Max hesitated.

"Oh Christ, Max, get some self-esteem. We're going to be working together—the least you can do is sit beside me on the way out."

"All right." Max sat down beside her as the hatch behind him swivelled shut and the sounds of the storm stepped back a few yards. With the storm farther and Mimi nearer, Max's eyes adjusted and he got a good look at the woman behind the voice. The years had been far kinder to her than to him: the line of her jaw and cheek was as smooth, her wide brown eyes as intelligent, her mouth as wide and generous as ever; and her jet-black hair, although tied back in a thick ponytail, showed none of the grey that had begun to fleck through Max's thinning mane over the past few months. No, Dr. Mimi Coover looked every bit the innocent woman-child she had been when, as a young Canadian marine biologist, she first signed with *Wylde's Kingdom* as technical consultant on the televised slaughter of the last three living St. Lawrence beluga whales.

"Prison seems to have agreed with you," said Max.

"Careful, Maxie," she said. "There but for the grace of God . . ."

"I meant it kindly," said Max.

Mimi shrugged. "Doesn't matter. I didn't actually serve much of my sentence; my skill set's in short supply these days, and GET snapped me up pretty quickly for their oceanographics lab. Serving my sentence saving the environment I was so bent on destroying. And with only a little social engineering . . ." Max grimaced ("social engineering" was Mimi's euphemism for "alcohol-assisted seduction") ". . . gaining access to an otherwise classified library of abstracts and raw data you would not believe."

"Lucky you," said Max.

"You don't know how lucky," said Mimi. She flashed a wide, white-toothed smile with a larcenous glint that erased any illusion of innocence. "I'm putting us back on the map, Maxie. The things I've found . . ."

"I do not want to know," said Max.

"Think," said Mimi, "*Nautilus*."

"What does an exercise machine have to do with anything?"

"*Nautilus*. You know—Captain Nemo? *Twenty Thousand Leagues Under the Sea*? The giant—"

Max couldn't hear what Mimi said next—the turbines had begun to cycle up for takeoff, and it took a second for the noise-dampers to kick in.

"—Well I've found a nest of them!" finished Mimi. "A nest! Filled with *hundreds* of them! *Hundreds*, Max! Nobody's been able to find more than one in nature, and here we've got a nest! Jerry is positively thrilled. That's why he wanted you back—this is going to put *Wylde's Kingdom* back on the charts."

"Whatever," said Max. "I'm tired."

"Tired, hmm? We'll see about that." Mimi sidled closer as the VTOL lifted off the pad and started its queasy ascent over the storm. She rested her head on Max's shoulder, and her hand fell on Max's thigh. He felt her fingernails through the cloth of his jeans. "You weren't being literal about being a castrated rodent? Were you, *Jim*?"

"Actually," said Max, "yes. Pretty literal."

Max settled back in his seat as Mimi's hand withdrew and she sighed. The old survival instinct, Max thought, was finally kicking in. It was about time.

The world looked better at ten thousand feet.

For one thing, Max could see the sun—and some uninterrupted blue sky. He couldn't remember the last time he'd seen blue sky and taken it for granted. Atlantica and its bastard offspring had darkened the planet's surface pretty effectively, and every time the clouds moved you went out and basked in it, melanoma be damned. It was tough to get worked up about something as trivial as skin cancer under the too-rare brightness of direct sunlight.

From up here, even Atlantica didn't look so bad—clean white cotton balls marching off forever, mixing into a vortex so wide you needed to be in orbit to see it for what it was: the beast that had wiped out close to half the Earth's population over the past decade and set the other half on the fast track to a soggy and wind-ravaged stone age.

It was no wonder, thought Max, that Jerry Wylde's star was waning under such a cloud: Atlantica had made the so-called Last Great White Hunter redundant.

In Jerry's first season, Atlantica wasn't charted as anything more than a grouping of hurricanes in the mid-Atlantic: Hurricane Colin, Hurricane Donald, Hurricane Elroy; then Freddy and Gerhardt and Helmut; Irving and Jacob and Kenneth and Lothar; Marvin and Noel and Otto. Only when it persisted past the usual hurricane season, crested the alphabet at Zoe and survived past Christmas, did Weath-Net name it for what it was—Atlantica, Earth's answer to Jupiter's spot—the world's first persistent superstorm.

Then, Jerry Wylde was already halfway through the twenty-six-episode first season of *Wylde's Kingdom*, building his studio on the *S.S. Minnow*, a loaded-down oil tanker anchored off British Columbia, and fending off subpoenas from a dozen different governments. With the help of Max and a team of zoologists, he had identified and exterminated eight species of animals that were headed that way anyway.

The first season was a good one for Max. He didn't even mind being only addressed as Jim by everyone he saw: hell, in half a season he'd become more famous as Jerry Wylde's athletic animal troubleshooter than he'd become in six seasons as *Shoorsen*'s pink-bellied second banana.

Jim did everything: jumped from helicopters into alligator-infested swamps, staged commando raids on lion prides, reprised his debut with the rhinos on an African veldt in the two-part special *Rhino Revenge*—this time armed with a Russian-built hammergun and benefiting from some heavy-duty air support. He even had his own line of action figures—which sold like hotcakes—and a prime spot in the *Wylde's Kingdom* console game, which, although less successful than the show, still made Jerry Wylde a mint.

By the end of the show's first season, Atlantica had taken a sizable chunk out of the Eastern Seaboard of the United States and reduced the islands of the Caribbean to little more than a few depopulated atolls.

As Jerry and his crew were preparing for the second season with a trip to the fragile, still-icy regions of the Antarctic, the Global Ecological Trust was beginning to mobilize. It probably shouldn't have surprised anyone that the multinational force sworn to restabilize the planetary ecosystem by persuasion or force should target Jerry Wylde and his nose-thumbing television program as public enemy number one.

One person it didn't surprise was Jerry himself. It turned out he had good reason for locating his studios on board an oil tanker: when the GET gunboat pulled up alongside the *S.S. Minnow*, demanding Wylde surrender to the justice of the world court, Jerry asked hypothetically how many years they thought he'd get if he were to blow the stopcocks on the tanker's two million barrels of crude oil and spread it all across the West Coast salmon beds—which he said would be easy to do before, as he put it, "you get a single one of your Greenpeace-surplus Zodiacs into the water, you tree-hugging candy-ass dupes."

Predictably, the GET ordered the gunboat's withdrawal, and the second season of *Wylde's Kingdom* kicked off without further harassment—although Jerry was effectively Polanskied from GET-signatory nations ever after.

And so it went. Tidal waves exfoliated Hawaii and the Philippines after California made good on its century-old promise to slide into the ocean. Waters continued to rise, with the ever-swelling Atlantica egging them on. Meanwhile, Jerry and Jim slogged their way through season two, then season three, and then half of season four.

Jim probably could have stayed on for longer quite comfortably. The nice thing about working with Jerry was it didn't require you to think much: Jerry had it all worked out. On Jerry's advice, Jim fired his agent and lawyer, and let the *Wylde's Kingdom* accountants look after him so he could concentrate on the work.

Max had been used to keeping himself in shape, but only as the camera demanded. Jim, on the other hand, had to not only look good, but *be* good. Sit-ups and weight training with a Hollywood-refugee personal trainer wouldn't cut the mustard—so Jim spent his every waking moment not in the infirmary in the *Minnow*'s training maze with the former SAS team that made up Jerry's personal guard.

So, yes, Jim probably would have continued in such a way indefinitely, a willing lapdog to the *Wylde's Kingdom* entertainment machine, were it not for the arrival, in the middle of the fourth season, of the new crew of naturalist consultants led by Dr. Mimi Coover.

In *I, Jerry*, the ghostwriter professed not to have a clue about what drove the wedge between Jim and Jerry Wylde. A third of chapter twelve was devoted to a maudlin and accusatory meditation on the falling out: "Did I neglect Jim in some horrible, horrible way? Did I miss a single feeding, fail to exercise him, neglect his entertainments for even a second? Was I such an irritating seatmate on the trans-Atlantic flight of life that there was no other way?"

Ah, if only Jerry had known. Sitting on the shuttle, Max studiously avoided looking at Mimi—although he was hotly aware of her gaze on him. On board the *Minnow* he had fallen in love with her, and he had to admit he was deathly afraid of repeating the mistake here in the stratosphere.

As Jim, Max had lived the life of an aesthete. Between training and performance, there wasn't much time remaining in his day for anything but sleep. Although Max later learned his inbox was overflowing with every imaginable kind of sexual offer, Jerry never gave Jim a chance to read a word of it.

So when one night Mimi stole down to Jim's dressing room, dressed in nothing but a pair of retro-porn cutoff jeans and a lumberjack shirt with several of the buttons strategically removed, Jim was defenseless. And when she breathlessly informed him she had watched him in action since she was a child—spotting his heroic potential in the very first season of *Look Out for Shoorsen!*, then seeing it realized past even her pubescent dreams in *Wylde's Kingdom*—Jim was lost to her.

Yet if it were as simple as that—a beautiful groupie, a secret rendezvous in the dressing room, followed by a few more secret rendezvous in the training room, on the bridge, in three of the *Minnow*'s lifeboats . . . just that, and Jim would have been fine. But Dr. Mimi Coover was more than a groupie. She was a marine biologist; the kind of marine biologist who would sign on board the *Minnow* to work for Jerry Wylde. And she had . . . ideas.

"Do you ever wonder," she said one rainy night as they lay sweating underneath the tarpaulin of Lifeboat 6, "why Atlantica?"

"Yes," said Jim immediately.

"And California? Why now?"

"They'd been predicting a quake like that for years," said Jim, then, when he felt the sweat-damp skin of her thigh peel disappointedly from his own, added hastily: "But, yes, I do wonder why now."

Mimi rolled over onto her stomach, propped up on her elbows so she looked down at Jim. "It's true what you say, though. We have been predicting a massive, continent-splitting earthquake along the San Andreas fault—and for *decades*, not just years. Just like we've been anticipating a superstorm like Atlantica for years, and we've been warning about the rising of the oceans, and we've been worrying about mutant viruses like the ones vectoring across North America and Asia right now. So I guess I shouldn't be surprised?"

"Guess not," said Jim.

"I shouldn't be surprised," she continued, "that half the Earth's population is drowned or starved or dead from disease; that the United Nations is gone, replaced by an ecologically overcompensating military machine that throws you in jail if your car doesn't pass emission standards and shoots you without trial if you cut down a tree in your backyard. And I guess I shouldn't be surprised Jerry Wylde and his throwback hunting show, which seems to be doing nothing but hastening the process of planetary death, is the ratings hit that it is."

Mimi got up and pulled the tarpaulin back. Cool, sharp rain pummelled down on their naked bodies, and Mimi swivelled her long legs over the gunwale and jumped onto the *Minnow*'s deck. No slouch in the jumping department himself, Jim followed easily. But Mimi was still halfway to the nearest hatch.

"I'm sorry!" he shouted, feet slapping the metal deck plates as he hurried to catch up with her. Mimi stopped and turned.

"For what?" she demanded.

"For—" Jim paused, searching for some kind of culpability "—for hastening the planetary death!"

Mimi laughed, and threw her arms around him. "Hastening the *process* of planetary death, is what I said. God, Jim, you are so malleable. You're like the soft top of a little baby's skull—I could draw a happy face there with my finger, and it would stay that way until the day you died."

Jim's mouth opened and closed, but no words came out—his mind was filled then with the horrifying image of Mimi's thin finger digging happy-face furrows on newborns' heads. Her flesh suddenly felt as cold and clammy as the fish she studied. But she only held him tighter when he tried to pull away.

"Here's the secret," she whispered. "The world *is* dying, Jim. It's a terminal case—the life that's infested it, become it, has run its course, and the world is reverting to its older, more natural geological state—joining its stately brethren of rocks and ice and gas-balls circling the sun. The world's dying, and the world knows it. It's obvious, and we should welcome it."

Jim reached up and pulled Mimi's arm from his shoulder. He stepped back. Mimi was grinning at him through black strands of hair washed over her face like seaweed in the storm.

"No way," said Jim.

"Oh, don't be stupid, Jim," she shouted. "The world is ending—Jerry Wylde is finishing it off, and you're right there with him! And now so am I! Centre stage!" She threw her head back so the rain ran into her eyes, her mouth. Lightning flashed paparazzi-silver across her naked body, made an apparition of her—ribs standing out in sharp relief, eyes shadowed into black and unknowable pits, mouth wide and streaming water as her head came back down to look at him.

"Centre stage," said Jim.

"Centre stage," repeated Mimi. "Good, Jim. You're catching on."

She took two more steps forward, and her hand came to rest on Jim's bare buttock. The tips of her fingers pressed furrows into the muscle there. "Let's make a baby," she hissed through bared teeth.

Jim thought about that for a minute; and thinking about procreating made him think about too many other things he'd never, ever considered. The inevitability of the end of the world. Jerry Wylde's complicity in that end. His own complicity. Mimi Coover's sharp fingertips digging drawings into their baby's skull. Jerry Wylde filming it for season five.

A sudden wave of conscience and self-loathing flooded him, like a tsunami over a Thai whorehouse.

Jim reached around, grabbed Mimi's wrist, and pulled her hand off his behind. "Forget it," he said. "I'm out of here."

Within a week, Jim was indeed out of there—gone without a trace, in fact—and Max Fiddler was alone in Lifeboat 6, firing off the last of his signal flares, calling for someone—anyone in the thinning population of the dying planet—to rescue him from the storm-swollen waves of the rising sea.

EPISODE 2:
A NIGHT AT THE ZOO

The shuttle dropped from the stratosphere and lanced back through the cloudy flesh of Atlantica. The cabin pitched and went dark for a second before the cabin lights came up.

"Where are we going?" said Max.

Mimi clapped. "A question! The eunuch vole wonders after its fate!"

Max shrugged. "The world is ending, and we might as well welcome it. That doesn't rule out curiosity."

"Fair enough." Mimi grinned. "We're going to the top of a mountain."

He raised his eyebrows. "That's interesting," said Max. "Jerry finally sold his tanker?"

Mimi's smile broke into a laugh. She mimed a firing handgun with her forefinger. "Gotcha," she said. "It's a sea mountain. On the Eastern Scotian Shelf."

Max blinked.

"Near Nova Scotia?" Mimi blinked back.

"So we are going to the *Minnow*?"

"Where else?" said Mimi. "Oh, you are going to *love* this, Maxie."

The shuttle banked on its descent, and Max thought he saw lights below them in a tanker-shaped oval, shining through the thinning cloud and thick sheet of rain.

"I cannot wait," he said, and looked away.

They were greeted on the deck pad by a couple of raincoated production assistants and a video crew. The PAs shouted non-sequiturs into headsets hidden under their hoods as they led Max and Mimi through a Stonehenge of crates and equipment across the broad plateau of the tanker's mid-deck, under a wide, corrugated-steel awning. Max was still wiping the rainwater from his eyes when the studio lights kicked in and the video crew pulled back for a wide shot.

Mimi elbowed him: "Stand up straight," she hissed. "You're live."

Max didn't have to be told twice. He'd spent the better part of three decades in the business, and his instinct in this area was even more deeply ingrained than his survival instinct. Max's spine straightened like a zipper pulling closed, and he felt his lips slide back like covers off a missile silo, to launch a white-toothed grin he thought he'd shelved for good the day they stopped booking him on *The Tonight Show*.

Max bounded across the floor of Jerry Wylde's soundstage, up the three shallow steps to the set, and landed perfectly on the sofa beside Jerry's desk, which had been faced with a single word, sea-green lettering on a midnight-black screen: *KRAKEN!* Nuremberg banners reading the same hung behind the set, illuminated from below with white-hot spots.

Somewhere deep within himself, Max Fiddler screamed.

But he was in character now, deep in character, and the scream was a quiet thing. Jim certainly didn't hear it. He reached across the desk and clasped the thin, hairless hand that belonged to Jerry Wylde. Jerry was wearing a hot pink double-breasted Armani and his pith helmet. Without a thought, Jim told him how sharp he looked tonight. Outside the still-open hatchway, lightning flashed close. But the lights in here were bright enough that Jim could ignore the flash. The neo-primitive cargo cult tribe that made up Jerry Wylde's studio audience were loud enough Jim didn't have to ignore the thunder that followed. He couldn't even hear it. They were chanting something he couldn't quite make out and twirling their arms around their heads in tightly choreographed mayhem, and they looked quite terrifying with their Frisbee-stretched lips and sponsor-scarified foreheads. Jim waved.

"Ahoy there, Jim!" yelled Jerry as the audience settled down.

"Ahoy yourself, Bwana Jerry," said Jim. He'd started calling Jerry *Bwana* at the start of the second season but hadn't used the word since the beginning of the third. The audience let out a nostalgic cheer. Jim crossed one lipo-weakened leg over the other and threw his head back in a near-perfect execution of the talk-show laugh.

On cue, the audience started to chant again. This time Jim understood what they were saying: "Kra-ken! Kra-ken! Kra-ken!"

"Right," said Jim.

Jerry put his hand over the mike. "Ah, it's time," he said into his lapel. "Let's go to clip, Jeffrey."

Jeffrey, whoever he was, didn't take even a heartbeat to shift gears. The studio went dark for barely an instant, and then the CGI projectors fired up and everything became a mottled green. The studio audience went into a panic with the unscripted change, but the projectors faded them to shadowy ghosts, and the dampers made their shouts into distant gurgles. Shit, thought Jim, his survival instinct grumbling. This was too real: every sense but smell told him they were under water.

"The deep blue sea," said Jerry, standing up and beckoning Jim to do the same. "You ain't seen nothing like this recently, have you, Jim?"

A heads-up prompter appeared in glowing red letters a few inches from Jim's eyes. Marks the same colour bled up through the floor. As with the prompter, these glowed like brand tips to Jim but wouldn't be picked up at all on camera.

"I haven't seen anything *but* this, Jerry," read Jim, moving to mark 1 and facing the direction of the arrow. "The whole world's sinking, in case you haven't noticed."

Jerry shrugged expansively. "Why Jim," he said, "I'm not talking about the water. I'm talking about . . ." and Jim moved to mark 2, just a step away and facing the opposite direction ". . . this!" finished Jerry, his face obscured behind a silvery tumult of virtual bubbles.

This time Jim screamed along with Max.

He was facing a giant, glowing mass of tentacles—some of them must have been a dozen or more feet long—and staring into what seemed to be an immense eyeball, as big as a soccer ball. And then it was gone, jetting past him, and Jim saw the creature's full cigar-shaped body, the tentacles at one end, a wide fin as big as a ship rudder at the other. The behemoth had snuck up behind him while he was reading his prompter. *Jee-sus*, thought Max. It must have been sixty feet long, glowing like a motel road sign from end to end; the suckers on its tentacles were each big enough to wrap a baseball.

"Captain Nemo," whispered Max, momentarily shocked out of character and into recollection. "A kraken. *Twenty Thousand Leagues* . . ." The welds on Max's vault of suppressed Disney memories slipped open, and Max peaked inside long enough to remember the movie: *Twenty Thousand Leagues Under the Sea* . . . James Mason and Kirk Douglas and a submarine and, yes, a great big rubber squid.

Jerry elbowed him in the ribs. "Line," he hissed.

"What the hell was that?" read Jim, a little too quickly. "Some kind of sea monster?"

Then Mimi stepped out of the murk, eyes focused on her own cue cards. She had changed into a form-fitting yellow wet suit and was carrying a drum-loading spear gun over her shoulder.

"In a way," she read, once the audience had applauded her entrance. "That's a giant squid, Jim."

"Aww, Doctor Mimi," said Jerry, aping disappointment with his usual brazen subtlety, "I wanted to see a *kraken*."

The muted audience went back at the chant with renewed vigour.

"Well, Jerry," read Mimi, "that may be just what you're looking at—there's every reason to believe the legendary kraken, which were supposed to have plagued shipping routes for hundreds of years, were actually foraging giant squid, who . . ."

Jerry's eyes shifted their focus to some point beyond the horizon.

". . . mistook early sailing vessels . . ."

Jerry wandered after the squid, leaving Jim and Mimi alone on-set.

Mimi, ever the trouper, finished her line: ". . . for food."

"Boy," read Jim, "I can't wait until I take on one of these things for real, in a battle broadcast live around the world—" he swallowed, his throat incongruously dry given the illusion of ocean around them, before he read the next set of words "—just three days from now."

"*One* of them?" Jerry shouted from the murk—probably behind the A camera. "Just *one*? You know what they say, Jim: you can't have just one!"

The air around Jerry was disrupted by a burst of bubbles and motion. Max stumbled and almost fell as the image of the squid came back for a second pass—something he should have anticipated. But it wasn't the one giant squid that freaked him out—it was the seven others, as big or bigger, that followed in the first one's wake.

"Jee-sus!" he yelled. "What the hell's that?"

He'd missed his cue again—the prompter flashed angry red and white—so he read: "Are my eyes deceiving me? Or are there eight giant squid down there?"

"At least," read Mimi. "What you saw was an image-enhanced holo we took just yesterday afternoon, from a divebot array just eight hundred feet below this ship. There could be more down there. *Far* more, in my professional opinion."

The audience *ooh*ed.

"Far more," said Jerry, rubbing his hands together with a sandpaper sound that gave lie to the illusion of water around them. "Like the sound of that, don't you, Jim?"

Can't have just one, thought Max/Jim crazily before the dark, frothing sea went darker behind his eyes, and he fell to the studio floor in a dead faint.

EPISODE 3:
THE CABINET OF DOCTOR JERRY

They gave him a shot of something to wake him up for the welcome-back party, and whatever it was it certainly did the trick—Max was so alert that he felt like he could kill every one of the thirty-seven houseflies crawling in and out of his ears if he wanted to, with nothing more deadly than the rock-hard tip of his newly rigidified tongue. He walked into the retrofitted mess hall unaided and sidled up to the bar.

Max looked around the room for some conversation, but he was a little dismayed to realize he recognized almost no one in the room. Max sighed and took careful sips from the drink the barkeep placed in front of him. It could have been anything from mineral water to goat's urine to his drug-benumbed taste buds.

It was actually okay not knowing anybody to talk to; Max was in no mood for conversation anyway. All he would get would be some armchair-producer critiques of Jim's last season on *Wylde's Kingdom*; or, worse, some liposucking fanboy gushing over just how dangerous a giant squid really was, reeling off statistics and little-known facts about how big their beaks were and how long their tentacles could reach, and marvelling at how much balls Jim—they would call him Jim, not Max, always Jim, because Max was a nobody and in their formative years Jim had been the next best thing to a positive role model—just exactly how much balls Jim had going up against the kraken, and not just one, but seven . . . ten . . . a hundred—Christ, who knew how many? *Did he have a plan?*, they'd ask. *Would this be Jim's last hurrah?*

"Sure'y no'," said Max to himself, his tongue about as agile as an ice-splintered tree stump. He must have said it louder than he'd intended; he drew uncomfortable stares from nearby conversations. Max took another sip of his drink.

He began to wonder what he was doing here in the first place. It was true, there wasn't really much he could have done to resist the AbSucker attack, and he could be excused for a certain amount of lassitude in its aftermath, as they ferried his sagging skin to the shuttle pad. And once on board the shuttle it would have been tricky for him to do anything, really, but wait until they landed. And once on board the *Minnow* Jerry had tricked him with lights and cameras, so, even had he wanted to, there wasn't anything to be done then either.

But now—was he going to wait until Jerry dropped him into a nest of giant squid, or whatever it was he was planning for him, before he took some kind of decisive action?

Action.

Max spotted two exits: the one he'd come in from, which led to the dressing rooms and studio after a few turns and ladders; and the washrooms, which Max recalled had a second exit leading through to an old barracks room, which, after some doing, led to the main deck and the lifeboats.

Max made up his mind. He swallowed the last of his mysteriously flavoured drink, got up, and headed for the washrooms, trying his best to look nonchalant. It must have worked—not a soul even looked up as he left his party. Once out of the room, Max hurried along the narrow corridor, past the doors with the stick-figure sign and through to the barracks room. It was being used as a storeroom for the bar and was filled with crates of whiskey and beer and Pepsi. Max stepped gingerly around them and hurried down the hall. He took a deep, optimistic breath. Things were going smoothly—just up a ladder down this corridor, through a galley—or maybe a studio— and there he was: right next to the exit.

Once on deck, it would be a simple repetition of his last escape: into a lifeboat, row like the devil's behind you and, after a couple of hours, make with the flare gun and hope for the best.

Max's optimism flagged for an instant at that thought.

The last time he'd tried this stunt hadn't actually gone that well. A Japanese fishing trawler had picked him up after two days at sea, and the crew had recognized him instantly. Initially, Max had thought that was a good thing—Jerry had always led him to believe that *Wylde's Kingdom* was universally revered: the only real critics were the fanatics at GET, said Jerry. But the truth was more complicated. The crew of this trawler were indeed regular viewers of the show, but as it turned out there were sharp divisions of opinion on just what kind of contribution Jerry and Jim were making to the world of televised entertainment and, following from that, the world in general. The long and the short of it saw Max barricaded on the bridge with a half-dozen rabidly loyal fans while the majority of the crew gathered mutinously below decks. The more reasonable of their number merely demanded the captain conduct a trial-at-sea for crimes against the planet. Others were ready to go so far as scuttling the ship, if it meant ridding the world of even a portion of the evil *Wylde's Kingdom* franchise.

Max was better off with the fans, but only marginally. The captain had damn near shattered Max's elbow in a marathon arm-wrestling match, and the cook had been agitating for a karate tournament—the *Wylde's Kingdom* website apparently claimed that yellow-belt Jim was a black-belt world champion, and the triple-black-belt cook wanted to try him out.

Max had been lucky: the trawler was part of a Sony-owned fleet, and *Wylde's Kingdom* still had enough cachet that Max was more valuable to the company's media division alive than dead. So the Sony security forces squashed the mutiny, rescued Max from his fanboy-allies, and moved him to a Tokyo hotel suite, all within a few hours.

Max found the ladder that led up to the kitchen or studio and paused.

The ratings of *Wylde's Kingdom* being what they were these days, Sony would not be as quick to pull Max's fat from the fire a second time.

"Fug i'," said Max. He scurried up the ladder and came out in one of the galleys. It was busy, all steam and sizzle and shouting, as Jerry's craft services team prepared tray upon tray of the particularly bland cheese and fish canapés that Jerry favoured. One of the chefs there did notice Max, and for a moment he feared he was discovered. But the woman took Max's arm, led him to one of the doors, and kindly explained that Jerry had declared craft services off limits to him until after the show.

"Sorry, Jim," she said. "I'll make you up a nice fish broth later if you like."

"'Kay," said Max, relieved. He stepped out the door, and then opened another door, and then he was on deck. Lightning flashed at him in greeting, and the hard rainwater drenched him immediately. He walked stiffly out into the dark storm.

There were no lights in which to hide here, no trickery to bring about his transformation into Jim. Max was alone with his thoughts. A bank of lifeboats swung in the wind, and he thought about lowering himself in one of those. He thought about the two days or more he would spend in his stolen lifeboat. He thought about the Grand Banks fishermen who plied these parts, and the *60 Minutes* segment he'd seen on them last year. He thought about the prospects of being rescued by one of their boats and just what they'd do to him when they found out who he was. And he thought about giant squids, and what they'd do to him by comparison.

"Fug i'," said Max.

He stepped back through the hatch and shut it behind him.

Max took a deep breath and headed for the *Minnow*'s aft decks— where last he remembered they kept the gymnasium, the infirmary, and his old training maze.

⊷

Max had been working out for barely an hour before Jerry showed up with the med team and the video crew. The intrusion pissed him off: three days was a hopelessly short time to train to begin with. He couldn't afford to be doing live segments with Jerry today if he were supposed to be doing live segments with giant squid in three days. When the unit producer sidled up to the thigh-sculptor machine to tell him he was on in five, that was what he told her.

"Don't worry," said the producer, a woman with a horse-long face and thinning red hair. "Just keep doing what you're doing. You with me, Jim?"

Max sighed and mentally stepped back.

"I'm with you," Jim said.

Jerry was standing slack-faced in the arch of the entryway sipping from a bottle of vintage spring water. He nodded when the producer signalled him, then came over by Jim's side. The videographer followed him. Max could tell that they started rolling: Jerry's slack features came alive, with the same demon-jester grin that adorned all his merchandise.

"Jim," he said. "Jim Jim Jim Jim Jim."

Jim started another set of extensions, wincing at the pain of tearing muscle and stretching ligament as the hydraulics hissed in the bowels of the machine. "Hey, Jerry," he said.

"Just keep doing what you're doing," said Jerry, and turned to the camera. "Jim is preparing for the fight of his life. So he doesn't have time for idle chit-chat—isn't that right, Jim?"

"Right," said Jim.

"Shh! Every extension, every contraction of those atrophied muscles of yours puts you one tiny step closer to being a match for the kraken, and I don't want to stand in your way—so shh!" Jerry put his finger to his mouth. "Shh! Remember, Jim, the giant squid is probably the fastest animal on the planet—it's got nerves as big around as your little finger, and that's a bandwidth to beat. And its suckers? They have little ridges of chitin around them that work like drill bits on your skin." Jerry made his hand into a claw and turned it back and forth like he was unscrewing the lid of a jar. "Let one get ahold of you, and it'll bore a hole into your flesh. So be strong, Jim! Be strong!"

Jim nodded. "You got it, Jerry."

"Okay," said the producer, "cut it. How was that, Mr. Wylde?"

Jerry's face sagged. "Fine," he muttered. "Send the team over. Time to juice him up."

———

Max barely felt the injection when it pricked his arm. Jerry and the TV crew walked out as the steroidal spasmodics kicked in. The med team stayed behind, putting a roll of padding between Max's teeth and helping him onto a restraining stretcher so he wouldn't injure himself in the early stages of the muscle-building phase.

"You rock, Jim," said one of the medics. "I just wanted to say that before your hearing goes."

"Temporarily," added the one who'd administered the injection.

Max's back arched in hyper-orgasmic fervor as the spasmodics went to work on the weakened muscles in his lower back. He made happy death-throe noises through his clenched teeth as the ringing started in his ears.

———

The spasmodics worked and kneaded Max's musculature for about six hours before they let him go, and at the end of it Max felt exhausted but good: the AbSucker had over-depleted him, but the spasmodics set the balance right. This cocktail was better than anything he'd used before; Jerry had obviously found a better supplier. These new drugs left his face and back smooth and acne-free, while strong, telegenic muscles rippled and twitched along his arms and legs and abdomen.

"I'm ready for anything," said Max. "Even your ridiculous squid, with their finger-thick nerves and their suckers that remove chunks of flesh like a drill bore."

Mimi ran a razor-nailed finger appreciatively along Max's left pectoral.

"That's the spirit," she said. Mimi had shown up about an hour earlier, on the spasmodics down curve, as his hearing was beginning to return, to talk about the shooting schedule and go over the equipment Max would have at his disposal. He hadn't been able to ask questions during the briefing, but there wasn't any need to: aside from the military-issue dive armour, everything on the list was gear that Jim had used many times before. The explosive-tipped spearguns; the razor-wire net pellets; the hum-knives and trank-spears and suit-mounted mini-torpedoes.

He might have asked more questions when Mimi started talking about the squid themselves—but they wouldn't have been any more in-depth than "Is there some point to telling me all this?" Or "Who cares?" But the questions wouldn't have been any more effective than the grunts and moans that were all Max could manage: Mimi had developed a theory, and the only way Max could stop her from explaining it to him would be to escape in a lifeboat again.

Mimi's theory was that they were sitting on top of an ancient hatchery—and that a shift in ocean currents had raised the temperature in that hatchery by the few degrees it would take to inflate the birth rate and, combined with the Wylde-hastened extinction of their natural enemies the sperm whales, had the effect of unlocking the gate on the kraken population explosion. What she wasn't so sure about was how so many of the squid had managed to grow to maturity and remain in such a small area. These creatures were giants, after all, with giant-sized food requirements, and the biomass oughtn't to be able to sustain them in such a large population.

"The GET researchers had apparently found some evidence of cannibalism," she had said. "Squid-bits in the bellies of a few captured adolescents. But cannibalism is a population limitation as well as a sustainer: an adult squid would have to eat a lot of babies to keep himself going, and on a daily basis."

There, Max had thought between spasms, with the babies again.

Now, he sat up on his cot and took Mimi's hand from his chest.

"Why are you back here?" he said. "Aren't you violating your parole or something?"

Mimi laughed—a surprisingly harsh noise, sharper than her nails. It made Max wince.

"I have my reasons," she said. "The money being only one."

Perhaps it was the familiarity brought on by his new sheath of muscles, combined with his proximity to Mimi—but he was filled with the sudden recollection of his last sight of her those years past, naked and demonic on the deck of the *Minnow*, selling him on the beauty of emptiness.

"Those squid are an affront to you, aren't they?" he said.

Mimi raised her eyebrows but didn't say anything.

"You can't understand why they're thriving—and you can't abide by their thriving either. They're one more stopgap against the sterilization of this planet." When she didn't object or disagree, Max stepped back from her.

"Are you going to bolt again?" said Mimi. "Jump in a lifeboat and row back to the mainland? I should warn you, don't think about going home. That little Brazilian hideout of yours is under water now—according to Weath-Net, Atlantica is on the move, Maxie, redrawing the South American coastline as we speak."

Max felt something stretch and snap in his throat as a final spasm shuddered up his spine.

"No joke," said Mimi. "South America is *shrinking*."

Christ, he'd *lived* there, and he'd have been dead there if the liposucking-fans hadn't shown up. Come to think of it, if the liposucking-fans hadn't shown up, Max would have welcomed dying. In more than an abstract sense, that had been precisely what he'd been doing there: waiting to die, killing himself by lassitude.

And the fact was that nowhere he turned did Max find anyone with an even slightly more optimistic view. What was the point in living past the moment when the future held nothing but Atlantica? A giant storm and rising oceans and earthquakes and plagues? Hundreds of millions of people wiped out by Atlantica and its aftereffects? For the first time since the bubonic plague decimated Europe in the middle ages, the global human was in actual decline.

And so Max had taken a boat down the Amazon—a trip that less than a hundred years earlier would have been a trip of a lifetime, a jungle adventure with piranhas and anacondas and tapirs—but now followed a muddy shoreline washed clean of human habitation by a combination of clear-cutting and the river's constant flooding. He had ended up in Brazil, squatting in the upper storeys of a sunken apartment house on the edge of Serra Do Mar Bay, eating and sleeping and drinking away the last of his so-appropriately named kill fee, waiting for the end.

Even Max's unbeatable survival instinct, his "inner Jim," could only take him so far. It had required Jerry—or Jerry's employees anyway—to bring Max back from the brink of death.

"We're all you've got," said Mimi, closing the gap between them. Her hands grasped the back of his neck and pulled his face down to her half-open mouth.

Although the spasmodics had made him more than strong enough to fend her off, this time Max couldn't summon the will.

EPISODE 4:
KRAKEN!

The sky over the *Minnow* was incongruously clear the morning of Jim's dive into kraken waters. Jerry had prepped Jim with a full hour of on-air pre-show interviews, so by the time they led him out to the dive armour, Max was so submerged as to be nonexistent.

It wasn't the same for Jerry. His shoulders slumped as they went single file along the catwalk to the dive crane at the ship's aft section, and by the time they climbed the stairs to the dive crane platform he seemed positively dejected.

"What is it, Jerry?" said Jim.

"Goddamn Atlantica," he said. "It's back in the Caribbean, and that means, before too long, it's going to hit Texas and Florida and the whole Eastern Seaboard."

Jim slapped Jerry's shoulder—a gesture that was one of the first character tics in Jim's repertoire of stock responses to Jerry's antics. "Take it easy, big guy," said Jerry automatically.

"It seems pretty nice here," said Jim. In fact, it was gorgeous—the sky was a clear robin's-egg blue, and the morning sun drew colour from even the drab and ungainly *Minnow*. The small part of Jim that was Max basked in it and regretted that, in a few moments, that brightness would be left behind for a dive eight hundred feet under the ocean.

"Oh yeah, great for your suntan. But think about our audience," said Jerry. "If you even have a thought in that pin-shaped head of yours."

Jim slapped Jerry on the shoulder again.

"Who the hell's going to be watching us with Atlantica running that far inland?" continued Jerry. "Everybody on one half of the continental US is going to be busy nailing up plywood on their windows if we're lucky, and sucking seawater if we're not. The one thing they are not going to be doing is watching us hunt squid."

"You can't generalize," said Jim.

"Ah, screw you," said Jerry irritably.

He might have said more, but they emerged onto the dive crane platform and into the view of three cameras and the studio audience, who were seated on bleachers to either side of the equipment. Jerry lifted his hands in the air and led the chant: *"KRA-KEN! KRA-KEN!*

KRA-KEN!" Jim hollered along gamely, then slapped Jerry on the back one more time, and climbed up the few steps to the place where the dive armour hung, open at the back and resembling nothing so much as a giant cockroach, cut open and disembowelled, so only the exoskeleton remained. As they'd rehearsed, Jim raised his arms above his head, rose onto his toes and fell forward into the thing's belly. The servo-motors did the rest, closing the suit behind him and clicking the seals, making the carapace complete. Jim wiggled his arms and legs until the flesh fell against the biofeedback contacts properly. The suit's arms extended with his own, and the HUD flashed up test forms a few inches in front of his eyes. These were meaningless to him, but Jerry had assured him that the controls had been dumbed down and the HUD wasn't really more than a special effect. The important part was the cues, green on the red of the HUD, that told him what to say and when to say it.

"All systems are green," read Jim.

"And green means—" started Jerry.

"—Go!" finished the audience. The crane swung out over the gunwale of the ship, and then Jim felt a sharp jolt and fell. He hit the water with a spine-wrenching smack, and the suit took over.

When Max came to, the HUD told him he was already at four hundred feet—just halfway down to his rendezvous with the video crew and the deep-sea studio with its cable comlink to the surface.

Until he reached that studio, he would be utterly alone: just Max, the ocean, and the recorder in his suit. He took a breath of suit air and watched through the darkness for the star-cluster glow of the studio lighting rig that would eventually rise on its tether to meet him.

━━

"Hey, Jim," said Mimi. "You okay in there?"

Mimi was one of the five crew members in the studio sub. There would be a camera on her, and if Max had wanted to, he could have watched her on the head's-up display. But he didn't want to see Mimi right now. He read his lines. "Just fine, Doctor Coover—but I'm getting a mite peckish. Got anything to eat in there?"

"Maybe we'll have some calamari later on—together." She silkily ad-libbed that last word.

The studio was quite near now. It was a bubble sub, suspended in the middle of a geodesic titanium cage rimmed with lights and cameras. From the briefings, Max knew it was immense—something like a hundred fifty feet in diameter, with a cable of steel and polymer and fiber-optics a dozen feet thick extending up to the *Minnow*—but as close as he got, it resembled nothing more than a particularly garish Christmas-tree decoration to Max.

The whole massive bauble twisted slightly on its tether, sending spears of light sweeping through the dark water. The HUD flickered in Max's suit with a rejoinder to Mimi's ad-lib. But Max minimized it and peered out into the shifting gloom. Adrenaline sluiced through his arteries like quicksilver, as the light spears panned and flickered over the bellies of giants.

"Do you see that?" he whispered.

The bauble shifted again, and several of the lights winked out.

"Mimi—Doctor Coover?" said Max.

Mimi didn't answer him directly. But her microphone picked up enough of the frantic chatter of her crewmates—"Shit, we've lost the feed!" "—Forget the feed, Hank, we're—" "—pressure! We'll implo—"—to give her an excuse. The bauble was swinging erratically. The lights were winking out in a now-familiar shape of expanding pattern. Max had more than a clue as to what the problem was.

They'd hit pay dirt: the squid had arrived, apparently in force. At least one of them had a grip on the submarine and was yanking on its moorings—and one of them was heading straight toward Max.

"Jim." Max whispered it like an invocation, as his own suit lights winked on, the servo-cameras fired up and the HUD came back in deep crimson combat mode. The numbers and bar-graph displays blurred in front of his eyes, however, as he got his first good look at the creature in front of him.

It was impossible to tell scale exactly, but this thing looked far larger than the sixty-foot glow-monsters they'd used for the infomercials. From Max's perspective, it was a nebula of tentacles that filled the ocean, lined with suckers as big as dinner plates and centred around a beak that gleamed like sharpened mahogany.

Max flailed backward, the jets at his waist instantaneously translating the impulse into a rearward thrust that should have taken him far from harm's way.

It should have—but as fast as the suit's biofeedback chips were, the kraken's thigh-thick nerves were that much faster. A long tentacle lashed behind Max and wrapped around him like a boa crushing a muskrat. There was a sickening sound of tooth-on-metal as the suckers tried to bore into Max's armour.

Max watched in horror as the image of the beak grew larger in his faceplate, opening and closing, and then as a cloud of black—emerging from the squid's ink sac, no doubt—billowed toward him like a steroidal blackout. And then there was just the HUD, deep red on black, and the sound of more suckers going to work on his suit, and a terrible clicking sound coming up through his ribs, as the beak made contact with his armour. Max felt his eyes heat up with tears of despair.

His comlink crackled. "Okay!" shouted Mimi. "We've got the feed back! Jim—you all right?"

Jim was too busy to answer—and the power draw for the EelSkin jolt he'd activated wouldn't have let him transmit for a few seconds anyway. The HUD dimmed for a second while it powered to send its 150,000 volts through the suit's skin, and then went black for what seemed like an eternity for the discharge. When the display came up again, the beak-scraping and sucker-drilling sounds were gone, but the world was still black out there and Jim wasn't fooled into thinking the kraken was gone too. He made a fist, raised his right hand in front of him, and sent a torpedo speeding into the darkness. It made contact almost instantly, and, giving it another second to burrow a little deeper, Jim raised his thumb against the detonator pad.

This time it wasn't his jets that sent him backward. He tumbled head over heels through the darkness for what the suit said was eighty-three feet before he escaped the giant ink cloud. It hung above him in a black thunderhead, the dim glow of the burning phosphorous at its core flickering like lightning.

"Scratch one kraken," Jim improvised.

The comlink was silent. Jim tongued the cue-card HUD. <STANDBY>, it blinked back in green letters.

"Hey," said Jim. "Anybody read me? Mimi? Jerry?"

Still nothing. He minimized the cue card and called up the comlink status bar. The words <SIGNAL LOSS> blinked amber across his view, even as his depth gauge rolled higher.

"Ah," said Max Fiddler, "shit."

From *I, Jerry*:

Danger is a media-induced state.

All right—I'll grant you there was a time that this wasn't so. Back in the days when a bad weather forecast meant you should bring your umbrella to work and not a submarine, when ocean-view property was actually a selling point, when catching the flu meant taking a few days off work and not updating your will, yeah, all right, danger meant something. That's because danger is a study in contrast—it's the threat of something worse around the corner, a catastrophic disruption of your delicate equilibrium. And if you're going to disrupt that equilibrium, it goes without saying it must exist in the first place. No equilibrium, and people have nothing to worry about—nothing to disrupt. Shit just happens.

Except, that is, here by the screen. I'm constantly amazed at you zombies—drop my pal Jim on a savannah with a pack of pissed-off white rhinos, give him a box of hand grenades and a shoulder-cam, and suddenly you're all squirmy and alive again. You start thinking and worrying and fretting—"Holy crow, Ethel, you think old Jim's met his match this time?" "Oh Jeb, I don' know I jes' don' know. Them rhinos nearly finished him the first time, and this here's in their natural en-vi-ron-ment." For those fleeting moments in front of your screen, you morons actually start to give at least a vicarious fuck about someone's survival, if not your own.

I tell you—if Jim and I had come along thirty years earlier, that spark we're igniting every week might actually have given me some hope for this dying wreck of a planet.

Max stabilized himself at six hundred feet and switched on his armour's sonar to sweep the ocean above him. It wouldn't show him squid—they were too close to the ocean's density to register—but, with the ink-clouded water intervening, sonar was the only way he could find the studio and the comlink to the surface. He hung still and quiet, listening for the ping that would point him in the right direction.

Listening—and watching for another kraken.

But Max didn't hear anything but the rasping sound of his own breath, and he didn't see anything but the dark of the deep waters, the dying star of phosphor in the dissipating ink cloud. The sonar quacked as it finished its first hemispheric sweep of the motionless waters around him, adding final confirmation:

The kraken were gone—and so were the studio and his link to *Wylde's Kingdom*.

Christ, thought Max, *Jerry must be shitting himself*.

It was possible that the *Minnow* had managed to pick up a small portion of his battle with the squid—but even if the crew had managed to fire the whole thing up the cable, the fight had lasted barely a few seconds, and most of that would have taken place in the midnight cloud of ink. And the script hadn't anticipated a battle this early in the show anyway; Max had seven hours of air in his suit, and Mimi and the team of oceanographers had expected that a few hours would be spent on scripted chit-chat and a guided tour of the installation before any squid came up to investigate.

And now, just twenty minutes into Jerry's big ratings comeback— *Kraken!*—was all but over.

Max started to chortle at Jerry's unhappy misfortune—but at a soft ping from his headset, he stopped himself, listening for it to repeat.

The sonar pinged a second time, and then a third, and the dive computer flashed confirmation: it had located the studio sub, two hundred feet to the north of Max and below him by about four hundred feet. On the third ping, the computer announced that the studio sub was descending, and quite rapidly.

Max checked the dive armour's help file. The structure and the life-support and propulsion system were all rated for a mile and a half, but the harpoon gun was only good for half that, and the cameras weren't rated any deeper than a thousand feet. So as far as Jerry and the show were concerned, the studio and its inhabitants were already casualties.

Of course, by now *Wylde's Kingdom* would be a ratings casualty in and of itself. Max had been around long enough to know that people didn't tune in to Jerry Wylde to watch him get creamed.

Max hit the dive sequencer with his chin and told the suit to lock onto the studio's signature and follow it down. Strictly speaking, Max knew the decision was counter-survival, but that was fine with him: off the air in the depths of the Atlantic, Max's inner Jim really had no say in the matter.

———

The pings multiplied as Max and the studio descended farther: they were approaching bottom, or more accurately, side—moving in a neat diagonal toward the southern slope of the sea mountain. The dive computer correlated the pings with its oceanographics database and came up with a three-dimensional map of the mountainside, which it displayed in a small window at the top of the HUD. Max and the studio were represented by little red triangles. The graphic was gorgeous—it reminded Max of the time he and Jerry had made a tiger-bombing trek to the southern Himalayas—and Max became so engrossed in the memory that he nearly gave himself a concussion against the back of his helmet when one of the cameras popped with a crack like a gunshot at 1,287 feet.

Head throbbing, Max wondered just what he expected to do when he got down there. If he were serious about rescuing Mimi and the rest of the crew, he would have done better to surface and report on the situation to Jerry. If he were halfway responsible, never mind just survival-oriented, Max supposed, that's what he'd do.

The second camera imploded at 1,315 feet, but this time Max was braced for it and just winced.

The thing was, Max wasn't halfway responsible. What he was, apparently, was more than halfway suicidal. And no amount of AbSucker treatments or spasmodics or steroids or anything else could mask that.

But what he also was, he realized, was damn curious.

Because from the look of the graphic on his HUD, the sub studio had just come to a landing on a high ledge of the mountain Mimi believed to be a giant-squid breeding ground.

Max accelerated downward, toward the now-motionless sub. Once again, the lights emerged from the murk—not as many as before, but enough to see by—and Max made sure to film it, in the seconds before the suit's third and final camera cracked under the pressure.

———

"Mimi," said Max as he grew nearer. "Do you read me?"

"Jim?" Her voice sounded woozy, like she'd been drinking.

"Max," said Max.

"Max," said Mimi. "What the hell are you doing here? You should have broken for surface right away. Jesus, you should do that now . . . . It's trouble down here."

There was a lot of silt stirred up around the studio; all Max could make out was about a dozen shafts of light, tangled in an opening-night criss-cross. The shafts didn't move, but they flickered now and again, as though occluded by something very large passing over it. Something the shape of a squid.

Max thought about it: if the sub had only fallen, it should have fallen straight down, not on a diagonal—from what Max had gathered, it was essentially a diving bell, with no locomotive power of its own. Something had pushed it.

"Trouble," Max repeated. "How many squid?"

"Three," said Mimi. Her voice trembled, and he heard the ugly chuffing sound of a man's tears in the background. "One's about thirty feet, another one's just a baby—fifteen, seventeen feet. And a big one—I can't tell how big, but from the parts of it we've seen, I'd say it tops a hundred."

"Feet?" said Max.

"Feet," confirmed Mimi.

As if on cue, Max saw an immense tentacle pull itself out of the cloud and wave a moment in the water, trailing silt in gossamer threads. It was wrapped around an object—a metal triangle, very tiny in the huge tentacle. It was a piece, Max realized, of the squid cage.

"It's got a piece of the cage," observed Max.

"Yeah," said Mimi. "It's got quite a few pieces of the cage. They all do. The bastards are cooperating. . . . This makes no sense, Jim . . . Max. . . . Ah, shit. Squid shouldn't be smart enough for this. They're opening us. Listen."

The comlink went silent for a moment—and sure enough, Max heard an echoing sound of rending metal: both over his headphones and vibrating through the walls of his armour.

"Wow," said Max.

"Yeah," said Mimi, her voice taking on a weary affection. "*Wow*. God, Jim. You are *so* malleable."

Max nudged on the jets and inched forward. His heart was thundering, and his mouth was dry as a desert. What the hell *was* he going to do here? Three squids, and one of them big as Godzilla. The monster tentacle let go of the metal and descended back into the silt cloud, which itself immediately expanded away from a mysterious crash-and-scrape of metal-on-rock within it. One of the lights winked out, and then another, and one more.

Max hit the jets again, and now he shot down toward the cloud of muck. "Mimi!" he shouted into his comlink. "What's going on in there?"

Mimi spoke quickly, shouting herself over various alarms sounding in the background. "Shit! Shit! They've stripped away the cage! Ah, shit! It's gotten in! Jesus, Jim, *it's inside the cage!*"

Max entered the cloud, and his view filled instantly with dancing motes of dirt. Fearful of hitting the mountainside, he reversed the jets. "Jim, Jim, Jim," he muttered desperately. "You would know what to do." But there was no Jim: Jim was just a character Max played on television.

And this deep down, there was no such thing as television.

There was another crash, nearer this time, but it somehow sounded softer. It took Max an instant to realize why: he wasn't hearing it over the comlink.

"Mimi!" he shouted. The familiar amber <SIGNAL LOSS> was his only answer. It was followed shortly by a *crack!* and a monstrous belch.

The silt cleared for an instant, and Max saw the wreckage: a twist of geodesic titanium, two or three lights dangling from wire, surrounding a shattered tangle of metal and plastics, all beneath a galaxy of air bubbles shooting toward the surface.

And he saw the squids. The smallest of them was indeed inside the cage, tail sticking out of the wreckage as its tentacles rummaged greedily inside. A larger squid hung above, tentacles spread like a spider's web over the wreckage. And the third squid—the giant one, the hundred-footer—lay supine on the rock, its tree-thick tentacles lazily gripping torn pieces of the cage like they were toys. Its eye was as big as a manhole pit, and as black.

Max called up the heads-up display for the harpoon targeting system, and centred on the giant. It wouldn't be a difficult shot by any means. His thumb hovered below the trigger, and he was about to fire when the small squid emerged from the wreckage. It had something in its tentacles, Max couldn't help but watch.

It was one of the bodies, or most of one. Mimi? It was hard to tell—the body was not in good shape. It trailed blood like ink from its torn abdomen, and Max thought about babies—about the one Mimi had wanted to make with him. Maybe she had furtively conceived already. If it was Mimi's body, their little zygote would be mingled in with the cloud. Max shuddered.

The squid dragged the body behind it, wrapped in three long tentacles, over to the giant's head. The giant's tentacles rippled and spread apart, and the smaller squid disappeared within them, dragging the body behind it. There was a flurry as the tentacles shifted, and a tremor went along the length of the kraken's body.

Max swore softly. The little squid was *feeding* the giant. These creatures were cooperating, to pillage the wreck and eat the TV oceanographers. God, he thought: if only we were live now . . .

Of course, if they were live, it would have been Jim and not Max, and he would have pressed the trigger the second the targeting system showed a lock, and the whole thing would have gone up in a brilliant phosphorous explosion. Then, before the fires had even dimmed, Jim would be off looking for the hatcheries and planting some shaped charges there, and moving off just far enough to escape the blast, but not so far he'd lose the shot. Jim would not feel a pang of regret about the deaths of the people in the studio sub, particularly Mimi, who might have been pregnant with his child. Jim would be so caught up in the moment that he probably wouldn't have realized it had happened. And Jim would certainly not pause to wonder what the significance of giant squids cooperatively cracking open a studio submarine and sharing the meal meant about the way that squids' brains worked and just what kind of a hierarchy they'd managed to build for themselves down here in the aftermath of their unlikely population explosion.

And, thought Max as he heard the *click!* of chitinous squid-sucker boring against his armour and felt himself being drawn backward and up and then fast around, Jim would not have likely let a fourth squid get the jump on him from behind. Not as easily as Max just had.

The side of the mountain filled Max's view for only an instant before the impact came. It wasn't hard enough to rupture the suit, but it was surely enough to twitch his thumb. The ocean around him caught fire as the phosphorous harpoon tips burst and ignited in the deep-sea water.

—▬—

SERIES FINALE:
I, MAX

The GET team found him in the evening, a coal-black knob at the edge of the *Minnow's* spill. They were using hovercraft too small to haul the armour on board, so Max didn't actually see a doctor until one of the craft had hooked up a chain and hauled him back to the base at Sable Island and a team of GET engineers cut him out of the damaged suit.

Max was a mess. The hard-shell suit had protected him from nitrogen narcosis, but at some point Jerry's three-day regimen of spasmodics and steroids and liposuction had caught up with Max. When the med team cracked open the suit, they found him in full spasmodic flashback.

He'd already shattered his left elbow, cracked his collarbone, and nearly bit his tongue off. Apparently he'd been hallucinating as well.

Max's delicate condition led to a spirited but inconclusive debate among the command staff as to whether to press the same charges against Max as they planned to lay against Jerry Wylde, and ship them both back for trial immediately. Because there were far too many unanswered questions, and Max Fiddler might be persuaded to answer them if there was a chance that charges could be stayed.

Where, for instance, was enviroterrorist Mimi Coover? Was she alive or dead? Where were the files she'd stolen from GET when she took flight? And, of prime concern, why did Jerry Wylde, mid-broadcast, pull the stopcocks on the *Minnow*'s oil tanks and unleash the largest oil spill the planet had seen in three decades? All Wylde would say on the matter was the oil spill was the only way he could save his ship, but that didn't make sense; the threat of an oil spill was the only thing that had saved him from arrest for the better part of a decade. He'd done the equivalent of shooting all his hostages when he opened his tanks.

The only explanation they had to go on was the story that everyone in the world who wasn't battened down against Atlantica saw on their screens. And that, the staff agreed, was not an acceptable answer. Wylde's CGI squid-monster was more convincing than the one in the old Disney movie, but it was still pathetic: a desperate attempt to inject some life into a questionable property that should have been killed a long time ago. There was something else going on—and Jerry Wylde and what crew they'd managed to round up so far weren't saying what that thing was.

So they determined to wait for Max Fiddler to regain his senses and tell them what had really happened. Then, and only then, would they take him and Wylde outside, skip the trial, and shoot them both.

Waiting, as it turned out, carried its own risks.

Two days after they arrived, the sky over the GET base was a Jovian bruise, purples and golds and reds that swirled above them and mingled into a malevolent blackness in the east. The oil-dappled waters in the Sable Island shallows—where the complex's hadrosauric buildings perched on thick alloy legs—reflected the rare beauty of that sky like the mirror on a cokehead's coffee table.

No one stopped to appreciate that beauty. The sky told them all what the satellite ring would confirm once they reached the command polyp at the low-lying island's highest point. Atlantica was back on the move.

Max awoke to the roar of wind, the *crack!* of breaking glass, and a nail-tip pain in his elbow. Someone was tugging on his cast.

"Christ, Jim, get up. I can't do this by myself."

Max's eyes slurped open. "Ow," he said. "Jerry?"

"Fuckin' A, Jim-bo." Jerry pulled at Max's arm again. "I got a wheelchair here. Now come on, get up. The shit's hitting the fan here, and we gotta move."

Max winced and sat up. He blinked in the dim light of an infirmary room. Jerry was wearing orderlies' greens, and, sure enough, he was leaning against a gleaming chrome wheelchair. Max grimaced and swung his feet onto the floor, then swung his behind around and into the wheelchair. Jerry turned it around and pushed it out the door and into a darkened hallway. Behind them, there was another crack of breaking glass, then a howling, and Max felt an icy wind cross the back of his neck. Jerry hurried along the corridor.

"You saw something down there, didn't you?" said Jerry.

"Mimi's dead. So's the rest of the crew on the studio. They were eaten by squids. How do you like that?" Max took a deep breath as Jerry pushed him into a pair of swinging doors. Beyond was a waiting room, rimmed with high frosted windows and a thick metal door marked *EXIT* on the opposite side. There was a candy machine in one corner, the front of which had been smashed with the fire axe that now lay propped against it. Max and Jerry were the only people in the room.

"A lot of people are dead," said Jerry. "A lot of people are going to be eaten by squids. Squids won, we lost. Next!"

Max noticed water seeping under the exit door. The puddle grew as he watched, like a bloodstain.

"Atlantica," said Max. Last time they'd spoken, Jerry had mentioned the storm had moved to the Caribbean and was getting ready to take on the Eastern Seaboard. "It's here now?"

"Here," said Jerry, "there. Everywhere. But particularly here. The GET bastards evacuated this morning, before their harbour swamped."

"And they just left us here?"

"Just left us here."

Max thought about that. He leaned back in the wheelchair.

"Where's here?"

"Sable Island," said Jerry. "GET's got a base here."

"So they just left us here," said Max.

"The guard said I wasn't worth the bullet it'd take to shoot me," said Jerry. "Asshole. We gotta get out of here, Jim-bo. We're going down."

"You shouldn't have pulled the stopcocks on the *Minnow*," said Max.

Jerry shrugged. "What can I say? I freaked out. You didn't see all those squid—all grabbing at the hull, *scraping* it like fingernails on a blackboard. Like they knew I was the one. Like they were smart. And that big one . . . Jesus, he could have torn the *Minnow* up the middle, and he was getting ready to. I could tell, Jimmy, and I freaked, all right? Sue me." Jerry's eyes went wide. "I freaked."

"I see," said Max.

Jerry nodded, and smiled in a panicky way. "You would have handled it different, right, Jim-bo? Big survivor guy. You would have had a better plan. Shit, buddy, I wish I'd had you on the deck. I may know television—but you . . . you got an instinct for this stuff."

"I'm not Jim," said Max. "My name is Max Fiddler. I am an actor."

Jerry squinted at him. "We're not back to this, are we? All right, Max, Jim, whatever you say. Tell me what you saw down there. See where those smart bastards lived? Anything we can use?"

Max looked around him. The entire floor was covered in water now and more was coming. He thought about the mountain and the giant squid—and the glimpses he'd had of the rest of it: the quivering walls of eggs that clung to the upper slopes of the sea mountain and the adult squids that circled them, guarding against the hungry smaller ones; the spectacle of a thousand squid, diving back to their homes in the trench, in sensible retreat from the spreading oil slick around the *Minnow*; and the behemoth, large beyond scale, that fell past him in the sun-dappled waters near the surface, trailing black strands of the same oil slick that would coat Max's own armour just a second later; its great black eye as large as Max, with a depth to it that, at first, Max mistook for intellect.

Maybe it was partly intellect he saw in the squid's eye, but he also recognized something more intimately familiar—and ultimately far more dangerous.

Max wheeled himself over to the exit door. He braced the wheels with his hands and opened the door with his foot.

"Is this a plan?" Jerry asked hopefully. "Because we could sure use a survival plan right now, Jim."

Rain hit him in a sheet. Max squinted through it, at the raging Atlantica outside. The ocean had indeed come up to the doorstep—if it were clearer outside, he would no doubt be able to see to a flat watery horizon, interrupted by nothing but the tops of a few buildings, and perhaps the semi-circle of a radar dish, poking above the waves.

Behind him, Jerry Wylde shouted something, but it could have been a dog barking at his heel; the roar and thunder of Atlantica was all.

OOPS

A little electric contraption inside played a song every time you opened it. *Da, da da Da. Da, da da Da.*

He hadn't heard the song in nearly ten years, but he would have recognized it even if it hadn't been Sarah Michelle Gellar on the front of the card: wooden stake clutched in one hand, hovering over her breast—her airbrush-smoothed face unmistakably stricken.

Whatever had happened with that stake, she hadn't meant it.

Inside, one word:

OOPS.

Yeah, he thought: Not much to choose from in the Apology section of the Shoppers Drug Mart greeting card aisle, and why would there be? You bought cards because your friend had a birthday, or got a job, or turned forty, or was going to graduate from something. Not because you fucked up.

He closed the card, left it finishing the Buffy riff on the dark shelf as he made his way back to the prescription counter. He spied movement of light and shadow in back, behind the low shelves of stock. He craned his neck.

"Is it ready yet?" he called.

She emerged, flashlight dangling from one hand. "I'm still looking."

"Oxytetracycline. Under 'O'."

"*Oh.*" She showed him a middle finger. "We're not the fucking library."

"Come on. I'm erupting here."

She tilted her head, raised an eyebrow, as if to say: *No shit.* He caught a glimpse of himself in the little mirror by the reading glasses. Florid boils the size of grapes crawled up his neck, swirling around the largest one—the first one—glistening on the edge of real eruption, just beneath his left eye. "No shit," he said.

She approached the counter, where bars of afternoon sunlight hit it. Her long ginger hair hung matted down the shoulder of her white pharmacist's smock. She chewed on her lower lip, and as he noticed that, he noticed a small blemish at the corner of her mouth. She must have seen him looking; her hand drifted up to cover it.

"That must really hurt," she said. "You got painkillers? Tylenol Threes? Vicodin? I know where to find lots of those."

"That's not wise," he said, "all things considered. I'm more worried about the infection than the pain. Stick with the Oxytetracyclene, thanks."

"Just trying to help."

"Thanks."

She went back to the shelves and cupboards, clicked on her flashlight, and he wondered: *What was she even doing here? She sure as shit wasn't a pharmacist.*

He took out his own penlight, found his way back to Apologies. *Sorry We Missed You*, said a clean-cut young man sporting a vintage leisure suit and drawing a bow and arrow on a circa-1972 archery range. *How About a Do-Over?* was inside a card with a squalling baby wearing an upturned bowl of pasta on her head. *Don't Quack Up Over This* was behind a cartoon showing three ducks in straitjackets, in a padded cell, glaring at the ceiling. He clicked the penlight off and stood in the dim, grey light that was all the gathering storm outside would allow.

At least he had options.

"Hey," she called from the back, "do you have anything to drink?"

"I assume you don't mean fruit punch," he said, and she said, "Fuck no."

"You proposing a trade?"

"No. I'm talking celebration." She emerged again, and shone her flashlight on a candy-jar-sized container of pills. "See? Found it."

"Great." He dug into his backpack and pulled out a small silver hip flask. An indeterminate amount of scotch sloshed inside.

She had two small plastic cups ready by the time he made it up the aisle, and he measured a dram into each. She lifted hers, took a delicate sip, and made a face. "Nasty," she said, appreciatively.

"Not used to the hard stuff, are you?" he said, and she motioned to his cup with her flashlight: "Bottoms up," she said.

"Bottoms up."

He set the empty cup down and looked at the jar. There had to be a thousand capsules inside. He picked it up, hefted it. "I don't need all that," he said. "Give me a week's worth."

"How many's that?"

He squinted. "You're not from the pharmacy, are you?"

"I am. But I don't work—didn't work back here. I do cash. I was on cash when it happened."

He poured another dram into his cup. She still had lots left in hers and waved him away when he offered. That was fine; she was going to talk about it now. He let his mind wander as she told her story: about how she'd been on shift two hours when the lights seemed to flare, and dim, and then there came a swishing sound. She had been helping a customer, an older man in a light grey business suit. The swishing sound was the sound of the fabric collapsing in on itself, now that the man had vanished.

"Just *swish*," she said, and wiggled her fingers. "Not just him. Everybody. *Swish*."

"Almost everybody."

"Yeah."

"Why didn't you go home?" he asked, and she motioned to the glass storefront. The clouds were massing dark again. And, he saw, the insects were back. They tapped on the windows, and a cyclone of them swirled over the parking lot.

"You've seen it out there. You've *been* out there." She finished her scotch in a gulp, and this time didn't stop him when he poured some more. "I may be crazy but I'm not stupid. There's food in here. Lots of water, in bottles. And with the dispensary in the pharmacy—I thought I could do some good. Because that's important now—right?"

Important, yes. Too late—also likely.

But he didn't say that. "Right," he told her. "Have you done some good?"

She shrugged. "You're the first one to come by. It's been three days. So you tell me."

Although it hurt to do so, he smiled. "You've done some good."

"Think it'll make a difference?"

He sighed. "If I knew," he said, "I don't think I'd still be here."

She asked him more questions: Had he seen anybody else since it happened? When did the boils start? After the event? Had he tried to pray?

Yes, from a distance; and yes, the first one came as he stood alone at the bus stop outside his house, blinking at the flaring sun.

And yes. He had tried to pray.

"But before I get going too long, the question always becomes: What to say? At this point in the game—what do you say?"

She nodded, and announced that she thought she was getting drunk.

"I shouldn't be doing this," she said, flicking the edge of her empty cup with her thumb, knocking it over. "Maybe this is why—I'm still here."

"Drinking on the job?" He considered that. "Maybe."

"You should take one of those pills. Make you better."

"Maybe," he said, and unscrewed the top of the jar. He pulled out a capsule—half red, half yellow—and put it on his tongue. He swallowed it dry.

She got unsteadily to her feet, turned and went into a drawer. She came out with an empty pill bottle, and handed it to him.

"Fill it up," she said, and he did.

"Thank you," he said.

"You're welcome," she replied. "Is there anything else I can do for you?" And she repeated, in a pleading, accommodating tone: "Anything?"

"Yes," he said, and he was glad—and a little sad—to see what looked like relief in her eye when he told her what he needed most.

━━━

Da, da da Da.

I am sorry, though for what I do not know, he wrote as he stood on the sidewalk outside the Shoppers Drug Mart. The locusts lighted on his shoulders, in his hair, before they were carried away in the hot wind that swirled over top the empty cars and trucks that sat empty in the parking lot.

Da, da da Da.

He looked at it again—and crossed it out, and wrote, *Forgive me.* Then he scratched that out, and circled OOPS!, and signed his name below that, and shut the card. He held it lightly between thumb and forefinger, and raised it over his head—and stood there until the music stopped, until the wind snatched it from him and carried it away with the locusts.

"Thank you for the pen!" he said, back inside. "Hey—thanks!" He took two more steps into the store. "Hey!"

In the end, he slipped the borrowed pen into the breast pocket of the pharmacist's smock where he found it, curled empty like a sleeping cat on the floor behind the counter.

THE NOTHING BOOK OF THE DEAD

Dearest Neal,
   You will receive many gifts through your long life, and all of them, you will find, are precisely what you make of them—nothing more and nothing less.
   I remain curious as to what you will make of this one.
   Love Forever,
   Grandmother
(from the frontispiece of Neal R. Smith's *The Nothing Book*, originally published 1974 by Harmony Books)

––•–

Dear ~~Granny~~
   Grandmother
Thank you for the nice present. I thought it might be a Hardy Boys book or an Alfred Hitchcock and the Three ~~Investigaters~~ **Investigators** book because it was about the right size. Imagine my ~~suprize~~ **surprise** when I opened the present and found that it was a book ~~abowt~~ **about** NOTHING. All blank pages! It is the most stupid present I ever got and mom made me ~~right~~ **write** you a thank you letter so I am writing it in this book and ~~sent it~~ sending it back to you as a lesson to send me something good next time.
   ~~Your Stupid Grandson~~
   Love
Neal
(from the dedication to Neal R. Smith's *The Nothing Book*, ibid)

––•–

Dearest Neal,

You are very welcome for your gift this Christmas and thank you for your wittily composed inscription. I promise in future years that I shall calibrate my choice in gifts so as to better accommodate your delicate sensibilities. In the meantime, I have taken the liberty of returning this one, and your inscription, with corrections in spelling appended. I have not for the most part commented upon your grammar and syntax, because I am one of those who believes such things accumulate into that rare and precious quality we name a writer's voice.

And so I return your Nothing Book, with notes appended and this brief inscription, and the remainder of the pages blank, that you might fill it with more fine prose such as this. Should you care to send me that prose, in whatever form you might choose, I would be very happy to read it and return comments.

Love Forever,

Grandmother

p.s. For your birthday, perhaps I shall send along a G.I. Joe playset, the one with the miniature Egyptian mummy. Doubtless you will think of me as you fiddle about with its vulgar contents.

(from the Introduction to Neal R. Smith's *The Nothing Book*, Ibid)

Chapter 1
The Vicars of Thun-Krakar

The many-jewelled city of Thun-Krakar boiled with the anger of its inhabitants. The swordsman went in through the front gate and immediately realized his mistake. Although he was the finest swordsman in all of Italy, he feared he was no match for the wrath of the evil Vicars of Thun-Krakar.

They stood in a line inside the gate. "Would you like to come round for tea?" said their leader, the imposing and deadly Father Postlewait.

A trap, thought the swordsman, whose name happened to be Eric. He pulled out his deadly blade Lasagne and rushed them. A lot of blood soon followed and Eric the swordsman stepped over the bleeding Vicars' bodies and made for the tavern.

(from Neal R. Smith's novel fragment entitled "An Italian in Thun-Krakar," *The Nothing Book*, Ibid)

Dearest Grandson,

What a wonderful attempt at the narrative form! Truly, you are a gem of a child; a genuine prodigy! Why, I see in this the influence of Edgar Rice Burroughs, Alfred Lord Tennyson, and Monty Python, all rolled up into one—with a marvellously discreet approach to violence so often absent in the films and novels of the past decade. I do wonder where Thun-Krakar might be located, in relation to Rome. Is it a Spanish town? Perhaps it is farther off in the other direction, in the Balkans perhaps, and the Vicars are English missionaries at work saving the souls of the perennially cross folk who make their homes there?

No, grandson, do not answer. Let my own imagination do the work. It helps to pass the hours in this accursed ward room.

Love,

Grandmother

(from the end-notes to Neal R. Smith's novel fragment entitled "An Italian in Thun-Krakar," *The Nothing Book*, Ibid)

A Potion to Cure All Illness

Mix Together In One Cauldron Made of Iron:

5 Fingernail Clippings from the Hand of a MURDERER
The Right Whisker of a BLACK CAT
1 cup, EPSOM SALTS
1 Teaspoon, GARLIC POWDER
1 shot, IRISH WHISKEY
1 can, ROOTBEER
Bring to a boil while chanting ~~EPLUBUM F'THAGIS SILFU G'TAUGH seven times.~~ This potion will CURE ALL ILLNESS.

(from Neal's R. Smith's "Tome of Power," *The Nothing Book*, Ibid)

Dearest Grandson,

Thank you for the kind thoughts—but I would much prefer to read another chapter of the adventure of Eric the Italian

swordsman, or perhaps a poem (it need not rhyme) as I recuperate in this dreary hospital room. Please write another of those. And please, whilst I am away, stay out of the attic, and my library there. That is for older boys and girls. And some of the books—such as the one which I intuit inspired this recipe—they are unwholesome. I should never have kept them. Especially not that one.

Please, Neal, do not inscribe anything else from that book. That, as I know your mother would say, is an order.

I think a poem is the thing now. Don't you?

Love,

Grandmother

(from the Introduction to Neal R. Smith's "Garden of Stupid Verse," *The Nothing Book*, Ibid)

There once was an old lady from Fen-a-lan
Who thought she knew stuff about channelin
But what she was hearing
Was not so endearing
It was just the Pied Piper of Hamelin
(from Neal R. Smith's "Garden of Stupid Verse," *The Nothing Book*, Ibid)

Dearest Grandson,
What a strange verse.
You're right, though; that's all it was.
Love,
Gran
(from the end of *The Nothing Book*, Part I, Ibid)

Dear Grandmother
I love you and miss you and I am sorry I did not come to the hospital in time. Mom was away from the house when the hospital called and it was three hours before she came back and I could tell her what they said. I waited for Mom instead of coming right over on the bus. Mom said it was okay but I know you would have wanted to see me before you died. We were too late by the time Mom came home and I could tell her. I am really sorry. So I am going to put this book

in the coffin like they used to do with the mummies in Egypt so you will have something to read wherever you are.

Hopefully nobody sees me do it because I don't want to get in more trouble.

Love

Your ~~stupid~~ grandson

Neal

(from the introduction to *The Nothing Book*, Part II, Ibid)

I SAW

(marginalia from the Introduction to *The Nothing Book*, Part II, Ibid)

December 15, 1979

This is the first entry in Neal Smith's journal. I am Neal Smith, obviously. I'm a Grade Ten student at Fenlan District Secondary School, and I don't know what I'm going to be writing in here. I thought this book was gone forever. But when I found it in the attic of the old house, while I was getting the Christmas lights, I thought I should start something in it.

My grandmother gave it to me when I was a kid. And I wrote some things in it, which you, who are reading this now, can look back and see. I am not doing that now myself because what I wrote was ~~pretty lame.~~**NO**

I said I am in Grade 10. I am in the Advanced stream, which means I can go to Grade 13 and university if I keep my grades up. So far so good. My average in Grade Nine was 83%. If I can keep it above 80 by Grade 12, I'll win an Ontario Scholar award. That would be cool.

I don't have a girlfriend right now but I think Cathy Gervais likes me. She has a locker two over from mine and says hi every morning. She's really pretty and really nice. The only trouble is she is going around with Mike Palmer, who is in Grade 11 and has a moustache. Maybe she is tired of him. In the cafeteria last week, I heard her make a joke that Mike was getting love handles from all the beer he drank on the weekend.

Maybe she will break up with him over Christmas.

(from "The Journal of Neal R. Smith," *The Nothing Book*, Ibid)

XOX

(marginalia from "The Journal of Neal R. Smith," *The Nothing Book*, Ibid)

December 18, 1979

We went to Toronto today to do Christmas shopping. Well to be honest Mom went Christmas shopping. She drove in with me and Kevin, and we all split up at the Eaton Centre for a few hours. Kevin and ~~me~~ I went up Yonge Street to look at Mr. Gameways Ark. It was cool; Kevin is a big-time wargamer and has been trying to get me to play Squad Leader with him. I wasn't going to at first but after spending some time at Gameways Ark I might just.

It is in a big old bank building, and on the top floor there is a club for gaming where mostly they play Advanced Dungeons and Dragons. That is not the cool thing about it (although I bought a set of dice and a lead necromancer miniature from Ral Partha, and checked out the Dungeon Master's Guide, which I will probably buy on Boxing Day with Christmas money). Someone had gone and built a full-sized mock-up of the bridge of the U.S.S. Enterprise right in the middle of the club. We took a picture, which when it is developed I'll stick in here, of me in the Captain's Chair. I wish there was one of these closer to Fenlan. Maybe not this one though; Kevin told me that they run a witch's coven here at night. I believe him.

But that wasn't the biggest news of the trip. On the way back we went into Sam the Record Man on Yonge Street. They should call it The World's Biggest Record Store, but maybe The World's Biggest Bookstore across the street has the trademark for that. Who do you think we saw there? Cathy Gervais!

She was with her cousin Pat, who is not as pretty and lives in Willowdale, which is just up the subway. Cathy said she was in town visiting for a week before Christmas. Kevin said we should hang around and we did for an hour. But Pat didn't like Kevin that much (I think) and whispered something to Cathy and Cathy said they had to go. But before they left she said, just to me, "I'm really sorry Neal. Maybe we can hang out more when I get back to Fenlan."

It was a good day in Toronto. ~~Maybe~~ I will have a girlfriend by 1980.

December 22, 1979

I should be careful what I wish for. This afternoon at the mall Mike Palmer said he would beat me up. He told me to stay away from his girl. I told him nothing was going on but maybe something is going on because he called me a lying piece of shit and got ready to hit me. He only stopped because he saw a security guard coming. But he said he would get me later.

~~Maybe I should stay away from Cathy.~~

(from "The Journal of Neal R. Smith," *The Nothing Book*, Ibid)

December 24, 1979
Dear Grandson,
I have taken (Illegible). He will not (illegible) again.
Merry Christmas.
Love Forever,
(Illegible)

December 25, 1979
Who are you who is reading my journal?
(from the final entry of "The Journal of Neal R. Smith," *The Nothing Book*, Ibid)

Dear Grandmother,

It is New Year's Eve now. Mom is going out with a new friend so it is ~~just me here.~~ **just Kevin and I**. I just read through the whole book again. I was scared to, but I did. I remember now—I put the book in your coffin at the funeral home. No one saw me. Unless Mom snuck up and took it out when I wasn't looking, there is no way it could have gotten to the attic.

I saw that it is all marked up—some of it from when I was a kid and would show it to you. But some too after you died. The handwriting is the same as before. I think you are trying to talk to me from wherever you are. Maybe you are stuck in between this world and the next one.

~~Maybe you should go to the light?~~

Love
Neal

Dear Grandmother,

You crossed out my last sentence. Is it because there is no light where you are?

Love Neal

Send Kevin away. Write me a poem.
Did you hurt Mike Palmer? He is in the hospital you know.
A poem.
(from an untitled section dated December 31, 1979, *The Nothing Book*, Ibid)

———

O spirit of the Underworld, who walked in the form of Beatrice Paulson when upon the earth, make thy presence known. I, Norman Fuller, High Priest of the Gameways Order of Light, do call upon thee with the strength of this circle to make thyself manifest here in the sacred aerie of the Ark.

(handwritten note accompanying a pentagram illustration, rendered using red ballpoint pen and a math-set compass, *The Nothing Book*, Ibid)

———

Dear Grandmother
These people want to help you. They know what they are doing. Please do as they ask.
Love,
Neal
There once was an old lady from Fen-a-lon.
Who thought she knew stuff about channelin.
Stop, Mister Norman Fuller. You cannot trick me. I know it is you telling Neal what to write in that book.
I'm sorry, Grandmother. It's me now. Mr. Fuller wanted to speak with you. I made him give me the book back. Please stop hurting him.
Send him away.
He's gone.
How did you get there?
Kevin drove.
Is he old enough to drive?
Yes.
Liar.
(text accompanying an illustration in the style of Jackson Pollock in deep red ink, applied so intensively that the paper has torn in several places, *The Nothing Book*, Ibid)

———

January 13, 1980

The trip to Mr. Gameways Ark went fine. Kevin drove there and back in his dad's Nova. We listened to the Sex Pistols and Bauhaus on the tape deck. Kevin was an excellent driver.

I bought the Dungeon Masters Guide with the Christmas money. And I took the Nothing Book upstairs. We all know what happened after that. The guys up there were cool. They aren't going to make me pay for the Captain's chair and Norm got cleaned up in the washroom fine after his nosebleed so we didn't have to call an ambulance. We just got out of there.

Up until last night, I hadn't told Mom about any of this. But when we got back, I made up my mind to tell her. It was easy to do. She was already worried because we were gone so long. So when she asked if it really took ten hours to buy a Dungeon Masters Guide, I took the Nothing Book out of the bag and sat her down at the kitchen table.

I was afraid she just wouldn't believe me. But she just read through it and cried and gave me a hug. She said that she'd had no idea that I'd put the book in the coffin. She didn't know how it got into the attic. She recognized the handwriting though. She believed me all right. She said it was just like something her mother would do.

Then she told me that she almost forgot: Cathy Gervais had been calling all day. Under the circumstances, she asked, did I really want to call her back, because she had sounded upset.

I called her but I am not going to get into what we talked about because it's private. And this book isn't private, right Grandmother?

We all agreed on one thing though. ~~We aren't going to be scared.~~

(from "The Journal of Neal R. Smith," continued, *The Nothing Book*, Ibid)

———

April 5, 1983

Hello Mother,

If you're there, still, I hope that you're doing well in whatever place it is you're dwelling.

It's your daughter here—Andrea—Mrs. Smith—the mother of Neal. Your beloved grandson. Do you still recall names, I wonder, after so long in Limbo?

If you're reading the date inscription above, you will realize that it's been some time since anyone opened your Nothing Book—or rather, Neal's. After the last entry, we had a very long talk about what to do. I'll be honest, Mother, we considered destroying it: tossing it onto a fire, or dousing it in a tub of acid. Neal wouldn't have it, though. He had given some thought to the metaphysics of the book, and come to believe it was at the very least a portal to the afterlife, but possibly more disturbing, that the book was the afterlife itself: a tiny universe that existed within the pages of the book, where upon your death you came to inhabit. Books can be powerful things, in the hands of the right reader, can't they? The authors of those old books that Neal showed me in the trunk in the attic certainly make that claim.

We didn't destroy the book (obviously). Instead, I slipped it into a large freezer bag, removed all the air from it, and froze it in a bucket of water. That's right; for the past three years it has been sitting at the bottom of the freezer, underneath what's left of the wedding cake.

What's left of my wedding cake. I've been thinking about my wedding, and the few years after it that I was able to spend with Neal's father. The two of you never got on, did you? Remember when we told you that we were going to be married? What was it you said? "Good. The koi pond needs cleaning. He looks like he has a reasonably strong back." That may have been about the kindest thing you ever said to him. The happiest I'd ever seen you around him was when he got sick. In retrospect, I'm amazed that you managed to keep a straight face at the viewing.

I wonder if he's with you there. I can't imagine he is.

Neal's not with you. He's gone away from here, for now. He's in school—I'll give you that much. He's a smart young man, and he kept his grades up and scholarships are helping out. He's studying journalism—in spite of, rather than because of, the typically heartless notes you gave him when he was a little boy. And that girl he fancied—Cathy? They did wind up "going around" in high school. Again, no thanks to you. She stood by that boy you hurt (I'm assuming it was you) while he recuperated, and it was a year before she noticed Neal again and he was heartbroken the whole time. When they got together they lasted about two weeks. And then it was heartbreak all over again.

What a wonderful gift you gave your beloved grandson.

I'm having a glass of wine right now. It's Merlot, from California. I remember how you used to like your Merlot. Well you can't have any now.

I see you're not marking up my letter. I wonder, will you do it later tonight? When I've closed the covers and you can tear my words apart at your leisure? Or do you only do that for Neal?

Or are you truly dead now?

Let's say you're not. Let's say that when Neal wrote that funny little incantation in the book—the one you crossed out—next to that recipe that he took mostly from Page CVII of that other "nothing" book—the untitled one with the crumbly pages and all the criss-crossing stitch-work on the leather cover—the unwholesome one—let's say that incantation made a place for you, wherever it is you are.

Well, how about, while you're busy marking up that last run-on sentence, we take a look-see through that book, and see what else we can find?

How about this one?

(from the Epilogue, accompanying a large red stain, partially occluding a matrix of hieroglyphs alongside a marginal note of limited legibility, *The Nothing Book*, Ibid)

DRAKEELA MUST DIE

The drakeela hid in the cloakroom during recess. It didn't like fresh air, and of course the sun was poison to its kind: they all knew that, even Lucy who wasn't allowed to watch the Sunday Monster Movie and had to be told what a drakeela was. At 10:30 a.m. the bell rang, and Mrs. Shelby said line up everyone. Mrs. Shelby looked up and down the line and wiggled her fingers as though she were counting. But she never counted the drakeela as it crab-crawled between the fluorescents over the art tables and twanged its thick dark fingernails on the sheet-metal ductwork that hung over the make-believe kitchen.

Leonard, their official leader, charted its progress along the ceiling and down the corridor to the far end of the cloakroom. There it hunched, resentful and out of breath, as the rest of them pulled on their galoshes and did up their snowsuits and tried not to look up.

They met behind the garbage dumpster near the gym every recess, and Leonard would make every one of them report, like secret agents.

It was Susie's job to watch the drakeela when it arrived, because she was the only one of them who lived across the street and could be at school before sunrise. The drakeela came with its father, who drove a big white sports car with tinted windows and always hid its face under a heavy coat and wide-brimmed hat. No one could tell who came to take the drakeela home—even Susie wasn't allowed to stay up that late.

Jason's job was to follow the drakeela whenever it put up its hand and asked to go make a pee-pee. If there was someone else in the washroom, Jason peered through the grill at the bottom of the door and watched as the drakeela pounced. It pushed its victim against the urinals or the sinks or the side of a toilet stall, gripped the face with its long-fingered hands and slipped its hollowed-out baby fangs high up the victim's nostrils. There would be a struggle, then the victim would relax as the blood and nose-spit began to flow. Later, Mrs. Shelby would get out a fresh Kleenex, wipe up the blood and scold the drakeela's victim for picking his nose so much. Jason had watched the drakeela do this five times, and hadn't been caught once.

Lucy watched the drakeela when it was in the classroom. Mrs. Shelby always gave the drakeela extra attention, and whenever anyone was mean to it she would get angry.

"Timmy Slitzken is a special child," she would shout, waving her finger. "Don't you go bothering Timmy." When Mrs. Shelby was away from it, Lucy reported, the drakeela spent a lot of time folded up in the long wooden toy cupboard that was under the blackboard. Sometimes it would lurk around the pretend-kitchen, making noises while the girls tried to play.

Reading and printing was a year away for all of them, so Leonard had to keep the reports in his head. It was a good thing, they all agreed, that Leonard was the smartest boy in the morning kindergarten and remembering wasn't hard for him.

On the first Tuesday in February, Leonard thought he had compiled enough reports to make a plan.

The sky was slate grey and it had snowed for two days straight, and on Tuesday most of the children in morning kindergarten brought their crazy carpets. Jason wanted to join the rest of them on the steep hill at the back of the yard, but Leonard overruled him. The plan was ready and they all had to be there for it and that was final.

The space behind the dumpster was choked with a high drift of powdery snow, and Leonard and Susie dug away enough of it so they could all squeeze in. "Everybody here?" said Leonard. "Then good. Here's the plan."

Leonard unzipped his Ninja Turtle backpack and began handing out the equipment. That morning, Leonard had glued together four wooden crosses from Popsicle sticks, and he passed them around. He hadn't been able to find any garlic, but his mother used garlic salt on everything, and before school he made a quick pass by the spice rack. He threw the salt on everyone, then pocketed the shaker and took out his G.I. Joe canteen. All the Catholic kids in town went to school down by the river at St. Cyprian's and wouldn't even talk to public school kids, so Leonard had filled his canteen at the drinking fountain in the Presbyterian church his parents went to. The holy water tasted stale and plasticky, but according to every one of Mr. Hammer's Drakeela movies you had to have it, so they all took a swig anyway.

Then Leonard handed out the rulers.

They were twelve-inch wooden rulers from the Grade One-Two classroom down the hall and were covered in drawings of machine guns and jet airplanes and trucks. Leonard and Jason had worked on these all Sunday afternoon in Jason's dad's garage. Now, where they would have said "12," the rulers were sharpened to a point. Jason said, "Watch out for slivers." Lucy giggled but Leonard said, "Mind what Jason says," in a voice that was very grown-up even for Leonard. Lucy stopped giggling and paid attention.

"These are for the drakeela," said Leonard, holding up the rulers. "They go straight into his heart, just like on TV."

Next he lifted the cross.

"The drakeela's ascared of these, so if he comes at you, hold it up."

He held the cross in front of him to demonstrate, then put it away too.

"Don't look in its eyes. It doesn't like mirrors. Stay together. Drakeelas getcha when you're alone. Drakeelas hate daytime. You can't shoot it with guns 'cause it just laughs. You ready?"

Jason nodded first, then Susie and finally Lucy.

On a bathroom trip that morning, Susie had propped open the door to the gym, and now she skipped around the dumpster and pulled it open.

With Leonard taking the lead, the four of them filed into the dark gymnasium.

When they came to the door to kindergarten, Lucy said she was scared and wanted to wait for Mrs. Shelby to get back from the Staff Room.

"That won't work, dummy," said Jason. "She's the teacher, she'll make us stop."

Leonard didn't even comment. He lifted his cross and pulled the door open a crack.

The drakeela had turned off the lights and shut the blinds when everyone left, and the rooms beyond were shadows of black and grey. He opened the door wider, so they could all see. The classroom, at the far end of kindergarten, was only visible in the dusty light that filtered through the venetian blinds. Closer, the little corridor that led to the washrooms and the cloakroom was impenetrably dark.

Leonard stepped inside, and motioned the others to follow. Their snow pants whisked nervously as they moved along the corridor into the cloakroom. They left a trail of dirty water and their boots squeaked. Ahead in the dark, Susie heard a sound like flies.

"Shhh!" hissed Leonard, and held his hand to Jason's chest as though they were a pair of G.I.s sneaking up on an enemy camp. The buzzing oscillated—loud and soft, high and low. Lucy was still scared, but she kept quiet.

The fly-sounds stopped abruptly as they entered the cloakroom. Now all four of them had their crosses out, and they held them high in front, like the Sunday TV matinees by Mr. Hammer said to.

"Think holy thoughts," said Leonard. "They can't getcha when you're pure."

The light fixtures rattled in the ceiling over their heads, and Susie gasped as she realized: the drakeela was moving, over their heads, back behind them.

"It's getting away!" Susie squealed, and in spite of herself Lucy giggled again. The rattle in the fixtures stopped, and an instant later they heard the claw-on-metal sound of the drakeela crawling over the ductwork in the main room.

"Get him!" yelled Leonard.

"Come on!" Jason hollered.

Hearts pounding, the four of them turned on their heels and, slipping only a little through the muddy water trail they'd left coming in, ran back into the kindergarten. They were all breathless and hot in their snowsuits, and when they looked around, the drakeela was nowhere to be seen. Leonard frowned.

"Drakeelas are tricky," said Leonard. "Watch everywhere at once. You never know where they'll be."

They watched everywhere at once. Lucy watched the toy cupboard, which was halfway open and so dark that it could be holding three drakeelas and she would never be able to tell. Susan watched the art table, draped in big sheets of construction paper that hung off the sides and wafted back and forth in the breeze from the radiators. Jason paid attention to the cloakroom hallway, which also led to the washrooms where the drakeela had pounced at least five times. Leonard kept his eyes up, watching the shadows of the blinds as they crisscrossed the ceiling.

They watched everywhere, and all at once, but Leonard was right about the drakeela being tricky. It had hidden underneath Mrs. Shelby's desk, where Mrs. Shelby put her knees. While the four of them watched the ceilings and cupboards and tables and washrooms, the drakeela cricked its back and bent its knees and with a breath like a winter wind pulled itself up to its full height over the desktop.

"Hum!" Susie exclaimed, putting her hand to her mouth as she saw the drakeela and it saw her. Its feet were on Mrs. Shelby's chair, so it loomed almost as high as a grown-up. Its big orange eyes glowed in the dim light, and its jaw clicked as it opened and closed. It made a noise like a little kitten. And then it started to buzz.

Leonard swallowed hard. The drakeela reached down to the desktop, and its long-nailed fingers closed around something. It buzzed louder as it lifted the thing into the air, swooped it back and forth. Susie and Lucy had a hard time recognizing it, and Leonard wasn't paying attention, but Jason got it immediately.

The drakeela was holding the Concord. It was plastic and grimy; its stickers had been coming off since Halloween and it was not even as long as the twelve-inch ruler Jason held in his fist. Until Christmas, the Concord was Jason's favourite toy in the toy cupboard. The drakeela stopped buzzing.

"Play?" Its bright orange eyes blinked, and it leaned forward so far that Jason thought it might fall on its face. But the drakeela kept its balance and made the Concord do a loop-the-loop.

"Hi," said the drakeela. "Play?"

Jason barely heard the twelve-inch ruler as it fell from his hand and clattered on the linoleum floor. He took a step toward the drakeela, and then another.

"Sure," said Jason. "Lemme see that."

He put out his hands, and the drakeela stretched and bent so that only its toes were touching the top of Mrs. Shelby's desk. The drakeela's clawed hands swung down on Jason, and he reached to the Concord that it held.

"Wolton! "Leonard yelled. Wolton was Jason's last name, and Leonard only used it when he was so mad he was going to beat Jason's head in. This time, though, Leonard wasn't mad. He only knew he had to get Jason's attention away from the drakeela—when you look into a drakeela's eyes, it's got you. Leonard yelled "Wolton" again, and this time it got Jason's attention.

"Hey!" Jason looked away, and then he looked back, and then his face crumpled into a hot red ball and he started to cry. The drakeela remained above him, still offering the Concord.

"Play. Here." The drakeela pushed the Concord down on him. "Take it."

But Jason just sat down and wept. The other three stood and watched. Susie wanted to go and get Jason a Kleenex or something, but Lucy stopped her.

Leonard was getting his cross ready.

"Come on. We got 'im."

The drakeela was almost on top of Jason now, pushing and prodding him with the wing of the Concord. The three of them lifted up their Popsicle-stick crosses and marched forward in a straight line.

"Hey! Drakeela!" said Leonard. "Look at this!"

The drakeela looked, and as it saw the three crosses its eyes became wide and round as pool balls. The drakeela dropped the Concord, lifted away from Jason and fell back against the desktop. Papers went flying as it scrambled to get away.

"You like that?" yelled Leonard." Stupid stupid drakeela head?"

Lucy and Susie joined in, in sing-song:

"Stupid stupid drakeela head," they all sang as the drakeela stumbled off the far side of the desk.

"Stupid stupid drakeela head," they sang as Lucy and Leonard circled around either side of the desk. Jason wheezed and sobbed and picked up the twelve-inch ruler he'd dropped when the drakeela took control of his mind. Then he stood up and joined the chorus:

"Stupid stupid drakeela head, stupid stupid drakeela head!"

The drakeela managed to get to its feet before Lucy and Leonard could get around the desk. It had nearly made it to the toy cupboard by the time they had caught up with it. Susie touched her cross to the drakeela's hand, and it screamed with a sound like a strangling kitten. When the wood came away, there was a burn mark on its knuckles, like it had been branded.

The drakeela stuck its head into the cupboard and tried to get inside, but Leonard managed to get ahold of its legs. When it kicked, it nearly sent him flying. Leonard reached into his belt-loop for the twelve-inch ruler and tried to stick the drakeela with it, but it was too far inside.

"I can't hold on!" yelled Leonard.

"I'm coming!" hollered Jason.

"Wait for us!" squealed Lucy.

It was a tough fight, but together, Lucy and Leonard and Susie and Jason managed to pull the drakeela out of the toy cupboard and lay it on its back. It thrashed back and forth, its legs going like pinwheels, and its fangs nearly gave Leonard a cut on his hand.

Leonard got his twelve-inch ruler. He took a deep breath. Susie took hold of the pointed end and put it against the drakeela's chest.

"That's where its heart is," said Susie. "I know 'cause I'm a doctor."

The drakeela's eyes were screwed shut. Its shoulders and knees trembled where Jason and Lucy held it pinned.

"You're not a doctor," said Leonard.

"Am too," said Susie. "Ask Lucy. She's a nurse."

Leonard was about to ask Lucy when a shudder went through the twelve-inch ruler and he almost lost his grip. The drakeela coughed, and its mouth spasmed open. Its two thin fangs slipped out from beneath its leathery lips for the barest instant. They looked like nails, Leonard thought. Little nails like his mom used to hang pictures in the living room.

The drakeela's lips folded back over its mouth, and its eyes opened. Their glow was diminished by shadows, but the eyes still reached up to Leonard. They pleaded, and tried to draw him down.

"No way!" screamed Jason. He let go of the drakeela's knees, reared up on his own knees and slammed his hand down on the top of the ruler. The fabric of the drakeela's T-shirt pushed in as the tip of the ruler slipped over a rib, but Jason's weight wasn't enough to push the stake in by itself.

Leonard shook his head rapidly and said, "That was close." He put his hands on top of Jason's and added his own weight.

The drakeela's T-shirt began to redden.

Lucy let go of the drakeela's shoulders and grabbed hold of the ruler as well. The drakeela flailed, and it snapped and bit and shrieked as the splintering tip of the ruler pierced its ribcage. It was harder than any of them had imagined—on Mr. Hammer's matinees, the stake always went in after one or two whacks from a mallet, and the drakeela just hissed a bit before it got killed. Killing this drakeela was hard work.

Finally, Susan piled on top. Combined, the weight of the four of them was enough to send the ruler the rest of the way into its chest, and the drakeela's cold, congealing blood shot up like a geyser. Its eyes shut tight, then opened wide, and then they became still, their orange glow extinguished.

Jason started to sob. He had pressed down too hard on top of the ruler when he jumped on it, and now his own hands were bleeding freely. The other three were fine, but hearing Jason, one by one they followed suit. Leonard was the last, and his tears came reluctantly.

The recess bell rang at 10:50 a.m., but Mrs. Semple, the vice-principal, told the kids from the morning kindergarten to stay outside for a while longer. When one of the kids said she had to go to the bathroom, Mrs. Semple had one of the older children take her around to the big kids' washrooms on the other side of the school.

Mrs. Shelby stayed in the kindergarten until the police and the ambulance came. She ordered the hallway from the gym to the door to the schoolyard sealed off, so that no one could get to the kindergarten but her.

She looked at little Timmy Slitzken for what seemed like a long time. They were all so small at this age, and this one . . . There was something precious in the special ones, wasn't there? Mrs. Shelby knew that she should have called the parents already, but she couldn't bring herself to. Not right away.

The parents of the special ones had seen so much pain already. Who knew what Mr. Slitzken would do in the face of this tragedy? Mrs. Shelby felt a February chill as the door to the yard opened for the paramedics' stretcher, and she shivered.

BLACK HEN À LA FORD

We cooked her, feathers and all, during the last hundred miles of that long drive to Agatha's Perch . . . and oh, her fume filled the cab with such a wonderful, peaceable scent. One might drift off to sleep by it—and that is precisely what I did.

I dreamed of the kitchen, hot with the afternoon sun and fire of the wood stove, the steam off the slowly cooling meat pies on the sill. . . . Gudrun, my dear sister, humming an old chant as she rolled out dough for more—out of sight, in the pantry. . . .

Were it not for that, I almost might have forgotten—what I'd come to do.

———

William had gutted her with an old scaling knife. After wiping the blood off, he applied the blade to coring crab-apples we'd filched from the same farm as we'd found her. He stuffed them up inside the cavity until she was ready to burst. He shoved salted roast peanuts and some pork rinds up between skin and breast, and he took two layers of thick-gauge tinfoil, wrapped her up tight and wedged her against the exhaust manifold. Then he turned the oven on—that's to say the oven of his truck, by driving it fast on the straightaways and too fast on the turns, into the foothills, up to the Perch.

"Black Hen à la Ford," he said when he finally cracked the hood and pulled her free.

She was hot in her bright shell, and he tossed that hen from hand to hand as we all gathered in the late afternoon haze, in the shade of that old house on the ridge.

"Voila!" he hollered, and we all howled.

William is a good grandson. Not the best, but I'd never dream of telling him that.

There were a lot of grandchildren at the Perch already and more to arrive before nightfall. Grandchildren, and nieces and nephews—great-grandchildren, maybe even a great-great-grandchild.

I lose track of them all, but I know the families: Alfred's and Rainer's, Kerr's and Lars's, and of course Gunnar's.

It was their turn this time. So of course they were there.

Janet, Gunnar's wife, had set up long tables on the front lawn, and dangled paper patio lanterns above them from the tree branches. She'd even arranged for two old blue plastic privies, side by side next to the old garden house.

Not far from that, a long green hose dribbled water into the grass. It was a good idea; you could wash up after doing your business, without ever feeling need of setting foot indoors.

Janet took the chicken from William and ran up the path to the house so William could go to the back and get my things.

There wasn't much to get: just an old suitcase with a new frock and a set of iron fry-pans—wrapped up in newspaper and covered in a green garbage bag. I packed them myself two days back, with great care. Wouldn't do for them to rust; it'd taken decades to season them right.

William carried them in one trip to the long porch, set them down next to where Janet had laid his offering. Then it was off to the privy. It'd been a long drive and we'd only stopped the once. Janet took me by the arm, hauled me over to a big green Muskoka chair at the head of the first table.

She said, "You look good, Granny Ingrid," which I didn't care for. No one tells good-looking people they look good.

Janet, now. What Janet looked was tired. There were new lines around her eyes, and her face was red with sunburn. She had probably earned it. The drive was long enough for William and me. We weren't hauling a trailer up the mountain road; there were no children in William's truck. William was young enough to have reserves. I'm old enough to know my limits. Janet, stuck between us, would have wrung herself dry with work, and with worry.

"Where are the girls?" I asked.

She pointed over to the Lookout. My great-grandchildren were there, on their toes, peering over the stone wall that came up to their chins. That was good. The drop off the lookout was fierce and far, and Lars and his boys had built it so even a grown man would have to mean it, to tip over that edge.

"They're getting big," said Janet. "Amanda's going to be in high school next year." She saw my perplexity, and pointed to the one on the left, coppery hair cropped short at her shoulders. She was bigger than I remembered. But it had been five years. One can't expect time to stand still, where a child's concerned.

"Mandy. And Lizzie—" the smaller of the two, with darker hair braided down her back, was bending down to pick up a pebble "—is she talking yet?" I asked. Last time, Liz only spoke to scream, and there were no words. She was five years old. We'd made a chant then—one of so many—that she wouldn't grow up a retard, but I hadn't much hope for her.

"She is," said Janet. "We put her in a special program at school. Now you can't shut her up."

Liz flung the pebbles overhand, and they rattled through the branches of the poplar trees below.

"Well that's a blessing."

Janet smiled, and waved to her daughters. "Come on over and see Granny Ingrid!"

Amanda waved back, and nudged her little sister, who looked over at us with a stricken expression.

"Oh, let them have their fun. I should go unpack," I said, "before the rest get here."

Janet smiled thinly, and nodded toward the porch.

"That's been taken care of," she said, and I looked over and saw it was true.

The porch was empty. While we were talking, Gudrun had collected my things, William's bird—and carried them all inside.

"I've got lots to do," said Janet. "Talk to your great-granddaughters. She . . . your sister can wait."

Janet left just as her girls arrived. I made a smile for them, and gave them both hugs, and asked them only a few questions before they set in with their talk.

Amanda was enrolled in a basketball program and she was very good at it, thank you very much. Lizzie was learning how to play chess and she wasn't very good yet, but would be soon. Amanda and Lizzie were both fond of a series of novels about a girl a few years older than they were, and her lover, a young man a few years older than she. According to Lizzie, Amanda had let a boy who was also a few years older than she kiss her, and when Amanda shouted no, Lizzie said all right, Amanda had kissed the boy, and asked if that was better? I believe Lizzie was trying to shock me, but it didn't work.

"Are you going to cook today?" asked Lizzie, and Mandy said, "You don't have to," and thought about what she said, and added, "I didn't mean that I don't like your food," which scarcely made matters better.

"We'll see how it goes," I said.

"Mandy means you can let Granny Gudrun do it if you're too tired," said Lizzie.

"I don't think that would do," I said, and lied: "The recipes take two to make their magic work."

"Magic!" said Lizzie. "Black magic!" Her sister shushed her.

"It's just cooking," said Mandy, and then she said to me: "It's not black magic." And after a heartbeat or so, she asked:

"Are you angry with us?"

Now that made me smile. Mandy had put her arm around Lizzie and her eyes were round. Lizzie was a step behind her sister, but as I watched, tendrils of worry crossed her face, like cloud over moon.

"I'm not angry," I said finally. "I'm not tired either. I had a wonderful nap in your Uncle William's truck on the way up. I'm ready for whatever the night brings. Black magic or not."

Mandy tried to smile, tried to laugh, failed at both. Lizzie did better just keeping quiet. I could barely see her trembling as I heard the familiar footsteps approaching behind me.

"You're good girls," I said. "You can run along now."

"They don't have to be told twice," said Gunnar as he stepped around the chair and bent to give me a kiss. "Help your mother!" he called after them as his daughters ran toward their family's van.

Gunnar opened a canvas chair beside me and sat in it.

"You look good," I said, and I *wasn't* lying. Gunnar's daughters had grown beyond recognition, splendid little weeds that they were; Janet's sunburned face was gradually taking on the texture of cowhide, and she was, to be honest, going to fat. Yet Gunnar—here was the same handsome, strapping lad I'd hugged the last time we'd gathered here. He had cut off most of his long blond hair, and shaved the little pirate beard he'd been so proud of. Past that—the years had treated my eldest grandson tenderly. One might even say neglectfully.

"I don't know what you said. But you scared the noses off my girls," he said.

"They scared their own noses off." I reached over and tapped the end of his nose, and finished with that old trick that had made him laugh so when he was but a tyke: lifted my fist, with thumb poked out, nose-ish, between index and middle fingers. "I'll give them this one. They can fight over it."

And that was all it took to make my Gunnar laugh again. But the laughter passed too quickly.

"You have to go in soon," he said.

Soon didn't mean right away. Before I went, I made sure Gunnar brought me up to date.

It had been a good five years since the last hootenanny. Gunnar began the first year still working for Mr. Oates at his construction company. By the end of the year, he was promoted, and in the middle of the second year was promoted again to a job in the office. At three years, Mr. Oates named him his second-in-command. Four years in, and he was a partner. Last year, Mr. Oates took ill, and went home, where he would probably stay until the end. Fingers crossed, I said to Gunnar.

They had a house now. In its back yard was a swimming pool. At the side was a garage, big enough for the minivan and one other car, a fast little red machine that was Gunnar's alone. The house backed on to a shallow ravine with pine trees. It wasn't too far from the office. The girls were happy there, as was Janet.

I too was very happy about all that and said so. I kept my peace when Gunnar leaned close and told me about Marissa, the accommodating young girl from the city that Gunnar would visit twice a week. I couldn't say anything—for that too had been on his list, five years ago. Whatever I might think of it, he had wanted that too.

And then it was time to go inside.

"Good luck, Granny," he said, and gave me a hug. I held it longer than he offered it—though not a quarter as long as was my due.

***

I found more offerings on the porch when I climbed the steps: a ring of green Jell-O, inside of which were suspended slices of frankfurter, three daisies and perhaps a dozen insects, including a hornet and an enormous dragonfly; long links of a black blood sausage, coiled on a green-tinted plastic platter; a casserole dish, covered in tinfoil and smelling not unpleasantly of paint thinner. It was heavy as a pile of bricks when I tried to lift it. So I left it with the sausage, and carried the Jell-O ring into the foyer.

Not much had changed here in five years. The wallpaper was the same geometric pattern, unlovely three decades ago. It smelled sweet, of pastry and cabbage. I let the door shut behind me, and the smell intensified.

"Hello, Ingrid."

"Hello, Gudrun." She was in the doorway to the kitchen where sunlight silhouetted her. She was sitting, slumped a bit. "Wheelchair now?" I asked.

She coughed, but not in a worrying way. "Wheelchair now. Yes. What's that?"

"Gelatin," I said, and she said, "Bring it here to me."

Gudrun was as fat as one would expect, living her days here at the Perch. Fat was what put her in the wheelchair as much as the years. She held her hands out for the gelatin. I helped her bring it down to her lap, jiggling with its bugs and its meats and its petals. She oohed at it like it was a newborn.

"Oh, this is *lovely*. Who made it?"

"I don't truly know. I didn't see who set it there."

She sniffed at it. "Well it's very creative. It will do fine, I think. Better than the chicken."

"Nothing wrong with the chicken," I said, and she smiled so her lips drew back under her teeth, and squinted down at the offering.

"I suspect Rainer's daughter. Always partial to the insectile. But it will all sort out. We'll take it all up to the Perch later," she said, meaning, of course, I would take it. I lifted the gelatin away and the wheels on the front of her chair squeaked as she turned around, leading me back into the kitchen.

It was not much changed—or to put it another way, what changes there might be were too small for me to be certain of. For years, we had all but lived here—hauling firewood, cleaning floor and countertop, doing the work of the young. . . . But I had not been by for five years now, then five years before that, then five again and again and again. Did the ceiling always warp down so, over the refrigerator? Were there so many flyspecks in the bowl of the lights? Did the wood stove gleam so brightly, as the light struck it from the high windows on the west wall? Had the shelves that covered three walls been painted, again?

And as to the smell of it . . .

Did the larder always smell so?

"Now," Gudrun said, taking her place in the middle of the floor, where the sun always hit this time in the afternoon of a hootenanny, "it's time to work, little sister." She clapped her hands, and grunted. "Find your apron. Fetch the knives. There are mouths to feed."

Gudrun surprised me then. For I was hoping for her to sit there in the warm sun, reminding me where things were, correcting my kitchen chants, demanding spoonfuls of broth for inspection, watching me sweat and bleed and cry, from her wheeled throne.

But no. That had not been our way for many years. And so—

She tilted her head, and drew a long and sore breath . . .

. . . and up she got, swaying and tottering on her thick, inadequate legs. Her grin was fierce as ever as she stumbled to the counter, caught and steadied herself. Huffing, Gudrun held out her hand, and I pulled a long steel flensing knife from the block, passed it to her.

"More and more mouths," she said when she caught her breath, "every time."

Carcasses were first. They were stacked on the counter between the sink and the stove, on long platters: goose and pig and sheep, venison and rabbit. The beasts had been skinned and gutted, but not very much butchered. We set at them fast and hard, Gudrun with knife, I with cleaver. There was a technique to it—we had been rending the carcasses for the better part of a century, Gudrun and I, and we knew our way around a butcher block—but it was not a mindful thing. If blood and gristle splattered—well, that is why we wore aprons, and tied our hair high. We were deft enough that the blades didn't slip, and none of the blood would be ours. In the end, the meat would be ready, stacked in glistening piles of fowl and swine and vermin, ready for flame.

There were vegetables to prepare—a bushel of potatoes mingled with other roots as we required—long stalks of rhubarb and a bucket filled with water, where leeks floated like the pale fingers of children. But we stopped a moment, to rest. I pushed the wheelchair closer so Gudrun could sit in it, but she swatted it away.

"Embarrassing." She looked at the hallway, the windows. Like someone might be watching. Someone might be, I thought, considering it.

"Fine," I said. "I'll sit in it myself." And I plunked myself down in the chair. Gudrun turned so she leaned against the counter. Her face was as slick as the meat; she was sweating like a farmhand.

"It suits you," she said, "better than me."

I laughed, but dutifully.

"You might learn a thing or two," she went on. "Be a better person for it."

I shook my head and smiled. Gudrun could try all she wanted; she wouldn't draw me out.

Still she tried. She ran water in the sink and filled two glasses for us, and wondered how it would have gone with Sam, my first husband, if my spine had stayed bent. I sweetly suggested he might have gone with Gudrun. "He wouldn't have found comfort in *my* bed," she sniffed as she handed me my water in an old jelly glass. "Not my sort."

We set to work on the vegetables then, peeling and chopping with fresh knives, and Gudrun set about reminiscing, with an eye to enumerating all the ways Sam wasn't her sort. He drove like an old woman, she said; he was too thin, and couldn't dance well, nor could he play an instrument. "I don't trust a fellow who's not at least musical. I don't see the sense of one," she said. "It's uncomely."

"He's gone now," I said.

"Yes. We didn't chant *him* well, did we?"

I took a breath, and bore down on the potato. It split like a stump under the weight of the knife, and me.

I might have returned fire. I might have wondered at Gudrun's own marriage, and the way her life had been warped around it. We had never properly shared Sam; he was mine. But for a time—for quite a time—we'd both shared a bed with the master of Gudrun's house.

Of course, pointing that out . . . well, that would be too cruel. So I kept my peace.

The flames had lived in the stove since dawn. But I threw in another log after we put the meat in the ovens—before we started work on the sauce.

We had branches of rosemary—garlic cloves, peeled and ready to crush under a stone mortar; pink runoff from the carcasses, collected in narrow grooves on the butcher block's edges; and in a tall glass jar, salt, grains as thick as pebbles. . . .

Sauce always being improved with salt.

Gudrun stopped goading me now that we put down our knives and stood before the fire. I set one of my pans over the firebox then, and we added parts, taking turns, and calling back chants at one another, stirring and stoking. It was work now, and tricky work at that. Everything could be undone if we missed a note, a beat. . . .

We got on best at moments like these.

———

The sun crossed the kitchen as it filled with smoke and fume, and we sang and chanted the usual storm: begged for health and well-being for the assembled families—good pay, light work for the fathers . . . for dire circumstances to fall on those who might stand against them. We put our heads together and got nearly all the names right, and Gudrun had a list of them tacked onto the refrigerator so we'd be sure. We poured off the sauce, tar thick, the colour of beets, into an urn, and I slid it into the warming oven next to the first platter of meat.

"They'll be getting hungry," said Gudrun. "It's nearly eight."

I nodded. "Later than usual, but not much."

Gudrun wiped her arm across her forehead, and motioned for the wheelchair. I brought it, and helped her back into it. She was sweaty and slow, and her breathing was shallow.

"You watch the roasts," I said. "You can do that from the chair."

"Not if I have to haul them out I can't."

"There's time on them yet." I looked out the door to the hall, the stairs. "But you're right. They will be getting hungry. I'd best get up there."

She didn't argue this time. Just settled back, folded her hands and drew in the scent of the cookery.

"Don't forget the Jell-O," she said, and pointed to the table where I'd put it, hours ago. The evening light refracted around the wieners and insects, and made it glow.

———

Three trips up and down two flights of stairs and a ladder, and I was ready. At the north corner of the widow's walk, I set the Jell-O. The southern corner, underneath the rooster weather vane, was where I left the blood sausage. I uncovered the casserole dish, and set it in the east.

And William's chicken—that I carefully unwrapped, and took it to the western corner—where I set, cross-legged, with the bird in the lap of my apron.

The sun was low enough that the flat spot on the roof was actually in shadow, though no tree drew this high. Peering over the edge, I could see the entire world it seemed, to the far horizons; green farmers' fields nearest, dotted with woodlots and finally stretching far to clots of housing. Houses such as that were the due of the families—Gunnar kept his family in one such as that. From the Perch, those modest homes did not seem so much to ask.

Stars began to appear. From below, I heard the families, their murmured conversations, some laughter. It was hard to make out precisely what was being said, from so high. But I knew my progeny. They were hungry, they were. Hungry for life; for wealth; for one another, finally.

These offerings they had made—they weren't offerings, not really. They were demands.

The air was sweet up on the Perch. An evening breeze blew across the treetops, light as a young boy's touch on my cheek. I lifted the chicken William—William and I—had made, into the breeze. The hour was about right now—soon, they would come.

The first lighted on the rooster. Its wings were wide, like rumpled paper. They were maybe wide as my hand. Thick antennae turned toward me, sniffing the offering. I stretched as high as I could without standing. And the moth took off, and circled overhead.

I felt the second on my hand, like the brushing of a curtain.

More would come soon.

When Gudrun and I were young, so many came—Gudrun claimed she near to suffocated under their weight, as they made a blanket over us. It was all I could do not to leap off the Perch, tumble down the steep roof. Oh, such terror—such terror as grows on the flesh of the young. It seemed then that death might have been preferable to the wings of the moth.

In my head, I remember that terror so well. In my heart—it fades.

———

It was all done in an hour—more, or less.

Put it this way. The stars were fulsome when I could see again. The breeze had shifted, and was cooler on me. Below, the families had become boisterous, percussive—pounding with their fists on the outside of that plastic privy, it sounded like. They all howled like hounds.

In the kitchen, as I stole past, to the celebration outside: silence. Blessed, final silence.

An hour would be about right.

———

William caught me coming out. He was dangling a beer bottle between two fingers and wiping his face with a sleeve as he climbed the steps to the porch. He'd been into the meat.

"Good food," he said, and I smiled at him, patted his arm. He wanted to ask me how the hen had gone over—how he, *we*, had fared. I could tell. But he wouldn't ask. So we walked quietly down to the families, for the most part gathered under the fickle glow from the paper lanterns.

The meat was all out now, on rows of platters along three picnic tables pushed together. There were a half dozen of our folk lined up on both sides of it. Flesh drooled off their plates, and still they stacked more.

"They don't know when they're full," said William.

"Oink oink," I said, and he laughed. "I'd like some meat myself. I'm surely not full. Could you gather me a plate?"

I let go of his arm then and took charge of one of the lawn chairs. William scooted off to the tables, to do as he was told. I settled down on my own—I'm surely not so old, either—and I leaned back in the chair, tilted my head back to look up into the glow in the branches, from the lanterns. For a time—for a short time—they left me alone, to count the crooks in the branches of the maple tree here. When I'd come here first—the tree mustn't have been more than a sapling. It would be fine to say I remembered that sapling, but really—I couldn't say such a thing. Agatha's Perch has so many trees on it. One's liable to lose track.

"Thank you, Granny Ingrid."

I brought my eyes back down, and looked at Liz. She had crept up on me. I made to smile. "Did you enjoy the meat?"

Liz shrugged her shoulders and rolled her eyes. "I guess," she said. Her mouth was clean of grease—she hadn't had that much, all things considered.

"You *guess*. Did your mother tell you to come over and thank me?"

"No," she said. "Dad did." When I didn't answer, she went on: "Dad said you gave me a holy gift with this meal. He said you blessed all of us with this meal. He said I should say thank you."

"And you have."

I looked back up into the branches.

"Granny," said Liz.

"Yes, child?"

"It seems like a lot of work to do what you do."

"It is a lot of work."

"Why do you do it for us?"

"Love," I said. "I do it out of love."

"Oh Granny!"

And before I could do anything to prevent her, the wretched child—the dear little *retard*—had grappled me around my shoulders, and pressed her face into my breast, and cried out: "I love you too!"

It took all the will I had—but I kept my peace.

William made me a modest plate. There was a thigh-bone from one of the ducks, and a glistening slice of pig belly—and the haunch of a rabbit. I took it, and set the plate on my lap.

"Is that all right?" he asked, and I said, "Just fine."

He stood quiet a moment, rocking back and forth on his heels as I cut into the duck, and finally, he dared ask: "How'd the hen go down?"

I chewed the duck flesh carefully—wouldn't do to choke on it. And then, since he'd asked . . .

"Gudrun's dead."

He nodded. William couldn't really do anything else—he had killed the hen and wrapped it up and tossed it into the belly of his own truck—the same truck he used to bring me here. He'd wished his own wishes, same as I'd wished mine.

"She's in the kitchen," I said.

"She was old," said William, uncertainly.

"She was. The gathering's a lot of work. Even with help."

William started to work it out, and I pursed my lips and nodded.

"I should go in," he said, and I said, "Yes. There's cleaning to be done."

"I should go," William said again. He backed away and half-ran back to the porch. William is a good grandson. When the work becomes clear, William sees to it.

I didn't finish the plate, but others finished theirs, and the night went on. Rainer went into the back of his truck and pulled out his twelve-string guitar, and the children gathered 'round him as he began to play. Rainer fancied himself a blues player, but what he really was, was undisciplined. Fifteen years ago, he had baked a cat into a pie-shell, and brought it to the gathering. I wouldn't touch the filthy thing, but Gudrun carried it to the Perch, and set it out properly, and when the moth-wings were gone—so was the pie.

Rainer made two record albums and one of them was very popular with certain sorts. But he lacked the discipline to take it any further. So now, he shared his gift with the family, at the gathering, and that was all. Although it is not my cup of tea, I must admit it does have its effect.

Rainer had two young sons, and one of them joined him on harmonica, while the other—little Peter, just five years old—pounded on a tambourine. His daughter Freya sang along. Lizzie and Mandy hung close—the older boy, James, would be a handsome specimen in a few years. At twelve, he already had his two young cousins hypnotized.

If they were my daughters, I would have just pulled them away.

But their mother, Janet, scarcely noticed them.

She hung at the very edge of the lantern light. Her shoulders were slumped—her head bowed into one hand.

I might have wondered if she hadn't just heard about Gudrun—if she hadn't some reason for mourning my elder sister. She seemed like a woman grieving. I might have gone to her, and put my hand on her shoulder, and said, *there there, dear*, the way that people are wont.

As I watched, she stepped back from the circle, and moved off. At this, I pushed myself from my chair, and make to follow her. And as I did so—I did wonder.

Could she have heard of Gudrun's fate? Could someone else have seen my sister, slipped past the quiet kitchen as did I—and told Janet?

Was that how it was to be? In spite of myself, I drew a breath, sharply. She climbed the steps to the porch, and cast about, as though looking for someone—as though making certain someone was *not* there.

I should not have been there. I should have let matters unfold as they were laid out. A watched pot never boils, yes? But of course that's not true. A flame will heat water, whether it's eyeballed or not.

She walked along the porch—peered into a dark window—ran her hands through her hair, as though making up her mind. As if it hadn't already been made up, for her.

I might have joined her on the porch. I might have told her how well she had planned the gathering—how beautiful the lanterns were, how the picnic tables were just right . . . how wonderful a touch were the privies, set so far from the old house that old Agatha had bequeathed us, when we all came here those hundred years past—

with nothing but bad luck and worse debts.

I might have told her how so very *worthy* she was.

But I didn't. I held back as she went back to the screen door, pulled it open, and went inside.

I stood still on the dark lawn, as Rainer finished his song and a cheer went up. "Another one!" cried a child, and Rainer laughed and said, "Well, one more," and started to pick at his guitar again, and a light went on in the window. Was William finished? It was difficult to tell, for there was no commotion that followed, as more lights went on—as Janet explored her new home . . . met her new master.

I found myself humming along with Rainer's song. It was a French song and I don't speak French, but it had a happy tune. It was time to turn from the house, and I continued down the path—until I stood at the lookout. The music grew quieter, and I heard birdsong—the cool breeze rattling the branches of the trees down the deep slope.

The wall here was high. It wasn't meant to be easy to go over it . . . you had to really mean to clamber up, and launch yourself into the air off Agatha's Perch. By the time you were up, you'd know whether you had reason to stay.

I drew a deep lungful of the night air, and placed my hands on the round river rocks that made the wall, and I held that breath. It wasn't long, although it seemed an eternity.

When I exhaled, I turned and saw Gunnar. He stood tall, and shirtless—smeared with congealing grease and sweat, and gristle. The moonlight made hollows of his eyes. His mouth hung open.

I opened my arms for him, and dutifully, he came to me. And he kissed me, my favourite grandson did, as I had always dreamed and wished and hoped.

ORLOK

(A prelude to *Volk*, the sequel to *Eutopia: A Novel of Terrible Optimism*)

"Was he beautiful?"

As though he had just registered his own nakedness at that instant, Gottlieb blinked and covered himself.

"Beautiful? No. He was compelling. Huge. Very muscular."

"And you were sexually attracted to him."

"Of course I was."

The doctor allowed a dozen beats of the metronome before he spoke the obvious: "He was not like you."

"No."

Gottlieb was grasping at his penis. The doctor made no attempt to disguise his observation of that fact and noted with satisfaction that Gottlieb didn't seem to care. He was as guileless as a babe then. Could a metronome tick triumphantly? The doctor let it, twice more.

"Describe to me the ways he was like you."

Gottlieb drew a deep breath and turned to the windows. They were open a crack to clear the air from the morning's session, and the sweet smell of apple blossom wafted in. The doctor was used to the smell—this was a room in which he spent a great deal of time—but he noted it, along with the flaring of Gottlieb's delicate nostrils.

"How was he like you?" asked the doctor again.

"I don't really know," said Gottlieb. "I didn't know him for very long."

"Anything."

"All right. He was German like me. And he was my age."

"How old were you then?"

The slightest frown. "Twenty-two."

The doctor looked again to the window. A conversation was drifting in along with the apple blossom scent. Two of the girls—Heidi and Anna? Yes. He recognized Anna's lisp, and she and Heidi were inseparable. Ergo . . .

They weren't too distracting—they would barely register on the recording. If they lingered, or became silly, he would have to stand and shut the window, and risk disturbing Gottlieb. But the pair were on their way somewhere, and within four ticks of the metronome were gone. The doctor settled back.

"His hair was brown," said Gottlieb. "Like mine too."

Three ticks.

"And he was homosexual," said Gottlieb.

Four more ticks now.

"But not like me."

"Tell me how he is not like you."

"As to his homosexuality?"

"If you like. Yes."

"He is a masculine force. He looks at me and causes me to feel as if . . . as if I am not. Not masculine."

The doctor smiled. The last time Gottlieb had spoken of this moment, he'd immediately denied his homosexuality. They were progressing very well, at least as measured against their stated objective of delving into Gottlieb's neurosis. The doctor started to reach for a pencil where his breast pocket would have been, but stopped himself and settled his hands back in his lap. He spoke quietly, calmly, in rhythm. Like a lullaby. "He is looking at you now," he said.

Tick. Tick.

Gottlieb flushed and, as his hand came away from his penis, the doctor was pleased to see it was flushed too.

"In the beer hall, yes?" said the doctor.

Gottlieb stretched his slender legs on the chaise longue, and his eyelids fluttered shut. A breeze from the window lifted the drapes, and raised gooseflesh as it passed. The air in the beer hall would not have been so fresh as this alpine breath.

"In the Bürgerbräukeller," said Gottlieb.

"What does it smell like?"

"Many things. Food . . . there is a basket of schnitzel nearby. There is some smoke. I mean from tobacco. And the whole place stinks of old beer. Of course. Men have been drinking beer all day."

The doctor waited until it seemed as though Gottlieb might drift off to sleep, before prodding:

"Where is he?"

Gottlieb smiled. "He is leaned against a pillar. By himself, across the hall from me. He is a very ugly man—his eyebrows meet in the middle of his forehead, so it seems he is scowling into his beer mug."

The doctor shifted in his chair. The towel he'd placed on the leather cushioning had moved, and in the warmth of the day the bare skin of his buttocks was sticking there. But he fought to contain his discomfort, his growing impatience. The metronome ticked seven times more before Gottlieb was ready to continue.

"My friends are sitting with me at one of the round tables in the middle of the great room. There is Gunther and Alex and Haydn. Gunther is getting fat, somehow. His hair is still blond, but is starting to go up front, and in a patch at his crown. Alex is a little fellow—smaller than me. His moustache is long, and covered in foam from his mug. Black hair. Haydn? Always licking his lips. No foam there. Otherwise handsome enough. He works in a warehouse by the Isar. Keeps him strong and from fat.

"Are they properly my friends? Gunther maybe: we fought alongside in the War and he liked me well enough to have me at his wedding when it was done. Alex and Haydn were Gunther's boyhood friends from Augsberg. They were good fellows and they tolerated me, but they preferred to reminisce with Gunther about this or that when they were all bachelors. They never had much to say to me. I didn't mind.

"We are drinking a round of lagers and Gunther is telling his story about the end of the War—set after Armistice, but just a few days. It is a little true, but for the most part a lie: he talks about how we met a company of British soldiers in No Man's Land. We shared our rations with them because they were so pitiable . . . nearly starving . . . literally begging for our aid.

"Gunther tells it boastfully, so as to illustrate his honourable nature. I remember the night differently—that we were all cold and hungry, and we all ate our own rations. It was still a good night—we refrained from slaughtering one another, kept our insults to ourselves. But no one begged. There was no . . . undue generosity. Not a whiff of charity, from Gunther or any of us.

"But I don't correct his lie. We are all becoming a little drunk, and this talk is preferable to political talk. Or, yes, a brawl.

"And yes. I am distracted.

"What is he wearing now? It is . . . a grey shirt, yes, open-necked over a white undershirt. He has a cap but he is not wearing it. It is stuffed into the belt of his trousers. I don't know what kind of trousers. Brown? Brown. A dark brown. I cannot see his boots, but later, I remember—

"All right. In the moment I cannot see his boots. There is a table of men in front of him, I think they are veterans too—two of them have helmets from the War, on the table before them. They are emptying their mugs quickly and having a very serious talk. I cannot hear what they are saying. But he is smiling at it, looking from one to the other as they argue among themselves.

"I imagine they are talking politics. Probably about the Weimar and the Jews, because of course later—

"Quite right, doctor. In the moment. In the moment.

"He looks up and sees me looking. But he doesn't seem surprised. I think he has known that I am looking at him for a long time. Maybe since I started. Maybe he saw me even before.

"He grants me a little wink, then takes a deep drink from his mug. And he is gone.

"Disappeared into thin air? No. There is a commotion around him—nothing serious. A gang of men arrive—more veterans, I think. They crowd into the discussion, grabbing the shoulders of the men in the midst of talk. One of them has a platter of sausages and sets it down on the table, and by the time they've moved out of the way, he is lost in the commotion.

"Now Gunther claps me on the shoulder.

"'Hey, Markus,' he says, 'you look pale. Don't tell me you're done drinking.'

"On the other side of me, Alex empties his cup and grins at me. His moustache is dripping beer.

"I finish my drink. There is not much left anyway. 'Another round?' asks Gunther. It is his turn to buy. 'Fine,' I say, 'but I need to return some of this round first.'

"'Don't take too long,' Gunther says. 'Little Alex is thirsty. He'll drink his and your beer too if you dawdle.'

"I laugh at that and so does Haydn. Alex smiles but I don't think he likes being called little. Or maybe he sees through my ruse. Because yes, maybe it is a ruse. I don't have to piss or I don't have to piss very much. I get up and go all the same.

"I cross the room. It feels as though the men here are looking at me as I go, but that is rot. Why would they? I become a little fearful, I admit, as I move through here, slip beneath the shadow of the balcony, past the pillars, thinking that I . . .

"I . . .

"I am outside now. In the beer garden. What is the weather? What kind of question is that? It is November. Just before six. It will get colder, much colder but right now the air is pleasant enough—I can feel the gooseflesh on my arms, which are bare, but that is fine, because the cool air is just what I need. I could probably use a splash of ice water, come to that. I have had too much to drink, maybe, after all. And part of it—a state of arousal, yes, that is part of it.

"The wind gusts now. It is coming from the southwest. A winter wind. From the mountains. The few that are outside getting air like me look for shelter from it, back in the hall. Not me. Not him either.

"He is sitting on one of the tables, feet propped on the bench, spread apart, forearms resting on his knees. His forefingers and thumbs are rubbing together, as though to make warmth. His cap is on his head.

"Oh—I can see his boots now. They are old army boots. Laced up high. He has tucked his trousers into them. He is looking right at me. I look away but only for a moment because I cannot look away for long.

"'You are a Jew?' he asks me.

"I tell him I am not.

He points back at the hall with one hand. 'Your friends. Jews?'

"'None of us are Jews.'

"'Are you certain?' he asks. 'Have you sucked all their uncircumcised cocks?'

"How does that make me feel?

"Fearful.

"Angry.

"And helpless.

"And no, I do not care for any of those feelings. What sort would enjoy that? What a question. But I also know it for what it is: a crude flirtation such as men make with one another. I despise this part, the beginning. But there is no other way.

"I tell him a joke: that they are all too busy sucking one another's cocks, and I must wait my turn. I laugh at it, my own joke, but he remains serious.

"'Come here.' That is what he says, then turns one great hand up and beckons me over. He might mean it as a command. I take it as permission.

"I am sitting on the bench where he is resting his feet, leaning back against the table where he is perched. He is saying something, but there's some kind of commotion from the street. . . . It sounds like a flock of great birds taking off. But that can't be right. . . . I cannot hear what he says because of it whatever the sound is. His hand comes down on my shoulder and squeezes. He is looking down at me. I tell him my name, because maybe he was asking that. I think he was asking that.

"'Good enough,' he says. 'What town?' I tell him. 'Then what are you doing here in Munich?' And I tell him about the book that I am writing. He wonders why I could not write that book at home, and I tell him some of that story. He doesn't say anything to that, but his hand doesn't leave my shoulder. Aah, his grip is so tight.

"'I sometimes write,' he tells me finally. 'Is your book true?' I tell him it is not true. It is a novel. 'Writing books that are not true is easy,' he says to me. 'True books are more difficult.' That is not my experience, I tell him. Fabrication is more difficult than just saying what's so.

"A group of men are walking past us, toward the beer hall. There are . . . maybe a dozen of them? Maybe less. They are dressed well. He loosens his grip on my shoulder, sits up as he looks over at them, but they don't seem to pay us any heed. Who are they? I ask.

"'Who knows?' he says. 'I don't like them, though.' He slides off the table then, and slaps my back.

"'Inside,' he says. 'Not good to be outdoors right now.'

"We are walking back to the beer hall. He is opening another door than the one from which we came. It is an exterior door that goes directly to the cellars. We are at the top of a wooden staircase. There is one bare bulb lighting the way down, set in the wall. We are climbing down the stairs. I am first. He is . . .

"He is . . ."

—◼—

Nearly sixty ticks of the metronome and the doctor dared clear his throat. Gottlieb seemed to be dozing, and if he was, the throat-clearing would rouse him. But based on his experience, the doctor suspected something other: a phenomenon he had observed not infrequently in the course of his work. In certain instances, the patient would inhabit the memory so deeply that there would be no words for it. The patient might recollect these deep fugues, later, and might write those memories in a journal, and might share that journal with a trusted psychotherapist. And that might be as near a psychotherapist would get to the nub of that deep, crucial memory. The only thing to do until that resolved, in the doctor's experience, was to wait.

The doctor reached and lifted the needle from the Dictaphone. He set about replacing the cylinder, which was more than three-fourths finished. Then, as quietly as he could manage but by no means silently, he shut and fastened the windows. Before he did, he drew in a last breath of the valley, and regarded the circle of smooth-skinned girls and boys, sunbathing by the riverbank. The doctor savoured the breath, imagining he was capturing a last whiff of their virility . . . their fecundity.

From the chaise longue, Gottlieb gasped. The doctor didn't need to look to confirm: He had ejaculated.

"Herr Gottlieb," whispered the doctor after he had set the needle back on the fresh cylinder.

Gottlieb's naked torso twisted, the pale droplets of semen distending into ghostly rivulets down his belly, and his eyelids fluttered over a gaze that was still focused elsewhere.

"Tell me his name," said the doctor.

Gottlieb's lips parted, so his tongue could wet them, because they were very dry.

<hr/>

"I cannot say now. I do not know it. He has not said it.

"We are deep in the cellar. I am lying close along his flank. My head is resting in the crook of his shoulder, my nose pressed into the damp fabric of his undershirt. I can smell him, even as his taste is still fresh on my tongue. . . .

"We are resting in the crook of two stacks of barrels. He has taken me to the darkest corner, past high stone arches and thick pillars. There is some light—from the far end of the cellar—and there is some sound . . . men talking, perhaps, at that end of the cellar . . . the noise of the beer hall above us? No. It is the scurrying feet of rats. That is what he says.

"'The true fathers of Munich,' he says. 'When those men are gone'—his hand leaves my shoulder to gesture upward, to the beer hall above us—'the rats will hold a feast.'

"'Do you not think they are holding one now?' I ask him, and finally he laughs at a jest I make.

"'It is true. I have never seen a starved rat. They have that advantage over we men: they will eat *anything*.'

"He pushes me away from him, just enough that he can straighten against the wall. He kicks away our trousers, where they are balled at our feet. Then he asks me: 'Do you know your blood type?'

"I do not know it and he scolds me. 'If you find yourself in a hospital, needing a transfusion, you had better know it. There are different types. There is A, there is B, there is AB, and there is O. Mix it up, get the wrong blood in you . . . that's it!'

"'Why do you say this now?' I ask. I am thinking all of a sudden about *Nosferatu*—the moving picture. I had watched it not even a year earlier. The blood-drinking cadaver, who arrives in town on a ship of rats.

"Rats . . . blood type . . .

"'You can tell about a fellow from his blood type,' he says. 'Type O . . . I think you are Type O.'

"'I don't know what type I am,' I say. 'What type are you?'

"'I am Type AB. I,' he says, 'can take any transfusion . . . transfuse to nearly anyone. Most of the time.'

"'Most of the time? Have you done this often, swapped blood?'

"'No. Hardly at all.'

"'What does your blood type say about you?'

"'It says . . .' he starts the answer but seems to consider. He pulls me closer again, and takes my wrist, and pulls it over to his penis. It is hard again already. I tug at the foreskin with my thumb, and begin to caress it.

"'I can travel anywhere,' he says, 'speak with anyone, although I am never truly *of* anyone. I can see the truth of matters, when others are blind to it. As I saw the truth of you.'

"I ask him what that means.

"'You think that there is greatness in you—you have thought this since you were very small. But it is hard to discover, yes? You followed the Kaiser into war and thought there might be greatness there. But there was nothing but mud, and blood, and death. You write lies in a book that you hope others will read one day. Perhaps they will venerate you. Perhaps, through words bound together in a cloth cover, your greatness will be assured. But true to yourself, you know that words in a book won't carry you any more than deeds in the War did. Not so long as the only words you write are lies.'

"'I have a confession,' I say, and I kiss his throat, insinuating myself closer. 'I am not writing a novel.'

"'Ah,' he says. 'The truth of you. As I sensed. Thank you for that.'

"And now he takes my face in his hand and draws me nearer, and kisses me on the mouth. . . .

"And . . .

"Oh.

"Light!

"Light has filled the room—another bulb in the ceiling, switched on. There are three men. They wear brown shirts and ties. One has a stick, like a walking stick.

"One says: 'What is this here?'

"Another: 'My God—look there. A pair of deviants!'

"The third says nothing, but reaches down and grabs my shoulder, pulls me half to my feet. He has short hair, almost no hair . . . he is not much taller than I—but bigger around the middle. He has a wide moustache.

"'Look at this,' he says, and pushes me to the ground. 'Bare-bottomed, hey? You a man or a woman?'

"I try to get to my feet. The walking stick hits me. I think that is what it is. Who knows? I fall.

"'We need to get them out of here,' says one. 'Tonight of all nights.'

"'Teach them a lesson.' The one with the stick. He strikes me again. In the chest this time. I feel a boot in my stomach. Another in my ribs. Someone laughs. I'm rolled over onto my stomach. The stick slaps my backside. I cry out—but not loud enough for anyone to hear.

"This has happened before, yes. In Stuttgart. Before the war. Then it was a whipping. I am recalling it. How I was made to scream. Manfred and I! Manfred!

"I will not scream at this. No. No screams. Tears—nothing to do for that. But no screaming. Not from me.

"But there are screams.

"Two gunshots, first. Like little barks from a dog, a room away. Maybe from upstairs. In the beer hall. Men screaming upstairs—the scraping of chairs on the floor above us . . . something is happening upstairs.

"Then . . . a moment of quiet. But barely that before . . . There are screams *everywhere*."

━━▄▬▬

Gottlieb's eyes were wide and he sat upright. Was he still entranced? Or had the recollection of the events in the cellar—the admixture of the beating in Stuttgart—pushed him back to consciousness, or perhaps into a mania?

"Herr Gottlieb," the doctor said. "Markus. It is necessary that you breathe."

Gottlieb did breathe—he drew a deep gulp of air, taken as though he were preparing to dive beneath the river.

"Let the breath out slowly," said the doctor. "Slowly. And with it, let the memories of Stuttgart go too."

The doctor knew about Stuttgart already. They had discussed this shortly after Gottlieb arrived here at the estates. *Surrender your garments first, and then your story*. And oh, Gottlieb may have been shy about those garments, but he told his story easily—a tale of how his father and uncle had found him and his cousin Manfred in an act of sodomy. Manfred denounced Gottlieb, and Gottlieb believed that because of that, the flogging had gone harder for him than Manfred. In fact, claimed Gottlieb, it had been Manfred who had instigated the encounter. Gottlieb was not blameless—yet nor was he guilty.

The doctor frankly did not care one way or another.

"Leave Stuttgart," he commanded. "Return to the cellar. That is where we are."

Gottlieb drew another breath, and lowered himself back to the couch, and although his eyes did not close, they refocused on the ceiling.

"The screaming," he said as the metronome ticked, "is everywhere."

—————

"He has pulled one of the men to the ground, tripping him between his legs first and then grabbing his belt, and then hauling him closer and grasping his head, by both ears. He holds it like an accordion, squeezing in. The man shouts. He twists. The man's legs twitch madly. It happens very quickly—so quickly the other two barely see what is happening before their friend is dead. This is a difficult thing to do, it is nearly impossible . . . to kill a man by twisting his neck. But he is very strong, stronger than anyone.

"The one with the stick swings at him now. But he catches the stick in one hand and twists it out of the man's hand. Then he stands, and spins it in a blur, high enough to strike and shatter the lightbulb hanging over us. It is darker again.

"And . . . *crack!* The stick strikes bone. And a second man falls, nearly in my lap. Yes. I am turned over now, coughing, watching the third man—the one who took hold of me, I think—running between the pillars, shouting "Help!" And he runs after that one, very fast. They don't get far before he overcomes the other. He leaps on him, straddling him from behind as he draws the stick around the front of his throat and kills him.

"I get to my feet. I find my trousers. The one who hit me with the stick might still live. I do not look to see. I do not care.

"I am not blameless. But I am not guilty either. He, after all, was the one who struck me.

"My . . . my lover, that is what he is, isn't he? He returns and bids me help him drag the third man back to the shadows here.

"'The *frauen* rarely come back here,' he says. 'It is filled with spiders and rats. We can leave these men here for a time.'

"He gathers his clothing and does up his trousers. 'But we should be tidy,' he tells me, and I ask him what he means, and he shows me.

"He takes the man he just killed and hefts him into the crook of barrels where we had just been. He takes the second man, and lays him next to him. The third man—who had hit me—he we stack on top of the other two both. As you would stack wood for the winter.

"'We ought to take our leave,' he tells me. 'It has been some time. Do you think your friends are still drinking?'

"'I don't want to drink with them.'

"'Better to do so,' he tells me. 'Unless they have chosen to leave.'

"We do not get to the beer hall—not right away," said Gottlieb.

"No," said the doctor. "That would have been difficult."

"We leave the way we came: back to the beer garden. But now . . . there are more men outside. They are dressed in the same coloured shirt as the men we left below. They are standing in a row near the gate to the street. Seeing them like this makes sense. They are S.A."

"Storm troopers."

"Storm troopers. One of them steps forward. He is very tall. He demands to know where we came from.

"We tell him that we were pissing. In the cellar? he asks, and I shrug, drunkenly enough to convince him. But he is not finished with us, this one.

"'There is a revolution taking place,' he says. 'Inside, we have Herr Kahr. He is even now acceding to our Fuhrer's demands. The government will change. Things will improve for some. Others will get what is coming to them. You had better be ready for that. Now: who are you for?'

"'Germany,' I say.

"'Clever answer. That can mean anything.' He stands close enough to smell us. 'All right, clever fellows. Tell us your names.'

The doctor leaned forward. He wanted to prompt Gottlieb: what does his mysterious lover say? But he knew better: drawing a sliver hastily simply embeds it more deeply.

A smile twitches across Gottlieb's face—oddly shaped, almost tentative, yet one of the few he'd spared the doctor since arriving.

"I tell him: 'I am Harker. This is my friend Orlok. We are just here for a drink.'"

<hr>

The doctor finished Gottlieb's session without the metronome—but the Dictaphone continued to spin. Gottlieb had laughed so hard at his own joke that the trance was broken for the day.

They spoke about the session, and the doctor allowed Gottlieb to talk about the things he believed he had learned from it and thereby generate his own theories. This filled the remainder of the cylinder. Gottlieb spoke at some length about the nature of his homosexual proclivities, and although it irritated the doctor after a time, he held his annoyance in check. So far as it concerned Gottlieb, his homosexuality was a symptom of a disease of the mind, for which he sought cure here. And the doctor had given Gottlieb no indication that matters stood any other way.

So Gottlieb theorized that his homosexual attractions were a manifestation of the violence in his life, and finally concluded: "Had my father and uncle not beaten me so, I might have forgotten the sweet curve of Manfred's arse. And then . . . well there was the War . . . and that night at Munich, where we killed the six storm troopers! It has cemented my erotic fixation, yes?"

"You said three," said the doctor. "Three storm troopers."

"Three? Oh yes, of course."

"Were there others that night?"

Gottlieb shook his head firmly. "I meant to say three," he said.

"And you know that those three were storm troopers how precisely?"

Gottlieb shrugged. "They wore the same coloured clothing. And storm troopers surrounded the beer hall that night, while Herr Hitler riled up the crowd within."

"What did you think of Hitler?"

"Hitler? I'd seen him speak before. This night . . . he was very loud. Almost shrill. Ugly little man. Hard to look away from, though."

"And your friend? What was his name?"

"Oh, he never cared for Hitler. He thought Hitler was a liar. One night, after things had settled down and they'd put Hitler and his Nazis behind bars . . . he told me that he would like to fuck the lies out of Hitler, and would if he got the chance."

"Like he fucked the lies out of you?" asked the doctor.

Gottlieb appeared to study his hand, frowning at the slight webbing between his fingers as he held it to the light of the window.

"He never properly fucked those out of me, doctor. He went off long before that could happen."

"And you do not know where he went?"

"It was a sudden departure."

"Of course."

The doctor cleared his throat, and tried one last time for the day. He put it to Gottlieb, directly.

"You know," he said, "it is interesting that for such an impression that this man left upon you, you cannot summon his name to your lips. Can you tell me his name, please?"

Gottlieb's fingers bent, then closed into a fist, casting a shadow across his face.

"I don't see what that has to do with anything," he said.

Daylight lingered over the grounds of the estate for some hours after Herr Gottlieb left the doctor's rooms. The doctor himself did not linger there long after. It was a beautiful summer's day in the valley where the estate stood, and the doctor thought to himself that he would not waste it, brooding over this troublesome patient.

He splashed water on his chest, beneath his arms, closed up his lavatory and then shut his office, and crossed the hall to the front steps. The outside air was cool, but welcome after the oppressiveness of the office, of his session with poor, broken Gottlieb.

As he walked, he passed Anna, her long blonde hair tied in braids that fell halfway down her naked back. She waved as he passed.

"Where is Heidi?" he asked, and she shrugged.

"I will meet up with her at supper," she lisped. "Will we see you at dinner, Herr Doctor Bergstrom?"

He patted his bare stomach. "I must watch my belly. But I will be there if you are."

She smiled—then glanced below his belly, and looked away from what she saw there. Now the doctor shrugged. Anna was a very healthy girl, despite her speech impediment, and she would soon become accustomed to all that her beauty inspired.

"We will see each other later, then, doctor," she said and hurried off.

As he watched her retreating backside, the doctor wondered whether Gottlieb would ever consider that one the way he contemplated Manfred's boyish rump. That was certainly Gottlieb's hope—that he could undo his nature, as though it were simply a neurosis, and take a wife with something approaching enthusiasm. The doctor remained a skeptic.

He set off through the orchards, which would lead to the river bank, where the others here might be found, doing their afternoon calisthenics. And having contemplated that happy prospect, he turned his mind away again from Gottlieb, and pondered his true patient, if one could call such as he a patient. . . .

The doctor smiled to himself and shook his head fast, as though to dislodge something that had fixed itself there.

He could not call that one a patient. He had never laid eyes upon him. The doctor could list what he knew of him, on one of those index cards they used in America.

He was a huge man. Brown haired. A single eyebrow. Very ugly. But muscular. And fearless. With fantastical charisma. But he was a man with no name or identity yet—not one the doctor could decode, until he could break through with Gottlieb, and the amnesiac French girl, and perhaps some others as his associates in Belgium might uncover. For the time being, the doctor had nothing with which to find him . . . next to nothing, beyond that description and what was almost certainly his phylum:

Übermensch.

(To be continued in *Volk*, available 2016 from
ChiZine Publications)

ABOUT THE AUTHOR

David Nickle is the author of numerous short stories and several novels. His 2011 novel *Eutopia: A Novel of Terrible Optimism* was a finalist for the Sunburst, Aurora, and Compton Crook Awards. He is a past winner of the Bram Stoker, Aurora, and Black Quill Awards. He lives in Toronto, where he works as a political journalist covering Toronto municipal politics.

PUBLICATION HISTORY

"Looker" first appeared in *Chilling Tales*, edited by Michael Kelly, 2011

"The Exorcist: A Love Story" is original to this collection

"The Radejastians" first appeared in *Tesseracts Thirteen*, edited by Nancy Kilpatrick and David Morrell, 2009

"The Summer Worms" first appeared in *Northern Frights 3*, edited by Don Hutchison, 1995

"Knife Fight" first appeared in *Masked Mosaic: Canadian Super Stories*, edited by Claude Lalumière and Camille Alexa, 2013

"Basements" first appeared in *Tesseracts Fourteen*, edited by Brett Alexander Savory and John Robert Colombo, 2010

"Wylde's Kingdom" first appeared in *Tesseracts Twelve*, edited by Claude Lalumière, 2008

"Love Means Forever" first appeared in *On Spec*, 1996

"Oops" first appeared in *No More Potlucks* #10, 2010

"The Nothing Book of the Dead" is original to this collection

"Drakeela Must Die" first appeared in *Valkyrie Magazine*, 1996

"Black Hen à la Ford" first appeared in *Chilling Tales 2*, edited by Michael Kelly, 2013

"Orlok" is original to this collection

ACKNOWLEDGEMENTS

In the acknowledgements to *Monstrous Affections*, my first story collection, I thanked my parents Olga Nickle and Lawrence Nickle for their general, if sometimes bemused support of my writing habit. I want to repeat those thanks, and expand on them a little as pertains to my dad Lawrence.

Last year, eighty-three years old, his health took a turn for the worse, and just days into this year he gave it up and died (I would say he passed away, or left us, or something else implying an immortal soul that might live beyond the flesh, but that would have offended him, inveterate atheist that he was. And in case he was wrong about that, I don't want to take any chances in having a pissed-off ghost peering over my shoulder). I've dedicated *Knife Fight* to him in memory, but not just in memory. This is the last round of fiction I have to publish that was written while he was alive, and therefore infused with his ongoing influence and support. Lawrence spent his life as an artist, one of the last plein-air painters in Canada. From his graduation from the Ontario College of Art in the 1950s to his death, I don't think he earned a penny from anything other than painting pictures and teaching others what he knew. I've followed his example by a bit of a stretch—I've not earned anything since graduating Ryerson that didn't involve putting words to paper or telling others how I thought they should do it. As we got older, my dad and I would tell each other how we thought the other should write stories or paint pictures respectively—but money never changed hands, so we kept it pure that way. I'll miss him.

I want to thank my partner and fiancée Madeline Ashby for her ongoing support. She's a hell of a writer and a hell of a partner, and as had Lawrence in his time, also doesn't charge for her excellent writing advice.

This is a story collection, and a lot of these stories have had life thanks to the encouragement and acceptance of some excellent and open-minded editors. Don Hutchison, Michael Kelly, Claude Lalumière, Camille Alexa, Brett Savory, John Robert Colombo, Liz Holliday, Nancy Kilpatrick, David Morrell, Ellen Datlow, and the crew at *On Spec Magazine* all share some credit and also blame for the stories that are reprinted here.

ChiZine Publications co-proprietors Brett Savory, and also Sandra Kasturi, share credit and blame for the new stories—of which there are two (three if you count that last bait-and-switch we pulled with the *Volk* prologue, "Orlok"). Both of them also added some previously absent polish to the reprinted stories. Peter Watts contributed not only the introduction, but also the rare scientifically accurate portions of "Wylde's Kingdom" (no one who knows Watts should be surprised that he is the go-to guy for giant squid lore). Erik Mohr's cover, as has been the case for five books of mine now, makes the whole thing look better than it has any right to, and hopefully has helped sway your purchasing decision in my favour.

The members of the Cecil Street Irregulars writers workshop and the annual science fiction writing retreat/workshop at Gibraltar Point have my gratitude for their input into these stories and others besides.

And as always, I'm indebted to Monica Pacheco who's ably represented me for many years now through Ann McDermid & Associates in Toronto.

―――

I would also thank Toronto Mayor Rob Ford, had he any direct influence on the title story in this collection. As he did not, I think it best to simply wish him well.